THE BLACK WITCH

Books by Laurie Forest
available from Harlequin TEEN

The Black Witch

LAURIE FOREST

THE BLACK WITCH

 HARLEQUIN® TEEN

ISBN-13: 978-0-373-21231-6

The Black Witch

Printed in U.S.A.

HARLEQUIN®TEEN
www.HarlequinTEEN.com

To my mother, Mary Jane Sexton,
artist, creative genius, intellectual
(1944–2015)

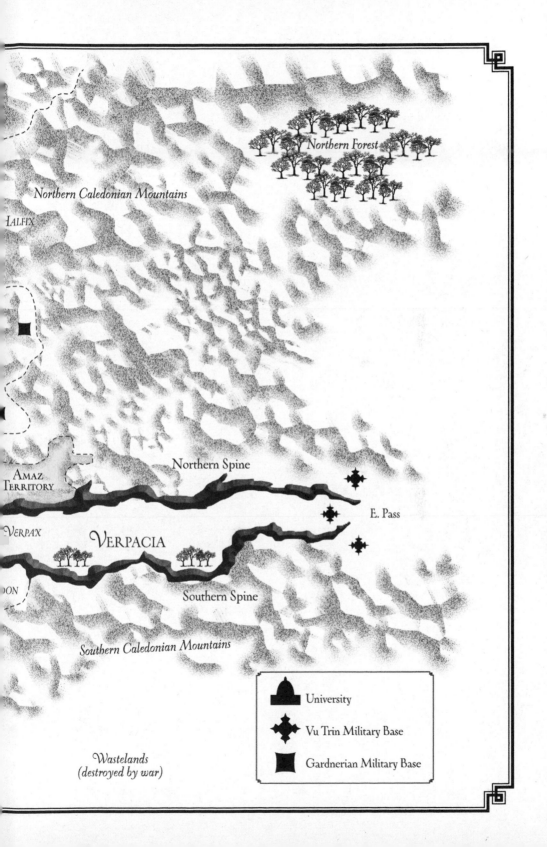

Northern Forest

Northern Caledonian Mountains

IALFIX

Northern Spine

AMAZ
TERRITORY

E. Pass

VERPAX

VERPACIA

Southern Spine

DON

Southern Caledonian Mountains

Wastelands
(destroyed by war)

University

Vu Trin Military Base

Gardnerian Military Base

PART ONE

PROLOGUE

The woods are beautiful.

They're my friends, the trees, and I can feel them smiling down at me.

I skip along, kicking at dry pine needles, singing to myself, following close at the heels of my beloved uncle Edwin, who turns every so often, smiles and encourages me to follow.

I am three years old.

We have never walked so far into the woods, and the thrill of adventure lights up my insides. In fact, we hardly *ever* walk into the woods. And Uncle Edwin has brought *only* me. He's left my brothers at home, far away.

I scramble to keep up with him, leaping over curved roots, dodging low-hanging branches.

We finally stop in a sunny clearing deep in the forest.

"Here, Elloren," my uncle says. "I have something for you." He bends down on one knee, pulls a stick from his cloak pocket and presses it into my tiny fist.

A present!

It's a special stick—light and airy. I close my eyes, and an image of the tree the stick came from enters my mind—a big, branchy tree, soaked in sunlight and anchored in sand. I open my eyes and bounce the stick up and down in my hand. It's as light as a feather.

My uncle fishes a candle out of his pants pocket, gets up and sets the candle on a nearby stump before returning to me. "Hold the stick like this, Elloren," he says gently as he bends down and holds his hand around mine.

I look at him with slight worry.

Why is his hand trembling?

I grasp onto the stick harder, trying my best to do what he wants.

"That's it, Elloren," he says patiently. "Now I'm going to ask you to say some funny words. Can you do that?"

I nod emphatically. Of course I can. I'd do anything for my uncle Edwin.

He says the words. There are only a few of them, and I feel proud and happy again. Even though they're in another language and sound strange to my ears, they're easy to say. I will do a good job, and he will hug me and maybe even give me some of the molasses cookies I saw him tuck away into his vest before we left home.

I hold my arm out, straight and true, and aim my feather-stick at the candle, just like he told me. I can feel him right behind me, watching me closely, ready to see how well I listened.

I open my mouth and start to speak the nonsense words.

As the odd words roll off my tongue, something warm and rumbling pulls up into my legs, right up from the ground beneath my feet.

Something from the trees.

A powerful energy shoots through me and courses toward the stick. My hand jerks hard and there's a blinding flash. An explosion. Fire shooting from the tip of the stick. The trees around us suddenly engulfed in flames. Fire everywhere. The sound of my own screaming. The trees screaming in my head.

THE BLACK WITCH

The terrifying roar of fire. The stick roughly pulled from my hands and quickly cast aside. My uncle grabbing me up, holding me tight to his chest and racing away from the fire as the forest falls apart around us.

Things change for me in the forest after that.

I can feel the trees pulling away, making me uneasy. And I begin to avoid the wild places.

Over time, the childhood memory becomes cloudy.

"It's just a dream," my uncle says, comforting me, when the burning scene returns in the dark of sleep. "About that time you wandered out into the forest. During that lightning storm. Think on pleasant things, and go back to sleep."

And so I believe him, because he cares for me and has never given me a reason not to believe.

Even the forest seems to echo his words. *Go back to sleep*, the leaves rustle on the wind. And over time, the memory fades, like a stone falling to the bottom of a deep, dark well.

Into the realm of shadowy nightmares.

Fourteen years later...

CHAPTER ONE

Halfix

"Take *that*, you stupid Icaral!"

I glance down with amusement at my young neighbors, a basket of freshly picked vegetables and herbs balanced on my hip, a slight near-autumn chill fighting to make itself known through the warm sunlight.

Emmet and Brennan Gaffney are six-year-old twins with the black hair, forest green eyes and faintly shimmering skin so prized by my people, the Gardnerian Mages.

The two boys pause from their noisy game and look up at me hopefully. They sit in the cool, sunlit grass, their toys scattered about.

All the traditional characters are there among the brightly painted wooden figures. The black-haired Gardnerian soldiers, their dark tunics marked with brilliant silver spheres, stand valiantly with wands or swords raised. The boys have lined the soldiers up on a wide, flat stone in military formation.

There are also the usual archvillains—the evil Icaral demons with their glowing eyes, their faces contorted into wide, malicious grins, black wings stretched out to their full size in an effort to intimidate, fireballs in their fists. The boys have lined these up on a log and are attempting to launch rocks at them from the direction of the soldiers with a catapult they've fashioned from sticks and string.

There are assorted side characters, too: the beautiful Gardnerian maidens with their long black hair; wicked Lupine shapeshifters—half-human, half-wolf; green-scaled Snake Elves; and the mysterious Vu Trin sorceresses. They're characters from the storybooks and songs of my childhood, as familiar to me as the old patchwork quilt that lies on my bed.

"Why are you here?" I ask the boys, glancing down into the valley toward the Gaffneys' estate and sprawling plantation. Eliss Gaffney usually keeps the twins firmly near home.

"Momma won't stop crying." Emmet scowls and bangs the head of a wolf-creature into the ground.

"Don't tell!" Brennan chastises, his voice shrill. "Poppa'll whip you for it! He said not to tell!"

I'm not surprised by Brennan's fear. It's well-known that Mage Warren Gaffney's a hard man, feared by his fastmate and children. And the startling disappearance of his nineteen-year-old daughter, Sage, has made him even harder.

I look to the Gaffneys' estate again with well-worn concern.

Where are you, Sage? I wonder unhappily. She's been missing without a trace for well over a year. *What could have possibly happened to you?*

I let out a troubled sigh and turn back to the boys. "It's all right," I say, trying to comfort them. "You can stay over here for a while. You can even stay for supper."

The boys brighten and appear more than a little relieved.

"Come play with us, Elloren," Brennan pleads as he playfully grabs at the edge of my tunic.

I chuckle and reach down to ruffle Brennan's hair. "Maybe later. I have to help make supper, you know that."

"We're defeating the Icarals!" Emmet exclaims. He throws a rock at one of the Icarals to demonstrate. The rock collides with the small demon and sends it spinning into the grass. "Wanna see if we can knock their wings off?"

I pick up the small figure and run my thumb across its unpainted base. Breathing in deep, I close my eyes and the image of a large tree with a dense crown, swooping branches and delicate white flowers fills my mind.

Frosted Hawthorne. Such elegant wood for a child's plaything.

I open my eyes, dissolving the image, focusing back in on the demon toy's orange eyes. I fight the urge to envision the tree once more, but I know better than to entertain this odd quirk of mine.

Often, if I close my eyes while holding a piece of wood, I can get the full sense of its source tree. With startling detail. I can see the tree's birthplace, smell the rich, loamy carpet beneath its roots, feel the sun dappling its outstretched leaves.

Of course, I've learned to keep these imaginings to myself.

A strange nature fixation like this smacks of Fae blood, and Uncle Edwin has warned me to never speak of it. We Gardnerians are a pure-blooded race, free from the stain of the heathen races that surround us. And my family line has the strongest, purest Mage blood of all.

But I often worry. If that's true, then why do I see these things?

"You should be more careful with your toys," I gently scold the boys as I shake off the lingering image of the tree and set the figure down.

The sound of the boys' grand battles recedes into the distance as I near the small cottage I share with Uncle Edwin and my two brothers. I peer across the broad field toward our horse stables and give a start.

A large, elegant carriage is parked there. The crest of the Mage Council, Gardneria's highest level of government, is artfully painted on its side—a golden *M* styled with graceful, looping calligraphy.

Four military guards, real-life versions of Emmet and Bren-nan's toys, sit eating some food. They're strapping soldiers, dressed in black tunics with silver spheres marking their chests, with wands and swords at their sides.

It has to be my aunt's carriage—it can't possibly be anyone else's. My aunt is a member of our ruling High Mage Council, and she always travels with an armed entourage.

A rush of excitement flashes through me, and I quicken my pace, wondering what on all of Erthia could have possibly brought my powerful aunt to remote Halfix, of all places.

I haven't seen her since I was five years old.

We lived near her back then, in Valgard, Gardneria's bustling port city and capital. But we hardly ever saw her.

One day, clear out of the blue, my aunt appeared in the front room of my uncle's violin shop.

"Have you had the children wandtested?" she inquired, her tone light, but her eyes sharp as ice.

I remember how I tried to hide behind Uncle Edwin, cling-ing to his tunic, mesmerized by the elegant creature before me.

"Of course, Vyvian," my uncle haltingly answered his sister. "Several times over."

I looked up at my uncle with confused surprise. I had no memory of being wandtested, even though I knew that all Gard-nerian children were.

"And what did you find?" she asked probingly.

"Rafe and Elloren are powerless," he told her as he shifted slightly, cutting off my view of Aunt Vyvian, casting me in shad-ows. "But Trystan. The boy has some magic in him."

"Are you sure?"

"Yes, Vyvian, quite."

And that was when she began to visit with us.

Soon after, my uncle unexpectedly soured on city life. With-out warning, he whisked my brothers and me away to where we now live. In tiny Halfix. At the very northeastern edge of Gardneria.

Right in the middle of nowhere.

As I round the corner of our cottage, I hear the sound of my name through the kitchen window and skid to a stop.

"Elloren is *not* a child anymore, Edwin." My aunt's voice drifts out.

I set my basket of vegetables and herbs on the ground and crouch low.

"She is too young for wandfasting," comes my uncle's attempt at a firm reply, a tremor of nervousness in his voice.

Wandfasting? My heart speeds up. I know that most Gardnerian girls my age are already wandfasted—magically bound to young men for life. But we're so isolated here, surrounded by the mountains. The only girl I know who's been fasted is Sage, and she's up and disappeared.

"Seventeen *is* the traditional age." My aunt sounds slightly exasperated.

"I don't care if it's the traditional age," my uncle persists, his tone gaining confidence. "It's still *too young*. She can't *possibly* know what she wants at this age. She's seen nothing of the world…"

"Because you *let* her see nothing of it."

My uncle makes a sound of protest but my aunt cuts him off. "No, Edwin. What happened to Sage Gaffney should be a wake-up call for all of us. Let me take Elloren under my wing. I'll introduce her to all the best young men. And after she is safely fasted to one of them, I'll apprentice her with the Mage Council. You *must* start to take her future seriously."

"I *do* take her future seriously, Vyvian, but she is still much too young to have it decided *for* her."

"Edwin." There's a note of challenge in my aunt's smooth voice. "You will force me to take matters into my own hands."

"You forget, Vyvian," my uncle counters, "that I am the eldest male of the family, and as such, I have the final say on all matters concerning Elloren, and when I am gone, it will be Rafe, not you, who will have the final say."

My eyebrows fly up at this. I can tell my uncle is treading on thin ice if he has decided to resort to *this* argument—an argument I know he doesn't actually agree with. He's always grousing about how unfair the Gardnerian power structure is toward women, and he's right. Few Gardnerian women have wand magic, my powerful grandmother being a rare exception. Almost all of our powerful Mages are men, our magic passing more easily along male lines. This makes our men the rulers in the home and over the land.

But Uncle Edwin thinks our people take this all too far: no wands for women, save with Council approval; ultimate control of a family always given to the eldest male; and our highest position in government, the office of High Mage, can only be held by a man. And then there's my uncle's biggest issue by far—the wandfast-binding of our women at increasingly younger ages.

"You will not be able to shelter her forever," my aunt insists. "What will happen when you are gone someday, and all the suitable men have already been wandfasted?"

"What *will* happen is that she will have the means to make her own way in the world."

My aunt laughs at this. Even her laugh is graceful. It makes me think of a pretty waterfall. I wish I could laugh like that. "And how, exactly, would she 'make her own way in the world'?"

"I've decided to send her to University."

I involuntarily suck in as much air as I can and hold it there, not able to breathe, too shocked to move. The pause in their conversation tells me that my aunt is probably having the same reaction.

Verpax University. With my brothers. In another country altogether. A dream I never imagined could actually come true.

"Send her there for *what?*" my aunt asks, horrified.

"To learn the apothecary trade."

A giddy, stunned joy wells up inside me. I've been begging Uncle Edwin for years to send me. Hungry for something more than our small library and homegrown herbs. Passionately envious of Trystan and Rafe, who get to study there.

Verpax University. In Verpacia's bustling capital city. With its apothecary laboratories and greenhouses. The fabled Gardnerian Athenaeum overflowing with books. Apothecary materials streaming into Verpacia's markets from East and West, the country a central trade route.

My mind spins with the exciting possibilities.

"Oh, come now, Vyvian," my uncle reasons. "Don't look so put out. The apothecary sciences are a respectable trade for women, and it suits Elloren's quiet, bookish nature more than the Mage Council ever could. Elloren loves her gardens, making medicines and so forth. She's quite good at it."

An uncomfortable silence ensues.

"You have left me with no alternative but to take a firm stand on this," my aunt says, her voice gone low and hard. "You realize that I cannot put one guilder toward Elloren's University tithe while she is unfasted."

"I expected as much," my uncle states coolly. "Which is why I have arranged for Elloren to pay her tithe through kitchen labor."

"This is *unheard of!*" my aunt exclaims. Her voice turns tight and angry. "You've raised these children like they're Keltic peasants," she snipes, "and frankly, Edwin, it's disgraceful. You've forgotten who we are. I have *never* heard of a Gardnerian girl, especially one of Elloren's standing, from such a distinguished family, laboring in a *kitchen.* That's work for Urisk, for Kelts, *not* for a girl such as Elloren. Her peers at University will be *shocked.*"

I jump in fright as something large bumps into me. I turn as my older brother, Rafe, plops down by my side, grinning widely.

"Surprise you, sis?"

It's beyond me how someone so tall and strapping can move as quietly as a cat. I imagine his extraordinary stealth comes from all the time he spends wandering the wilds and hunting. He's clearly just back from a hunt, his bow and quiver slung over one shoulder, a dead goose hanging upside down over the other.

I shoot my brother a stern look and hold up a finger to shush him. Aunt Vyvian and Uncle Edwin have resumed their wand-fasting argument.

Rafe raises his eyebrows in curiosity, still smiling, and tilts his head toward the window. "Ah," he whispers, bumping his shoulder into mine in camaraderie. "They're talking about your romantic future."

"You missed the best part," I whisper back. "Earlier they were talking about how you would be my lord and master when Uncle Edwin is gone."

Rafe chuckles. "Yeah, and I'm going to start my iron-fisted rule by having you do all my chores for me. *Especially* dish-washing."

I roll my eyes at him.

"And I'm going to have you wandfasted to Gareth." He continues to bait me.

My eyes and mouth fly open. Gareth, our good friend since childhood, is like a brother to me. I have no romantic interest in him whatsoever.

"What?" Rafe laughs. "You could do a lot worse, you know." Something just over my shoulder catches his eye, and his smile broadens. "Oh, look who's here. Hello, Gareth, Trystan."

Trystan and Gareth have rounded the cottage's corner and are approaching us. I catch Gareth's eye, and immediately he flushes scarlet and takes on a subdued, self-conscious expression.

I am mortified. He obviously heard Rafe's teasing.

Gareth is a few years older than me at twenty, broad and sturdy with dark green eyes and black hair like the rest of us.

But there's one notable difference: Gareth's black hair has a trace of silver highlights in it—very unusual in Gardnerians, and read by many as a sign of his less-than-pure blood. It's been the source of relentless teasing all throughout his life. "Mongrel," "Elfling" and "Fae blood" are just a few of the names the other children called him. The son of a ship captain, Gareth stoically endured the teasing and often found solace with his father at sea. Or here, with us.

An uncomfortable flush heats my face. I love Gareth like a brother. But I certainly don't want to fast to him.

"What are you doing?" my younger brother, Trystan, asks, confused to see Rafe and me crouched down under the window.

"We're eavesdropping," Rafe whispers cheerfully.

"Why?"

"Ren here's about to be fasted off," Rafe answers.

"I am not," I counter, grimacing at Rafe, then look back up at Trystan, giddy happiness welling up. I break out into a grin. "But I *am* going to University."

Trystan cocks an eyebrow in surprise. "You're kidding."

"Nope," Rafe answers jovially.

Trystan eyes me with approval. I know my quiet, studious younger brother loves the University. Trystan's the only one of us with magical power, but he's also a talented bow maker and fletcher. At only sixteen years of age, he's already been pre-accepted into the Gardnerian Weapons Guild and apprenticed with the military.

"That's great, Ren," Trystan says. "We can eat meals together."

Rafe shushes Trystan with mock severity and motions toward the window.

Humoring us, Trystan bends his wiry frame and crouches down. Looking ill at ease, Gareth does the same.

"You're *wrong*, Edwin. You can't possibly send her to University without wandfasting her to someone first." My aunt's domineering tone is beginning to fray at the edges.

"Why?" my uncle challenges her. "Her brothers are unfasted. And Elloren's not a fool."

"Sage Gaffney wasn't a fool, either," my aunt cautions, her tone dark. "You know as well as I do that they let in all manner of unsuitable types: Kelts, Elfhollen...they even have two Icarals this year. Yes, Edwin, *Icarals*."

My eyes fly up at this. Icaral demons! Attending University? How could that even be possible? Keltic peasants and Elfhollen half-breeds are one thing, but Icarals! Alarmed, I look to Rafe, who simply shrugs.

"It's not surprising, really," my aunt comments, her voice disgusted. "The Verpacian Council is full of half-breeds. As is most of the University's hierarchy. They mandate an *absurd* level of integration, and, quite frankly, it's dangerous." She gives a frustrated sigh. "Marcus Vogel will clean up the situation once he's named High Mage."

"*If*, Vyvian," my uncle tersely counters. "Vogel may not win."

"Oh, he'll win," my aunt crows. "His support is growing."

"I really don't see how any of this pertains to Elloren," my uncle cuts in, uncharacteristically severe.

"It *pertains* to Elloren because the potential is there for her to be drawn into a *wildly* unsuitable romantic alliance, one that could destroy her future and reflect badly on the entire family. Now, if she was *wandfasted*, like almost all Gardnerian girls her age, she could safely attend University—"

"Vyvian," my uncle persists, "I've made up my mind about this. I'm not going to change it."

Silence.

"Very well." My aunt sighs with deep disapproval. "I can see you are quite decided at present, but at least let her spend the next week or so with me. It makes perfect sense, as Valgard is on the way from here to the University."

"All right," he capitulates wearily.

"Well," she says, her tone brightening, "I'm glad *that's* settled. Now, if my niece and nephews would kindly stop crouching under the window and come in and join us, it would be lovely to see everyone."

Gareth, Trystan and I give a small start.

Rafe turns to me, raises his eyebrows and grins.

CHAPTER TWO

Aunt Vyvian

The Gaffney twins buzz past as I make my way into the kitchen, which is now full of friendly, boisterous noise.

My aunt stands with her back to me as she kisses Rafe on both cheeks in greeting. My uncle shakes hands with Gareth, and the twins are practically hanging from Trystan while holding up their toys for his inspection.

My aunt releases Rafe, stops admiring how tall he's become, and turns toward me in one fluid, graceful movement.

Her gaze lights on me and she freezes, her eyes gone wide as if she's come face-to-face with a ghost.

The room grows silent as everyone else turns their attention toward us, curious as to what's amiss. Only my uncle does not look confused—his expression grown oddly dark and worried.

"Elloren," Aunt Vyvian breathes, "you have grown into the absolute *image* of your grandmother."

It's a huge compliment, and I want to believe it. My grandmother was not only one of my people's most powerful Mages, she was also considered to be very beautiful.

"Thank you," I say shyly.

Her eyes wander down toward my plain, homespun clothing.

If ever there was anyone who looks out of place in our tiny kitchen, it's my aunt. She stands there, studying me, amidst the battered wooden furniture, soup and stew pots simmering on our cookstove and bunches of drying herbs hanging from the ceiling.

She's like a fine painting hanging in a farmer's market stall.

I take in her stunning, black, formfitting tunic that hangs over a long, dark skirt, the silk embroidered with delicate, curling vines. My aunt is the absolute epitome of what a Gardnerian woman is supposed to look like— waist-length black hair, deep green eyes and swirling black wandfasting lines marking her hands.

I'm suddenly acutely aware of the sad state of my own appearance. At seventeen, I'm tall and slender with the same black hair and forest green eyes of my aunt, but any resemblance ends there. I'm dressed in a shapeless brown woolen tunic and skirt, no makeup (I don't own any), my hair is tied into its usual messy bun and my face is all sharp, severe angles, not smooth, pretty lines like my aunt's.

My aunt sweeps forward and embraces me, obviously not as dismayed by my appearance as I am. She kisses both my cheeks and steps back, her hands still grasping my upper arms. "I just cannot *believe* how much you look like *her*," she says with awed admiration. Her eyes grow wistful. "I wish you could have gotten to know her, Elloren."

"I do, too," I tell her, warmed by my aunt's approval.

Aunt Vyvian's eyes glisten with emotion. "She was a *great* Mage. The finest *ever*. It's a heritage to be proud of."

My uncle begins scurrying around the kitchen, setting out teacups and plates, clunking them down on the table a little too loudly. He doesn't look at me as he fusses, and I'm confused by his odd behavior. Gareth stands rooted by the woodstove, his muscular arms crossed, watching my aunt and me intently.

"You must be tired after your trip," I say to my aunt, feeling nervous and thrilled to be in her lofty presence. "Why don't you sit down and rest? I'll get some biscuits to go with the tea."

Aunt Vyvian joins Rafe and Trystan at the table while I fetch the food, and Uncle Edwin pours tea for everyone.

"Elloren." My aunt pauses to sip at her tea. "I know you overheard my conversation with your uncle, and I'm glad you did. What do you think about being fasted before you go to University?"

"Now, Vyvian," my uncle cuts in, almost dropping the teapot, "there's no point in bringing this up. I told you my decision was final."

"Yes, yes, Edwin, but there's no harm in getting the girl's opinion, is there? What do you say, Elloren? You know that most of the young girls your age are already wandfasted, or about to be."

My cheeks grow warm. "I, um…we've never talked much about it." I envy Trystan and Rafe as they sit playing with the twins and their toys. Why isn't this conversation about Rafe? He's nineteen!

"Well—" my aunt shoots a disapproving look at my uncle "—it's high time you *did* discuss it. As you overheard, I'm taking you with me when I leave tomorrow. We'll spend the next few weeks together, and I'll tell you all about wandfasting and what I know about the University. We'll also get you a new wardrobe while we're in Valgard, and your brothers can meet up with us for a day or two. What do you say to that?"

Leaving tomorrow. For Valgard and the University! The thought of venturing out of isolated Halfix sends ripples of excitement through me. I glance at my uncle, who wears an uneasy look on his face, his lips tightly pursed.

"I'd like that very much, Aunt Vyvian," I answer politely, trying to keep my overwhelming excitement at bay.

Gareth shoots me a look of warning, and I cock my head at him questioningly.

My aunt narrows her eyes at Gareth. "Gareth," she says pleasantly, "I had the privilege of working with your father before he retired from his position as head of the Maritime Guild."

"He didn't retire," Gareth corrects, stiff challenge in his tone. "He was forced to resign."

The kitchen quiets, even the twins sensing the sudden tension in the air. My uncle catches Gareth's eye and slightly motions his head from side to side, as if in caution.

"Well," says my aunt, still smiling, "you certainly speak your mind very frankly. Perhaps talk of politics is best left to those of us who have finished our schooling."

"I have to be going," Gareth announces, his tone clipped. He turns to me. "Ren, I'll come by to see you when you're in Valgard. Maybe I can take you sailing."

My aunt is studying me closely. I blush, realizing what conclusion she must be forming in her mind about the nature of my relationship with Gareth. I don't want to respond too enthusiastically, to give the wrong impression. But I don't want to hurt Gareth's feelings, either.

"All right, I'll see you there," I tell Gareth, "but I might not have time for sailing."

Gareth throws a parting, resentful look at my aunt. "That's okay, Ren. Maybe I can bring you by to say hello to my family at least. I know my father would love to see you."

I glance over at my aunt. She's calmly sipping her tea, but the corner of her lip twitches at the mention of Gareth's father.

"I'd like that," I say cautiously. "I haven't seen him in a long time."

"Well, then," Gareth says, his face tense, "I'll be off."

Rafe gets up to see him out, the legs of his chair squeaking against the wooden floor as he pushes it from the table.

Trystan gets up, too, followed by my uncle and the twins, and all the males make their way out of the kitchen. I sit down, feeling self-conscious.

My aunt and I are alone.

She's tranquilly sipping her tea and studying me with sharp, intelligent eyes. "Gareth seems to take *quite* the interest in you, my dear," she muses.

My face grows hot again. "Oh, no...it's not like that," I stammer. "He's just a friend."

My aunt leans forward and places a graceful hand on mine.

"You aren't a child anymore, Elloren. More and more, your future will be decided by the company you keep." She looks at me meaningfully, then sits back, her expression lightening. "I am *so* glad your uncle has finally come to his senses and is letting you spend some time with me. I have a number of young men I am *very* eager for you to meet."

Later, after we have eaten supper, I make my way outside to bring the leftover scraps from dinner to the few pigs we keep. The days are getting shorter, the shadows longer, and a chill is steadily creeping in, the sun less and less able to fight it off.

Before, in the light of day, the idea of attending University seemed like an exciting adventure, but as the tide of night slowly sweeps in, I begin to feel apprehension coming in with it.

As eager as I am to see the wider world, there's a part of me that *likes* my quiet life here with my uncle, tending the gardens and the animals, making simple medicines, crafting violins, reading, sewing.

So quiet. So safe.

I peer out into the distance, past the garden where the twins were playing, past the Gaffneys' farmland and estate, past the sprawling wilderness, to the mountains beyond—mountains that loom in the distance and cast dark shadows over everything as the sun sets behind them.

And the forest—the wild forest.

I squint into the distance and make out the curious shapes of several large white birds flying in from the wilds. They're different from any birds I've ever seen before, with huge, fanning wings, so light they seem iridescent.

As I watch them, I'm overcome by a strange sense of foreboding, as if the earth is shifting beneath my feet.

I forget, for a moment, about the basket of pig slop I'm balancing on my hip, and some large vegetable remnants fall to the ground with a dull thud. I glance down and stoop to gather them back into the basket.

When I straighten again and look for the strange white birds, they're gone.

CHAPTER THREE

Goodbye

That night I'm in my quiet bedroom, softly illuminated by the gentle glow of the lantern on my desk. As I pack, my hand passes through a shadow, and I pause to look at it.

Like all Gardnerians, my skin shimmers faintly in the dark. It's the mark of the First Children, set down on us by the Ancient One above, marking us as the rightful owners of Erthia.

At least, that's what our holy book, *The Book of the Ancients*, tells us.

The traveling trunk Aunt Vyvian has brought for me lies open on the bed. It hits me that I've never been away from my uncle for more than a day, not since my brothers and I came to live with him when I was three, after my parents were killed in the Realm War.

It was a bloody conflict that raged for thirteen long years and ended with my grandmother's death in battle. But it was a necessary war, my beleaguered country relentlessly attacked and ransacked at the beginning of it. By the time it ended, Gardneria was allied with the Alfsigr Elves, ten times its original size, and the new, major power in the region.

All thanks to my grandmother, The Black Witch.

My father, Vale, was a highly ranked Gardnerian soldier, and my mother, Tessla, was visiting him when Keltic forces struck. They died together, and my uncle took us in soon after.

My little white cat, Isabel, jumps into my trunk and tries to pull a string from my old patchwork quilt. It's the quilt my mother made while pregnant with me, and it's linked to the only vivid memory I have of her. When I wrap myself in it, I can hear, faintly, the sound of my mother's voice singing me a lullaby, and almost feel her arms cradling me. No matter how bad a day I've had, just wrapping myself in this quilt can soothe me like nothing else.

It's as if she sewed her love right into the soft fabric.

Next to my trunk stands my apothecary kit, vials neatly stacked inside, tools secured, the medicines meticulously prepared. I've inherited this affinity for medicinal plants and herbs from my mother. She was a gifted apothecary, well-known for several creative tonics and elixirs that she developed.

Beside my apothecary supplies lies my violin, case open, its amber, lacquered wood reflecting the lantern light. I run my fingers along the violin's smooth surface.

I made this instrument, and there's no way I can part with it. I'm not *supposed* to know how to make violins, since women aren't allowed in the music crafter's Guilds. My uncle hesitated to teach me, but as time went on, he became increasingly aware of my natural talent and relented.

I love everything about violin-making. My hands have always been drawn to wood, soothed by it, and I can tell just by touching it what type it is, whether or not the tree was healthy, what kind of sound it will support. I can lose myself for hours on end carving, sanding, coaxing the raw wood into the graceful shapes of violin parts.

Sometimes we play together, my uncle and I, especially during the winter evenings by the light of the hearth.

A polite knock on the door frame breaks my reverie, and I turn to see my uncle standing in the open doorway.

"Am I disturbing you?" My uncle's face is gentle and softer than usual in the dim, warm light. His words, however, have a troubling edge of concern to them.

"No," I reply tentatively. "I'm just finishing packing."

"Can I come in?" he asks, hesitating. I nod and take a seat on my bed, which looks forlorn and foreign without its quilt. My uncle sits down next to me.

"I imagine you're feeling quite confused," he says. "Your aunt sent word a few months ago that she might be paying us a visit at some point, to discuss your future. So I started to make arrangements with the University. Just in case. I knew it was possible that she'd come for you someday, but I was hoping it wouldn't be for a few more years at least."

"Why?" I ask. I'm incredibly curious about why Aunt Vyvian has taken such a sudden interest in me—and why Uncle Edwin is so rattled by it.

My uncle wrings his clasped hands. "Because I *do not* believe what your aunt wants for your future is necessarily the best thing for you." He pauses and sighs deeply. "You know I love you and your brothers as much as if you were my own children."

I lean over onto his shoulder. His wool vest is scratchy. He puts his arm around me, and some of the stray hairs from his scraggly beard tickle my cheek.

"I've tried to shelter you, and protect you," he continues, "and I hope that your parents, if they were here, would understand why I've made the decisions that I have."

"I love you, too," I say, my voice cracking, my eyes filling with tears.

I've wanted to venture out for so long, but it's suddenly hitting me—I won't see my uncle or my loving home for a long time. Maybe not until spring.

"Well, now, what's this?" he asks, rubbing my shoulder to comfort me.

"It's just all so *fast*." I sniff back the tears. "I want to go, but... I'll miss you. And Isabel, too." Isabel, perhaps sensing my need for comfort, jumps onto my lap, purring and kneading me.

And I don't want you to be lonely with me gone.

"Oh, there now," my uncle says, as he hugs me tighter. "Don't cry. I'll take good care of Isabel, and you'll see her soon enough. You'll be back before you know it, with tales of all *sorts* of grand adventures."

I wipe at my tears and pull away to look up at him. I don't understand the urgency. He's always been so reluctant to let me go anywhere, always wanting to keep me here at home. Why has he made such a quick decision to finally let me go?

Perhaps seeing the questions in my eyes, my uncle lets out a deep sigh. "Your aunt can't force the issue of wandfasting as long as Rafe and I are here, but she *can* force the issue of schooling— unless I choose first. So I'm choosing. I've some contacts in the University's apothecary school, so it was no trouble finding you a spot there."

"Why don't you want me to apprentice at the High Mage Council with Aunt Vyvian?"

"It doesn't suit you," he explains with a shake of his head. "I want you to pursue something..." He hesitates a moment. "Something more *peaceful*."

He looks at me meaningfully, like he's trying to convey a secret hope and perhaps an unspoken danger, then he reaches down to pet Isabel, who pushes her head against him, purring contentedly.

I stare at him, confused by his odd emphasis.

"If they ask you," he says, focused in on the cat, "I've already wandtested you, and you have no magic."

"I know, but... I don't remember."

"It's not surprising," he says, absently, as he continues to stroke the cat. "You were very young, and it wasn't very memorable, as you have no magic."

Only Trystan has magic, unlike most Gardnerians, who have no magic, or weak magic at best. Trystan has *lots* of magic. And he's trained in weapon magic, which is particularly dangerous. But since my uncle won't allow wands or grimoires in the house, Trystan's never been able to show me what he can do.

Uncle Edwin's eyes meet mine, his expression darkening. "I want you to promise me, Elloren," he says, his tone uncharacteristically urgent. "Promise me that you won't leave school to apprentice with the Mage Council, no matter how much your aunt pressures you."

I don't understand why he's being so grave about this. I want to be an apothecary like my mother was, not apprenticed with our ruling council. I nod my head in agreement.

"And if something happens to me, you'll wait to wandfast to someone. You'll finish your education first."

"But nothing's going to happen to you."

"No, no, it's not," he says, reassuringly. "But promise me anyway."

A familiar worry mushrooms inside me. We all know that my uncle has been struggling with ill health for some time, prone to fatigue and problems with his joints and lungs. My brothers and I are loath to speak of this. He's been a parent to us for so long—the only parent we can really remember. The thought of losing him is too awful to think of.

"Okay," I say. "I promise. I'll wait."

Hearing these words, some of the tension leaves my uncle's face. He pats my shoulder approvingly and gets up, joints cracking as he stands. He pauses and puts his hand affectionately on my head. "Go to University," he says. "Learn the apothecary trade. Then come back to Halfix and practice your trade here."

Some of the creeping worry withdraws its cold hands.

That sounds just fine. And perhaps I'll meet a young man. I

do want to be fasted, someday. Maybe, after I'm fasted, my fast-mate and I could settle here in Halfix.

"All right," I agree, bolstered.

This is all sudden and unexpected, but it's exactly what I've wished for. Everything will work out for the best.

"Get some sleep," he tells me. "You've a long ride ahead of you tomorrow."

"Okay," I say. "I'll see you in the morning."

"Good night. Sleep well."

I watch him leave, his shy, friendly smile the last thing I see before he gently shuts the door.

CHAPTER FOUR

The White Wand

I'm awakened by a sharp rapping at my window. I jerk up from my bed, look toward the window and am startled by the sight of an enormous white bird sitting on a branch outside, staring intently at me.

One of the birds I saw flying in from the mountains.

Its wings are so white against the blue light of predawn, they seem otherworldly.

I creep out of bed to see how close I can get to the bird before spooking it, but don't get far. As soon as I lose contact with the bed, the bird silently spreads its massive wings and flies out of sight. I rush to the window, fascinated.

There, I can still see it, staring fixedly at me, as if beckoning me to follow.

It's across the field, near the long fence that separates our property from the Gaffneys' estate.

I haphazardly dress and run outside, instantly consumed by the strange blue light that covers everything, transforming the familiar landscape into something ethereal.

The bird is still staring at me.

I walk toward it, the odd-colored scene making me feel like I'm in a dream.

I get quite close to the creature when it flies away again, past the garden, where the fence to my left disappears briefly into some dense bushes and trees.

I follow, feeling a thrill course through me, like I'm a child playing hide-and-seek. I round the corner to a small clearing, then jump with fright and almost bolt in the opposite direction when I see what's there.

The white bird, along with two others, sits on a long tree branch. Directly below stands a spectral figure in a black cloak, its face hidden in the shadow of an overhanging hood.

"Elloren." The voice is familiar, halting me before I start to run.

Realization of who this is crashes through me.

"Sage?" I'm amazed and confused at the same time, my heart racing from the jolt of fear.

She stands, just beyond the fence. Sage Gaffney, our neighbor's eldest daughter.

Warily, I make my way toward her still figure, aware of the watchful birds above. As I get closer, I begin to make out her face in the blue light, her gaunt, terrified expression startling me. She was always a pleasant, healthy-looking girl, a University scholar and daughter of one of the wealthiest men in Gardneria. Her zealously religious family fasted her at thirteen to Tobias Vassilis, the son of a well-thought-of Gardnerian family. Sage had everything any Gardnerian girl could ever dream of.

But then she disappeared soon after starting University. Her family searched for her for over a year to no avail.

And yet here she is, as if risen from the dead.

"Wh-where have you been?" I stammer. "Your parents have been looking *everywhere* for you…"

"Keep your voice down, Elloren," she commands, her eyes fearful and darting around restlessly. She seems poised and prepared for escape, a large travel sack hanging from her back. Something is moving beneath her cloak, something she's carrying.

"What's under your cloak?" I ask, bewildered.

"My son," she says with a defiant lift of her chin.

"You and Tobias have a son?"

"No," she corrects me, harshly, "he is *not* Tobias's." She says Tobias's name with such pure loathing, I wince. And she keeps the child hidden.

"Do you need help, Sage?" I keep my voice low, not wanting to spook her any more than she already is.

"I need to give you something," she whispers, then reaches with a shaking hand for something hidden under her cloak. She pulls out a long, white wand that rises up from an exquisitely carved handle, its tip so white it reminds me of the birds' wings. But my eyes are quickly drawn away from the wand to her hand.

It's covered with deep, bloody lash marks that continue up her wrist and disappear beneath the sleeve of her cloak.

I gasp in horror. "Holy Ancient One, what happened?"

Her eyes are briefly filled with despair before they harden again, a bitter smile forming on her mouth. "I did not honor my wandfasting," she whispers acidly.

I've heard tales of the harsh consequences of fast-breaking, but to *see* it...

"Elloren," she pleads, the look of terror returning. She pushes the wand out at me as if trying to will me to take it. "*Please.* There's not a lot of time! I'm supposed to give it to you. It *wants* to go to you."

"What do you mean, it *wants* to go to me?" I ask, confused. "Sage, where did you get this?"

"Just *take* it!" she insists. "It's incredibly powerful. And you can't let *them* get it!"

"Who's *them*?"

"The Gardnerians!"

I force out a disbelieving breath. "Sage, *we're* Gardnerians."

"Please," she begs. *"Please* take it."

"Oh, Sage," I say, shaking my head. "There's no reason for me to have a wand. I've no magic…"

"It doesn't matter! *They* want you to have it!" She gestures with the wand toward the tree above.

"The birds?"

"They're not just birds! They're *Watchers*. They appear during times of great darkness."

None of this makes any sense. "Sage, come inside with me." I try to sound as soothing as I can. "We'll talk to my uncle…"

"No!" she snarls, recoiling. "I told you, it only wants *you!*" Her expression turns desperate. "It's the *White Wand*, Elloren."

Pity flashes through me. "Oh, Sage, that's a children's story."

It's a religious myth, told to every Gardnerian child. Good versus Evil—the White Wand pitted against the Dark Wand. The White Wand, a pure force for good, coming to the aid of the oppressed and used in ancient, primordial battles against demonic forces. Against the power of the Dark Wand.

"It's not just a story," Sage counters, teeth gritted, her eyes gone wild. "You *have* to believe me. This is *the White Wand.*" She lifts the wand again and thrusts it toward me.

She's mad, completely mad. But she's so agitated, and I want to calm her fears. Relenting, I reach out and take the wand.

The pale wood of the handle is smooth and cool to the touch, strangely devoid of any sense of its source tree. I slide it under my cloak and into a pocket.

Sage looks instantly relieved, like a heavy burden has been lifted.

Movement in the distance catches my eye, just inside where the wilds begin. Two dark figures on horseback are there and gone again so quickly, I wonder if it's a trick of the light. There are so many strange, dark shadows this time in the morning. I glance up and look for the white birds, and I have to blink twice to make sure I'm not seeing things.

They're gone. With no sound made in leaving. I spin around on my heels, searching for them. They're nowhere in sight.

"They're gone, Elloren," Sage says, her eyes once again apprehensively scanning around as if sensing some impending doom. She grasps my arm hard, her nails biting into my skin.

"Keep it secret, Elloren! Promise me!"

"Okay," I agree, wanting to reassure her. "I promise."

Sage lets out a deep sigh and releases me. "Thank you." She looks in the direction of my cottage. "I have to go."

"Wait," I beg of her. "Don't go. Whatever's going on... I want to help you."

She regards me mournfully as if I'm dauntingly naive. "They want my baby, Elloren," she says, her voice cracking, a tear spilling down her cheek.

Her baby? "*Who* wants your baby?"

Sage wipes her eyes with the back of her shaking, disfigured hand and casts a sidelong glance at my cottage. "*They* do!" She looks over her shoulder and gives her own home a pained look. "I wish... I wish I could explain to my family what's really going on. To make them *see*. But they *believe*." Her frown deepens, and she sets her gaze hard on me. "The Council's coming for him, Elloren. They think he's Evil. That's why your aunt's here."

"No, Sage," I insist. "She's here to talk to me about wandfasting."

She shakes her head vehemently. "No. They're coming for my baby. And I have to leave before they get here." She looks away for a moment as if desperately trying to compose herself. She hides her hand back under her cloak and cradles the small bundle inside. I wonder why she won't let me see him.

I reach out to touch her arm. "You're imagining all this, Sage. There's no way anyone would want to hurt your baby."

She glares at me with angry frustration, then shakes her head as if resigned to madness. "Goodbye, Elloren," she says as if she pities me. "Good luck."

"Wait…" I implore as she begins to walk along the fence line in the direction of the great wilderness. I follow her brisk pace, the fence separating us, leaning over it to reach her as she veers away, her back receding into the distance—a dark, ghostly figure making her way through the last of the morning mist.

The trees swallow her up into their darkness just as the sun rises, transforming the eerie blue dreamworld of early morning into the clear, sunlit world of day.

My fingers fumble under my cloak for the wand, half expecting it to be gone, expecting to find that I was sleepwalking and imagined all of this. But then I feel it—smooth and straight and very much real.

I rush back to the house, the sunlight steadily gaining strength.

Shaken, I'm desperate to find Uncle Edwin. Surely he'll know what to do.

As I round the trees, I'm surprised to see Aunt Vyvian standing in the doorway watching me, her expression unreadable.

A small wave of apprehension washes over me at the sight of her, and I immediately slow my pace, struggling to turn my expression blank, as if returning from an uneventful morning stroll. But my mind is a tumult.

Those marks on Sage's hands—they were so horrible. Maybe Sage is right. Maybe the Council is planning to take her baby away…

Aunt Vyvian tilts her head and eyes me thoughtfully as I approach. "Are you done packing?" she asks. "We're ready to go."

I stand awkwardly in front of her, not able to move forward as she's blocking the doorway. "Yes, I'm done." I'm acutely aware of the wand, my hand involuntarily drawn to it.

My aunt's eyes flicker in the direction of the Gaffneys' farm. "Did you visit with Sage Gaffney?" Her face is open, welcoming me to confide in her.

Shock flashes through me. How does she know that Sage is here?

I glance back toward the wilds, my heart thumping against my chest.

Sage was right. Aunt Vyvian isn't just here for me. Clearly she's here for Sage, too. But surely she would never harm a baby?

Aunt Vyvian sighs. "It's all right, Elloren. I know she's here, and I realize it must be terribly upsetting to see her. She's...very troubled. We're trying to help her, but..." She shakes her head sadly. "How is she?" Her tone is one of maternal concern. Some of my tension lightens.

"She's terribly frightened." The words rush out. "The baby. She thinks someone wants to harm him. That someone from the Council is coming to take him away from her."

My aunt doesn't seem surprised by this. She fixes me with the type of look adults use when they are about to reveal to a child some unfortunate, troubling fact of life. "The Council *is* coming to take custody of her baby."

I blink in shocked surprise.

Aunt Vyvian lays a comforting hand on my shoulder. "The child is deformed, Elloren. It needs a physician's care, and much more."

"What's wrong with it?" I breathe, almost not wanting to know.

Aunt Vyvian searches my eyes, hesitant to tell me what I know will be something monstrous. "Elloren," she explains gravely, "Sage has given birth to an Icaral."

I recoil at the word. *No! It can't be.* It's too horrible to imagine. One of the Evil Winged Ones—like giving birth to a grotesque demon. No wonder Sage didn't let me see her child.

The dull thud of horses' hooves sounds in the distance, and I spot another Mage Council carriage rounding the hills and making its way down into the valley toward the Gaffneys' estate. It's followed by eight Gardnerian soldiers on horseback.

"Can the child be helped?" My voice comes out in a shocked whisper as I watch the carriage and the soldiers nearing the cottage.

"The Council will try, Elloren." My aunt reassures me. "Its wings will be removed and a Mage Priest will do everything he can to try and save the child's twisted soul." She pauses and looks at me inquisitively. "What else did Sage say to you?"

It's a simple enough question, but something pulls me up short, some amorphous fear. And Sage has enough problems already.

Clearly she's stolen this wand. It can't possibly be the wand of myth that she imagines it to be, but it's obviously an expensive wand. Probably belonging to Tobias.

I'll wait until all this dies down and find a way to return it to him. And I don't mention that Sage has run off into the woods—I'm sure the Council will find her soon enough on their own anyway.

"She didn't say much else," I lie. "Only what I've told you."

My aunt nods in approval and lets out a small sigh. "Well, then, enough of this. We've a big journey ahead of us."

I attempt a small, resigned smile in return and bury Sage's secret deep within, as well as my guilt in keeping it.

CHAPTER FIVE

The Selkie

I stare out the window of my aunt's grand carriage as the scenery gradually changes from wilderness interspersed with farmland to small towns with more horse traffic. We sit opposite each other on green silk-cushioned seats, windows to our sides. A red, tasseled cord hangs from the ceiling that can be pulled to get the driver's attention.

I run my fingers nervously along the polished wood that lines my seat, its smooth touch soothing to me. An image of its source tree suffuses my mind, delicate, pointed leaves sparkling gold in the sunlight.

Star Maple.

I breathe in deep and let the tree anchor me.

All throughout the morning and well into the afternoon, my aunt quietly works on Mage Council paperwork on a small table that folds out from the wall.

Aunt Vyvian's the only woman to ever sit on our ruling Mage Council. She's one of twelve Mages there, not counting our High Mage. You have to be important to be on the Mage Council, and it's usually made up of powerful priests or Guild leaders, like Warren Gaffney, who's the head of the Agricultural Guild. But Aunt Vyvian has especially high status, being the daughter of the Black Witch.

Aunt Vyvian dips her pen in an inkwell with a sharp tap, her script graceful as a professional calligrapher's.

Glancing up, she smiles at me, then finishes up the page she's working on and places it into a large, important-looking, black leather folder, the Mage Council's golden *M* affixed to its front. After clearing the table, she collapses it back against the wall, smooths her skirts and turns her attention to me.

"Well, Elloren," she begins pleasantly, "it's been a long time since we've seen each other, and an even longer time since we've had a chance to talk. I really do regret that your uncle left everything to the last minute like this. It must be very confusing for you, and I suspect you have some questions."

I ponder this. Sage's deformed hands are foremost on my mind.

"When I saw Sage this morning," I begin, tentatively, "her hands were wounded...horribly wounded."

My aunt looks a bit taken aback. She sighs deeply. "Elloren," she says, her face solemn, "Sage left her fastmate and ran off with a Kelt."

A rush of shock runs through me. The Kelts killed my parents. They oppressed my people for generations. How could kind, gentle Sage have run off with...a Kelt?

My aunt's brow tightens in sympathy. "I know this must be hard for you, since you were friendly with the girl, but wand-fasting is a *sacred* commitment, and breaking that commitment has serious consequences." Her face softens when she sees my troubled expression. "Do not despair, Elloren," she says to comfort me. "There is hope yet. Tobias is willing to take Sage back, and there may be hope for her child, as well. The Ancient One is full of compassion when we truly repent and beg for forgiveness."

I remember Sage's defiance and think it highly unlikely she will beg for anyone's forgiveness, least of all Tobias's. I've hidden Sage's white wand inside the lining of my travel trunk, so at least being in possession of a stolen wand won't be added to her horrific troubles.

"It doesn't hurt to be fasted, does it?" I ask Aunt Vyvian worriedly.

My aunt laughs at this and leans forward to pat my hand with affection. "No, Elloren. It's not painful at all! The priest simply has the couple hold hands before waving his wand over them and reciting a few words. It's not something you feel, although it does leave an imprint on your hand, which you've seen before." My aunt holds out her hand, which is marked with graceful black swirls that extend to her wrist.

Unlike my uncle, who never married, most Gardnerian adults have some variation of these marks on their hands and wrists, the design unique to each couple and influenced by their Mage affinity lines. Hers are quite beautiful; undimmed by time and the death of her fastmate in the Realm War.

"Do not let Sage's unfortunate situation color your view of wandfasting," my aunt cautions. "Wandfasting is a beautiful sacrament, meant to keep us pure and chaste. The lure of the Evil Ones is strong, Elloren. Wandfasting helps young people such as yourself to stay on the path of virtue. It's one of the many things that sets us apart from the heretic races all around us." She motions toward me with both hands, palms upturned. "*That* is why I would like to see you wandfasted to someone you find appealing, someone who would be right for you. I'm having a party at week's end while you're in Valgard. Let me know if there is any young man who particularly catches your fancy." My aunt smiles at me conspiratorially.

A heady anticipation ripples through me.

What if I meet a young man I like at my aunt's party? Might he ask me to dance? Or to walk with him in a beautiful garden? There's a dearth of young, unfasted men in Halfix, and none that I fancy. Meeting a young man in Valgard is a thrilling thought, and I spend a fair bit of time dreamily considering it.

It takes several days to reach Valgard, and we stop often to change horses, stretch our legs and retire in the evening to sumptuous lodging. My aunt picks only the best guesthouses—delicious food brought to our rooms, fresh flowers gracing the tables and soft bedding stuffed with down.

Over meals and during the long carriage rides, Aunt Vyvian tells me about the people she's invited to her party: the various young men, along with their accomplishments and family connections, as well as the young women I will be meeting and who they're wandfasted to. She also speaks about her hopes for the rise of Marcus Vogel to High Mage, our highest level of government. Our current High Mage, Aldus Worthin, is elderly and getting ready to step down in the spring.

Marcus Vogel's name catches my attention. I remember a conversation my brother Rafe recently had with Uncle Edwin about him. Uncle Edwin was surprisingly strident in his dismissal of Vogel, calling him a "rabid zealot."

"Half the Council is still behind Phinneas Callnan for our next High Mage," Aunt Vyvian tells me, her tone clipped. "But the man has no spine. He's forgotten his own faith and how we were almost destroyed as a people." She shakes her head in strident disapproval. "If it was up to him, I suspect we'd all be slaves again, or half-breeds." She pats my hand as if I need consoling on this point. "No matter, Elloren. The referendum's not until spring, and Vogel's support grows every day."

My political ignorance aside, it's easy to sit back and fall under Aunt Vyvian's congenial spell, and she brightens in response to my rapt attention. She's a wonderful traveling companion, charming and vivacious. And she paints such vivid pictures of each person she describes that I imagine I'll be able to recognize them on sight.

She seems particularly fond of a young man named Lukas

Grey—a powerful, Level Five Mage and rising star in the Gard-nerian military.

"He's the son of the High Commander of the entire Mage Guard," she tells me as we roll along, a spectacular view of the Voltic Sea to my right, the late-afternoon sun sparkling on its waves. "*And* he's a top graduate of the University."

"What did he study?" I ask, curious.

"Military history and languages," she crows.

I can tell from the way her eyes light up when she speaks of him that he's her first choice of fasted partner for me. I humor her, doubting that this much-sought-after young man will spare even a glance toward a shy girl from Halfix. But it's enjoyable to listen to her enthusiastic descriptions, nonetheless.

"Only three years out of University and *already* a first lieu-tenant," she gushes brightly. "There's talk that within a year's time, Lukas Grey could be the youngest commander in the his-tory of the Guard."

My aunt prattles on for a long time about Lukas and several other young men. As she speaks, I glance out the window and watch the scenery go by. Gradually, the buildings of the towns we pass through are becoming taller, grander and closer to-gether, and lanterns are lit to welcome the twilight. Our prog-ress is now slowed by heavier carriage and horse traffic. We crest a hill, pass through a wooded area, and then, suddenly, it's before us—a sloping valley leading straight to Valgard, Gard-neria's capital city.

Like an elegant cloak clasp, gleaming Valgard rings the Malt-horin Bay. A glorious sunset lights the ocean beyond and bathes everything in the rich colors of a well-stoked fire. Tiny ships speckle the water. Valgard's docks resemble the curved half of a long fishbone.

I can scarcely breathe as I take it all in, the city glittering in the fading light, points of illumination sprouting throughout, like fireflies waking. Our carriage weaves down into the valley, and before long, we're in the heart of the capital.

I slide the carriage window open and stare.

Buildings made of luxurious, dark Ironwood rise up around me, the progressively wider upper stories supported by richly carved ebony columns. Curling emerald trellises thick with lush, flowering vines flow out over the rooftops and down the buildings' sides.

I close my eyes and breathe in the rich Ironwood. It's traditional for our homes to be made of this wood and styled in designs that look like forests and trees—a symbol of the Ancient One's creation of my people from the seeds of the sacred Ironwood Tree, giving us dominion over all the trees and all the wilds.

We pass an open-air restaurant, dining tables spilling out onto a promenade surrounded by decorative fruit trees, all of it lit by diamond-paned lanterns. The smell of rich food wafts into the carriage—roasted lamb, sautéed fish, platters of herbed potatoes.

A small orchestra plays beneath a plum tree.

I turn to my aunt, thrilled by the beautiful music. I've never heard an orchestra before. "Is that the Valgard symphony?"

Aunt Vyvian laughs. "Heavens, no, Elloren. They're employees of the restaurant." She eyes me with amused speculation. "Would you like to hear the symphony while you're here?"

"Oh, yes," I breathe.

There's an endless variety of shops, cafés and markets. And I've never seen so many Gardnerians together before, their uniformly dark garb lending an air of elegance and gravity to their appearance, the women's black silken tunics set off by glittering gems. I know it says right in our holy book that we're supposed to wear the colors of night to remember our long history of oppression, but it's hard to keep such somber thoughts in mind as I look around. It's all so wonderfully grand. I'm seized by a heady excitement, coupled with a desire to be part of it all. I glance down at my simple, dark brown woolen clothing and wonder what it would be like to wear something fine.

The carriage lurches, and we turn sharply to the right and make our way down a narrow, darker road, the buildings not as lovely as the ones on the main thoroughfare, the storefront windows mysteriously harder to see through, the lighting a moody red.

"I had my driver take a shortcut," my aunt says by way of explanation as she flips through more Council papers, the golden lumenstone in the carriage lantern growing in brightness in response to the dark.

I marvel at the lumenstone's rich, otherworldly light. Elfin lumenstone is incredibly expensive, the golden stone the rarest. I've only seen swampy green lumenstone in the Gaffneys' outdoor lamps back home.

Aunt Vyvian lets out a sigh and pulls down one of the blinds. "This isn't the best part of town, Elloren, but it will shave quite a bit of time off our journey. I suggest you close the window. It's not an attractive area. Frankly, it should all be razed and rebuilt."

I lean forward to close my open window and draw the blind as the carriage slows to a halt. It's been a constant stop and go ever since we reached the city because of the heavy street traffic.

A split second before I'm about to pull the cord, something hits the window with a loud smack—a white bird's wing, there and gone so fast, I swear I imagined it. I press my face to the window and try to locate the bird.

They're not just birds, they're Watchers! Sage's words echo in my mind.

And that's when I see her—a young woman only a few feet away from me.

She is, by far, the most beautiful person I've ever seen, even dressed as she is in a simple white tunic. Her long, silver hair sparkles like sun glinting off a waterfall and spills out over translucent skin so pale, it's almost blue. She has a lithe, graceful figure, her legs folded together to one side, her weight supported by slender, alabaster arms.

But it's her eyes that are the most riveting. They're huge and gray as a stormy sea. And they're filled with wild terror.

She's in a cage. An actual, locked cage, only big enough for her to sit in, not stand, and it's placed on a table. Two men stand staring at her while engaged in some private conversation. On the other side of the cage, two boys are poking at her side with a long, sharp stick, trying for a reaction.

She doesn't seem to even register that they're there. She's looking straight at *me*, her eyes absolutely locked on to mine. Her look is one of such primal fear, I pull back from the sheer force of it, my heart beginning to pound against my chest.

The woman lunges forward, grabs fiercely at the bars in front of her and opens her mouth. My head jerks back in surprise as slender rows of silvery slits on both sides of the base of her neck fly open, her skin puffing out around them.

Holy Ancient One—she has *gills*!

The woman lets loose a high-pitched, earsplitting croak, the likes of which I have never heard before. I have no idea what she's trying to scream, what's happened to her voice, but still, her meaning is clear. She's crying out for my help.

The men jump at the sound, put their hands over their ears and shoot her a look of annoyance. The boys laugh, perhaps thinking they provoked her cry. The boys push the stick into her once more, harder this time. Again, she doesn't flinch. She just keeps her eyes locked on mine.

My eyes dart to the sign on the storefront above her. *Pearls of the Ocean*, it reads. Suddenly the carriage lurches forward, and she's gone.

"Aunt Vyvian," I cry, my voice strained and high-pitched, "there was a *woman*! With...*gills*! In a *cage*!" I point to the window on the side where she had been, my heart racing.

My aunt glances quickly in the direction of the window, her

expression one of mild disgust. "Yes, Elloren," she says, sighing. "It was hard to miss the screeching."

"But, but...*what*..." I can barely get the words out.

"Selkies, Elloren, it's a Selkie." She cuts me off, clearly not wanting to discuss it further.

I'm stunned by her nonchalance. "She was in a *cage!*" I point again at the window, still not believing what I just saw.

"Not everything is how it appears on the surface, Elloren," she says stiffly. "You'll have to learn that if you're going to be part of the wider world." She peers over at me and studies my troubled face, perhaps seeing that a longer explanation is unavoidable. "They may look like humans, Elloren, but they aren't."

The very human-looking, terrified eyes of the young woman are burned into my mind. "What are they?" I ask, still shaken.

"They're seals. Very fierce seals, at that." My aunt pauses to lean back against the elaborately embroidered cushions. "Long ago, the Selkies were enchanted by a sea witch. Every full moon they come to shore somewhere on the coast, step out of their seal skin and emerge in human form. For many years they caused a great deal of havoc—attacking sailors, dismantling ships. It was terrible."

"But she looked so frail."

"Ah, it's like I just said. Appearances can be deceiving. Selkies, in possession of their skins, are stronger than the strongest Mage, and like most seals, they are very dangerous predators."

"And without their skins?"

"Very good, Elloren." My aunt looks pleased. "You've gotten right to the heart of it. Without their skins, they can be easily controlled."

"Why?"

"Because they lose their strength, and because they cannot transform back into seals without them. Without their skins, they cannot get back to the ocean. Being wild animals, no matter how long they are kept in human form, they desperately want to get back to their ocean home. They're not human, Elloren. It's only an illusion. Don't let it trouble you."

"But why was she in a cage?"

My aunt grimaces at my question, like she's detected an unpleasant odor. "Some people like to keep them...as pets."

I scrutinize her face. She's not looking at me. She's now glancing toward the window impatiently.

"She...she looked so *terrified*," I say, upset.

My aunt's expression softens. "Well, caged wild animals are never a pleasant sight. I am completely and utterly against the Selkie trade and am doing everything I can to wipe it out." She pats my hand reassuringly.

I feel some measure of relief wash over me.

"There are better ways to deal with Selkies that are *far* more humane than keeping them in cages, forcing them to...act human," she explains thoughtfully as she splays the fingers of one hand in front of herself and scrutinizes her lovely nails.

I'm so glad she feels this way. I know my brothers would agree. They're staunchly against the abuse of animals. Rafe, especially, hates the sight of wild animals confined or shackled in cruel ways.

"So you'll help her?" I press.

"Yes, yes, Elloren. Of course I will." My aunt impatiently straightens her sleeve cuffs. "Once Marcus Vogel becomes High Mage, it will be possible to put an end to this sort of thing."

I try to be consoled by this, but it's all so troubling.

She sets her eyes on me. "But really, Elloren, I didn't bring you here to talk about the local wildlife. There are so many more pleasant things to speak of."

I nod silently as my aunt points out her favorite shops and historical landmarks, but the face of the Selkie stays fresh in my mind, and I can't shake the chill I now feel for the rest of the ride.

CHAPTER
SIX

Valgard

A starlit sky overhead, we arrive, the carriage pulling up before
Aunt Vyvian's three-story home, arching windows lit golden
and an expansive, dark wooden staircase spilling toward us in
welcome.

Lush gardens arc along the curved entrance road, and I breathe
in their heady, sweet scent as the carriage slows. Ironwood trees
are bursting with glowing Ironflowers that cast the road in their
soft blue luminescence.

Our carriage glides to a smooth stop.

Two Urisk serving women stand on either side of the carriage door as I exit, their straight violet hair tied back into tidy
braids, their ears coming to swift points and their skin the soft
lavender hue of the Urisk upper class. Their coloration is new
to my eyes—the only Urisk I've ever seen are those toiling at
the Gaffneys' farm. Those women have the white, rose-tinted
skin, hair and eyes of the Urisks' lowest class—so pale they
could almost pass for Alfsigr Elves, were it not for the faintly
pink sheen of their skin and hair. These upper-class women's
linen uniforms are crisply starched, snow-white tunics over long
gray skirts, their expressions neutral.

Suddenly self-conscious, I grasp at the rough wool of my tunic hem. *I'm shabbier than even the servants.* I crane my neck up, amazed at the height of the house, and swallow apprehensively, feeling small and insignificant in contrast to this grandeur.

Aunt Vyvian's mansion is the same style of architecture I saw throughout Valgard—a climbing, multistoried building hewn from Ironwood; the broader, higher floors supported by curved, wooden columns; the roof topped with expansive gardens and multiple potted trees, vines of every variety spilling over the sides.

Like a giant tree.

It sits on elevated land with a panoramic view of the ocean to the back, and down onto twinkling Valgard and the Malthorin Bay to the side.

It's so beautiful.

Heady with anticipation, I follow at Aunt Vyvian's heels as she briskly makes her way up the stairs, the double doors opened for us by two more Urisk servants.

She holds herself so elegantly straight, I adjust my posture without thinking and hasten my pace to keep up with her. I wonder how she manages to walk so confidently and gracefully in her slim, tall heels, her skirts swishing around her feet.

I'd probably fall clear over on shoes like that.

My own feet are covered in sturdy boots made for gardening and caring for livestock. I secretly hope I can try feminine shoes like hers.

We pause in the most beautiful foyer I've ever been in: tables set with fresh bouquets of red roses, the tilework beneath my feet set in a black-and-green geometric design and a pair of stained-glass doors patterned with climbing vines.

A flutter of excitement rises in me to be in the middle of such luxury.

Aunt Vyvian riffles through some papers on a silver tray held by one of her serving women. "I apologize, Elloren, but I must leave you to get settled on your own." She pauses and examines one of the papers with shrewd eyes. "Fenil'lyn will show you to your rooms, and then we'll have a late dinner once you've unpacked." She sets down the letter and smiles expectantly at me.

"Of course. That's fine," I respond eagerly. I glance around and break into a wide grin, looking at her with appreciation and a heightened desire to win her approval. "It's...it's so lovely here," I say falteringly, suddenly giddy with nerves.

My aunt nods distractedly as if she's suddenly lost interest in me, then motions toward the servants and strides away, trailed by three of the Urisk, her heels clicking sharply on the tile floor. One stays behind—Fenil'lyn, I assume.

Aunt Vyvian's aloof dismissal has a small sting to it.

If I had magic, would I be of more interest to her? I let out a small sigh. On the carriage ride here, my aunt repeatedly brought up her disappointment that I take after my famous grandmother in looks only. *No matter,* I console myself. *It's a huge honor that she's chosen to single me out and bring me here.*

I follow straight-backed Fenil'lyn down a long hallway decorated with small, potted trees, and out into an expansive central hall. I skid to a stop, stunned by the sight that lies before me.

A central staircase spirals three stories up around a life-size tree sculpture. Wrought-iron grating, stylized to look like flowering vines, encloses each story's circular balcony.

I quicken my steps to catch up with Fenil'lyn and follow as she starts up the staircase. I take in the lifelike carved leaves, fascinated, and brush my fingers along their textured surface as we ascend.

River Oak.

An image of the source tree lights up my mind like the summer sun, moss-covered branches undulating out.

Reaching the top floor, I wordlessly follow Fenil'lyn onto the top balcony. She stops before two expansive wooden doors and pushes them open.

I peer inside and have to blink to believe my eyes.

A roaring woodstove pumps out a crackling heat, a crimson-canopied bed directly across from it. Sanded trunks and branches rise up near the walls, hewn from dark wood, giving off the smell of their rich beeswax coating, the domed ceiling painted to give the illusion of a starlit sky. I step inside and am immediately enfolded in delicious warmth.

Everything already done for me, no wood to lug.

Directly before me, two cut-crystal doors sparkle gold in the reflected lamp and firelight.

I pause to touch the smooth silk of a golden tassel that hangs from my bed's canopy, to stare in amazement at the intricate tree design embroidered on the scarlet quilt.

I reach the crystal doors, open them and find a curved sunroom just beyond, its walls made of glass that looks straight out over the ocean, a geometric glass ceiling giving me a panoramic view of the real night sky.

Two snow-white kittens play with a ball of string in the center of the sunroom's floor. They're fluffy white, with sky blue eyes. Just like my own cat, Isabel.

Enchanted, I stoop down and pick up one of the kittens. She kneads me with needle-sharp claws as a tiny, rumbling purr emanates from her small chest. The other kitten continues to worry the ball of string.

"For you, Mage Gardner," Fenil'lyn informs me with a polite smile. She's slender, with gorgeous eyes the color of amethysts. Her violet hair is streaked with a single stripe of gray. "Mage Damon felt you might be missing your pet."

My chest floods with a grateful warmth. *How incredibly thoughtful.*

Happily, I rise and turn to Fenil'lyn, hugging the purring kitten against my chest, the animal's tiny head tickling under my chin.

"You can call me Elloren," I tell her, grinning from ear to ear.

She stiffens, her smile freezing in place. "Thank you, Mage Gardner. But that would show disrespect." She tilts her head gracefully and gives a small bow. "Please allow me to honor you with your proper title."

It's odd to be in the presence of an Urisk woman who speaks the common tongue. Odder still to experience such deferential treatment, especially from someone who might be older than Aunt Vyvian. I'm momentarily ill at ease.

"Of course," I defer, the woman's frozen smile softening into an expression of relief.

"If you have need of anything, Mage Gardner," she tells me brightly, "simply ring the bell." She motions toward a golden-tasseled rope hanging by the door with a practiced wave. "I'll be back shortly to bring you to dinner."

"Thank you," I say, nodding.

She quietly leaves, and I take a deep breath, overcome by my surroundings.

Setting the kitten down in a basket with its littermate, I open the sunroom's side door.

The salty ocean breeze kisses my face the moment I step out onto a curved balcony. The stone balcony follows the arc of the sunroom, the rhythmic whoosh of waves lapping the dark rocks below. I peer over the balcony's edge, down two stories toward another, broader balcony, where servants are busy setting out an elaborate dinner.

Our dinner, I realize. Nothing to cook. Nothing to clean.

Breathing in deep, I take in the refreshing, salt-tinged air.

I could get used to this.

I wander back into my rooms and skim my finger over the spines of the books in a small library that's set into the wall, all the texts related to apothecary medicine.

A thread of amazed gratification ripples through me.

She's created a custom library just for me.

I remember the runehawk messenger bird Aunt Vyvian had

her guard send out to bring word of our arrival, but still, I'm stunned that so many personal touches have been pulled together in two days' time.

I slide a volume off the shelf and open the cover, the new leather resisting my pull. The drawings of herbs are hand-painted and look so lifelike, I can almost smell their scent.

I wonder if she'll let me take some of these books to University with me—they'd be of incredible use to me in my studies. A sitting table near the bed has a mirror rimmed with stained-glass roses. On the table sits a gilded brush and comb set, along with brand-new bottles of perfume, their spritzers tasseled with crimson silk.

So many pretty things. Things I never had in a house full of messy males.

I pick up one of the glass bottles, spritz it in the air and inhale. *Mmm.* It smells like vanilla and rose.

As the mist falls and dissipates, my eyes light on a shelf set into the wall, a cabinet beneath. Set on the table are two marble statues.

I walk over to them and pick one of the statues up, the polished base cool against my palm. It depicts my grandmother, her wand in her belt, leading Gardnerian children to some destination, smiles on the children's upturned, adoring faces. I look closely and trace my finger over the face's sharp features, her thin nose.

It's me. Or certainly a close likeness.

The second statue is my grandmother again, powerful and fierce, her delicate wand raised, her hair flying out behind her, a dead Icaral demon crushed beneath her feet.

An Icaral, like Sage's deformed baby.

I pause, troubled, my brow tensing. The thought of Icaral demons is so jarring in the midst of the comforting warmth, the sweet kittens, the luxury cushioning me all around. It makes me want to hide the statue away in a closet and never set eyes upon it again.

Shaking off the dark image, I clean myself up and prepare to meet my aunt for dinner.

"Are the rooms to your liking, Elloren?"

Aunt Vyvian beams at me as I join her at the balcony table. Fenil'lyn bows and graciously takes her leave.

"They're lovely, thank you," I reply, a bit dazzled. "I've never seen anything like..." I look out over the spectacular view of the ocean. "Well, like any of this."

She smiles, pleased. "Well, it's your birthright. Enjoy it. Your uncle's deprived you for far too long." She gestures toward a chair with a light wave of her hand. "Please. Sit. Enjoy the view with me."

Delighted, I take a seat opposite her, a deep green rug beneath our feet covering the gray stone of the balcony. Lanterns hang on multiple stands and cast the table in a soft glow that reflects off the fine porcelain with tiny, golden pinpricks of light.

A plate's been made up for me—slices of a citrus-glazed pheasant, precarved on a side table, thin lemon slices decorating the succulent bird; wild rice with dried fruit and nuts; baby carrots. Fresh bread steams between us alongside a dish of butter molded into flowers. A pitcher of mint water and a basket of fresh fruit also adorn the table. And a small table by the balcony's side wall holds a steaming pot of tea, a tower of small pastries and a bouquet of red roses in a crystal vase.

A servant stands still as a statue by the tea set, a young blue-skinned Urisk woman with vivid sapphire eyes who stares straight ahead into the middle distance, her expression carefully blank. It's hard to remember she's a person and not a statue, she's that still.

Aunt Vyvian's gaze wanders over me as she sips her water.

I find myself longing for her approval. I try to sit straight, my hands folded lightly on my lap, mimicking her graceful posture. My clothing may be shoddy, but at least I can try to mirror her refined ways.

"Tomorrow I'm sending you to the premier dressmaker in Valgard to have an entire new wardrobe fitted," she tells me with a small smile. "You can take it to University with you."

It's like she can read my wishes, and I'm overcome with gratitude. We've never had enough money for fine clothing. A warm rush rises in my neck and cheeks as I blush at her kindness. "Thank you, Aunt Vyvian."

"Unfortunately, I won't be able to accompany you." She sets down her glass and cuts into her pheasant. "I've Mage Council business to attend to, but I'm having three young women join you. They'll be your peers at University."

"Oh." I'm nervous and elated by the thought of meeting fellow scholars. I take a bite of the pheasant and it falls apart in my mouth, the glaze bright with lemon and spiked with fresh herbs.

"You'll like Paige Snowden and Echo Flood a great deal, I'm sure of it," she muses, taking a neat bite of her food. She dots her mouth with her napkin. "They're the daughters of Mage Council members. Lovely young women. Pleasant and morally upstanding."

But—she mentioned *three* young women. I blink at her in confusion, wondering if I heard her wrong.

"And the third?"

Aunt Vyvian's mouth grows tight, her face darkening, eyes cool. "That would be Fallon Bane, dear. I very much doubt you'll like her."

I gape at her. "Then…why…?"

"Her father is Malkyn Bane. He's a military commander and has a great deal of Council influence. He's also a Level Five Mage." She says this with the gravity it's due, and I nod and take note of it as I pull a warm piece of bread from the basket.

Level Five Mages are not common, which is why my Level Five brother Trystan is a full-fledged Weapons Guild Mage at the tender age of sixteen.

"Malkyn Bane's children are *all* Level Five Mages," Aunt Vyvian continues with great significance.

I freeze, bread and butter knife in hand. "You can't mean his daughter, too?"

Aunt Vyvian slowly nods. "Fallon Bane is a Level Five Mage, as are her two brothers." She gives this a moment to fully sink in.

I gape at her. "A *female*? With that much power?" That high level of power is almost exclusively held by males, with the notable exception of my grandmother.

My aunt's face fills with bitter frustration. "That kind of power rightfully belongs in *our* line. Especially with how much you look like Mother." She shakes her head, her brow going tight. "But even Trystan, with his great promise, is no match for Fallon Bane. Especially since he got such a late start in his training, due to your uncle's negligence on that front." She lets out a frustrated breath and gives me a level look. "Fallon's only eighteen, and she's already on the outer reaches of Level Five, Elloren. Much like your grandmother was at her age."

I remain frozen as realization washes over me. "She's the next Black Witch."

Aunt Vyvian's eyes darken. "*No.* I refuse to believe it. One of your children will hold that title. Or Trystan's. But *not* Fallon Bane. That power is *our* legacy. *Ours alone.* No matter how much Fallon Bane and her family like to strut about and pretend they're the heirs to it."

I knit my brow in question. "But even if she's not the Black Witch…if she's so dangerous, and if you dislike her so—then why is Fallon Bane going dress shopping with me?"

It seems almost comically bizarre.

Aunt Vyvian leans forward and looks me straight in the eye

as if conveying something of deep importance. "Because some-times in this world, it's good to know what you're dealing with."

"I don't understand."

Her eyes narrow. "Fallon is obsessed with Lukas Grey."

Ah, him again.

"So...they're courting?"

"No," she puts in flatly. "Not to my knowledge. From what I've seen, Lukas has little interest in the girl." My aunt's face twists into a disgusted sneer. "Even though Fallon throws her-self at him *quite wantonly.*"

Warmth spreads through my cheeks as I start to realize where all this is going. Lukas is a prize. And Aunt Vyvian is actively plotting for me to win him. Away from Fallon Bane.

"You want me to spend time with Fallon Bane so I can size up the competition?" I say, disbelieving.

Her eyes take on a sly gleam. "There is an opportunity here, Elloren."

Worry pricks at me. *I might not even like this Lukas Grey, so there's that. But there's an even larger concern.*

I set my bread and knife down and level with her.

"Aunt Vyvian. You've really gone out of your way for me. And I don't want to disappoint you." A nervous dismay ripples through me—I don't want to lose her kind regard. I've been hungry for a mother figure for so long, for female guidance. *But she has to know the truth.* "I have no experience in society. There's just no way I can...swoop down into it and...fit in with this Lukas Grey, or anyone else, for that matter." I slump, los-ing heart as I take in the tiny, elaborate braids that decorate her long hair. I'm hungry for knowledge of such pretty ways. "I don't even know how to do my hair. Or use makeup properly. Or...*anything.*" *If I had my mother...*

Aunt Vyvian pats my hand and gives me a warm, maternal smile.

"You don't have to know anything, dear." She gives my hand

a gentle squeeze. "I've taken you under my wing. And that's the best place to be. Simply sit back, enjoy it and follow my lead."

I smile shyly, encouraged, as I hold on to her cool, smooth hand.

CHAPTER
SEVEN

Fallon Bane

"Have you kissed him?"

"Excuse me?"

"Gareth Keeler. Have you kissed him?"

I'm facing an audience of three young women—the University scholars Aunt Vyvian has chosen to be my companions for the day. They sit staring at me with rapt attention, waiting for my answer.

To the most embarrassing question I've ever been asked.

Inappropriate, personal questions like this were not acceptable in Halfix, and I inwardly draw back from them in discomfort.

It's early on my first morning in Valgard, and we are in Aunt Vyvian's carriage, headed toward the shop of the premier dressmaker in Gardneria. The ride is smooth, the carriage surrounded by twelve armed, high-level Mage soldiers.

Twelve.

Charged with protecting Fallon Bane—our next Black Witch. Aunt Vyvian might not want to believe that she's the one, but it's clear from our armed escort that most other Gardnerians don't agree with this view.

Fallon is, by far, the most intimidating young woman I've

ever met. She's beautiful, with full lips, curly black hair down to her waist and large eyes that shine with the whole spectrum of green. But everything else about her flies in the face of convention. For one thing, she's dressed in a military apprentice uniform modified for a female—the traditional slate-gray silk tunic over a long, gray skirt instead of pants, and marked with a silver Erthia sphere embroidered over her heart. And the arms of her uniform are marked with a Level Five Mage's five silver bands. Fallon watches me, her legs splayed open, aggressively taking up as much room in the carriage as possible.

She's the one asking the questions, a slightly contemptuous smirk on her face. My obvious discomfort, given away by the blush I feel forming on my face, seems to greatly amuse her.

"Why are you asking me about Gareth Keeler?" I ask Fallon defensively.

"Your aunt says you know him."

"I do," I tell her. "He's my friend."

Fallon shoots sly, sidelong glances at both Echo and Paige before setting bright eyes back on me. "Have you looked closely at his hair?"

I bristle, my view of Fallon quickly coalescing into a hard ball of dislike. "His hair is black."

Fallon smirks wider. "So...if you haven't kissed Gareth, have you ever kissed *anyone*?"

I struggle to keep my expression neutral, greatly put off by her intrusive behavior. "Of course not. I'm unfasted." *And not in the habit of throwing myself at young men, unlike you.*

Fallon flashes a devious look at Echo, which sends my dislike of Fallon flaring higher. Then she turns her mischievous gaze back on me, her tone thick with condescension. "You're not in the backwoods anymore, Elloren. It's okay to kiss a boy."

Echo purses her lips at Fallon. "Some of us have morals," she chastises. "Even in Valgard."

Fallon spits out a disdainful laugh and rolls her eyes at me, like I'm an old chum.

Echo's regarding me now, with serious, owl-like eyes, as if measuring my worth. She's garbed in the manner of the most religious Gardnerians, her black tunic double-layered and very high in the collar, a small Erthia sphere hanging from a silver chain around her neck, her hair unadorned and parted straight as a pin.

Noticing Fallon's and Echo's unfriendly expressions, Paige smiles at me encouragingly. She's the only truly pleasant person in the group, her curly black hair escaping from jeweled barrettes, spilling out over round, rosy cheeks.

Fallon takes note of Paige's happy expression. "*Paige* has been kissed," Fallon teases, her tone unkind.

That wipes the smile clear off Paige's face. "Well...umm..." Paige stammers as she looks down at the marked hands that fidget in her lap. "I'm fasted."

"She's been fasted since she was *thirteen*," Fallon leans in and whispers to me, as if this is a delicious secret.

"You have?" I'm surprised. Thirteen seems *awfully* young. But then I think of Sage—she was fasted at thirteen.

"I'm... I'm fasted to Fallon's brother, Sylus," Paige mumbles, seeming less than overjoyed by this.

Fallon throws an arm around Paige and hugs her tight with mock affection. "We're going to be *actual* sisters!"

Paige glances meekly at Fallon and forces a small, quavering smile.

I motion toward Echo's marked hands. "Have you been fasted a long time?"

Echo's solemn stare doesn't waver. "To Basyl Dorne. Five years ago."

I study her, trying to catch a glimpse of how she feels about this, but Echo's as private and unreadable as a statue.

My eyes wander to Fallon's unmarked hands. "So… I see you're not fasted."

Fallon's expression turns cold, and she fixes me with a belligerent stare. "Not *yet*." She says it like a challenge.

"Fallon likes Lukas Grey." Paige giggles nervously. Fallon swivels her head smoothly toward Paige and stares her down. Paige's smile vanishes. "Well…you *do*…like Lukas, I mean."

I remember my aunt's gushing praise of Lukas Grey, the prospective fasting partner she seems to want most for *me*. I'm amused that Aunt Vyvian actually thinks I could compete with Fallon Bane for anything—and win.

"He's *really* handsome," gushes Paige, "and his father is the High Commander of the *entire* Mage Guard. He comes from a *very* important family, *and* he's a Level Five Mage."

Fallon is watching me closely, a gloating look on her face, like she's won some prize.

"When are you getting fasted to Lukas?" I ask.

Fallon's smile freezes, and she narrows her eyes at me. "Soon. *Very* soon." There's warning in her inflection. *Stay away from Lukas. He's mine.*

I wonder why she's so insecure about him, and whether or not she knows Aunt Vyvian ludicrously wants him for me. I find myself even more curious about my aunt's party, if only for the chance to meet the mysterious Lukas Grey. My eyes are drawn to the wand that sticks out from Fallon's belt like some great thorn.

"So—" I gesture toward the wand "—you've quite a bit of power, I've heard."

She bares her teeth. "A little."

I can tell by the incredulous looks Echo and Paige throw her that she's being wildly sarcastic.

"I've never seen magic used," I tell her.

Her feral smile inches wider. "You've no magic, then?"

I shake my head, bothered by the gloating look on her face.

In one smooth, deft movement, Fallon pulls out her wand, holds it straight up and murmurs a spell.

A loud crack sends Echo, Paige and me recoiling back against our seats as a flash of blue light bursts from Fallon's wand. The sound jars me to the bone, and I gasp as the light quickly coalesces into a whirling, glowing sphere that floats just above the wand's tip, its rhythmic, deep *whoosh* a jagged scrape to my ears, the carriage rapidly cooling, frost forming on the windows.

"*Stop it*, Fallon," Echo snaps as she glares at Fallon with annoyance, all of us cast in sapphire light. "You'll freeze us to death."

Fallon lets out a contemptuous laugh but relents. She murmurs more strange words and the iceball instantly morphs into a roiling, white vapor that quickly explodes into a frigid, odorless mist and disappears.

Fallon sits back and grins, a triumphant gleam in her eyes.

"That's amazing," I breathe, swallowing hard, fighting back a shiver.

"That's *nothing*," Paige says, eyes wide. "You should see what *else* she can do. She's a Level Five Mage. One of the best of the *whole* Guard."

"It sounds like you and Lukas Grey are well suited for each other," I tell Fallon placatingly, wanting to be struck clear off her list of potential enemies.

Aunt Vyvian needs to abandon her absurd dream of matching me with Lukas Grey. All she's going to do is place me directly into scary Fallon Bane's line of fire.

Fallon seems pleased by my comment. She nods approvingly, sets her wand back into her belt and relaxes against her seat.

Echo shoots Fallon a look of mild disapproval, then glances down at my unmarked hands and frowns. "I don't understand why you're not fasted."

"My uncle wants me to wait until I'm older," I tell her, increasingly put off by Echo's judgmental approach. And besides,

Fallon looks to be about the same age as me, and she isn't fasted, either.

"Oh, what fun you'll have," Paige enthuses with a dreamy look of longing. "All the parties and dances and your *first kiss!*"

"Have you met *anyone* you're interested in?" Fallon probes, sizing me up to see if I'm competition for Lukas, no doubt.

"No." I shake my head. "I haven't really had a chance to, being from Halfix. It's so isolated there. And this is only my first full day in Valgard."

Fallon regards me with renewed interest. She narrows her eyes. "Have you ever been around *any* men...other than Gardnerian men?"

My brow knits tight and I feel myself growing defensive over my sheltered upbringing. "What do you mean?" I ask guardedly.

Fallon spits out a short laugh. "I mean, have you ever been around Keltic boys? Or Elves? Or... *Lupine?*"

I eye her with astonishment. "There aren't Lupines at the University, are there?" That strikes me as incredibly dangerous. Lupines are vicious wolf-shifters. Stronger than the strongest Gardnerian, and completely immune to our magic.

"I'm afraid there are," Echo replies, a grave expression on her face.

"That's rather shocking," I say, shaking my head. "I'm really surprised." But then I think back to Aunt Vyvian's conversation with Uncle Edwin, and her outrage over the University's misguided racial integration—even Icaral demons are allowed to attend.

Paige is worriedly chewing at her bottom lip, her eyes round as two saucers.

Fallon leans in toward me with obvious relish, her voice a scratchy whisper. "Lupines don't ever marry, did you know that? They simply grab whomever they like and mate with them in the *woods.*"

"Like *animals,*" Echo chimes in, with great indignation.

"Really?" It's all so scandalous. And troubling.

"*I've* heard," continues Fallon, "that sometimes they grab young women, pull them into the woods and mate with them... as *wolves!*"

Paige gasps, one hand flying up to cover her mouth.

"Is that even possible?" I question, aghast.

Fallon laughs and settles back into her seat. "Stay away from the Lupine boys."

"They don't always mate in the woods," Echo informs me darkly as she fingers her sphere pendant.

Paige shrinks down, clearly apprehensive to hear what Echo is about to say, as Fallon eyes me with gleeful anticipation, everyone waiting for me to ask the obvious question.

I blink at them. This is the most outrageous conversation I've ever had and, despite myself, I'm overcome by lurid fascination. "Where...um...where do they..." I motioned with my hands to finish.

Echo seems to approve of my reluctance to just come out with it. She leans closer. "My father used to be the Council's ambassador to the Lupines, and he's actually *visited* the Lupine Territory. I overheard him talking to my mother about them, and *he* said that when Lupines are about our age they get their whole pack together—that's what they call their societies, like a pack of wolves—and they stand up in front of everyone, pick out someone to mate with and mate with them *right there*, in front of *everyone*. Even the *children*."

My face is growing very hot. This is the most sordid thing I have ever heard in my entire life. "Won't it be sort of...dangerous? To go to University with them?" I wonder.

"There's only two of them." Fallon flicks her hand dismissively. "Brother and sister. Twins."

Well, that's a relief. Only two Lupines. How dangerous could only two Lupines be?

"What about the Elves?" I ask. My brothers have told me

they make up about a quarter of the scholars at the University. "What are they like?"

"Complete opposite," Fallon says with a shake of her head. "*Very* prissy." She snorts in derision. "It's amazing they ever get around to ever having children. They're *extremely* protective of their women, though. If a boy of another race so much as *touches* one of their women..."

"Like anyone would *want* to," scoffs Echo.

"I think the girl Elves are pretty," Paige confesses sheepishly. Fallon throws her a quick, withering glance. "They *are!*" Paige insists. "They have those dainty pointed ears. And white hair, and white clothes...kind of the opposite of us..."

"Very *much* the opposite of us," Echo cuts in. She looks to me. "They're idol worshippers."

"Aren't they our allies?" I put in, keeping my voice carefully neutral.

Fallon pins me with her eyes. "For now."

Well, that's interesting. "And the Kelts?" I wonder, looking to Echo. "What are their men like?"

Fallon snorts derisively as Echo regards me somberly, her fist closed tight around her Erthia sphere. "Their blood is polluted with *all types* of filth—Fae blood, Urisk...even *Icaral.*" Echo waits to see if I'm appropriately horrified before continuing.

Sage's Icaral baby immediately leaps to mind, casting a pall over everything. I remember how troubled and terrified she was. *A Kelt. The demon baby's father is a Kelt. And she met him at University.*

"Priest Vogel says the Kelts are cast out and no longer First People like us," Echo continues stridently. "They've secretly aligned themselves with Evil Ones, like the desert heathens and the Urisk."

"Look out for the Urisk women," Fallon warns as a side note. "They may look all innocent, but they *love* going after our men."

I've heard Warren Gaffney going on about this on more than

one occasion. The fact is, Urisk women don't have any men of their own to go after. The Gardnerian government killed all their males during the Realm War.

Urisk males are powerful geomancers, able to harness the full, destructive powers of stones and gems. Their existence would pose a serious threat to our country. The women, on the other hand, are completely devoid of magic and are allowed to live in Gardneria as guest workers.

It's a horrible thought, though—the Urisk boy babies being killed. It's a subject I've never been able to discuss with Uncle Edwin, as he becomes visibly upset if I try to broach the topic, once to the point of tearing up and clutching at his chest.

Male Urisk warlords viciously attacked our country when they had power, seeking to wipe us out, but still, it's all so troubling.

Echo sighs. "At least Urisk half-breeds only have weak magic, at best."

Paige nods to her in agreement, but Fallon is ignoring them both. Instead, she's watching me with a silent intensity so unnerving that it raises the hairs on the back of my neck. My initial dislike of her deepens.

"Be careful with those mixed-breeds," Fallon tells me, a sly smile spreading across her face. I bristle, realizing she's once again alluding to Gareth and his silver-tipped hair. She slides her thumb along the length of her wand. "Mixed-breeds are everywhere," she purrs. "You just can't be too careful."

Textured Silk

"Stand up straight, now. That's better..."

Mage Heloise Florel pulls the measuring tape tight around
my waist as I drown in embarrassment. An imperious, square
woman about sixty years of age, Mage Florel is the proprietor
of the dress shop. Her own long, dark tunic and skirt are exquisitely made, her gray hair plaited and tied back into a neat bun,
her eyes like little green searchlights that take in every last detail.

I'm standing on a pedestal right in the center of her fitting
room with Fallon, Echo and Paige looking on. In my *underwear*!

"All right. Now lift your arms above your head..."

Mage Florel, to my mortification, begins measuring above
my breasts, around my breasts and under them as she calls out
numbers to a quiet Urisk girl. The girl, who looks to be about
my age, takes down every number on a small piece of parchment, her face as blank as snow. Fallon makes a show of reading
the girl's notes over her shoulder and then whispering to Paige
and Echo, her lips shielded with her hand, a nasty smirk on her
face. I just know she's commenting on my measurements and I
flush with embarrassment.

I glance around at the dark sea of fabric bolts surrounding me, trying to shut out Mage Florel's poking and prodding. Everywhere I look, lining every wall to the ceiling, is luxurious fabric, much of it embroidered with intricate designs. I'd never have imagined there could be so many variations of black cloth, the colors ranging from the deepest black of night, to hues just on the edge of gray, the textures spanning from silk so shiny you expected to see your reflection in it to matte velvet.

"You've got quite a nice figure," Mage Florel remarks, eyeing my chest. "Too bad you've been hiding it away underneath all of those...*clothes*." She nudges my discarded pile of garb with her foot.

I can feel my face growing even hotter, but this time my embarrassment is mixed in with gratification at the compliment, and how sour Fallon looks in response to Mage Florel's praise.

Privately, I'm aware that I have a pleasing figure, but no one has ever publicly commented on my body before. Growing up with an uncle and two brothers, my body has always been very private, and, in the Gardnerian tradition, completely covered—from my neck to my wrists down to my feet. I've never shown so much as a bare ankle in public. When I reached the age when I needed more tailored clothing, I took to sewing my dresses myself.

Finally, to my immense relief, the ordeal is over and Mage Florel orders me to get dressed, then dictates some notes to the Urisk girl regarding alterations and appropriate trim.

It's hard not to stare at the young Urisk woman—she's so lovely. Like the upper-class servants at Aunt Vyvian's house, she has lavender skin, long, pointed ears and startlingly lovely eyes that glimmer several shades of amethyst. Her violet hair is pulled back into one long braid, and she's simply dressed in a white linen tunic and white underskirt.

I think of the Urisk women who work the Gaffneys' sprawling farm. They've always been a bit of a mystery to me, the Urisk farmworkers, with their Uriskal language and tendency to disappear as soon as the harvest work is done for the season. And they are, all of them, wizened and bedraggled. Nothing at all like this beautiful girl.

The Urisk girl hands the parchment to Mage Florel, who squints at it through half-moon spectacles attached to a long, pearl necklace. "Very good, Sparrow," she comments. "Go fetch Effrey."

Sparrow nods and leaves, her movements graceful. Within a few seconds, another Urisk girl, a skinny, frantic little thing with deep purple skin, hair and eyes, runs into the room and skids to an abrupt halt in front of Mage Florel, Sparrow shadowing close behind. The child looks to be about eight years of age.

The older woman stares down at the child uncertainly, then directs her to fetch some fabric. A few minutes later the child returns carrying two bolts of cloth that are coming unwound around her legs, one ebony silk flecked with small, golden threads, the other a muted blue-black. They're large bolts, and the girl looks to be out of breath from the effort.

Mage Florel lets out a disgusted sigh. "*Textured silk*, Effrey, I wanted it *textured*."

The girl's eyes fly open in panic.

"Let's make this easier," Mage Florel offers, the girl looking about ready to burst into tears. "Get me the sample booklets instead. They're easier to carry than the bolts."

Little Effrey sprints out of the room, seeming eager to correct her mistake.

Mage Florel turns back to us, shaking her head in consternation. "I'm sorry," she confides. "She's new. And she's been *extraordinarily* difficult to train. She just doesn't listen carefully."

Fallon snorts as she runs her hand along some velvet. "You'd think with ears *that* big, she'd be able to listen just fine."

My head jerks toward Fallon. Mage Florel, Echo and Paige join me in looks of shocked surprise.

Fallon eyes us incredulously just as little Effrey stumbles back into the room. The child is lugging a thick sample book under one arm, frayed fabric edges poking out the sides. Fallon spits out a laugh and gestures widely toward the little girl. "Oh, so we're supposed to pretend she doesn't look like an overgrown *bat?*"

Effrey comes to a wobbly stop. She glances up at Fallon, her lip quivering into a miserable frown, her ears seeming to droop at the points. I watch as Sparrow shoots Effrey a swift look of serious caution, the older girl standing just behind Fallon Bane. Effrey immediately averts her eyes and looks down at her feet.

"Girl!" Fallon barks at Effrey with exaggerated force, then stifles a laugh when the girl jumps and whips her head up. Fallon flicks her fingers toward herself magisterially. "All right, then. Hand it over."

The child lowers her head deferentially as she offers the sample book up to Fallon. I notice her hands are trembling.

"Thank you," I say gently, in an effort to soothe the girl. I shoot Fallon a look of censure, bewildered by her cruelty.

Mage Florel is regarding Fallon with a pained expression, and she makes a point of dismissing little Effrey as soon as Fallon has the sample book in hand. I don't wonder at Mage Florel's deference to Fallon Bane, the presumptive heir to my grandmother's power.

Fallon sets the sample book on a wooden stand and opens it. She takes her time, monopolizing the booklet as everyone silently waits. Eventually, she lights on fabric of interest to her. "Oh, here we go, Elloren," she says, her voice dripping with faux sweetness. She pulls a dull black rectangle from the book and holds it up.

It's ugly, rough wool. Of worse quality than the clothing I arrived in.

"I think this would be good for you," Fallon beams, *"especially* for your aunt's party. Don't you think so, Paige?"

Paige looks at the fabric sample, her brow knitting tight. She glances over at me and blinks uncertainly. "Um...well...*maybe it could work*..."

I can't figure out if Fallon is joking. She has to be. "I was thinking of something...different," I venture.

Fallon widens her eyes in mock affront. "But...this is *Gorthan wool*. It's *very* much the style." Her gaze flicks toward Echo and Paige mischievously.

Before I have a chance to respond, Fallon slams the sample book shut and hands it, along with the piece of wool, to Mage Florel. "I think you should make her dress out of this," she says decidedly, shooting me a wide grin. "In fact, I think you should make her whole wardrobe out of it."

A sharp spike of resentment wells up inside me, my heart speeding up as I eye Fallon's wand. "Wait," I say, addressing Mage Florel directly. "I'd like to see the samples for myself."

Fallon's smile morphs into a half sneer. "Good heavens, Elloren." She gestures around the room at the fabric surrounding us. "It's *all* black."

I meet her eyes. "I'd still like to see them for myself." The room goes so quiet, one could hear the prick of a pin.

Fallon's eyes bore down on me, and I actively resist being cowed by her. They're mesmerizing, her eyes, striped as they are with alternating lines of light and dark green, the lighter green streaks so light they're almost white. They make me think of icicles. Sharp as spears.

After a moment of tense deliberation, Mage Florel sets the book down on another raised table beside me. "Of course, dear," she says, her eyes flicking toward Fallon warily. "Go ahead."

I open the book, uncomfortably aware of Fallon's icy glare. I flip through the fabric, a violet-black square of velvet momentarily catching my eye, soft as a baby hare.

"Oh...look at this," I gasp, half forgetting about Fallon as I turn to the next sample, the black silk lighting up red and yellow around the folds as it moves. "It's extraordinary." I turn the fabric this way and that, tipping it toward the closest wall lantern to watch the colors change.

Mage Florel nods her head in satisfaction. "Ishkartan goldweave," she says as she removes the swath and cradles it. "Brought in from the Eastern Desert. Flame-gold worked right into the weave. Very fine. Very rare."

I look down at the scratchy brown wool of my tunic from home. It's like trying to compare the finest violin with some coarsely carved instrument.

Mage Florel smiles at me. "You've lovely taste, Mage Gardner."

I flip through the next samples and come to an abrupt stop as my eyes light on the loveliest one of all. Midnight black silk. Patterned with vines woven through so subtly you have to look carefully to make them out. But once you do...

I run my finger along the textured silk. "It's so *beautiful*."

"Salishen silk," Mage Florel says reverently. "From the Salishen Isles. They're master weavers, the Salish. True artists. And all of their embroidery is as exquisite as this."

I glance up at her. "Do you think you could use this?"

"Of course, Mage Gardner," she replies, obviously thrilled by my choice.

Fallon's hand comes down on the fabric. "You can't use this," she says, her tone hard.

I blink up at her in resentful surprise. "Why?"

"*Because*," she replies, her voice syrupy with condescension, "this is what *my* dress is being made of."

"Ah, what a pity," Mage Florel sighs. She pats my shoulder sympathetically. "I've others, Mage Gardner, don't you fret. We'll find something *just* as lovely for you..."

Heart racing, I put my own hand down firmly on the fabric sample, right next to Fallon's. I meet Fallon's stare and hold it. "No. I want *this* one."

Everyone gapes at me.

Fallon leans in a fraction and bares her teeth. "You *can't have it*."

I try to ignore the slight trembling of my hand. "Oh, come now, Fallon," I say as I gesture at the fabric around us, mimicking her sneering tone. "It's *all* black. And I'm sure the cut will be different." I look over at Mage Florel, whose eyes are as wide as everyone else's. "Can you make sure it's very different from hers?"

Fallon spits out a sound of contempt. "My dress isn't being made *here*. I have my *own* dressmaker."

"Well, then," I tell her. "That simplifies things." I turn to Mage Florel. "Can you make it for me in time? With this fabric?"

Mage Florel gives me an appraising look, her eyes darting toward Fallon as if weighing the options. She lifts her chin. "Why, *yes*, Mage Gardner. I think I can." She smiles coldly at Fallon. "Why don't you tell me what your dress is like, dear? I'll make sure it's *quite* different."

I'm surprised and bolstered by Mage Florel's support. But when I turn back toward Fallon, her grin startles me. It's wide and malicious. She jerks her hand away from the fabric sample and seems pleased when I flinch. "I'm leaving," she announces, keeping her eyes tight on mine.

Echo and Paige fly to her and try to placate her and convince her to stay.

I look away and flip through the samples, barely seeing the fabric. I know it's a mistake to say more. But I think of her treatment of the little girl and can't help myself.

"Don't worry, Fallon," I say, careful not to look at her, struggling to keep my voice even. "Maybe your tailor can make you another dress. In Gorthan wool. I hear it's very much the style."

I glance up at Fallon just in time to catch her look of pure, undisguised hostility. Her fist tight on her wand, Fallon stalks out and slams the door behind her.

Out of the corner of my eye, I catch Sparrow's mouth twitching into a fleeting grin.

CHAPTER NINE

The Black Witch

"You look just like Carnissa Gardner. You're *perfect.*"

Paige gushes as I stare at the stranger looking back at me from the full-length ornate mirror.

We're in the luxurious bedroom Aunt Vyvian has given me, the crystalline doors and the sunroom's windows propped open, a balmy ocean breeze wafting in on the night air, the white kittens tussling on my bed. I've met with Paige a number of times over the past few days, lunching with her and Aunt Vyvian twice in the city and shopping together once for shoes. I greatly prefer her company to both Echo's and Fallon's.

For the past hour, Mage Florel has been primping and painting me while Aunt Vyvian stands watch, arms crossed. My aunt directs Mage Florel with the seriousness of a master painter overseeing a work of vital importance, and before long, it seems as if I'm not really in the room. As if I'm staring at someone else, disbelief washing over me.

The messy hair I've never known what to do with now hangs past my shoulders, woven into intricate braids, my eyes rendered large and mysterious by heavy makeup. My eyebrows, which have been plucked and shaped, heighten the effect. My lips are now full and scarlet, my cheekbones accented with blush. It's amazing—all of the unpleasant, sharp lines of my face transformed into a vision of powerful elegance. And that's not all—my ears and neck are graced with gold-set emeralds, and the gown Mage Florel made for me...

It's breathtaking. The subtly woven vines appear and disappear as the fabric moves, the shimmering tunic like a second skin flowing out over the underskirt.

My grandmother, more than any other woman, was the standard bearer of Gardnerian beauty. Known as "The Black Witch" by our enemies, she was one of the most powerful Gardnerian Mages ever. Intellectually brilliant, artistically gifted, stunningly beautiful and a ruthlessly effective commander of our military forces—she was all of these things.

And I don't just resemble her. I'm her *absolute spitting image*.

"Yes," Aunt Vyvian breathes, "that will do. I think our work here is finished, Heloise." She gets up and smiles broadly. "Elloren, you will come down to the party in an hour's time. Paige will escort you." She turns to Paige. "Bring her down the central staircase. I want her to make an entrance." My aunt pauses to take me in once more, then leaves with Mage Florel, the two women chatting amiably as they go.

I go back to staring at myself in the mirror, dumbstruck.

"You must be *so* proud," Paige says reverently. "Your grandmother was such a great woman. You must have a calling to follow in her footsteps, Elloren, or else the Ancient One wouldn't have blessed you with her looks. Wait until everyone sees you!"

I follow Paige through the winding hallways, populated only by the occasional, harried Urisk maid rushing past and deferentially ignoring us.

As we step out onto a cherrywood-banistered mezzanine, I feel my throat go dry. I pause at the crest of a sweeping staircase and look down over a mammoth, circular hall.

A sea of important-looking Gardnerians lies before us, uniformly garbed in black. Roughly half of them are in military uniform, most high-ranking, a few wearing the silver-edged cloaks of the magically powerful.

First, there are a few curious glances our way. Then someone gasps. A hush falls over the room.

I blink down at them, distracted by the enormous chandelier that dominates the foyer—hundreds of candles set on the branches of a carved, inverted frostbirch tree hung with leaf-shaped crystals. It suffuses the entire room with a dancing, changeable glow.

My eyes circle around the foyer, my gaze drawn toward a man standing in its center. He's tall and slender and wearing a long, dark priest's tunic, the image of a white bird emblazoned on his chest. He's younger than most priests, with compelling razor-sharp features, a high forehead and straight black hair that falls to his shoulders. His green eyes are so intense and vivid, they seem to glow white-hot, as if lit from within.

He's staring at me with a look of recognition so strong, it throws me.

An image bursts into view—the scorched shell of a tree, black limbs rising up against a barren sky.

Sucked into the image's dark void, I grasp at the balcony for support.

The tree flickers then sputters out.

I squint up at the chandelier and let out a deep breath. Perhaps a trick of the light. It had to be a trick of the light.

Heart pulsing, I glance back down at the priest. He's still staring at me with disconcerting familiarity. My aunt is standing close beside him. She beckons me to join their circle with one graceful, outstretched hand, her dark tunic and skirts winking sapphire.

Paige puts her hand on my shoulder, her voice soft and encouraging. "Go ahead, Elloren."

Feeling rattled, I force one foot in front of the other and focus on the rich, emerald carpeting of the stairs that mutes my footsteps and blessedly keeps me from slipping on my new, slick heels, my hand tight on the shiny railing. The cherrywood steadies me, the source tree solid and strong.

As I step off the last stair, the wide-eyed, appreciative crowd parts, and soon I'm standing before the young priest. The image of the lifeless tree sputters to life once more. Thrown, I blink hard to clear the image, and it rapidly fades to nothing.

There's something so wrong here. It's like I'm standing before a deep forest, everyone sure that nothing's amiss. But a wolf is waiting in the shadows.

I meet the priest's overpowering stare.

"Elloren," my aunt beams. Her hand sweeps toward him. "This is Marcus Vogel. He sits on the Mage Council with me and may well be our next High Mage. Priest Vogel, my niece, Elloren Gardner."

Marcus Vogel reaches out with serpentine grace, takes my hand and leans to kiss it, fascinated curiosity lighting his gaze.

I fight the urge to slink back.

His skin is oddly warm. Almost hot. And he's looking at me as if he can see clear into the back of my head to the image of the tree still reverberating there.

"Elloren Gardner," he croons, his voice unexpectedly throaty. There's a subtle, seductive quality to him that sets off a prob-ing heat deep in my center—like an eerie invasion. I tense my-self against it.

Vogel closes his eyes, smiles and takes a deep breath. "*Her* power. It *courses* through your veins." He opens his eyes, his gaze now riveted on my hand. He traces a finger languidly over the skin of it, and an uncomfortable shiver works its way up my spine. Vogel lifts his gaze to mine, eyes intent, his voice a lull. "Can you *feel* it?"

I'm cast into a troubled confusion. "No," I force out as I try to unobtrusively tug my hand away. He holds firm.

"Has she been wandtested?" His question to my aunt comes out thick as dark honey.

"Yes, several times," my aunt assures him. "She's powerless."

"Are you *sure*?" he asks, his unflinching eyes boring down on Aunt Vyvian.

My confident, unflappable aunt visibly wilts under Vogel's penetrating stare. "Yes...yes, quite." Aunt Vyvian falters. "Her uncle assured me of it. He had her formally tested again only last year."

I look to my aunt, astonished by both her cowering behavior and her words. No one wandtested me a year ago. I haven't been tested since I was a small child.

Why did Uncle Edwin lie?

Vogel's black void presses into me, warm and relentless, and I inwardly shrink back from it, eyeing his fiery stare with mounting trepidation.

Why does he unnerve me so much when Aunt Vyvian and so many other Mages clearly worship the ground he walks on?

Vogel releases my hand and I pull it back protectively, fingers repeatedly clenching, trying to throw off the disturbing feel of him.

"What a pity," he laments, reaching up to touch my face with deft, artist's fingers. I resist the urge to recoil. He tilts his head in question and breathes deeply, as if smelling the air. "And yet... there is something of Carnissa's essence about her. It's *strong*."

"Ah, yes," my aunt assents with a wistful smile, "she *does* have some of Mother in her." Aunt Vyvian proudly launches into a description of my musical accomplishments, my easy acceptance into University.

Vogel's half listening to her, his eyes fixed on my hands. "You're not fasted," he says to me, the words flat and oddly hard.

Defiance flares, deep in my core. I look straight at him. "Neither are you."

"Good Heavens, child," a neatly bearded Council member puts in, a golden Council *M* pinned to his tunic. "Mage Vogel's a *priest*. Of *course* he's not fasted." The Council Mage shakes his head and titters a nervous, apologetic laugh toward Priest Vogel.

Vogel ignores him. "She needs to be well fasted," he says to my aunt, his eyes tight on mine.

"She will be," Aunt Vyvian assures him.

Vogel briefly turns to my aunt. "To someone of considerable power."

She smiles conspiratorially. "Of course, Marcus. She's under my wing now."

"Has she met Lukas Grey?"

Aunt Vyvian leans to whisper something into Vogel's ear, her stiff skirts rustling. The other members of their circle fall into easy conversation with each other.

I barely hear them, distracted by the feel of Marcus Vogel's penetrating stare.

The sound of a boisterous group entering finally draws my attention away.

Fallon Bane sweeps into the room. She's surrounded by a throng of handsome military apprentices in slate-gray uniforms, as well as her military guard and a few other officers decked out in soldier black. Orbiting them is a smattering of lovely young women.

But none is more beautiful than Fallon.

If she possessed a gown made of the same fabric as mine, she quickly abandoned it. The lush gown she now wears is a spectacular, glittering affair that flies in screaming defiance of the accepted dress code—scandalously purple on the edge of black, rather than black on the edge of purple. The two military men she's flanked by possess her same features, stunning eyes and smug grin. They must be Fallon's brothers—one of them taller, his uniform black, while the other wears military-apprentice gray. And they both bear five stripes of silver on their arms.

Fallon instantly zeroes in on me. She lifts a hand as if taunting me, and sends a spiral of smoke rising up that flashes a rainbow of colors. The crowd erupts into delighted "oohs" and "aahs" as all the attention in the room pivots toward her. The older military men in our circle eye her with wary deliberation. Military apprentices aren't supposed to use magic unless they have permission—it can be grounds for dismissal from our Mage Guard.

The military commander near my aunt gestures toward the officer beside him with a subtle patting of the air—*let it go*. My head starts to throb. Apparently Fallon Bane isn't just powerful. It seems she exists independent of all the usual rules.

Fallon jerks her wand, and the colored smoke disappears in a riot of multicolored sparking. The young people surrounding her laugh and applaud.

Fallon resheathes her wand, narrows her eyes at me, leans in toward her taller black-clad brother and murmurs something as the others listen in. They all give each other looks of surprise, then turn to peer at me with expressions of amused disgust.

I clench my toes stiffly, heart sinking, and wonder what lies she's spreading about me.

CHAPTER TEN

The Prophecy

After my aunt gives us leave, Paige leads me quickly away. Her arm's threaded through mine as she pulls me through a pair of open, ornate doors and into a huge ballroom. Orchestral music swells around us, and I find myself quickly caught up in the grandeur of it.

We're surrounded by well-to-do Gardnerians, some whirling on the dance floor. Many of the people we pass gasp at the sight of me, smile appreciatively and come forward to extend compliments to my "most excellent family." Some Urisk servants in smart white tunics circulate with golden trays of small delicacies. Other Urisk serve food from a large table that holds a wide assortment of offerings set off beautifully by vases of red roses, everything richly lit by the multiple branched candelabras that grace the table.

Paige leads me through the crowd toward the food, then gives a start as she spots Fallon and her friends entering, surrounded by Fallon's military guard. Paige hurriedly grabs two plates, throws some candied fruit on them both and pulls me into a dim corner, the two of us partially hidden by a gigantic potted fern.

"Is that Sylus next to Fallon?" I ask as Paige hands me a plate.

Paige's brow goes tense as she nibbles at a sugared gooseberry. "Yes, that's him."

I shoot her a sympathetic glance as I take a bite of candied cherry. If Sylus Bane is anything like his sister, it's the worst of luck for mild Paige to be fasted to him.

I glance around as Paige picks at the berries, her fingers quickly becoming sticky from the sugary fruit. My eyes widen in surprise as I catch sight of familiar faces.

"It's... Sage Gaffney's parents," I murmur to Paige in astonishment. They're in the broad hallway just off to the side of the ballroom, dressed in their usual high-necked, dour, conservative garb. Their expressions are solemn and pained, and they're being hugged by a series of well-wishers, the peoples' faces full of grave concern. I scour the room for other members of their family and find Sage's oldest brother, Shane. He's at the other end of the food tables, standing beside another potted fern, dressed in his soldier's uniform and glowering at the crowd.

Paige places her hand on mine in caution. "Elloren, you can't say her name. And you shouldn't go to them. Something *terrible* has happened..."

"I know," I tell her. "I know all about it. But I don't understand. Why can't I say her name?"

Paige swallows, her eyes flitting toward the Gaffneys fretfully. "She's been *Banished*."

"*Banished?*" I blanch, my mouth falling open. It's a ritual cutting off. Like a funeral. Reserved for those whose actions are so heinous, their very existence is to be erased to restore honor and purity to their family. "But...my aunt told me they're trying to help her."

Paige glances over at Sage's family, her expression mournful. "I guess she didn't want to be helped."

I remember how mad Sage was. Giving birth to an Icaral demon—it's enough to drive anyone mad. An image fills my mind of Sage weaving me wreaths of ribbons and meadowlark flowers when I was a child. Of Sage letting me play with her little goats. And later, as teens, of Sage patiently teaching me how to embroider intricate designs. We'd sit under the broad oak tree that lies halfway between her estate and my cottage, quietly sewing Ironflowers along the hems of our garments. I always admired her for her quiet grace and artistic ways.

I set my plate down. "I'm going to speak to her brother."

Paige fidgets. I can see she wants no part of this, that she's scared by the Gaffneys' proximity to a real-life nightmare, but she doesn't stop me as I cross the ballroom to Shane's side.

Shane's hand is grasped around a crystal cup tightly as if he's trying to decide whom to throw it at. He's shorter than most of the young soldiers here, but compensates for it with the wiry, athletic build of a fighter—all lean muscle and angry, coiled energy.

"Shane," I say carefully as I approach, looking around and keeping my voice low. "I heard about Sage."

He grimaces sharply. "Don't you know you're not supposed to say her name?" He gestures toward his family with his cup, a disgusted look on his face. "They might Banish you, too."

I glance over at the Gaffneys, troubled. "What happened to her? Is she okay?"

His expression darkens with worry and he shakes his head. "I don't know, Elloren. I don't know where she is. No one knows. And my younger sisters have run off with her."

My breath catches tight. *Her sisters, too!* I remember the surreal sight of Sage heading into the wilderness and feel a sharp spike of guilt. *Oh, Ancient One, I should have said something...*

He shakes his head again in disbelief. "They sent the *entire* Fifth Division out after them. But they couldn't find them. It's like they all disappeared into thin air."

The Fifth Division is made up of the best Gardnerian trackers. It's impossible to hide from them. They gained notoriety during the Realm War, ferreting out secret enemy bases, locating hidden groups of dangerous Fae. It's rumored that the best of them can read a week-old trail left behind in the woods. I know all this because they've been actively recruiting my brother, Rafe, for a few years now.

"Isn't that your division?" I ask. "Why aren't you out with them?" Shane's a tracker. And a talented one at that. Just like Rafe.

Shane's face twists into a mask of bitterness. "Well, Elloren, it seems they thought I lacked the necessary level of detachment needed to kill my own sister."

My face blanches. "*Kill* her?"

Shane's expression turns pained. "She didn't just give birth to an Icaral, Elloren. They believe she's given birth to *the* Icaral."

I'm frozen into stunned silence.

We all know of the Prophecy, set down by the late Atellian Lumyn, one of the greatest Seers our church has ever known.

A Great Winged One will soon arise and cast his fearsome shadow upon the land. And just as Night slays Day, and Day slays Night, so also shall another Black Witch rise to meet him, her powers vast beyond imagining. And as their powers clash upon the field of battle, the heavens shall open, the mountains tremble and the waters run crimson…and their fates shall determine the future of all Erthia.

Lumyn was considered to be a prophet, his writings read by all pious Gardnerians and second only to our holy scripture, *The Book of the Ancients*. He died when I was a child living in Valgard, and I still remember the crowded streets on the day of his funeral, the communal outpouring of grief.

Mage Lumyn accurately predicted the rise of my grandmother to power and her battle with an Icaral demon. He set down his final Prophecy soon after my grandmother's death and the end of the Realm War, and it sent waves of shock barreling through Gardneria. My people thought the Icaral demons were defeated. That they were finally safe from the Icarals' terrible fire and winged darkness. But now an even greater demonic threat loomed on the horizon.

"The time is here," Shane rasps in a harsh whisper. "The Church Seers have confirmed it. And not just *them*. The Seers of other races, too. They've all read the same message—the Icaral of Prophecy is here. A male, possessed of his wings and full powers. Every other male Icaral has been captured and stripped of its wings. Don't you see, Elloren? It *has* to be my sister's baby."

"No." I shake my head, desperate to refute this. It's too awfully bizarre. How could kind, thoughtful Sage give birth to the demon of Prophecy? "It can't be…"

But I know from his expression that it can.

Shane looks down at his punch glass, barely able to contain his misery. "Did you know he beat her?"

"Who?"

"Who do you *think*? *Tobias*. Quite the temper that one has." He looks around at the crowd, anguish breaking through. "You know, she did everything they ever wanted her to do. *All* of them. He started in on her soon after she got to University. That's why she ran off with that *Kelt*." Now he's grasping his glass so hard I fear it might shatter. "He took advantage of her," Shane grinds out, fury swimming in his eyes. "Isn't that just like a *Kelt*? He *used* my sister, forced his *filthy self* on her and *now…*" He breaks off, his eyes glazing over with angry tears.

I reach out for him, but he flinches away from me.

"Shane, it can't be," I press, undaunted. "The Prophecy isn't just about an Icaral. There has to be a Black Witch, too, and there isn't anyone with that level of power…"

Shane shoots me a look of wild incredulity. "Of *course* there is. Or there will be." He glances pointedly across the room at the Banes.

My throat tightens. *Fallon Bane.* The next Black Witch. Sent to kill the demon baby of Sage Gaffney. It's the stuff of nightmares.

I turn back to Shane, my voice weak. "Do you really think Fallon Bane could become that powerful?"

"Yes, at the rate her power's growing." Shane's face closes down, his voice going hard, devoid of all hope. "There's nothing that can be done about it, Elloren. It's all over for my sister. Go back to your family. This isn't your affair."

I look toward Fallon.

She pulls out her wand and mock points it at a thin military apprentice. He freezes and goes pale, the others in her party growing silent and tense.

This isn't allowed. Apprentices are forbidden from pulling wands on each other.

I'm stunned. There are officers dotting the entire ballroom and, again, no one rebukes Fallon for a flagrant violation of the rules.

Fallon laughs and resheathes her wand, diffusing the tension, the onlookers breaking out into nervous laughter. The young apprentice gives them all a thin, frightened smile before slinking away.

Fallon watches him leave, then fixes her eyes on me. Her smile is slow and deliberate, her message unmistakable.

Careful, Elloren Gardner. That could easily be you.

CHAPTER
ELEVEN

Aislinn Greer

Shane takes his leave, and in an effort to calm myself down, I walk over to the refreshment table to get something to drink.

I pour myself some punch but find that my hands are shaking, the glass ladle chattering against the crystal cup as I fill it with sweet, red liquid dotted with edible flower petals. Summoned by Sylus, Paige has reluctantly gone to join him, leaving me all alone.

Suddenly aware of someone's eyes on me, I glance to the side.

A slight, plain young woman with intelligent green eyes is regarding me calmly from where she sits, a book open and facedown on her lap, her hands resting on it. She's dressed like Echo Flood, in a conservative, multilayered frock with a silver Erthia sphere hanging from it. No makeup. I notice that the hands resting on her book are unmarked, like mine, and it seems incongruous. Her dress pegs her as a girl from a very conservative family, yet she's unfasted.

"Fallon doesn't seem to like you," she comments as she glances over at Fallon, who's laughing and eating with her friends. She smiles at me sympathetically, her eyes kind. "You're brave, you know. In your choice of enemies."

"You don't like her, then?" I ask, surprised.

The young woman shakes her head. "Fallon? She's mean as a snake. So are her brothers." She shoots me a look of caution. "Mind you, if you tell anyone I said that, I'll deny it."

I raise my eyebrows, relieved to finally be meeting someone outside Fallon's social circle. I extend my hand to her. "I'm Elloren Gardner."

She laughs and takes my hand in hers. "*That's* obvious. I've heard all about you."

"Let me guess," I say guardedly. "I'm the girl who looks exactly like my grandmother?"

"No," she laughs, "you're the girl who's been living under a rock somewhere up north. But I think your *real* claim to fame is that you've never been kissed."

My face going hot, I sigh and reach up to massage my aching forehead. "I should never have told her that."

"Don't worry," she says, trying to comfort me. "I *have* been kissed, and it's overrated."

I stop rubbing my forehead. "Really?"

"*Really*. Two people, smushing their mouths together, tasting each other's spit, possibly with food bits mixed into it. It's not at all appealing, when you really think about it."

I let out a short laugh. "You're a dyed in the wool romantic, aren't you?"

"I am not the least bit romantic," she affirms, somewhat proudly. "Romance just complicates life, sets up unrealistic expectations."

She sits there so neatly, her discreet dress perfectly pressed, her long black hair carefully brushed and pulled back off her face with two silver barrettes.

"Maybe you just haven't met the right young man yet," I offer.

"No, I've met him," she says, matter-of-factly. "We'll be wandfasted by the end of the year. He's over there." She gestures with her chin toward the entrance to the large ballroom. "The one just to the right of the door."

He's much like all the other young men who are milling about. Square jaw, black hair, green eyes.

I turn back to her. "So you've kissed him."

"Yes, it's expected." She sighs with resignation. "They wait so long for...other things, our men. We're supposed to throw them a bone every now and then, I guess."

"But you don't like it."

"It's not *awful*, don't get me wrong. I mean, it's *tolerable*."

Her lack of enthusiasm makes me laugh. "You make it sound like doing chores!"

"Well, it kind of *is*." She's smiling at me good-humoredly.

"You feel this way, and you're okay with fasting to him? With *marrying* him?"

She shrugs. "Oh, Randall's all right. He'll make a good fastmate, I suppose. My parents picked him out for me, and I trust them."

"You mean you had no say in the matter?"

"I don't need to have a say. I trust them. I knew they wouldn't pick someone mean. They chose fastmates for my two older sisters, as well."

I'm fascinated by her complete acceptance of this. "Don't you want to choose your own fastmate?" Uncle Edwin would never just pick someone for me. Maybe he'd introduce me to someone nice, but he'd certainly leave the decision solely with me.

She shrugs. "It doesn't really matter who chooses. Most of them are pretty interchangeable anyway. I mean, look at them." She gestures toward a group of young men dismissively. "It's hard to even tell them apart."

She has a point. Looking around the room, I have to admit I'd be hard-pressed to find a memorable face, one that stands out in true contrast.

"What are you reading?" I ask, noticing her book again.

She flushes. "Oh, it's just a book for University," she explains, a little too innocently. "I'm getting a head start on my reading."

The cover confirms what she's told me: *An Annotated History of Gardneria.* On second thought, though, the paper cover doesn't fit the book *exactly*, hanging a bit over on the sides.

"What are you *really* reading?" I probe.

At first, her eyes widen in surprise, and then she slumps back in her chair, sighs and hands the book over in mock defeat. "You can't tell anyone," she whispers conspiratorially.

I peek under the cover and flip through it. "Love poems!" I whisper back, chuckling. I hand the book back to her and smile. "I thought you weren't romantic."

"Not in real life," she clarifies. "I guess I like the idea of it, though. But I realize it's pure, unadulterated fantasy."

"You're funny," I say, smiling at her.

She cocks her head to one side, considering me. "And you're completely different than how I expected you'd be. I'm Aislinn Greer, by the way. My father sits on the Mage Council with your aunt. We'll be fellow scholars at University."

"Elloren, I see you've made a new friend."

I turn to find my aunt gliding up to us.

"Good evening, Mage Damon." Aislinn greets my aunt respectfully as she covers the book with both hands.

"Good evening, Aislinn," Aunt Vyvian beams. "I was just speaking with your father. So nice to see you here." She turns to me. "Elloren, I'd like you to go fetch your violin. Priest Vogel would like to hear you perform for us this evening."

My stomach drops straight through the floor. "Perform? Now? For *everyone*?"

"Your uncle has told me time and again how extraordinarily talented you are."

"I'm sorry, Aunt Vyvian... I... I *can't*..." I've never once performed for a crowd, and just the thought of it makes me feel sick with apprehension.

"Nonsense, child," Aunt Vyvian says dismissively. "Run along and fetch your instrument. *No one* keeps the next High Mage waiting."

CHAPTER
TWELVE

Lukas Grey

It's a relief when I finally leave the crowded ballroom for the private hallway that leads to my room, my feet cramped in my pinching shoes. I briefly ponder escape.

I enter the deserted room and my breath immediately catches tight in my throat.

There, lying open on my bed, is a violin case. Within, nestled comfortably in green velvet, is a Maelorian violin—the highest-quality violin in the Western Realm, made by Elves in the northern Maelorian Mountains from rare Alfsigr spruce. There's a note card carefully slid under the strings, a message written in my aunt's flowing script.

Make the family proud.

I sit down beside the violin and stare at it. How Aunt Vyvian obtained the use of such an instrument, I can't begin to imagine. When I finally take it in my hands, I feel as if I'm lifting a holy object. A picture of a tapering Alfsigr spruce tree set on a sloping mountainside caresses my mind as I gently pluck at the strings.

Perfectly in tune.

A tingling excitement bubbles up within me as I tighten the bow, lift the instrument into position and slide the bow across the A string.

A perfect note sounds on the air, pure as a still blue lake.

A rush of joy quickens my heart. Overwhelmed, I set the instrument down, go to my travel bag and fish excitedly through the music folder for my favorite piece, *Winter's Dark*, quickly locating the stiff parchment. I stare at the crisp lines of notes, the music already dancing in my head.

I glance over at the door and my euphoria rapidly implodes, my unwelcome task waiting to press down on me like a miller's stone.

Steeling myself, I make a decision. If I'm going to go down in flames in front of half of Valgard, I might as well go down in flames to the tune of the most beautiful piece of music ever composed for the violin.

I carefully secure the violin, tuck my music under one arm, force myself to my feet and purposefully walk out to meet my doom—well, as purposefully as one can possibly walk in the most uncomfortable shoes ever invented.

I reenter the crowded ballroom and immediately begin to fall apart at the seams, my mouth becoming dry, my gut clenching and worst of all—my hands start to tremble.

My aunt regards me with a polite smile as I approach. She's speaking with Priest Vogel and a group of Mage Council members. Marcus Vogel stares at me with unblinking intensity, and I wonder again if he can read my mind.

"Thank you for the use of this…amazing violin, Aunt Vyvian," I say, my voice quavering.

"You're quite welcome, dear," she beams. "We're ready for you." She gestures toward a gold music stand positioned next to the orchestra and in front of a magnificently carved piano, the ebony of its wood cut into the likeness of multiple trees that support the piano's broad surface on leafy branches.

Aunt Vyvian leads me to the music stand. The members of the orchestra dip their heads and smile in greeting. I stoop down to fumble with the violin case as the trembling in my hands worsens.

"This is Enith," my aunt says. I look up to see a young Urisk girl with wide, sapphire eyes and bright blue skin. "She can turn the pages for you."

"Pages?"

My aunt looks at me like I've taken leave of my senses. "Of your *music*."

"Oh, yes...of course." I straighten up and reach under my arm, handing the parchment to the Urisk girl. She takes in my shaking hands, her brow knit with worry.

The conversation in the vast room gradually dies down to a hush as more and more of the guests notice my aunt waiting for their attention.

"I'd like to introduce my niece, Elloren Gardner," Aunt Vyvian says smoothly. "Some of you have had the pleasure of meeting her already. Some of you will be attending University with her this year."

I look out over the crowd and am horrified to see Fallon working her way to the front with a large group of young people.

I reach up to turn to the first page of my music and knock it clear off the stand, the pages scattering everywhere on the floor.

"Sorry," I choke out hoarsely.

I crouch down and fumble around for the pages, the Urisk girl stooping to help me. I can hear Fallon and her entourage trying to disguise their derisive laughter with coughing.

After what seems like a mortifying eternity, I rise. The Urisk girl grabs the music from my hands, perhaps not willing to let me ruin her designated end of the job.

I lean down again to lift the violin out of its case, rise, steady it with my chin and tense my bow arm to try and bring my trembling under control.

Fallon and her group watch me with wicked anticipation. Aislinn Greer, who's standing near the front of the crowd, nods with friendly encouragement.

I fear I might throw up right there in front of all of them if I hesitate any longer, so I begin.

My bow strafes the violin with a harsh screech and I wince, surprising even myself with how incredibly horrible I sound. I plow on, disastrously off-key, as I struggle to stay focused on the music, feeling like I'm rapidly losing all control of my shaking hands.

I stop, violin still poised, tears stinging at my eyes, too ashamed to look into the crowd.

More coughing and shocked laughter waft over from Fallon's direction.

The sound of their ridicule sends a spike of angry hurt through me, unexpectedly steeling my resolve. The violin's wood faintly pulses with warmth. The image of rough, strong branches flickers behind my eyes then retreats, as if the wood is trying to reach me.

Bolstered, I concentrate on relaxing my hands, force the trembling into submission and begin again. This time my bow slides smoothly across the strings and the melody begins to fall into place. I grit my teeth and play on, the quality of the instrument rendering the music nearly passable...

And then it begins.

Piano music from behind me, accompanying me.

But not just any piano music—*beautiful* music, twining itself around my feeble attempts at the melody.

I falter for a moment in disbelief.

The piano music catches me, slowing where I've stumbled, improvising where I've missed the notes. Another swell of warmth suffuses the wood as sinuous branches fill my mind, winding through me.

I relax and fall into the music, little by little, my hands steadying, the notes coming into focus. I close my eyes. I don't need to look at the music. I *know* this song.

The crowd in front of me fades then disappears until it's just me, the violin, the piano and the tree.

And then, no longer relying on the piano for a safety net, I suddenly take off, my hands now steady and sure, the music soaring. I continue beautifully on, even after the piano falls away, leaving me to dive into the long violin solo at the heart of the piece.

Tears come to my eyes as the melody reaches its crescendo, the music piercing through me. I let it flow, through the wood of the bow, the wood of the violin, as I gently, gracefully bring the piece to its mournful close.

I lower my bow, eyes still closed, the room stone silent for one blessed, magical moment.

The ballroom erupts into loud, enthusiastic applause.

I open my eyes as the crowd converges around me, the members of the small orchestra showering me with a cacophony of praise and compliments.

But perhaps the clearest measure of the quality of my performance can be seen in the expression on Fallon Bane's face. She stands, her mouth agape, looking horrified, while her friends regard me with newly blossoming approval.

I turn to find out who my savior at the piano is, and my breath hitches when I see him.

He is, by far, the best-looking young man I have ever seen in my life, with strong, finely chiseled features, the dashing attire of a Gardnerian soldier and absolutely riveting deep green eyes.

And he's smiling at me.

I can guess who this is without needing to be introduced. *Lukas Grey.*

He gets up from the piano seat in one fluid, graceful movement. He's tall with broad shoulders, the lean body of a natural athlete, and the controlled movements of a panther. And the sleeves of his black military tunic are marked with five silver bands.

As he approaches me, Fallon Bane immediately falls in next to him, threads her arm territorially through his and fixes me with a threatening glare.

Lukas glances down at Fallon's arm with surprised amusement, then looks back up at me and cocks one black eyebrow, as if we're old friends sharing an inside joke. Suddenly, my aunt appears at Lukas's other side and she focuses in on Fallon, a pleasant, yet calculating look on her face.

"Fallon, dear," she croons, "Priest Vogel and I need to speak with you."

Fallon's face goes pale and takes on an expression of sheer panic as her eyes dart back and forth from Lukas to me and back to my aunt again. She opens her mouth as if trying to formulate a protest, but nothing comes out. Lukas continues to look at me with those dazzling eyes, amused by the situation.

"Come along, dear." My aunt directs Fallon. She gestures across the room to where Priest Vogel stands surrounded by a bright-eyed, adoring throng. I cautiously meet the priest's piercing gaze, and he nods.

Fallon releases Lukas's arm like she's abandoning a hard-won treasure and shoots me a look of pure loathing. "I'll be *right back*," she snipes as she passes, her tone holding a thick edge of menace.

As my aunt leads her firmly away, Fallon glances back at us repeatedly, her face a mask of furious desperation.

I turn to Lukas.

Holy Ancient One, he's beautiful.

"Thank you for playing," I say with honest gratitude.

He places an arm casually on the top of the piano, leaning

into it. "It was a pleasure. It's not often that I get to play with a superior musician. It was a privilege, actually."

I laugh nervously. "I'm not the superior musician. I pretty much butchered the beginning."

His eyes glint. "Yes, well, you were nervous. But you quickly made up for it."

He languidly pushes himself up and holds his hand out to me. "I'm Lukas Grey."

"I know," I reply unsteadily, taking his hand. His handshake is firm and strong.

"You *know*?" he says, cocking an eyebrow.

"Fallon. When I saw her take your arm, I figured out who you were. She told me that you're about to be fasted to her."

"Oh, *did* she now?" He's grinning again.

"Aren't you?"

"No."

"Oh."

"She did corner me earlier to tell me all about *you*," he says, smiling.

"What did she say?"

"Well, the obvious. That you look exactly like your grandmother." He leans in so close I can feel his breath on my ear. "I've seen portraits of your grandmother. You're much more attractive than she ever was."

I gulp, mesmerized by him.

He straightens back up as my face starts to betray my quickening pulse by coloring.

"What else did she tell you?" I ask.

"She said that you're head over heels in love with Gareth Keeler."

A nervous laugh comes sputtering out of me. "Oh, for goodness' sake."

"So it's not true?"

"No!" I say, scrunching my face up in disbelief. "I mean… we used to take *baths* together!"

He grins wickedly.

"In a *washbasin!*" I splutter, making it worse.

"Lucky for him," he says, raising his eyebrows in delight.

"No, no…it's not at all what you're thinking."

"I'm thinking that I'm becoming more envious of Gareth Keeler by the minute."

"We were *small children*," I cry, desperately trying to exorcise the picture forming in his mind. "I've known him all my life. We grew up together. He's like a brother to me."

He just stands there, grinning, enjoying this way too much.

I sigh. "What else did Fallon tell you?" I ask, giving up.

"She told me that you've never been kissed."

I roll my eyes at this, mortified. "I should never have told her that. I think she's told everyone in the room."

He fixes me with eyes full of suggestion. "Well, that's easily remedied."

"What?" I say stupidly.

He steps back and holds out his hand. "C'mon," he says, grinning.

I can make out Fallon across the room, still cornered by my aunt, giving us a look of pure rage.

Heart pounding, I take Lukas's hand and follow as he leads me briskly through the crowd and out of the ballroom.

I pass Paige in the foyer, and her eyebrows shoot up. She frantically shakes her head from side to side and opens her mouth to say something, which comes out as an incoherent squeak. I know I'm infringing unforgivably on Fallon's territory, but this is, by far, the most thrilling thing that's ever happened to me.

I stumble a bit, trying to keep up with Lukas's long stride as he leads me around the foyer's staircase and down a series of halls. I catch glimpses of grandeur along the way—more chandeliers, a portrait of my grandmother, beautiful landscapes of the Verpacian mountains and the Voltic Sea.

The decor suddenly changes as we duck down a side hallway with deep maroon carpeting and burgundy walls suffused with the soft, amber glow of sporadic wall lamps. The hallway is deserted, the distant sounds of the party now muffled and far away. Lukas slows and leads me down the length of it, past where it curves to where it ends.

He stops and turns to face me, his grin returning. I step back and nervously feel for the wall behind me as I eye the ebony wand affixed to his belt.

He leans in close, places a hand on the wall beside me and reaches up to brush a loose tendril of my hair back behind my ear.

I swallow audibly, my heartbeat becoming erratic.

"Now," he says silkily, "what's this about your never having been kissed?"

I open my mouth to say something. To let him know that I don't know *how* to kiss, and that I'm probably very bad at it, but before I can say anything, he raises my chin, leans in and brings his lips to mine with gentle pressure, all of my concerns instantly disappearing into a puff of smoke.

He lets his lips linger on mine briefly before pulling away a fraction and bringing his mouth close to my ear. "There," he whispers softly. "Now you've been kissed."

I've fallen into a complete daze. *Aislinn was so very wrong about this.*

I reach up tentatively and place my hands on his shoulders. I can feel the warmth of him through the silk of his tunic.

"You're very beautiful," he breathes as he leans in for another kiss.

His lips are more insistent this time, and I'm growing warm to his touch in a way I've never experienced, feeling as if I'm floating deeper and deeper into a dream. He slides his hand around my waist and pulls me in close. It feels so good to be kissed by him, to be so close to him—dangerously good. Better than the feel of smooth River Maple. Better than the velvety bark of the Verpacian Elm. Better than anything.

The feeling swells into a strong flash of sensation as if every piece of wood surrounding us fleetingly blazes with torchlight. The fire courses through me from my feet, through my body, heating my lips as a vision of dark, primordial forest fills my mind.

I gasp and pull back, the fire immediately dampening, the image blurred then gone.

Lukas looks momentarily stunned, his eyes gone wide, his hands tight around me.

"They told me about you," I breathe, overwhelmed by the wild thrill of being with him. "They told me...that you're powerful."

Lukas's eyes narrow in on me intently and he flashes me a disconcertingly wicked grin. "I am," he says as he studies me. "But so are you. Perhaps even more so. I can sense it about you." His fingers lightly trace along the back of my neck. "Only you don't know it, do you?" His eyes darken. *"Yet."*

My breath catches as he teasingly runs his thumb just above the collar on the back of my dress. It's incredibly exciting and deeply alarming all at the same time.

I shake my head. "I only look like my grandmother. I've no magic."

"Really," Lukas says, cocking his head to one side contemplatively, his hand now resting loosely on my hip. "Have you ever picked up a wand, Elloren?"

"Not that I remember."

His face takes on a darker look, the edges of his lips curling. "Well," he says, pleased with this new knowledge, "we'll just have to take care of that, as well." He snakes his arm around my waist and leans in close. "You should be wandtested. By me."

"Lukas!" a male voice calls from the hallway.

My body stiffens, my face reddening. Lukas, on the other hand, seems completely unfazed.

It's Sylus Bane.

Sweet Ancient One, not another Bane. Not now.

Sylus's eyes widen when he realizes who I am, then his gaze narrows, his mouth lifting in a jaded smirk. "Well, if it isn't Mage Elloren Gardner! Fast work, Lukas. As usual, you have my complete and utter admiration." He spits out a short laugh. "Just *wait* until Fallon gets wind of *this...*"

A creeping dread shivers up my spine. *Fallon's going to kill me.*

"Is there a particular reason why you are so rudely interrupting us?" Lukas calmly asks.

There's a chilly edge to his tone, and Sylus Bane's smirk dampens. "Well," Sylus explains, "we're going...*out.* I assumed you'd be joining us. Unless, of course, you're much too busy here?"

Lukas sighs and gives me a somewhat reluctant look. He turns to face Sylus. "I'll meet you out front momentarily."

Sylus grins wickedly, as if he's won some secret contest, before he makes his exit. I relax a bit.

Lukas leans on the wall, one arm lightly around my waist.

I look closely at him. "Are you involved with Fallon Bane?"

He tilts his head and gives me a wry look. "I courted her. Briefly. Quite a while ago."

"Oh." I nod in complete understanding now.

He lets out a resigned sigh, his gaze level. "Our affinity lines clash. Disastrously, in my opinion, though obviously not in hers. She has a strong affinity for ice. I've none." He rubs his fingers along my lower back, a delicious heat trailing his touch. His mouth tilts into a grin. "I've more of an affinity for fire."

I hold his stare and imagine I could fall right into the smoldering green of it.

Trystan's told me all about Mage affinities, how magic runs

deep along elemental lines, every Mage possessing a different proportion of the five elementals: fire, earth, air, light and water, Trystan having leanings toward both fire and water magic.

I can sense Lukas's magic. I can feel his fire.

Lukas has grown quiet and appears to be considering something.

"Come to the Yule dance with me," he says.

"I don't know what that is."

"It's a dance held every Yule at the University for Gardnerian scholars and graduates. Come with me."

I swallow, not believing this is happening. It has to be a dream. "All right," I say, nodding dumbly.

He grins widely and reaches up to play with my hair. "We should be getting back," he says ruefully. "Your aunt will be wondering what became of you."

"Oh, I don't know," I say, drawn in by his languid touch. "She seemed pretty happy to see us leave together."

Overjoyed, actually.

"Yes, well..." he agrees, chuckling. He pulls away and offers me his arm. I thread my arm through his, part of me feeling oddly reckless, not wanting to leave, wanting to stay here alone with him, to feel the fire of his kiss light up the room.

When we reach the foyer, a group of young soldiers and military apprentices, Sylus amongst them, shout boisterously to Lukas. I look past them to see my brother Rafe approaching at a brisk pace, his eyes darting back and forth between Lukas and myself.

"Hey, Ren," he greets me warmly.

I let go of Lukas's arm and give my brother an affectionate hug.

"Where's Trystan?" I ask, overjoyed to be with my brother again, but self-consciously aware of Lukas by my side.

"Trystan is staying with Gareth and his family," Rafe tells me, smiling. "You know how much he loves large social gatherings."

I laugh at this. "Where's the harem that Trystan says you're usually trailed by?" I tease.

He grins mischievously. "I just got here." Rafe turns to Lukas, his smile becoming tight—less a friendly gesture, more a tiger bearing its teeth. "Giving my sister a tour, were you?"

"Something like that," Lukas replies evenly.

Although Rafe is still smiling, his right arm clenches, his hand closing into a fist.

"How's that bow arm of yours, Rafe?" Lukas asks pleasantly.

"Deadly accurate as ever, Lukas."

Lukas turns to me, ignoring the sudden tension in the air. "I keep trying to get your brother to apprentice with the military. He could be very successful. Best tracker, best hunter... best Gardnerian archer I've ever seen. He's a dangerous man, your brother."

"Oh, now, I'm not all that dangerous, Lukas," Rafe says, still smiling. "Not unless someone were to bother my little sister, that is."

Lukas laughs at this. "I seriously doubt that she needs your protection, Rafe."

Rafe's eyes flicker toward me questioningly before lighting again on Lukas.

One of the soldiers calls out for Lukas to join them.

"I'll let you two catch up with each other," Lukas says. He takes my hand and leans to kiss the back of it, a smile on his lips. His touch sends a delicious chill down my spine and I struggle to maintain my composure. "Elloren, it's been a pleasure meeting you," he says, his eyes locked on mine. He straightens and turns to my brother. "Rafe," he says as he tips his head to my brother in acknowledgment.

"Lukas," my brother replies coolly.

We both watch as Lukas strides off in the direction of his fellow soldiers and makes his exit with them.

Rafe turns to me, visibly relaxing. "I hear you were quite the star tonight." His face takes on a look of mock suspicion. "Who are you, and what have you done with my shy, reserved sister?"

"I'm her glamoured double," I laugh.

The foyer is now mostly empty, except for the two of us. It seems the party is dying down, the buzz of conversation emanating from the ballroom quieter, the music now absent.

"Hey, Ren," Rafe says, his voice uncharacteristically serious, "you know I wouldn't tell you how to run your life, right?"

I look up at him curiously, wondering what's prompted this comment.

He inhales deeply, as if wanting to choose his words carefully. "I know Aunt Vyvian wants you fasted, but…don't jump into anything with Lukas Grey, all right?"

I feel myself flushing and shrug evasively. "I'm *not*."

"I've known him a long time," Rafe cautions me. "And I know you're smart, but so is he. And he has more…*experience* in the world."

I purse my lips in embarrassed annoyance, wanting to ignore this.

Rafe lets out a long sigh and rubs at the bridge of his nose. "Just be careful, all right?"

"I will," I promise edgily.

Upon hearing this, Rafe seems to relax, and his usual easy expression returns. "All right, all right," he says, holding up his hands in mock defeat. "This concludes the overprotective older brother part of the evening."

"Good," I say with relief, attempting to bury his warning in the back of my mind. I notice a group of nice-looking girls hovering near the door to the ballroom, giggling and looking at Rafe.

"Hey, Rafe," I say, "have you ever met Aislinn Greer?"

"Not formally." He lifts one eyebrow in question.

"I just met her a while ago. I should introduce the two of you."

He laughs. "You're trying to set me up with her, aren't you?"

"Okay, I realize you don't need much help with that." I glance over at the knot of giggling girls. I suspect they'll converge around Rafe like a flock of geese as soon as I'm done talking to him. "Aislinn seems...different. She's smart...nice..."

"I'll tell you what," he bargains, amused. "There's a dance every Yule at University. You go with Gareth, and I'll ask Aislinn Greer."

"I can't," I say hesitantly, not wanting to displease my older brother. "I've already agreed to go with Lukas."

"Elloren." He reaches out to touch my arm, his voice once again serious. "I'm not kidding about Lukas Grey. Stay away from him. He's incredibly powerful. You're playing with fire there."

Maybe I want to play with fire.

"Thanks for the warning," I say, my tone completely and utterly noncommittal.

CHAPTER THIRTEEN

Wandfasting

"I received some correspondence this morning," my aunt informs me as we sit in her breakfast alcove.

We're surrounded on three sides by arching windows that overlook well-maintained gardens. A nearby display of blood-red roses pierces the gloomy, overcast day.

I can barely make out the sound of silverware on the gilded porcelain as my aunt neatly cuts into the omelete and spiced fruit before her. Her half-eaten scone sits pristinely on an adjacent plate. Everything she does—calligraphy, eating, dressing—is always so *tidy*. It's easy to feel disheveled and bumbling next to her constant perfection. I glance down at my own half-eaten scone, a circle of fine crumbs orbiting the plate.

"Correspondence from whom?" I wonder as I try to clean up my stray crumbs with the tip of my finger.

"Lukas Grey's parents."

My finger freezes. I look up, my aunt taking her time with this news as she tranquilly sips at her tea.

"Are you friends with them, then?" I ask, trying to keep my voice neutral.

My aunt shoots me a bemused smile. "Of course, dear. I've known Lachlan and Evelyn for *years.*"

I take a small bite from my scone, attempting to appear nonchalant.

"Apparently," she continues, as she cradles her teacup, "Lukas indicated to them last night that he would agree to fast to you."

I choke on the scone. *"What?"*

My aunt flashes a large, white smile at me, like a cat that has just eaten a canary. "It seems you made *quite* an impression."

"He wants to *wandfast* to me?" I sputter, crumbs flying from my mouth.

She eyes me quizzically. "Why are you so surprised? You're of age, Elloren. Most Gardnerian girls your age are already fasted, or are soon about to be…"

"But I've only just *met* him!"

"That's of no consequence," she says, waving her hand dismissively.

I stare at her, stunned. *Of no consequence. Seriously?*

"We should arrange for the two of you to be fasted as soon as possible," Aunt Vyvian states decidedly. "Enith…"

My aunt turns to the blue-skinned Urisk girl who helped me with my music last night. She stands against the wall, silent and expressionless, like a statue.

"Yes, ma'am?" Enith responds.

"Send word to the Greys," my aunt instructs. "Let them know that Elloren is *very* pleased to accept Lukas's proposal and that we would like to arrange for the fasting to take place as soon as possible. Perhaps after tomorrow's church service."

"Wait…" I plead, interrupting her. "I can't fast to Lukas."

Aunt Vyvian holds her scone in suspended animation. "What do you mean, you *can't?*"

Enith is glowering at me, wide-eyed and appalled, like I've just thrown a jar of preserves at both of them.

"I've known him exactly one day." *Sweet Ancient One, what could Lukas be thinking?*

"Elloren," my aunt breathes, setting her scone down, "this type of proposal, from a family such as this, from a young man such as Lukas Grey, does not come along every day."

"I'm sorry." I shake my head. "I can't. I've only just met him. And…and I promised Uncle Edwin…"

"Promised him *what*?"

"That I'll wait until I'm done with my education to fast to someone."

My aunt's mouth falls open. "But that's at least two years from now!"

"I know."

"Elloren," she says, her voice low, "you'd be a *fool* to turn down this proposal."

My resolve stiffens. "Perhaps if he likes me that much, he can court me first."

Her eyes take on a hard glint. "Perhaps I should send word to the Greys that they should reconsider their initial plan."

"What plan?"

"Why, to have Lukas fasted to Fallon Bane, my dear."

I freeze, completely thrown. "But," I counter, "Lukas told me he's not going to fast to Fallon."

My aunt makes a sound of derision. "Really, Elloren. Do you *honestly* think he'll wait for you forever?" Her gaze turns calculating. "I'm sure Fallon Bane would be happy to take your place."

An unbidden image of Lukas kissing smug, perfect Fallon forms in my mind, his back to me as he clings to her passionately, her eyes open, glaring at me with malicious triumph. *She* wouldn't hesitate to accept a wandfasting proposal from Lukas Grey.

But to fast to him after knowing him for only one day—that would be madness.

And Rafe has concerns. Enough to warn me off Lukas.

"Do you want to be alone all your life, Elloren?" my aunt coos, leaning forward. "Don't you want to be fasted someday? To have a family? Do you know how *unlikely* that will be if you go unfasted for much longer?" She sits back. "Of course there will be a *few* choices left after you finish University. The young men that no one else wants. But is that what you really want?"

Her words get under my skin, and I momentarily wonder if I'm making a huge mistake.

A chill starts from deep within me, and it has nothing to do with the damp outside. I suddenly very much want my uncle.

"I… I just can't," I say weakly.

She narrows her eyes at me. "What, pray tell, am I to tell Lukas's parents?"

"Tell them," I begin, my throat becoming constricted, "that I am very thankful for their proposal and I will consider it, but I need time to get to know Lukas a little better."

"It seems like you were getting to know him pretty well last night, my dear," she snipes as she takes a sip of her tea.

My face goes hot.

"Don't you think my servants tell me everything?" She purses her lips at me. "If you're going to indulge in *that* type of behavior, Elloren, you need to fast to the young man, and quickly."

I'm completely mortified.

"If you assume I'm going to sit idly by and watch while you go off to University *unfasted* and potentially disgrace your entire extended family by falling in with the wrong man, like Sage Gaffney did, you certainly don't know me very well." She sets down her tea and leans forward. "You forget, Elloren, that not only will I refuse to pay your University tithe while you are unfasted, I know and am on very close terms with the University's High Chancellor, in addition to most of the Gardnerian professors *and* the Lodging Mistress. If I need to, I can make things *very* unpleasant for you there." She collects herself and lets out a frustrated sigh. "I'm only doing this for your own good, Elloren. And for the good of our family. You do realize you can avoid all sorts of unpleasantness if you simply agree to fast to Lukas Grey."

It hurts that she would threaten me—like a sharp slap. "I'm not saying I won't consider it," I counter, thrown. "I just can't fast to him so quickly. I'd like to get to know him a little first."

If Uncle Edwin was here, he'd take my side.

"Honestly, Elloren," she says coldly, "you are making this *very* difficult for me."

My anger flares. "Then maybe it's lucky for you that you're not my official guardian."

Silence. The Urisk girl freezes, her eyes gone wide with shock.

Aunt Vyvian's gaze narrows. "My brother doesn't always have the firmest grasp on reality, my dear. I would *never* have allowed him to take you in if I had known..." She breaks off, her eyes angrily brimming with some unspoken thought.

"Known *what*?" I press, stung by her easy dismissal of my uncle.

She leans forward, teeth bared. "That you would grow up to turn down a fasting proposal that every girl in Gardneria would give her eyeteeth for!"

Her expression turns venomous and I shrink back, shocked by the frightening change in her demeanor.

My aunt quickly collects herself, regaining her careful sheen of control, like thick curtains being drawn around her true feelings.

"I shall simply have to find a way to help you change your mind," she states, her voice once again tranquil. She lightly taps her teacup.

The Urisk girl springs forward to fill it, as if her life depends on it.

My aunt takes her time, mixing some cream into her tea. "I

have found that *everyone* can be persuaded to do the right thing if the right kind of pressure is applied."

I stare at her with a new wariness, watching as she lifts the porcelain cup with long, graceful fingers.

"Everyone has a breaking point, Elloren. *Everyone.*" She regards me levelly. "*Don't* force me to find yours."

CHAPTER FOURTEEN

Icarals

The next morning our ride to church is uncomfortably silent, our carriage surrounded by Aunt Vyvian's personal guard. Dark clouds loom above Valgard and threaten a storm. I peer up at them, my cheek pressed against the cool glass of the carriage's window, wishing I was with my brothers and Gareth.

Aunt Vyvian is studying me icily, perhaps considering how best to bend my will. She's been trying to convince me to wandfast for every one of the fifteen days we've been together, and that pressure, after yesterday's wandfasting offer, has now turned markedly oppressive. She's keeping me with her until the last possible moment, desperate to have me buckle and wandfast to Lukas Grey before going off to University.

We're to arrive at Valgard's Grand Cathedral hours before morning service so that Aunt Vyvian can discuss some government business with Priest Vogel. Then she's insisting I attend service with her—where, I suspect, we'll conveniently run into Lukas and his family. I flush uncomfortably at the thought of seeing him again.

Later, after the service, I'm to make the carriage journey to

University alone. Rafe, Trystan and Gareth are long gone, having left together early this morning on horseback.

I long to be with them. I don't want to be in these fancy, restrictive clothes that necessitate slower carriage travel anymore. And I long to break free of Aunt Vyvian's unforgiving watch. I want to be on horseback with my brothers and Gareth, riding to Verpacia and the bustling University.

Soon, I remind myself. *You'll be out of here soon enough.*

The dark forest of buildings ahead gives way to an expansive, circular plaza, a larger-than-life marble statue of my grandmother dominating its middle. I focus right in on it, wondering if I'll be able to make out my own features in the marble face, but it's too far away.

Approaching the plaza, we make a sharp turn to the right, and I almost gasp as Valgard's Cathedral bursts into view, even grander than I remembered it.

Broad, sweeping columns rise skyward, eventually coalescing to form one, narrowing spire that supports a silver Erthia sphere at its zenith. The whole structure is wrought from Ironwood the color of wet earth. A mammoth central arch with two smaller, adjacent arches frames the entrance, the huge front doors richly carved with images from *The Book of the Ancients*.

The carriage halts just in front of the cathedral, and I almost trip down its steps as I disembark, my gaze riveted on the immense, vertigo-inducing structure. I crane my neck to take it all in, the silver sphere highlighted by the darkening sky.

My aunt ushers me into the cathedral and toward one of the countless, intricately carved pews.

"Sit here," she directs sternly.

I obey as her heels click down an aisle that leads to the broad dais and altar. Two priests in dark, flowing robes circle the altar, lighting candles and waving incense, the white bird symbol of the Ancient One emblazoned on their chests. Above the altar hangs another Erthia sphere.

My aunt approaches the priests, then launches into hushed conversation with them. They take turns surreptitiously glaring in my direction as my stomach twists itself into uncomfortable knots. And then they're gone, having exited together through a side door, leaving me all alone in the vast space.

I am bereft, my palms flat on the wood of my seat.

But soon the wood of the cathedral begins to lull me into a calmer state. Numerous columns, some straight, some diagonal and curving, rise toward an irregular ceiling covered with crisscrossing arches. It's like being underneath the root system of an enormous, otherworldly tree.

I close my eyes, slide my palms against the wood and breathe in its amber scent.

Soothed, I open my eyes to find a copy of *The Book of the Ancients* sitting beside me.

I pick up the black, leather-bound tome and run my finger along its gilded title. I know this book well. Unbeknownst to my uncle, who seems to disapprove of religion in general, I keep my grandmother's old copy under my pillow, the gilded holy book passed down to me by Aunt Vyvian when I was a small child. Sometimes, in the dark of night, when sadness comes, when the void left by my parents' deaths seems too painful to bear, *The Book*'s many prayers for strength in times of hardship and sorrow are of great comfort to me.

Just as the first rumble of thunder sounds in the distance, I open to the first page and read.

The Creation

In the beginning, there was only the Ancient One. The universe was vast and empty. And out of the great, unfathomable nothing-

ness, the Ancient One brought forth the planets and the stars, the sun and the moon and Erthia, the Great Sphere.

And on this Great Sphere, the Ancient One separated the land from the water and brought forth all manner of living things: the green plants, the birds of the air, the beasts of the field and forest and water.

And the Ancient One looked down upon it all and was pleased.

But the Ancient One was not finished. The breath of life was sent out over the Great Sphere, and from the seeds of the sacred Ironwood Tree sprang the First Children, who were to dwell on the Great Sphere; and the Angelic Ones, who were to dwell in the Heavens.

At first, all dwelled in harmony.

All of creation joined together to worship, glorify and obey the Ancient One.

But it came to pass that the Angelic Ones, winged as they were, began to feel that they did not need to obey. They began to feel that they were better than the Ancient One, and that they owned the Heavens.

And it came to pass that the Angelic Ones flew down to the First Children and pleaded with them to turn away from the Ancient One and to worship them instead. The First Children were angered by this betrayal and refused. The First Children told the Angelic Ones that they would worship and glorify none other than the Ancient One. The Angelic Ones, angered in turn by the refusal of the First Children, brought down a host of evil upon them: the shapeshifters who preyed upon them at night, the wyverns who attacked from above, the sorceresses who sought to mislead them and all manner of dark creatures and tricksters, thus scattering the First Children and sending them into disarray.

And it came to pass that the Ancient One looked down and saw the sufferings of the First Children, and that the Angelic Ones had become Evil Ones in their betrayal. In great fury and righteousness, the Ancient One smote the Angelic Ones and sent them hurtling down to the surface of the Great Sphere. And then the Ancient One spoke to the Angelic Ones, who were now Evil Ones, saying unto them:

"From now on, you shall no longer be counted among my children and will be known as Icarals, the most despised of all creatures. You will wander the surface of my Great Sphere without a home. My True Children, My First Children, will join together to smite you and to break your wings."

And thus it came to pass that the True Children once again joined together from all corners of the Great Sphere to smite the Evil Ones and to worship, glorify and obey the Ancient One.

So ends the first book of Creation.

I glance up at the stained-glass windows that shine between the columns as I remember the stories in the sacred text associated with each image, the normally vivid colors of the scenes strangely darkened by the stormy skies.

The first window depicts the Ancient One symbolized by a graceful, white bird, sending down rays of light to Erthia below. I take in a deep breath as the familiar, protective image fills me with warmth.

The images continue, all around: the reluctant prophetess, Galliana, astride a giant fire raven, leading our people from slavery, White Wand in hand; the First Children receiving the deep blue Ironflowers as a symbol of the Ancient One's promise to keep them free from oppression, the flowers offering magical protection from demon fire.

I briefly glance down at the familiar Ironflower trim worked into the hem of my sleeve, comforted by the flowers' symbolic promise of safety.

Next comes images of terrible battles: First Children slaying winged Icaral demons as the demons shoot fire from their palms; First Children soldiers combating bloodthirsty shapeshifters—wolf-shifters, fox-shifters and even a wyvern-shifter with slits for eyes and a forked tongue hanging from its mouth.

Above all these images, the Ancient One's light shines down.

As I ponder the religious teachings of my youth, movement near the stained-glass wyvern-shifter catches my eye.

Just above its reptilian head is a clear portion of glass, and I can make out two small eyes watching me through it. The eyes flick up and out of view, revealing a strong silver beak and then…nothing.

A Watcher.

Curious, I get up, walk toward the back of the church and exit through the mammoth front doors.

As the doors swing shut behind me, I'm instantly aware of a strange current in the air. I stare down over the empty plaza, searching everywhere for the bird.

There, in the plaza's center, stands the huge stone statue of my grandmother. The plaza is eerily quiet, the normally raucous seagulls absent. The odd colors of the sky shift slightly, and I hear another small, far-off murmur of thunder. I look up to see dark clouds slowly lumbering toward the church.

Halfway down the cathedral stairs, I see it. *The white bird.* It flies across the wide plaza and lands just behind my grandmother's statue.

I reach the statue of my grandmother and circle slowly around it, searching for the bird. Soon the huge marble monument completely blocks the cathedral from view. I pause in its shadow, riveted by it.

The soft rumbling of thunder jostles the silence like a faint drumroll.

My grandmother stands, larger than life, my identical features finely wrought by a master's chisel, every fold of her billowing robes perfectly rendered, so lifelike it seems as if I could reach up and move the fabric. Her left arm is raised in a grace-ful arc above her head, her wand arm pointing straight down at an Icaral that lies prostrate at her feet, his face a contorted mask of agony.

At this angle, it's as if she's pointing her wand not at the Icaral, but at me.

The clouds move above her head in the direction of the church, giving the illusion that she's the one moving instead, in-clining her head toward me reproachfully, sizing up this fraudu-lent copy of herself.

You could never be me.

The white bird pokes its head over my grandmother's shoul-der, startling me, its eyes filled with alarm. It moves its head from side to side in warning, as if a bird could make such a human gesture.

Suddenly, a strong, bony hand slams against my mouth. An arm flies around my waist and locks my elbows against my sides in a viselike grip. I fall backward onto a hard body, and a foul smell like rotted meat washes over me.

My fear is a delayed reaction, like the pain that hesitates briefly when you touch something so hot it will burn and scar. Catching up, my heart begins to beat wildly as a nasal, taunt-ing male voice hisses into my ear.

"Don't bother screaming, Black Witch. No one will hear you."

I struggle wildly, straining against the binding arm, kicking at him, but he's too strong. I can't wrench myself free, and I can't turn my head to see the face of my attacker.

The thunder becomes more insistent, the wind surging as the storm continues to move straight toward the cathedral.

I desperately scream against his hand and scan the plaza for help. But there's no one.

A second figure springs from the shadows between two nearby buildings and scrambles toward me on long, sickly thin limbs. It's bald and naked from the waist up, its flesh pale and emaciated, multiple gashes marking its chest and arms as if it's been lashed repeatedly, its face contorted into an evil smile, red lips surrounding decayed and pointed teeth.

But its eyes...oh, its eyes—they're a swirling, opalescent white, devoid of humanity, devoid of a soul...like the living dead. And there are grotesque stumps jutting out from its shoulder blades. The stumps move in and out rhythmically in a disgusting mimicry of flight, and a terrifying realization washes over me.

It used to have wings.

It's an Icaral demon. My screams turn to sobs of terror as I catch a glimpse of a dagger in its hand.

I raise my palms in supplication, a silent, desperate plea for mercy as I begin to grow faint.

The demon scuttles forward with surprising quickness and agility and grabs my wrist so hard, its long fingernails dig into my skin, piercing my flesh. I let out a muffled cry.

It holds tight onto me, its soulless eyes widening in shock. "It is She! It truly is the Black Witch!"

"Then do not hesitate!" snarls the creature restraining me. "Kill it, Vestus! Kill it before it can become like Her!"

My knees buckle as the creature called Vestus pulls his dagger back and raises it above his head. Thunder smashes against the sky.

"History will now be rewritten, Black Witch!" Vestus shrieks. "The Prophecy will be shattered, and the Icaral will live! You will die, and we will rise!"

Everything seems to happen in slow motion. The creature's hand jerks backward to ready his attack, but then a longer blade bursts through the creature's chest. A fountain of blood spurts out, covering me, and I'm falling, falling, the creature behind me also falling away, freeing me. I slam into the cold, hard ground, aware of the overwhelming, ferrous smell of blood.

And then a soldier is before me.

Lukas!

He pulls his sword out of the Icaral and pushes the creature forward, dead, its head slamming onto the stone tile inches from me with a sickening crack.

I whirl around just in time to see one of my aunt's guards dragging off the second Icaral, this one taller and more muscular than the other, but bloodied and unconscious. Thunder cracks loudly as the wind strengthens and pushes my blood-soaked clothing flat against my skin.

A movement beyond my aunt's guard catches my eye—just a small glimpse in a dark alley beyond the plaza, beyond the road.

Another Icaral looks at me for a split second, then disappears from sight.

A strong hand grabs my arm. I jump in fright and whirl around to see Lukas shouting something at me. I close my eyes tight and jerk my head from side to side, desperate to pull myself together, to focus. I open my eyes as all the sound around me rushes back in with a roar, like a dam opened.

"There's another one!" I cry to Lukas, pointing toward the alleyway.

Lukas pulls out his wand and aims it in that direction. A burst of blue-green lightning spears from his wand's tip and explodes into the alley. It incinerates the walls of the buildings on either side with a crackling boom that sends a sharp pain through my ears.

Lukas yells to the guards as four other Mages run toward us, their wands drawn, their cloaks edged with rows of silver lines.

Lukas calls out orders, and all of the Mages run off in the direction of the alley.

"Are you hurt?" Lukas shouts at me as the heavens open up and the rain pours down, the water mixing with the blood of the Icarals, forming dark, violent puddles. I nod, and Lukas pulls me to my feet. He braces me with a strong arm around my waist, his other hand still gripping his blood-stained sword. I grip my throbbing wrist as he guides me across the plaza.

Lightning flashes around us as we quickly make our way toward the cathedral. Soldiers fan out over the plaza, and a small crowd of Gardnerians, including my aunt and Echo Flood, look out from the open cathedral doors with horrified faces.

Marcus Vogel stands amongst them, the calm eye of the hurricane.

And the bird, the white bird, sits above the doorway in a hollowed-out, sheltered crevice, as still as the artwork adorning the cathedral.

Watching me.

Lukas paces back and forth across the room like a caged animal, glancing over at me every so often, his jaw set tight, face ruddy, his brow furrowed with angry impatience. Like me, he's soaked through with rain and blood, his sword sheathed and hanging at his side. His pacing is interrupted when one of my aunt's guards comes in to speak with him, the two of them talking so low I can't make out what they're saying. Lukas's hand is on his hip as he speaks to the man, both of them tense, the guard taking a subordinate stance as Lukas gives him a series of orders. The guard nods and leaves with a look of serious purpose.

I'm sitting on a wooden chair in Priest Vogel's cathedral sanctuary, shivering uncontrollably, feeling dazed and frightened, surrounded by black-robed priests.

Vogel is looming over me, holding outstretched hands above my head, his eyes firmly closed as he intones a prayer in the Ancient Tongue. An image of dark Icaral wings and lifeless trees flashes behind my eyes and sends a vicious chill through me.

The priest to the left of Vogel swings a gold ball filled with incense from a long chain. Pungent smoke wafts from holes in the sphere, burning my nose, my stomach clenching with nausea.

Even though they're closed, I can feel Vogel's eyes.

Echo sits next to me and holds my hand tight.

"What's he doing?" I ask, still in shock. *This can't be real. I'm trapped in a nightmare. None of this can be real.*

"Shhh, Elloren," she whispers kindly. She gives my hand a squeeze of solidarity. "You have looked into the eyes of an Icaral. To do this is to pollute your soul. Priest Vogel is exorcizing the stain."

My wrist burns where the Icaral dug its claws into my flesh.

"I want my uncle," I whimper, tears starting to fall. I feel lost among all these unfamiliar people, and frightened by the need for ritual purification.

And I'm scared of Vogel.

My aunt stands in the doorway with two more priests, old men with snow-white hair. They speak in hushed tones, their expressions grave.

I drop my face into my hands and begin to sob. My shivering gets worse as Priest Vogel drones on and on, rattling me with his remote chanting of prayers and the sense of his dark void swirling around me. I cry as the chanting falls away and the dark void subsides, only half aware of Lukas asking for a moment alone with me.

The room grows quiet.

"Elloren. Look at me."

I jump at the sound of Lukas's stern voice and the feel of his strong hand gripping my arm. I straighten and pull my tear-soaked hands from my eyes.

He's down on one knee, his head level with mine, eyes full of fire. *"Stop it."*

His harsh tone stuns me into astonished silence.

I choke back my tears as anger at his treatment wells up within me. Wasn't he right there? Didn't he see those...*things*? A dark fury takes root, replacing my fear with steel-cold anger.

"That's better!" Lukas snarls as I glare at him with as much hatred as I can muster. "You are *not* weak!"

"How can you say that?" I spit out, wanting to strike him. "You're wrong!"

"No, I'm not," he vehemently counters, still gripping me. "I can sense power in you. You look *exactly* like your grandmother, and her blood runs through your veins. Your uncle has done you a grave disservice by not preparing you for something like this."

"Don't you *dare* speak against my uncle!" I cry. I try to jerk my arm away from him, but he holds on tight.

"No, Elloren, it needs to be said. *He* did this to you by leaving you unarmed and ignorant!"

An uncomfortable doubt rises in the back of my mind. I beat it back.

"You don't know anything about my uncle," I say firmly. "You've never even *met* him!"

"They were at your uncle's house, Elloren."

I stop trying to wrench away from him. "What do you mean?"

"The Icarals. Galen got a confession from one of them before he killed it. They escaped from the Valgard Sanitorium. One of them was an empath. He found out about you from a worker there—someone who knows your aunt. They were waiting for this, Elloren—for the next Black Witch to be found. They went straight to your uncle's house, but you were gone. They found your uncle sleeping, and the empath read where you were from his thoughts by touching him. If your aunt hadn't pulled you from there, you'd be dead right now."

I stare at him, wide-eyed and frozen. *No, this isn't happening. This isn't real.* "I'm *powerless*. Why would those…*things* think that I'm the Black Witch?"

Lukas doesn't answer. He just keeps his unwavering stare fixed on me.

I already know the answer, though. It's my blood. *Her* blood— that's what the creature sensed. And I look just like her.

"The third Icaral," I finally say, my voice strangled. "Did they find it?"

Lukas takes a deep breath. "No."

"And my uncle?" I ask, almost in a whisper.

"He's fine," he says, his voice losing its angry edge. "They weren't after him, Elloren. They were after *you*." Lukas's hand loosens then falls away from my arm. "We've sent guards to your uncle's house as a precaution."

"But what about Rafe? And Trystan?"

"I've already sent guards to find them and escort them across Verpacia's border, if they haven't crossed already."

"And once they're across?"

His lips turn up at the edges. "You won't have to worry about them once they cross the border. It's ward-magicked. Verpacia's military force is formidable, and they have the help of the Vu Trin sorceresses. You'll be safe there, as well. You're safe now. The Icaral's weak. Its wings were amputated long ago. Your aunt's guards and I will escort you to University, and we've already sent word to the High Chancellor about what's happened."

My wrist is beginning to throb. Miserable, I turn it over for his inspection, bloody scratches and gashes ringing it where the creature gripped me. I wait for Lukas to express *some* sympathy.

He takes my wrist in his hand, his touch surprisingly gentle. His eyes meet mine and his expression goes hard. "You're lucky," he says. "It will scar and be a constant reminder to prepare yourself. These are battle scars, Elloren."

"Why are you so *harsh*?" I cry, wrenching my wrist away.

"Because," he grinds out as he grips both arms of my chair, "you do *not* need to be coddled!"

"You don't even *know* me!"

He shakes his head from side to side and takes a breath. "You're wrong," he says, his voice gone low.

He stands up, a horizontal line of blood splashed across the front of his tunic, short tendrils of wet hair plastered to his forehead. We're both damp and sweaty and smell like blood. The image of Lukas slaying the Icaral demon flashes into my mind, rapidly deflating the remnants of my anger.

He saved my life.

Lukas holds his hand out to me, and I reach up to take it.

"You *are* equal to this, Elloren," he says firmly as he helps me to my feet.

I raise my eyes to meet his. "I'm not the Black Witch, Lukas."

He sighs deeply and looks at me with resignation. "Let's go," is all he says.

A few hours later I'm in a carriage with Lukas, traveling to Verpacia, the two of us in clean, dry clothing.

"Lukas will protect you," Aunt Vyvian reassured me back at her mansion, as she directed Urisk servants to quickly pack my things into my travel trunk, plus an additional large trunk she's provided for me. "You'll be safer in Verpacia. Especially with Lukas as your guard."

She could barely hide her smug satisfaction at the way events have played right into her hands, pushing Lukas and me firmly together. But I'm too rattled to be anything but grateful for her assistance, and for Lukas's help and protection.

I think about how many things my aunt and the others tried to warn me about. It's just as it says in our sacred text, just as the images on the stained-glass windows portray things to be. The Icarals are hideous things of great Evil, and need to be destroyed before they destroy us. And Sage's baby, if this is its destiny—to turn into one of those *things*—then the Mage Council is right in wanting to take it from her, stripping it of its wings and its power.

Killing it, even.

I shudder to think of those creatures armed with over-whelming power at their disposal, and I know that if my at-tackers had been in possession of their wings, I'd be dead.

And if my aunt is right about this, and about my need to leave home, if her intuition is so good, maybe she's right about other things, as well. Maybe the Selkies are only dangerous, feral animals—just as horrible as the Icarals when they have their skins. And maybe she's right about Lukas and wandfasting.

I look over at Lukas as he sits in stony silence, staring out the window through the rain-battered glass, and a surge of gratitude washes over me.

Oh, Uncle Edwin, I anguish, *why did you leave me in the dark about what might be out here waiting for me? Did you have any idea? Why didn't you protect me?*

He didn't know, I realize. It turns out that my sweet uncle is dangerously naive about the world, cooped up in Halfix, isolated amidst his beehives and violins and childish good intentions.

As much as I love Uncle Edwin, I'm forced to consider that he's not only dangerously ignorant, but he may actually be wrong, too. About so many things.

And Aunt Vyvian might be right.

I resolve to find out the truth for myself.

CHAPTER
FIFTEEN

Verpacia

I stare out at the sheeting rain as I cradle my bruised wrist. After several hours I lose track of how long we've been on the road, all the farms and towns bleeding into each other. Lukas is equally silent and deep in thought.

My fear has settled into an anxious unease. I look over at Lukas and wonder what he's thinking. He's brooding and remote, but I feel a kinship with his aura of gravity that makes me feel less alone.

Eventually we slow, and I make out one of the Ironwood outposts of our military. A cloaked soldier waves us through.

"The border," Lukas informs me.

Three trade routes converge here, and we're gradually stopped by the traffic, most of the horses pulling wagons heavily weighed down by goods.

Thunder crashes, and I strain to see through the rain. A long, ivory wagon passes close by. It's surrounded by a large contingent of ivory-cloaked soldiers astride pale steeds. The soldiers have white hair, and their eyes are silver.

"Gold merchants," Lukas says, noting my interest.

Amazement cuts through my lingering haze of fear. "Are they Elves?"

"You've never seen them?"

I shake my head and look back out. The Elves' ethereal whiteness is pristine, as if the dirt and grime of this stormy day hasn't touched them at all.

My eyes are drawn upward by the shifting winds.

I can just make out the western edge of the Verpacian Spine, an impassable mass of vertical rock that borders the country of Verpacia. The white-gray rock seems to reach right up to the heavens and disappears into the storm clouds as the rain batters the bleached stone. Multiple guard towers are carved into the cliffs, hewn from the rock itself. Cloaked archers in pale gray uniforms the color of the Spine climb about the towers like nimble mountain goats. They appear to be keeping a close eye on the convergence of traffic seeking entrance into Verpacia through this break in the Spine.

Our carriage door opens, and an archer pokes his head in. He has a bow slung over his shoulder and rain drips copiously off the edge of his hood. He looks like an Elf, his eyes gleaming silver, but his hair and skin are a silvery-gray only slightly darker than his eyes.

"Lieutenant Grey," he says congenially, the words heavily accented. He glances over at me, and his smile is whisked right off his face. He blurts out something in what must be the Elfhollen language, his tone one of shock.

"Orin," Lukas says carefully, as if trying to calm him, "this is Elloren Gardner."

"She's not back from the dead, then?" Orin breathes, his eyes locked tight on mine.

Lukas smiles. "Only in appearance."

Then, to my surprise, they launch into a serious conversation in Elfhollen. Orin gestures sharply toward me several times, his expression deeply conflicted. I stiffen, rattled by Orin's confrontational tone.

Lukas shoots him an incredulous look. "Do you honestly think I'd bring her here if she had any power?"

I glance sidelong at Lukas, surprised. He's told me more than once that he suspects I have power. My heart thuds nervously, realizing that there's danger here. And he's protecting me.

Orin narrows his silver eyes at me one last time, shuts the door and waves us through.

I let out a breath of relief, then turn to Lukas in amazement. "You speak Elfhollen?" Even if he's well versed in languages, it's still a surprising choice.

Lukas smirks. "I have an odd talent for picking up the more obscure languages." He eyes me appraisingly. "How much do you know about the Elfhollen?"

I consider for a moment. "They're half-breed Elves, right? With Mountain Fae blood? I've read a little about them."

"It's a nice combination, really," Lukas muses as he throws his arm along the back of his seat. "Deadly archers with perfect balance. It's lucky for Verpacia that the Alfsigr hate mixed-breeds. The Alfsigr Elves were idiots to drive the Elfhollen from their land." He flicks his finger in the direction of the sentry towers and the agile Elfhollen soldiers stationed in and around them. "They're one of the only reasons Verpacia is able to keep control of the Pass. That, and the Vu Trin border wards." Lukas bears his teeth. "And the Vu Trin sorceresses."

I look over at Lukas, surprised by his matter-of-fact way of discussing mixed-breeds and sorceresses. And his friendly demeanor toward one of them. Most Gardnerians are as distrustful of mixed-breeds as the Alfsigr Elves are. It's understandable— we were almost wiped out several times. Of course we want to keep our race pure and intact.

All around us, the Elfhollen soldiers brave the icy rain to search through wagons: looking under secured wax cloth, opening up barrels, questioning the drivers. Some of the soldiers are accompanied by heavily armed women garbed in black, their hair and eyes as dark as their uniforms. Their uniforms bear glowing blue rune-marks that are so beautiful, I can't tear my eyes away,

"Are those Vu Trin soldiers?" I ask Lukas, transfixed by the sight of the lethal-looking women and their shimmering rune-marks.

Lukas nods, eyeing them with what looks like respect. "They're a guest military force here. They control the western and eastern passes through the Spine. Their presence is part of the treaty agreement that formally ended the Realm War."

"It's strange to me," I say, marveling at the curved swords the Vu Trin carry at their sides and the rows of silver throwing stars strapped across their chests. "Women as *soldiers*."

Lukas seems amused by this. "The men of their race don't have any magic. But the women more than make up for it, believe me."

A tall Vu Trin motions sharply for a group of Kelts on horseback to halt, her face steel-hard. Her uniform's arms are marked with lines of circular ward symbols that glow blue. A smaller Vu Trin woman, with only one glowing sleeve ward, searches the Kelts' saddlebags.

"What are they looking for?" I wonder.

"Smugglers."

"Of what?"

Lukas shrugs. "Weapons, spirits…pit dragons."

Spirits don't surprise me. Forbidden by our religion, they're illegal in Gardneria. A number of passages in *The Book of the Ancients* touch on the evil of intoxication. But my eyes widen at the mention of dragons.

"Pit dragons?"

"They're a particularly vicious type of dragon," Lukas explains. "Used as weapons. And for sport." He turns from the window to glance at me. "They're pure dragon. They don't shift."

I've only seen dragons twice. Both times were in Halfix, the dragons high in the sky. They were black Gardnerian military dragons, used for transport and as powerful weapons. But I know there are other dragons rumored to be somewhere in the Eastern Realm. Wyverns who can breathe fire and shift to human form. And Wyrm shapeshifters who breathe lightning and can control the weather.

Our carriage hits a bump and jostles me from my thoughts. It's all stop and go for quite a while, but soon the traffic lessens and we're on our way.

After a few hours the rain thins and I gasp as the tops of the northern and southern peaks of the Spine become visible, like two great walls bracketing the entire country of Verpacia. I've never seen anything as high as these snowcapped and intimidatingly beautiful peaks.

I'm glued to the window for the rest of the ride. There's so much to see, the thrill of the unknown lighting me up.

We pass a busy horse market full of foreigners, our carriage slowed to the pace of walking by the heavy road traffic. Fascinated, I take it all in.

Elves are showing off ivory mares, the Elves' hoods down to reveal gracefully pointed ears and long, white hair decorated with thin braids. Near the Elves are a group of muscular women garbed in black pants, boots and red tunics that shine brightly with fiery crimson rune-marks. The glowing symbols remind me of the blue rune-marks used by the Vu Trin sorceresses, though these women are a far more mixed group. Some are pale with blond hair, and others have skin in varying shades of brown and a rainbow of Urisk hues.

They're as heavily armed as the Vu Trin sorceresses, and many have facial markings shaped like the runes on their clothing, as well as some piercings. A gleaming metal hoop is stuck right through the bottom of one red-haired woman's nose, her ears sharply pointed and multiply pierced with dark metallic hoops.

"Amazakaran," Lukas informs me. "Horsewomen of the Caledonian mountains."

I stare at them, wide-eyed. "Are they as dangerous as the Vu Trin?"

Lukas laughs. "Just about."

"They look like they aren't really one race. Except they're all dressed similarly."

"The Amaz allow women of any race to join them." He smiles at me and motions toward them. "They'd let you in, Elloren. And train you to use an ax like that."

I gape at him, then look back toward the largest Amazakaran there. Her white-rose hair is braided and pulled back, and her face is heavily tattooed. She carries a huge, gleaming, rune-marked ax strapped to her back, and I jump slightly as the woman sets her fierce gaze on me, her eyes narrowed and dangerous. I whip my eyes quickly away from her, heart thudding, as the carriage gives a lurch forward and whisks the Amaz warrior from my sight.

We press on, and soon we're traveling through forest and down a winding road, the rain picking up. There's a clearing up ahead, and the Southern Spine comes into view, the forest falling away.

Rain-fogged Verpax appears, spread out before us, the countless domes and spires of the University city completely filling the immense valley. A haze of golden light from countless lanterns and torchlights hangs in the darkening fog. It's a gated city, surrounded by a stone wall, the gates bracketed by guard towers.

I stare out over the scene, excitement and trepidation rising in equal measure.

Lukas turns to me, his mouth tilting into a wry smile. "Welcome to Verpax."

PART TWO

PROLOGUE

"We cannot allow the Black Witch to be in possession of the White Wand."

"The White Wand chooses its own path. You know that, Kam. To interfere would be to court disaster."

The two women stand in the guard tower at Verpax's entrance gate. They watch through high-arched windows as an elegant carriage makes its way down the winding road that leads to the University. The carriage's horses press on slowly, their heads bowed by the rain and howling wind.

Every so often, thunder rumbles in the distance.

One of the women, a Gardnerian, is still and calm, her dark green eyes narrowed behind gold-rimmed spectacles as she peers through the diamond-paned glass, her ebony hair tied back into a neat bun.

The second woman, a Vu Trin sorceress, is garbed in a black uniform marked with glowing blue rune-marks. She wears a series of razor-sharp metal stars strapped diagonally across her chest, curved swords sheathed at her sides. Her eyes are dark, her skin a deep brown, and she wears her straight black hair tied into a tight, ropy coil, as is the custom of the Vu Trin soldiers.

"If she is indeed the one, we need to strike her down *immediately*," the sorceress says with fierce resolve. "Before she realizes her power. While there is still time." She sets her cold gaze back on the carriage as a streak of lightning scythes through the sky, flashing against the steel of her weapons.

The Gardnerian holds up a hand in calm protest as she watches the carriage. Thunder cracks overhead. "Patience, Kam. Patience. We must give the girl a chance."

The sorceress turns her head sharply to face her companion. "Have you forgotten the Prophecy?"

"The Prophecy is vague. The girl has a choice, as we all do. Her future is not fixed. She might not choose the path of darkness."

"And what of this girl's grandmother? What of *her*?" The sorceress's face grows hard. "Was she not once just a girl, as well? A girl with a *choice*? A girl who *chose* to kill *thousands* of my people!"

The Gardnerian takes a deep breath and slowly turns to face the sorceress, her expression one of grave sympathy. "I know how much you have suffered, Kam."

The sorceress's face flinches. "No. You do *not*."

The words hang in the air for one long minute as the women regard each other.

The Gardnerian places a comforting hand on the sorceress's arm, but the sorceress remains military stiff, her hands clenched tight on her swords as if ready to attack the very memory of atrocities endured. After a moment, the Gardnerian lets her hand drop and turns back to the window. Thunder rumbles again to the west.

"Now is not the time to strike her down, Kam," the Gardnerian states. "The Wand has chosen her. We must wait a bit to find out why—to see what this girl is made of. I do not plan on making her life here easy. Curiously, I have her aunt's cooperation in this."

The sorceress cocks a questioning eyebrow.

"Vyvian Damon has her own motivation for putting some pressure on the girl," the Gardnerian explains. "A wandfasting conflict. She wants the girl to fast to Lukas Grey."

"Rising star of the Gardnerian military forces. How fitting."

The Gardnerian chooses to ignore the comment.

"My assassins are restless," the sorceress cautions darkly. "I cannot promise you that the girl will be safe if they view you as complacent, not after what this girl's grandmother did to our people, and what she would have succeeded in doing had the Icaral not cut her down. And this girl—" she gestures in the direction of the carriage with a sharp jerk of her chin "—if she is indeed The One, she is prophesied to be even greater in power than Carnissa, perhaps the most powerful Mage that has ever existed."

The Gardnerian's mouth is pressed into a thin, hard line as she deliberates, the ticking of the clock on the wall reverberating in the silence. "I understand your dilemma," she finally says. She straightens and turns from the window to face Kam Vin. "If the White Wand chooses to leave Elloren Gardner, *or* if she makes any move to contact the Amazakaran, the Kinh Hoang may strike." Her eyes narrow, facing the sorceress down.

The sorceress meets the Vice Chancellor's intense gaze levelly, without blinking. "That will be sufficient for now," she says, pausing for emphasis. "But take care. We will not be patient forever."

Verpax University

With a jerking, forward lurch, our carriage finishes its winding descent into the valley, the city's lights glittering like jewels through the rain-soaked fog.

We slow down at Verpax's gated entrance, two stone guard towers bracketing it, and I crane my neck to take in the tops of the towers with their arching, diamond-paned windows. I can just make out two still figures standing inside the window, watching us. They're garbed in black, but the rain streams down the glass and renders their features wavy and amorphous.

"I'll be right back," Lukas assures me. He disembarks to talk with a pair of unsmiling Vu Trin sorceresses stationed at the gates, but my eyes are repeatedly drawn toward the watching figures.

"They've warded the border," Lukas tells me as he swings back into the carriage, his shoulders and hair damp from the rain. "You'll be quite safe."

Our carriage makes its way through the gates, leaving the watching figures and the Vu Trin guards behind as we enter the University city.

I'm instantly swept up in the exotic bustle of Verpax, even on this cold, rainy day.

Colorful Guild crests and banners mark the Spine-stone buildings, their designs a bright contrast to the gray sky and stone. The cobbled streets are narrow, which puts my window close to shops, taverns and passersby. On either side of us, knots of cloaked Gardnerians, Kelts, Verpacians, Elfhollen, Urisk and Elves hurry through the rain, some wearing forest green professorial robes, their heads bowed against the weather like the carriage horses'.

I'm wide-eyed over the sheer number and diversity of people.

And the cornucopia of shops and taverns and crafthouses.

There are glass merchants, cheese vendors, a Gardnerian wandcrafter's shop, cheerful lodging houses and even a swordsmith from the Eastern Realm. My nose bumps the glass as I take in the golden rune-marked, embroidered tunic of the man selling jeweled swords under a sheltering canopy, a green headband marked with more golden runes round his head.

And then I spot it—a gleaming apothecary shop, the Gardnerian Guild crest painted boldly on its front: a white mortar and pestle on a black shield, the mortar marked with a silver Erthia sphere, the image surrounded by a wreath of leaves. Neat bottles line the window, and I can just see the tight bunches of herbs hanging from the ceiling rafters in long rows. A smiling Gardnerian woman, her hair pulled back into a tight bun, talks with a customer.

My spirits rise. That could be me someday. With a beautiful shop like that.

Soon the road widens, we pass through the wrought-iron University gates and we're there. *Verpax University.*

We ride down several narrow streets, the crowds thicker here, more green professorial robes in sight. The carriage slows, and we come to a stop before a mammoth, multidomed building hewn from pure alabaster Spine stone—Verpax's central White Hall.

Craning my neck to take in the huge, rain-splattered dome, a wave of relief washes over me.

"My brothers?" I ask Lukas, turning to him. "They'll be here?"

"They should be," he says, then pauses. "I'll take you to them. And later you'll come with me. We'll ride up toward the Northern Spine, away from all this, and I'll wandtest you."

He says it calmly enough, but there's something in his eyes that brooks no argument. I nod in assent.

Satisfied, Lukas pulls his hood over his head, the carriage door opened for him by one of our guards. He steps out into the rain, turns and extends his hand for me to take.

For a moment I hesitate, afraid to expose myself to the open, but Lukas's aura of invincibility steadies me. I take his hand and pull my cloak tight against the icy rain.

Lukas steers me through the needling rain toward a wide staircase that leads to an arching doorway. Anticipation lifts my battered spirit.

Rafe. Trystan. Gareth.

They'll be there, just past the doors.

Lukas pulls the heavy door open for me while he gestures for our driver and the guards to continue on. As our carriage pulls away, I slide into the building's huge, torch-lit foyer and am quickly cast into confusion and deep alarm.

A large contingent of Gardnerian soldiers, Elfhollen archers and Vu Trin sorceresses swarm around me.

Lukas's hand clamps tight around my arm as he pulls me backward and whips out his wand.

A sickening metallic scrape tears through the air as the Vu Trin sorceresses unsheath curved, rune-marked swords and the Elfhollen nock arrows, all aimed at Lukas's head.

"*Stand down!*" orders one of the Elfhollen, his gray uniform marked with a single blue stripe down the center.

"What's this?" Lukas demands of a stern-faced Gardnerian

soldier whose uniform bears the silver markings of our High Commander—a wide silver band encompassing his upper arms and silver fabric edging the bottom third of his black cloak.

Lachlan Grey. Lukas's father.

Heart racing, I search the older man's face for something of Lukas, but can find little resemblance, except in the line of his jaw and his identical, fierce green eyes.

"It appears that Mage Elloren Gardner has never been formally wandtested," Lachlan Grey informs his son with barely concealed anger.

"That's not true. I have been tested," I protest shakily. "My uncle tested me more than once."

Which I don't remember. And he lied about formally testing me this past year. A thread of dizzying fear worms through me.

Lukas's hand tightens around my arm.

The Elfhollen commander steps forward. "She is on Verpacian territory, and I am taking her into custody," he grinds out to Lachlan Grey, ignoring my protest.

Lukas pulls me a fraction closer.

Lachlan stares the Elfhollen down. "She is a citizen of Gardneria," he counters. "You have no jurisdiction."

"She is potentially the greatest weapon in the Western Realm," the Elfhollen insists.

My mind spins in tumult, my heart hammering. *This is impossible. I'm no weapon. I have absolutely no power.*

"Tell your son to stand down, Lachlan," one of the Vu Trin puts in as she enters the foyer, her tone conversational. "You're outnumbered."

Lachlan Grey is unmoved. "I insist on bringing her back to Gardneria."

"Not until she is tested," the Elfhollen demands. "Right now. Under a joint guard."

A joint guard? To test...me? I look to Lukas imploringly, his hand still vise-tight around my arm.

Lachlan Grey's eyes cast around, visibly calculating the chances of successfully taking on so many Elfhollen and Vu Trin. "Stand down, Lukas," he finally relents.

Lukas's face is fierce as his eyes dart around the room, wand still raised. I begin to feel weak in the knees.

Commander Grey eyes him, furious. "Lieutenant Grey, I said *stand down!*"

After a long moment of deliberation, Lukas resheathes his wand but keeps tight hold of my arm.

My heart feels like it will pound straight through my chest.

"Very clever, Lachlan," the Vu Trin comments. "Hiding the girl in Halfix for so many years."

"Believe me, Commander Vin," Lukas's father replies as he glares at his son, "it was completely unintentional."

"No one was hiding me!" I insist with spiking alarm.

Lukas's quick look silences me, his eyes a warning.

"If she is found to be powerful," the Elfhollen puts in to Lachlan Grey, "we *will* be taking her into custody."

"No," Lachlan firmly counters. "What's to prevent you from killing her?"

Killing me? My gut clenches, and I stifle a cry. I move closer to Lukas and clutch at the side of his tunic.

"We could place her in the High Tower under a joint guard," the Elfhollen offers, "until we come to an agreement regarding what to do with her."

"Dismiss half of your guard, and I will consent to the girl's testing," Lachlan capitulates.

Commander Vin eyes Lachlan with amused suspicion, then gestures toward Lukas with her chin. "Dismiss *him*, and I will agree to it. We all know that your young lieutenant is equal to ten of us."

Lachlan's eyes flick back and forth from Lukas to the Vu Trin guard. "Very well. Lukas, you are dismissed."

Lukas makes no move to release my arm.

"Please," I beg them, the word bursting out. "I just want to see my brothers."

"Silence, Gardnerian!" Commander Vin snarls. Her hostility sends me inwardly reeling.

"Lukas," Lachlan says firmly, his eyes belying a steely confidence, "you will accompany the Vu Trin guard to their western base." He raises his brow at Commander Vin. "Agreed?"

Commander Vin nods.

Lukas stares hard into his father's eyes. His hand loosens from my arm.

I hold on to his tunic, heart racing. "No, *please*. Don't leave me!"

He turns to me and places both hands on my arms. "Elloren, they're going to test you, and then they will talk. There's enough of our Mage Guard here to ensure your safety."

"No!" I try to cling to him, but firm hands pull me back.

There's a flash of indecision in Lukas's eyes, but then his face hardens and he turns away. I watch, despairing, as he strides out of the room flanked by ten Vu Trin sorceresses and a contingent of Elfhollen.

Desperation takes hold. I struggle against the hands that restrain me, tears stinging at my eyes. "Let me *go!*" I insist. "My brothers are here. I need to find them…"

And then Commander Vin is before me. She stares me down, her eyes narrowed to hostile slits.

I stop struggling and shrink back from her.

"Elloren Gardner," she says, steel in her eyes, "you will come with us."

CHAPTER TWO

Wandtesting

They lead me to an underground military armory, the huge, circular room stocked with weaponry of every size. Swords, knives, terrifying razored chains and other objects of mutilation hang thick on the stone walls.

"Elloren Gardner," Commander Kam Vin orders as the door closes behind us, "you will explain the extent of your training."

"Training?" I croak out. *What on Erthia is she talking about?*

The Vu Trin sorceress narrows her eyes at me. "Yes, your training. In the martial arts."

"I... I don't understand," I stammer, bewildered.

She purses her lips and starts pacing, her black cloak billowing behind her, never taking her eyes off me, looking at me as though I'm a dangerous, unpredictable animal.

"What kind of wandwork have you done, Mage Gardner?" she persists.

I'm completely lost. "I don't...we never had wands..."

She stops pacing and points at me for emphasis. "Mage Gardner, answer the question! I will ask again. *What type of wandwork have you done?*"

"None!" I cry, holding my hands out, palms up.

"What about *swordwork*?" she asks slyly, as if she's caught on to the game I'm playing.

"None!" I insist. "Why are you asking me...?"

"Knife magic?"

"What? No!"

"Caledonian stick fighting?"

"No!"

"Asteroth staff work?"

She goes on and on through a list of about twenty more forms of fighting I have never heard of in my life. I'm lost in a wilderness of confusion.

"No!" I finally cry in frustration. "I've never done *any* of these things!"

She pauses and glares at me, her brow furrowing sharply before she continues pacing. "Your uncle, he has not given you *any* training in the martial arts?"

My confusion spikes. "No, of course not. He's a violin maker!"

"But surely he must have given you a wand."

I shake my head vehemently. "He didn't even allow them in the house." The image of Sage's white wand briefly flickers through my mind.

The sorceress eyes me with disbelief, one hand placed squarely on her hip. "Do not play games with me, Elloren Gardner! Your uncle must have armed you in some way."

"He *didn't*," I bite out. "Uncle Edwin doesn't like violence."

Commander Vin freezes in her tracks and looks at me like I've started speaking some unintelligible language. *"What?"* she spits out.

"Uncle Edwin doesn't like..."

"I *heard* what you said!"

"Then why did you..."

"What have you been *doing*, then?"

"What do you mean?"

"At your uncle's house!"

I glare at her, frustration boiling over. "Tending the garden, taking care of the animals." I'm careful not to mention the violins. Females aren't supposed to apprentice as luthiers, and I don't want to get Uncle Edwin in trouble with these horrible people. "I read, make herbal remedies. And...and sometimes I make wooden toys..."

"Toys?"

"Little animal figurines, mostly." I shrug. "Sometimes doll furniture. My uncle sells them at the market..."

The Elfhollen, who have been standing very still and regarding me coldly, venture small looks of surprise at each other.

"You are being evasive!" the sorceress grinds out as she points an accusatory finger at me. "Arm yourself, Gardnerian!"

One of the sorceress's underlings steps forward and hands me a smooth, polished wand of Red Oak.

Commander Vin points to a table across the room, where a small, unlit candle in a brass holder is placed. "You will now produce a flame."

I look down at the wand in my hand then back at her, dumbfounded. "How?"

"Mage Gardner, do not feign ignorance with me! It is the simplest of spells!"

"I don't *know* any spells!"

"Bring her the grimoire, Myn!" the sorceress barks in the direction of her underling.

Myn brings me a book and flips the worn pages open. "Aim your wand and speak these words," she instructs stiffly.

I look the words over. They seemed vaguely familiar. Like something from a dream. *A dream with fire.*

I lift the wand awkwardly and point it at the candle. *"Illiumin..."* I begin, my voice high and shaky.

Commander Vin lets out a sound of impatient disgust. "Elloren Gardner!" she barks. "You are holding the wand incorrectly. You must make contact with the palm, or the wand energy cannot flow through you."

I rearrange the wand so that one end is pressing against my palm and point it at the candle once more. My hand shaking, I lift the grimoire and begin to speak the words of the candle-lighting spell.

As soon as the words roll off my lips, a pure, crackling energy begins to prick at the balls of my feet, and the image of an immense tree bursts into the back of my mind. I gasp as a much larger jolt of energy shoots up through me toward the wand, slams against it and then violently and painfully ricochets backward through me.

I drop the wand and it falls to the floor with a sharp clank.

Stunned, I looked over at the candle.

Nothing. Not even a tendril of smoke. But my arm aches as if it's been burned from within.

What just happened?

Lachlan Grey and the other Gardnerian soldiers look heavily disappointed. The sorceresses and Elfhollen seem to be breathing sighs of relief. Only Commander Vin appears momentarily unnerved as she stares, eyes riveted on the painful wand arm I'm flexing to quell the discomfort.

"Well," Commander Vin begins, her momentarily rattled expression gone, her face once again impassive as she addresses Lukas's father. "It would appear, Lachlan, that Mage Gardner is definitively *not* the next Black Witch."

"I did try to tell you," I murmur, the pain in my arm having morphed into a throbbing ache. *But that monstrous energy. What was that?*

"Elloren Gardner," Lukas's father formally announces, "you are hereby placed at Gardnerian Wand Level One."

The lowest level possible—no magic whatsoever.

I stare at him as certainty rises within me like black water.

I might not be able to access power, but it's there. Some echo of the Black Witch. Deep inside me. Coursing through my veins.

Possibly waiting for release.

CHAPTER
THREE

Orientation

When Echo Flood enters the room, the soldiers look relieved to be handing me off to her.

My head spins with confusion. "Echo, why are you here? Why didn't my brothers come for me? And Gareth?"

"Lukas sent for me," she explains, her large eyes solemn with concern.

"My brothers," I ask, feeling lost. "Where are they?"

"They were delayed," Echo explains. "They were caught in the storm, and Gareth's horse panicked at the thunder. The horse threw him and he broke his leg. They had to double back to Valgard to find a healer."

"Oh, no." I struggle to fight back tears. *I need to see my family. I don't want to be alone here.*

"Come," Echo says softly as she places her hand on my arm. "The High Chancellor is addressing all of the scholars. We need to take our places with them."

I stay close to Echo's side as we step into the White Hall.

It's the largest interior I've ever seen, the vast sea of scholars momentarily overwhelming me, the smell of wet wool and lamp oil thick on the dank air.

We're in an open, curved walkway that rings the entire hall, the Spine-stone floor beneath us mottled with damp, overlapping bootprints.

The domed roof stretches high overhead, a bat wheeling back and forth across the vast space, paintings of constellations on a night sky set high into the sectional dome, a ring of huge, arching windows just beneath. Colorful Guild banners hang below every window, a cacophony of primary colors, silver and gold, some of the banners marked with foreign words in exotic, curling alphabets.

My eyes light on the Apothecary Guild banner. The Gardnerian Guild banners are easy to pick out with their black backgrounds.

Like spokes on some great wheel, long aisles connect the external curving walkway to a central raised dais, where an elderly, white-bearded man stands before a podium. His dark green robe is distinguished by golden trim, his thin voice echoing off the stonework as he directs two latecomer Kelts toward empty seats up front.

Echo leans in, her eyes set on the elderly man. "High Chancellor Abenthy."

Rows of green-robed professors flank the High Chancellor, their robes uniform, but their faces reflecting a multitude of races.

"Come," Echo prompts gently, motioning ahead. "I have seats for us."

I nod, my eyes furtively casting around. The storm-dimmed twilight seems to be seeping through the very walls, aisle lamps on long stands fighting against the shadows with small dandelion puffs of light.

The scholars are heavily segregated into ethnic groups, the darkly clad Gardnerians standing out in sharp relief against the

grouping of Elves, the Elves' blindingly ivory cloaks illuminating their section of the hall.

We start down a side aisle cutting through Gardnerian scholars to the left, Kelts to the right. Kicking up like dust, a small
buzz of conversation follows me, my grandmother's name whis-
pered over and over, awed looks from the Gardnerian side, dark
glowering from the Kelts. I stiffen, self-consciously aware of the
unwanted attention.

As I follow Echo by the Gardnerian sea of black, my eye is
drawn to a subsection of slate gray–uniformed Gardnerians.

Military apprentices.

And within their grouping is a lone, uniformed female, a ring
of black-clad Gardnerian soldiers seated around her.

Fallon Bane. And her military guard.

I catch her eye as we pass, and my stomach twists.

She shoots me a dark grin and discreetly reaches for the wand
fastened to her belt. She angles it toward me and gives it a small
jerk.

I exhale sharply as my foot painfully hits something solid and
I trip over it, toppling down to the damp floor.

Small sounds of surprise go up around me.

The floor is cold and gritty and smells like the bottoms of wet
boots, and my hands sting from smacking it. For a brief second
I lay there as embarrassment washes over me.

A strong hand grabs hold of my arm, effortlessly helping me
to my feet.

I look up into the most riveting eyes I've ever seen, even more
so than the Valgard Selkie's. They're bright amber and glow in
an inhuman way that seems almost feral.

The eyes belong to a lean, sandy-haired young man wearing simple, earth-toned clothing. His calm, friendly expression
stands out in bold contrast to those fierce eyes.

"Are you okay?" he asks kindly.

"Yes. Thank you," I say, heart racing. My head whips around

to see what I tripped over. There's nothing there. The aisle is clear. I glance over at Fallon, who's regarding me with a malicious grin, and a spasm of alarm shoots through me.

She did it. She tripped me.

Fallon's smile curls even farther upward as she sees the growing dread on my face.

I turn back toward the strange young man, gratitude washing over me.

"Unhand her," Echo orders him, glaring. "I'll help her the rest of the way."

There's a flash of hurt in his eyes before his face goes tight with offense. He releases me at once.

Echo grabs hold of me and decidedly tugs me away.

"He helped me," I whisper as she firmly guides me along, accusation in my tone. "What's wrong? Who is he?"

She glances over at me, her eyes sharp. "One of the *Lupines.*"

Startled, I look back to where the strange young man is now seated in with the Kelts. He gives me a small smile, which eases my alarm and piques my curiosity. Next to him sits a beautiful girl with long blond hair, plain clothing and the same wild, amber eyes. She sits like she's royalty, her chin held high, and regards me with barely disguised contempt.

The Lupine twins.

I remember the sordid gossip, the shocking stories about nudity and public mating. About how Lupine males go after any women they can get their hands on. I glance back toward the Lupines and wonder if there's truth in any of it. I'm so curious about them, but I also feel a twinge of guilt to be thinking about such indecent things.

Finally, we reach our place and Echo guides me, to my immense relief, toward a seat between herself and Aislinn Greer.

As I sit down, Aislinn puts her arm around me and hands me a stack of papers.

"What's this?" I ask, taking them.

"Maps," she says. "Your lecture schedule. Lodging and labor assignments. When I heard what happened, I went to the Records Master and got these for you."

"Thank you," I say, touched. I look to Aislinn and Echo with gratitude.

Echo pats my arm in solidarity, then focuses in with rapt attention as the High Chancellor begins his opening remarks.

I resentfully look back toward where Fallon is sitting. I can't see her through the thick crowd.

"When I was walking up that aisle," I whisper to Aislinn, "I think Fallon Bane tripped me...with magic."

"I can't say I'm surprised," she says, eyeing me gravely. "She's not too happy about...um... Lukas and you."

Where is Lukas? I grasp the papers in my lap and bite worriedly at my lower lip. What's he doing? Will he come for me at some point?

"Can Fallon do that?" I ask anxiously. "Can she conjure invisible objects? And trip people with them?"

"She's a Level Five," Aislinn replies with some incredulity. "Of course she can." Perhaps seeing how upset I am, Aislinn pats my shoulder. "She won't go too far, Elloren. You're Carnissa Gardner's granddaughter. If she hurts you, she'll be dismissed from the Guard." She eyes me ruefully. "Just...stay away from Lukas. Okay?"

I nod, fuming over Fallon's casual cruelty. But it's all easier said than done. How can I possibly stay away from Lukas with Aunt Vyvian bent on my wandfasting to him?

We fall silent as High Chancellor Abenthy begins lengthy introductions of each of the multitude of professors. He details their recent accomplishments to polite, scattered applause that blends in with the sound of the rain. The hall is so large, I have to strain to hear his thin, reedy voice.

Distracted by the wide variety of scholars, I venture a glance across the aisle toward the large grouping of Kelts. They're very varied in appearance, with a rainbow of light hair shades, eye coloring and skin tones.

The Kelts are not a pure race like us. They're more accepting of intermarriage, and because of this, they're hopelessly mixed.

I notice that the Kelts' clothing is varied as well, although uniformly not very fine. These are work clothes, homespun garb best suited for farm chores—the type I wear at home for comfort.

I suddenly feel weighed down and pinched in by my expensive layers of silk.

I miss Uncle Edwin and the comfort of home.

Does Uncle Edwin know about the Icaral attack? Has Aunt Vyvian sent out a runehawk to let him know what happened and that I'm okay?

My eyes are drawn to a stern-faced Keltic youth sitting directly across from us. He's lanky, with brown hair and starkly angular features. He's staring straight ahead with a look of great resolve as if it's taking a huge effort to focus on the High Chancellor and not on something else.

He unexpectedly turns and fixes his startlingly golden-green eyes on me with a look of hatred so intense, I flinch back.

I turn away quickly, my face growing hot, embarrassed to be caught staring at him and stunned by the violence in his emerald glare. I can almost feel the tension vibrating off him.

"Aislinn," I whisper, swallowing hard, "who's the Kelt sitting opposite us? He's looking at me like he wants to *kill* me."

Aislinn glances discreetly toward the young man.

He's turned away and is once again focused, with obvious effort, on the High Chancellor, his fists tightly clenched.

"That's Yvan Guriel," she informs me. "Don't let him rattle you. He hates Gardnerians."

Especially me, I think. *Especially the granddaughter of the Black Witch.*

I venture another look in his direction. He's still staring

straight ahead, his jaw flexing with pent-up tension. I sit there for a moment, a disquieting tangle of emotions swamping over me. My foot still smarts from its encounter with an invisible object, my head and wand arm are now throbbing in time with my pulse and my wrist is stinging from the Icaral's tearing grip. It's a wonder I'm still upright.

This Yvan Guriel doesn't even know me, I lament, glaring resentfully at him out of the corner of my eye. *He has no right to be so hateful.*

"What else do you know about him?" I ask Aislinn, feeling dejected.

"Well," says Aislinn, leaning in close, "he was almost expelled last year."

"Why?"

"Practicing medicine without Guild approval. On some Urisk kitchen workers. He's a physician's apprentice."

I risk another glance at Yvan Guriel, surprisingly stung by this stranger's undisguised loathing. He's still focused militantly toward the front of the room, practically seething with hostility.

Determined to ignore the hateful Kelt, I let my eyes wander back a few rows to a young man with deep brown skin who towers over everyone around him. There's an impressive stillness to the way he sits that speaks of military discipline. His dark purple hair is cut short, revealing pointed ears pierced with rows of dark metal hoops. But perhaps the most striking thing about him are the swirling black rune-tattoos that cover his face, which mirror the glowing red rune-marks on his crimson tunic.

"Who's the tall, tattooed man?" I ask Aislinn.

"Shhhh!" A slim, stern-faced Gardnerian chastises us with vast irritation, and both Aislinn and I shrink back, my face heating. We're quiet for a long moment.

"That's Andras Volya," Aislinn finally whispers.

"He looks like he's from the East," I puzzle out, "but his ears are pointed, and he has purple hair." I know many groups in the East have darker skin, but not pointed ears or purple hair.

"He's Amaz," Aislinn clarifies. "They're of all different races. Andras and his mother are part Ishkart, part Urisk."

I remember the tattooed women I saw at the Verpacian horse market and am confused.

"But…he's not a woman." Amaz tribes are made up *only* of women. They kill men who wander into their territory. I lean in toward Aislinn. "And I thought they used rune-magery to only have baby girls."

"They do," Aislinn concurs, "but it doesn't always work. Every now and then, a male is born. By accident." Aislinn gestures to the front of the room with her chin. "That's his mother—Professor Volya."

I scan the green-robed professors sitting silently in rows behind the High Chancellor and quickly locate a woman who greatly resembles Andras. Her face is similarly rune-marked, though her hair is black with streaks of purple.

"She refused to abandon Andras when he was a baby, so she was exiled from Amaz lands," Aislinn explains. "For a while she and Andras lived on their own in Western Keltania, but then she came here. About ten years ago. Andras has pretty much grown up here."

"What does she teach?"

"Equine Studies, of course. And Chemistrie. That's one of your classes." Aislinn reaches over and riffles through my papers, pulls one out and hands it to me. "I'm taking it, too."

I skim the paper.

APOTHECARY SCIENCES, YEAR ONE

Apothecarium I with Laboratory—Professor
Guild Mage Eluthra Lorel

Metallurgie I with Laboratory—Professor Guild Master Fy'ill Xanillir

Botanicals I—Professor Priest Mage Bartholomew Simitri

Advanced Mathematics—Professor Guild Mage Josef Klinmann

History of Gardneria—Professor Priest Mage Bartholomew Simitri

Chemistrie I with Laboratory—Professor Guild Master Astrid Volya

There it is. *Chemistrie. Professor Astrid Volya.* I glance back over at Andras.

"What's her son like?" I wonder.

"He's quiet," Aislinn whispers, looking over at him. "And he's amazingly good at every sport: sword fighting, ax throwing, archery, you name it. And he's a natural with horses, just like his mother. That's his job. He cares for the horses stabled here. The Amaz can talk to their horses, you know—with their *minds*. He's a skilled horse healer, too. Last year one of the Gardnerian military apprentices took a nasty fall on his horse, and the horse's leg was broken. The animal was so wild with pain, no one could get near it. But Andras could. Within a week, he had the horse good as new."

"How do you know so much about everyone?" I ask, impressed.

Aislinn smiles. "My own life is so incredibly boring, I have to live vicariously through everyone else's." She pauses and lets out a sigh for dramatic effect. "I suppose, seeing as how I'll be fasting to Randall, perhaps the most boring young man on the face of Erthia, I will always have to amuse myself in this way."

Around us, scholars are beginning to talk and get up, the High Chancellor having finished his presentation. Aislinn and Echo stand up, and I follow suit, glancing down at my pile of papers. Aislinn helps me search through them and pulls out one from the middle.

"You're supposed to meet with the Vice Chancellor," she tells me, handing the paper back to me. "Come. I'll bring you to her."

Reluctantly, I say my goodbyes to Echo and follow behind Aislinn, trying my best to ignore the Kelt, Yvan Guriel, as he sets his fiery green eyes on me and shoots me a parting, hostile glare.

CHAPTER FOUR

Vice Chancellor Quillen

Vice Chancellor Lucretia Quillen sits at her desk, efficiently finishing some correspondence as I arrive, motioning me in with a sharp flick of her hand. She's Gardnerian, with straight black hair pulled into a tight bun, her dark tunic finely made.

Her office is located high up in one of the White Hall's many towers, the diamond-paned windows providing a panoramic view of the lamp-lit University city.

I stare, amazed, at the breathtaking view of the entire valley and the mammoth Northern Spine beyond. It's clearing outside, the gray clouds breaking up, stars pricking through. There's a sea of domed Spine-stone roofs laid out before me, the cobbled streets like small paths from this height, a stone bridge below us connecting the third floor of the White Hall and another building.

All stone and so little comforting wood, I lament. *But still, it's beautiful.*

It's uncomfortably quiet, and I can make out the ticking of the clock that sits on the bookshelf behind the Vice Chancellor. There are framed maps of the Western and Eastern Realms hanging on the walls, as well as one of Verpax. A set of bookshelves below the windows holds a small library. The ceiling is a curved dome, much like the White Hall, and painted to resemble the night sky in a similar fashion.

I'm positively leaden, so exhausted I'm barely able to concentrate around a now-vicious headache.

The Vice Chancellor sets down her pen and regards me coolly over gold-wire spectacles. "You've had quite an eventful day, Mage Gardner," she observes in a voice full of authority not easily questioned.

My pulse throbs against my skull. "It's been very difficult."

"Yes, I imagine it was."

"I'll be happier when my brothers get here...and it'll be good to get some sleep."

The Vice Chancellor hands me a sturdy necklace—a gold disc hanging from a linked chain. "This is your Guild insignia. It will get you into the Apothecary Archives."

I turn the disc over in my hand and run my thumb along its bumpy design. Warm excitement wells inside me over my new status as an official Guild apprentice. I slip the chain over my head.

"You're to meet with the Kitchen Mistress tonight," she informs me levelly. "About your work assignment."

I riffle through the papers Aislinn has given me and find the one detailing my labor assignment. I hold it out for the Vice Chancellor's inspection. She gestures dismissively to indicate that she's already familiar with the details and does not need to see it. I lower it back into the pile of parchment on my lap.

"I'm supposed to be living somewhere called the North Tower?" I mention tentatively.

"Ah, yes," she says, turning briefly and pointing toward the windows behind her. "It's past the University's northern grounds, just beyond the horse stables. You can see it from here."

I peer out. I can just make out a gloomy stone structure at

the crest of a long hill, the open wilds visible at its back and the Northern Spine beyond.

"It looks like a guard tower," I say, heavily disappointed, wistfully remembering the richly lit lodging houses Lukas and I passed on the way in.

The Vice Chancellor purses her lips. "You entered late, Mage Gardner. Our lodging houses were full. In any case, you won't be alone. We placed you there with two other scholars."

"Ariel Haven and Wynter Eirllyn?" I ask, having seen them listed as my lodging mates on the papers I've been given.

The Vice Chancellor's eyes narrow at this, and a small smile twitches at the corner of her mouth. "Yes, they will be your lodging mates."

"Are they Gardnerian?" I wonder. Wynter is a strange name. I've never heard it before.

She gives me a cryptic look—the same look my aunt gave me when she explained that Selkies are sometimes kept as pets.

"Ariel Haven is Gardnerian," she replies slowly. "Wynter Eirllyn is Elfkin."

An Elf. That's unexpected, and despite my painful headache and aching wand arm, I find myself intrigued by the idea. I'll be lodging with an Elf. "Oh," is all I can think of to say.

The Vice Chancellor is still studying me closely as if she's trying to figure something out. "Your aunt was hopeful that you would someday follow in the footsteps of your grandmother," she says stiffly. "Apparently, this will not be the case."

My disastrous wandtesting. Well, at least the truth is finally out. "I think, because I resemble her…"

"You look *exactly* like her," she corrects sharply.

I'm thrown by her icy approach. "I've only seen paintings of her, and I was only three when she died, so…"

"So you have no clear image of her," she says, cutting me off. "Unlike you, I remember her quite well." She pauses a moment to stare at me, her lips pressed into a thin, tight line.

My brow creases in confusion. Why is she being so terse at the mention of my grandmother? Our greatest Mage. Our people's Deliverer. Most Gardnerians worship her memory.

She stands up unexpectedly and gestures toward the door. "Very well, Mage Gardner. It would seem that it's time for you to report for your labor assignment."

For a moment I just sit there, blinking at her, then realize I'm been summarily dismissed. I gather up my papers and make my departure.

CHAPTER FIVE

The North Tower

I follow my map to a long building near the White Hall, enter and make my way through the sizable dining area toward a door at the very end.

An engraved wooden placard on the adjacent wall reads *Main Kitchen*.

I push on the door, and it swings open on heavy iron hinges. The corridor it opens into is lined with shelves stacked full of cleaning tools, and the smell of soap is heavy in the air. I walk toward another door just ahead and peer through its circular window.

Warm light emanates from the kitchen and spills out over me like a cozy blanket, the smells of food and well-banked fires filling me with comfort.

It smells like home. Like the kitchen in my uncle's cottage. As if I could close my eyes, and when I opened them, I'd be home, my uncle offering me a mug of warm, mint tea with honey.

On a broad wooden table directly before me, a plump, elderly Urisk woman busily kneads a large pile of bread dough. She's carrying on a quiet conversation with three other Urisk women doing the same. Almost all of them look like the seasonal laborers at the Gaffneys' farm—rose-tinted white skin, hair and eyes. Members of the Urisk lower class.

The women laugh every now and then, the fragrant herbs hanging in rows from the rafters above their heads giving the kitchen the look of a friendly forest. A number of young Kelts joke with each other amicably as they go about washing dishes, tending fires, chopping vegetables for tomorrow's meals. A small Urisk child skips about, her rose-white hair braided, the kitchen laborers skirting around her, careful not to spill hot water or plates of food on her head. She can't be more than five years old. The little girl is holding some twisted wire and a small bottle, pausing every now and then to blow bubbles at people, the bread makers good-naturedly shooing her and popping bubbles before they can land on the piles of dough.

As I continue to watch the warm scene, relief washes over me.

To think Aunt Vyvian imagined working here would be so terrible. This is work I truly welcome. Peeling potatoes, washing dishes, pleasant people.

And then I see *him*.

Yvan Guriel.

The angry Kelt. The one who hated me on sight.

But he doesn't look angry now. He's sitting in a far corner in front of a table. With him sit four young women—three of them Urisk, one a serious, blonde Keltic girl—all of whom look to be about the same age as me.

There are books and maps open in front of them, and Yvan is talking and pointing to something on one of the pages, almost as if he's lecturing. Every so often he pauses, and the Urisk girls copy something down onto the parchment in front of them. Two of the Urisk girls nod at him when he speaks, concentrating intently on what he has to say.

These girls have rose-white coloration, like most of the Urisk in the kitchen, and are plainly dressed in aprons over work clothes, their hair pulled back into single braids. But the third

Urisk girl is different. She reminds me of the Amazakaran—her hair worn in a series of beaded ropes, her posture defiant, her emerald eyes as intense as Yvan's. And her hair and skin are as vivid green as her eyes.

The small, bubble-blowing Urisk child runs over to their table, to Yvan, and throws her arms around him, spilling almost the entire bottle of the bubble liquid down his brown woolen shirt.

I wonder what he'll do, intense and angry as he seems to be.

But he surprises me. He reaches up and puts a gentle hand on the small arm that's still wrapped around him, the little girl grinning at him widely. Then he turns his head to her and smiles.

My breath catches in my throat.

His broad, kind smile transforms him into a completely different person than the angry young man I saw earlier. He's dazzling— more boyish than Lukas, but devastatingly handsome. The flickering lantern light of the kitchen highlights his angular features, and his brilliant green eyes, so hateful before, are now so lovely to look at—brimming with intelligence and kindness. Seeing him like this sets off a sudden bloom of warmth in my chest.

He says something to the Urisk child and squeezes her arm affectionately. The child nods, still smiling, and skips off with her bubbles.

For a moment I can't take my eyes off him, and I imagine what it would be like to be on the receiving end of such a smile.

It's all so wonderful. Friendship. Cooking. Children.

And, the icing on the cake, a large, gray cat walks across the floor.

It reminds me of home. And I know that once Yvan gets to know me, he'll see that I'm not a bad person.

Everything is going to work out just fine.

I summon what little courage I have left, push open the swinging door and walk into the kitchen.

As soon as I enter, every last trace of friendly conversation snuffs out like a candle doused with a bucket of cold water.

My transient happiness evaporates.

Yvan stands up so abruptly he almost knocks his chair over, the look of hatred back on his face, his eyes narrowing furiously on me. The fierce green Urisk girl and the blonde Kelt girl shoot up, glaring at me with pure, undisguised loathing. The two other Urisk girls at the table take on looks of terror, glancing from me to the books and maps in front of them as if they're thieves caught with stolen goods.

I blink at them in confusion.

Are the books not allowed in here? And what about the maps? Why are they so afraid?

One of the older Urisk women pushes the little girl behind her skirts, as if shielding her from me. Everyone in the room begins casting secret, furtive glances at each other, as if they're trying, desperately, to figure out what to do.

Everyone except for Yvan, the heat in his rage-filled glare radiating clear across the room.

I struggle not to shrink back, an uncomfortable flush rising along my neck and cheeks.

The plump, elderly Urisk woman who was kneading bread comes forward, a forced smile on her face as she wrings her flour-covered hands nervously. "Is there something I can do for you, dear?"

"Um..." I hold out my papers to her with a quavering smile. "I'm Elloren Gardner. This is my labor assignment."

The blonde Kelt girl's mouth falls open in surprise. Beside her, the fierce Urisk girl eyes me murderously, and the small child peers out from her hiding spot curiously.

The elderly Urisk woman before me swallows audibly and keeps reading my labor assignment papers over and over, as if there's been some mistake, and if she only reads it through enough times she'll find it—as if my being there is just too awful to be true. The headache throbbing behind my eyes spreads out to my temples.

I can feel Yvan's glare boring into me. He's taller than I originally thought, and all the more intimidating for it.

"I'm supposed to find Fernyllia Hawthorne," I offer.

"That would be me, Mage Gardner," the old woman says, attempting another fake, wavering smile before carefully handing my papers back. "I'm Kitchen Mistress."

"Oh, well... I'm ready to work." I smile weakly at them, avoiding eye contact with Yvan. "Just let me know what you need."

"Oh, Mage Gardner, you're really not dressed for it," Fernyllia points out, gesturing toward my fine clothes.

"Yes, I know," I say apologetically. "I just got in and haven't had a chance to change." I look down at my intricately embroidered skirts. "My aunt bought these for me. These clothes. They're not very practical."

"Your aunt?" Fernyllia says faintly, like she's having a bad dream.

"Yes, my aunt... Vyvian Damon."

Fernyllia and some of the other kitchen workers wince at the mention of my aunt's name. Yvan's scowl hardens.

"Yes," Fernyllia says softly, "I know of her." She looks up at me imploringly. "I must apologize for my granddaughter being here, Mage Gardner." She gestures in the direction of the child. "Her mother's sick and...and I needed to mind her tonight. It won't happen again."

"Oh, it's okay," I reply reassuringly. "I like children."

Why would it matter that the child's here? Is there some reason she's not allowed in the kitchen?

No one's expression budges.

"And Yvan," she explains nervously, gesturing toward him, "he's getting a head start on his University studies. Such a good student he is. But I *did* tell him that he needs to get his work done elsewhere in the future. A kitchen is no place for books, what with all the things that can spill on them and such!"

I smile and nod at her in agreement, trying to prove myself worthy of their acceptance.

"I wish I was ahead in my studies," I tell Yvan, attempting a smile as I turn to him and meet his intense eyes. "I'm already behind, it seems..."

His glare goes scalding, as if he's wildly affronted. I can feel the anger radiating off him in thick waves, bearing down on me.

I swallow audibly, really hurt by his unrelenting, bizarre level of hatred. I blink back the sting of tears and turn to Fernyllia.

Ignore him, I tell myself. *Force yourself to ignore him.*

"So, what would you like me to do?" I ask with forced pleasantry.

Fernyllia's eyes dart around, as if she's trying to figure something important out quickly.

"Why don't I show Mage Gardner what to do with the compost buckets?" the fierce-looking Urisk girl offers in a slow, careful tone.

Fernyllia's eyes flicker in the direction of the books and back to me again. She puts on another false, obsequious smile. "That's an *excellent* idea, Bleddyn," she agrees. "Why don't you go with Bleddyn, Mage Gardner. She'll show you what to do. You don't mind being around animals, do you?"

"Oh, no," I respond with newfound enthusiasm. "I *love* animals."

"Good, good," says Fernyllia as she wrings her weathered hands nervously. "Just follow Bleddyn out, then. The scraps need to go out to the pigs. She'll show you what to do."

I feel like Yvan and everyone else in the room are holding their collective breath as I set down my books and papers and follow Bleddyn out of the kitchen and into a back room. A few large, wooden buckets filled with food scraps are lined up by a door.

"Grab two and follow me," Bleddyn orders icily, her eyes narrowed to slits. I notice that she makes no move to pick up buckets herself, even though there are several more waiting to be brought out.

Bleddyn opens the door with more force than necessary, and it slams against the outside wall of the kitchen with a sharp crack.

The door opens out onto a grassy pasture. Bleddyn grabs a lantern that hangs on a hook next to the door. It's not raining anymore, but everything remains damp and cold, and I can feel the icy moisture of the grass seeping over the edges of my fancy shoes.

Frost will come soon. I can smell it on the early-autumn air.

As we trudge in the direction of a series of low barns and livestock pens, I find myself yearning for my mother's quilt and a warm, dry room.

Soon. This day will be over soon. And then Rafe and Trystan and Gareth will be here, and they'll help me make sense of all the terrible things that have happened.

The storm clouds are breaking up into slender, dark ribbons, a portion of the full moon appearing, then disappearing and appearing again, like some malevolent eye going in and out of hiding. With all the moving clouds and shifting light, the sky seems very large and oppressive, and I feel small and exposed. I think of the Icaral, out there somewhere, hidden like this moon, waiting for me, and a chill courses down my spine.

Bleddyn's fast pace is creating a yawning distance between us, and I hurry to catch up, not wanting to be caught alone in the darkness.

I follow Bleddyn into one of the barns where pigs are being kept in a series of clean, spacious stalls that smell of mud, fresh hay and food scraps. It's poorly lit, and I can barely see my way around.

Bleddyn opens the latch on the gate to one of the stalls. She points to a far corner, where a long trough stands, along with a sow nursing a number of snorting, snuffling piglets jockeying with each other for position.

"There," she says, gesturing toward the trough. "Dump the scraps in there."

I tighten my grip on the two scrap buckets and walk into the stall, my shoes sinking into something soft. I make a concerted effort to ignore it.

I'll clean myself up later. And besides, I don't want this stern Urisk girl to think I'm some pampered Gardnerian who can't pull my weight. They'll soon see that I'm as hard a worker as any of them.

As I pull up one foot, the shoe makes an unpleasant sucking sound.

A hard kick to my rear sends me sprawling.

I fall forward into the mud and pig manure, the scrap buckets falling out of my hands and tumbling over, food remnants scattering everywhere, one of my shoes coming loose. The pigs oink excitedly as they frantically scramble about for the food.

I push myself up onto my knees and round on Bleddyn, my heart racing. "Did you just kick me?" I ask, incredulous.

Bleddyn is leaning against a wall, smiling darkly at me.

"Why did you kick me?" I demand as I pull myself up.

The blonde Keltic girl who was standing with Bleddyn in the kitchen walks in.

"She *kicked* me!" I exclaim to the blonde girl, pointing at Bleddyn.

"I didn't kick her," Bleddyn sneers. "She tripped. She's quite clumsy."

"I did *not* trip!" I vehemently contradict. "I was *kicked*!"

The blonde girl shakes her head from side to side. "Isn't that just like a Gardnerian? Blaming the help."

"They're all the same," Bleddyn agrees. "Bunch of black Roaches."

I flinch at the racial insult. It's a horrible name that mocks the black of our sacred garb. "Get away from me!" I spit out, turning to retrieve my shoe.

I should never have turned my back on them. Another kick sends me flying back down into the muck.

"Why are you doing this?" I cry, scrambling around to face them, my heart pounding. A curious piglet comes over to snuffle at my skirts.

"I *cannot* believe she tripped again!" Bleddyn exclaims.

"She really is dreadfully clumsy," the Kelt agrees.

"I think she needs a new labor assignment."

"Something that doesn't require walking."

They both pause to chuckle at this.

I'm stunned. Why are they being so cruel? I've done nothing to deserve it.

"Oh, and *look*, she's soiled her pretty, pretty dress," Bleddyn observes.

"Leave me alone!" I insist as I pull myself once more to my feet, every muscle tensed. "If you don't get away from me, I'll... I'll report you both!"

"Shut up!" the Kelt girl barks as she bursts into the stall, fists clenched.

I shrink back from her.

"Now, you listen to me, *Gardnerian!*" she snarls at me. "Don't think we don't know why you're here!"

"I'm here because I need money for University!"

A swift slap across my face sends me flying backward and into a state of shock. I've never been struck in my entire life.

"I told you to shut up, Roach!" she bellows.

Bleddyn stands behind her, smirking.

"How stupid do you think we are?" the blonde girl continues, her tone acid as I cradle my cheek.

"About *what?*" I cry, bursting into angry tears. "I'm here so I can pay my tithe. Just like you!"

"Liar!" she snarls. "They sent you here to spy on us, didn't they?"

Spy? What kind of strange world have I landed in?

"I don't know what you're talking about!" I choke out at her.

I think of the books. The maps hastily cleared away. What are they all involved in here?

"Look at me, Gardnerian!" the blonde girl demands.

Afraid of being struck again, I comply.

The blonde girl points an unforgiving finger at me. "If you so much as mention to anyone that you saw a child here, or any books or maps, we will find you, and we will break your arms and legs."

"I think it would be quite easy," Bleddyn observes, sounding almost bored. "She's very weak-looking. So willowy."

"Very willowy," the Kelt agrees.

"Not much she could do about it, either. She's a Level One Mage, did you know that?"

"How embarrassing."

"Her grandmother would be *so* disappointed."

I feel a spark of anger rise at their mention of my grandmother. I push it down and watch them carefully.

They eye me for a long moment. I wonder if they're done beating on me as I cower by the wall, exhausted, filthy and fighting back the tears.

"Anyway," the blonde girl finally says, "I think we've made ourselves clear. See you in the kitchens, Elloren Gardner."

"Bring back the buckets," says Bleddyn as they both turn to leave, "and try not to trip again."

After they leave, I sob for a minute or two before my anger sparks anew.

They can't treat me this way. They can't. I roughly wipe the tears from my face. I may be powerless, but I can report them to the Kitchen Mistress. I won't let them scare me into submission.

My outrage burning away at my fear, I take a deep breath and drag myself back to the kitchen.

I enter and am met by the same unified silence I departed from.

Bleddyn and the blonde Kelt girl stand bracketing Fernyllia and are both glaring at me menacingly.

Yvan looks momentarily stunned by my appearance.

Fernyllia and the others seem shocked, too, but they quickly recover, masking their dismay with carefully neutral expressions.

Only Yvan's eyes remain a storm of conflict.

I notice that the child is gone, and so are the books and maps that were on the table.

"They tripped me and slapped me!" I tell Fernyllia, my voice breaking with emotion as I point at Bleddyn and the Kelt girl.

"Now then, Mage, you must be mistaken," Fernyllia says in a conciliatory tone, but there's a hard edge of warning in her eyes. "I'm sure Bleddyn and Iris meant you no harm."

"They beat on me and threatened me!"

"No, Mage," Fernyllia corrects. "You *tripped*."

I gape at her, stupefied. They're all a united front—united against me.

Head spinning, I grasp for what to do. I could go to the Chancellor and turn every last one of them in. But first I have to get out of here safely.

"Why don't you take the rest of the night off, Mage Gardner?" Fernyllia offers, but there's a hint of a command behind her polite, subservient tone. "Get yourself settled in. Your shift here tomorrow begins at fifteenth hour."

My outrage collapses into an exhausted, browbeaten misery, everything around me going blurry with tears.

I grab my paperwork, which Fernyllia's holding out to me, and look squarely with undisguised accusation at Yvan.

He's holding himself stiffly, not looking at me now, his hands on his hips, his jaw tight, doggedly making his loyalties known.

Against me.

A flood of tears threatening, I turn away from all of them and flee.

Stumbling as I go, silent tears falling, I struggle to find my way toward the North Tower.

Shelter. Shelter's all I want right now. A place to sleep and hide until tomorrow, when I can find my brothers and get help.

The hatred in Yvan's eyes reverberates in my mind, but I feel better the farther from the kitchens I get.

Outside, the clouds have continued to thin and now resemble hundreds of slow-moving, dark snakes, the moon partially hidden by the shifting serpents. I make my way through the winding University streets and its small knots of cloaked strangers, past the Weavers' Guild building and then a series of damp fields, the cold air and brisk walk gradually calming me.

Some of the fields are home to sheep, huddled by feeding troughs in muddied masses, while others are horse pasture adjacent to long boarding stables.

And then I'm past it all, my steps halting as I stare up across a broad, barren field, the sloping expanse of it scrubby and deserted. A thin wind whistles.

The North Tower lies before me.

It sits clear across the field, a poorly maintained stone path winding up to it. Like a sentinel guarding the forest, this old military post is a last-chance stop before being enveloped by the wilderness to its back and sides, a weathered archer's turret placed high on the roof.

My new home.

It's gray and cold and foreboding—everything made of Spine stone, no wood. Nothing at all like Uncle Edwin's warm, comforting cottage. My heart sinks even lower at the sight of it.

Resignedly, I trudge through the huge field, the tower looming over me as I approach.

I open the sole door at the base of the tower, and it creakily swings open to reveal a small foyer, a spiraling staircase to the left and a storage closet to the right. The door to the closet is open and, by the dim light of a wall lantern, I can see it's full of buckets, rakes, extra lanterns and a variety of cleaning supplies. I'm heartened to see that it also holds both of my travel trunks and my violin.

I let out a long breath. *See, it'll be all right,* I reassure myself. *And I'm rooming with a Gardnerian and an Elf. No hateful Urisk or Kelts. Things will be just fine.*

I decide to leave my belongings in the closet for the moment and make my way up the staircase, the heels of my shoes almost slipping a few times on the polished stone, my steps echoing sharply throughout the eerily quiet tower.

When I reach the top, another door opens into a short hallway, also lit by a wall lantern. There's a stone bench placed against one wall and, on either end of the hallway, windows look out over the surrounding fields, the moon peering in. A metal ladder is bolted to the wall before me and leads to the archers' tower, the ceiling entrance long since nailed shut. There's another door at the end of the hallway.

That has to be my new lodging.

I wonder if my new lodging mates are asleep or absent, as I can't make out any light around the door frame. I walk down the deserted hallway toward the door, slightly unnerved by the quiet.

I pause before opening the door and glance out the window, the moon still watching, cold and indifferent. I stare at it for a moment until it's covered in the shifting clouds, the outside world plunged into a deeper darkness. I turn back to the door, curl my hand around its cool, metal handle and push it open.

The room is pitch-black, but I can make out a large, oval window directly before me.

"Hello," I say softly, not wanting to startle anyone who might be trying to sleep. The clouds shift, and moonlight spills into the room.

And that's when I see it. Something crouched just below the window.

Something with wings.

The blood drains from my face, and I'm overcome by a rush of fear so strong that it paralyzes me, rooting me to the spot.

An Icaral.

It's gotten in somehow. And I'm about to be killed. The thing in front of me emits the same smell of rotted meat as the Icarals in Valgard.

Slowly, it rises and unfurls ragged, black wings. And it's not alone. To the right of it, I see movement on top of what appears to be a dresser. Another winged figure, also crouching like it's waiting to attack.

Holy Ancient One, there's two of them.

"Hello, Elloren Gardner," the Icaral under the window says in a raspy, malevolent voice. "Welcome to hell."

CHAPTER SIX

Ariel

A jolt of energy shoots though me, wrenching me out of my crippling haze of fear as the Icaral advances toward me.

Terrified, I find my footing and bolt out of the room, down the short hallway, bumping against the stone bench, taking the spiraled stairs three at a time, almost falling.

When I jump to the bottom, jarring my ankle, a realization dawns on me with nauseating clarity.

Nowhere is safe.

If they're here, they're probably everywhere. Probably waiting for me outside, as well.

I throw myself into the cleaning closet, slam the door shut and begin barricading myself in with an old shelf, my travel case and finally my feet as I brace my legs against the barricade for leverage. I'm shaking with terror as I sit in the dark, the cold stone floor beneath me, the only light a faint glow rimming the door from the dimly lit foyer and the slight shimmer of my skin.

It's quiet.

Deathly quiet.

So quiet that my heavy, panicked breathing sounds obscenely

loud, my heart audible as it beats wildly against my chest. But I know they're out there. Waiting for me.

"I'm not the Black Witch!" I shriek at the door, spittle flying from my mouth.

For a moment there's no response. Only more quiet. When the reply finally comes, it's close.

"Oh, yes, you are," the thing hisses mockingly.

Oh, Holy Ancient One, it's on the other side of the door.

My trembling intensifies, and I begin to recite a prayer from *The Book of the Ancients* over and over again in a desperate whisper.

Most Holy Ancient One, In the Heavens Above, Deliver me from the Evil Ones...

As I beg for my life to be spared, the demon begins to scrape its nails down the length of the door. Very slowly. Again and again.

Then more silence.

A hard force slams up against the door, jolting me through the barricade, through my legs. I cry out and begin to sob.

"I *will* kill you," the voice snarls, "and *slowly*."

The scraping begins again, but this time sharper, as if the wooden door is being gouged by a knife.

"You have to sleep sometime, Gardnerian," the cruel thing sneers. "And when you do, I will *cut* you..."

The sound of wood being gouged intensifies, and I can feel the rhythmic pressure through my legs. The thing is dismantling the door, taking as much time doing this as it will when it kills me.

My panicked thoughts run wild in my head, like a crazed stallion. Images of Rafe, Trystan and Gareth arriving at school to find me dead in this closet, torn to shreds by Icarals. Images of my uncle's heart giving out when he discovers what's happened to me. Of Fallon Bane being overjoyed at my fate. And Sage's wand being found...

The wand!

I scramble around in the dark, feeling for the straps on my travel trunk, throwing it open, ripping the fabric liner with wildly shaking hands to get at the wand. Sage said it was powerful— maybe so powerful that it will work even for someone as weak as me.

I hold the wand in the way Commander Vin instructed, the end pressed against my palm, and point it toward the scraping sound. I can't recall the words to any spells. I can only remember some magic words from the tales of my youth. I try them all, tears streaming down my face.

Nothing.

I throw the wand on the floor and lose myself to fear's icy, suffocating grip. The scraping goes on and on late into the night, and I feel myself falling, falling, until everything fades to black.

I'm running through the North Tower's upstairs hallway.

It goes on and on so far, I can't see what lies at the end until finally, I come to my new lodging. This time the door is open, and the room is lit with a soft light that glows unearthly red. Heart pounding, I step inside.

Sage Gaffney stands near the window, a single candle with a blood-red flame beside her, casting the room in long shadows. She has a blank look, her eyes hollowed-out sockets.

"Sage," I say, confused. "Why are you here?"

She doesn't answer, only opens her dark cloak to reveal the bundle that's hidden underneath. Something moves inside the tightly wrapped blankets, and she holds it out to me.

I approach her warily, the bundle full of rippling movement, like a baby lizard about to break out of its soft eggshell, straining to be born. I feel a strong sense of revulsion.

Her baby.

The Icaral.

A macabre curiosity drives me on. After a moment's hesitation, I reach down and pull back the blanket.

A crippling fear seizes me as I face the monster Sage has given birth to, its head that of the Icaral in Valgard, its eyes white and soulless. The creature unfurls foul, black wings, pulls its mouth back into a snarl and lunges...

"No! No!" I scream as a woman's voice cuts through the image before me.

"Wake up, child!"

The dream fades like mist at daybreak, replaced by the face of an elderly Urisk woman kneeling before me, her broad, blue face so deeply lined it resembles a raisin, a brown kerchief holding back her gray hair.

I recoil from the wizened, bony hands that clutch at my shoulders. She releases me and leans back on her heels, her expression one of wary concern. I shake my head hard from side to side, trying to quickly rid myself of the lingering fuzziness.

Did I pass out?

Confused and disoriented, I glance wildly around.

I was dreaming. Was it all a nightmare?

The Urisk woman's eyes flicker over to something on the floor to the right of me. "You dropped your wand," she points out.

My heart leaps into my throat.

I grab up the wand and shove it back under the inner lining of my travel trunk, relieved that she doesn't seem suspicious that I would be in possession of an expensive wand. "I was attacked by Icarals," I inform her breathlessly.

She doesn't look surprised. Instead, she tilts her head, regarding me levelly.

"That would have been Miss Ariel, I suppose."

I shake my head vehemently. "No. They were Icarals. I'm sure of it."

"Miss Ariel and Miss Wynter *are* Icarals," she replies matter-of-factly.

I gape at her in confusion. I shake my head at her again, refusing to believe her. "No. That can't be. The Vice Chancellor told me that Ariel Haven is a Gardnerian and Wynter Eirllyn is an Elf."

She lifts her eyebrows. "That *is* true, Mage Gardner. But it is *also* true that they are both Icarals."

The blood drains from my face. "No. That's impossible," I say in a whisper, feeling like the room is beginning to spin out of control. "They...they *can't* be my lodging mates! They want to *kill* me!"

"Now, now, child," she chides, like I'm somehow overreacting. "You're making yourself hysterical. Miss Wynter wouldn't hurt a fly. Gentle as can be, that one. Now, Miss Ariel, she can come off a bit scary upon first meeting..."

"A *bit*?" I cry. "She clawed at this door all night long, telling me every way she wants to kill me!"

"I'm sure she didn't mean it, Mage Gardner," she reassures me.

I can't believe it. How can she be so blasé about Icaral demons?

"Where are they?" I demand, looking beyond her into the foyer.

"Gone, Mage. In class, I suppose."

"They're *scholars* here?" I cry, not believing this can be happening. But then I remember Aunt Vyvian talking about two Icaral demons. Here at the University.

My lodging mates.

The realization sets my head spinning.

The Urisk woman gets up off the floor and offers me a hand.

I ignore her and get up myself, not trusting her. Not trusting anything.

She lowers her hand, shoots me an unreadable glance, grabs a mop and bucket and waddles out into the foyer.

I hesitantly move toward the door of the closet, half expecting the Icarals to be crouched behind the walls bracketing the door, but when I see the Urisk woman setting down the mop and bucket, humming a tune to herself, I poke my head out of the closet.

The foyer is empty, except for us.

Sunlight streams through a long window halfway up the spiraling staircase. I can see puffy white clouds working their way across a crystal-blue sky. I venture out of the closet on shaky legs, glancing wildly around, listening intently for sound. Then I turn around and close the closet's door and immediately feel light-headed.

The scratching I heard, the gouging—it was all *real*.

The door is completely covered in writing etched deep in the wood by some sharp tool or knife. Over and over, the Icaral wrote "HATE" and "KILL" and a variety of obscenities that cover the entire door. I turn to the Urisk woman.

She's ceased her humming and is leaning on her mop, studying me calmly.

"Do you see this?" I ask her shrilly.

She makes a clicking sound with her tongue and shakes her head from side to side. "Miss Ariel's work, by the looks of it."

How can she be so calm?

"Ariel," I repeat incredulously. "My new lodging mate. The demon."

"She's a bit high-strung, Mage."

High-strung? Is this a University or a sanitorium?

"Don't you worry, Mage," she clucks. "I'll have that door replaced..."

Not able to stomach any more of her infuriating calmness I stalk past her, fleeing from the North Tower as fast as I can.

CHAPTER
SEVEN

Tournaments & Tests

I stumble out into the sunshine, my eyes smarting from the glare.

It's late morning, the sun high in the sky, and the fields, which were so gray the day before, are green and cheerful, rimmed by trees highlighted with the beginnings of vibrant fall color.

I rush down the broad, scrubby field that separates the North Tower from the rolling horse pastures, squinting into the sunlight.

A few curious sheep raise their heads as I hurry past their partitioned fields, the dirt path moist beneath my feet, the scent of mud and greenery on the air. The clacking of multiple looms and the buoyant sound of female conversation waft from the Weavers' Guild building, the doors propped open to let in the fresh air. Blonde Verpacian and silver-haired Elfhollen girls are coming and going, newcomers lugging baskets of brightly colored yarn. I fly past them all onto the cobbled walkways of the University city, the occasional groupings of scholars, laborers and professors breaking off midsentence to gawk at me.

There are flags flapping everywhere, affixed to buildings, streaming from windows, hanging from belts and saddles. Verpacia's four-pointed star on gray seems to dominate, with Gard-

neria's silver Erthia sphere on black a close second. The streets
are crowded, the passersby in a celebratory mood, and uniformed
soldiers of every stripe are out in force.

I suddenly remember that this week marks the beginning of
the Fall Tournaments. My brothers told me about them, the
contests ranging from archery and sword combat to weaving
and glasswork. Competitors come from all over Erthia to show
off their expertise and impress the various Guilds.

Breathless, I stop in front of the stately Merchants' Guild, the
flags of Gardneria and the pure white flag of the Elfin Alfsigr
lands bracketing the entrance. I'm jostled as the crowd surges
around me. My eyes dart from building to building as I try to
find my bearings in this sea of people, but nothing and no one
looks familiar.

"Are you all right?"

I turn to find a young, pointy-eared Elfhollen soldier staring
at me with his bright silver eyes.

"No," I tell him.

"Can I help you?"

I glance around blankly. "I need to find the Lodging Mistress."

"You're just across the street from her." He points to a squat
building festooned with Gardnerian flags. "It's over there."

Relief floods through me as I dodge pedestrian and horse traffic to get to the office of Mage Sylvia Abernathy, the woman
in charge of the scholar housing.

She's a fellow Gardnerian. She'll understand the gravity of
the situation, and I'm sure she'll help me.

A short while later I'm in a stuffy office sitting opposite Mage
Abernathy, a pinch-faced woman, our flag prominently displayed behind her long desk. Like the Urisk cleaning woman,
she's oddly unsurprised by my appearance or by my story, and
regards me with cold, calm eyes.

"You'll help me, won't you?" I plead, thrown by her composure.

For a moment she holds her pen in suspended animation over the stack of papers in front of her. "Why, that's entirely up to you, Mage Gardner," she says as she resumes her writing.

"I don't understand." I struggle to remain composed.

"Well, Mage Gardner," she replies absently, "your aunt has been in touch with me about your lodging arrangements. She sent a runehawk with instructions yesterday morn. Of course it would be possible to move you into a room with...more amiable roommates."

More amiable roommates?

Why isn't she outraged? I've been placed in a room with Icarals! And they tried to kill me!

I force myself to take a deep breath. I need to stay calm, even if all of the people here are completely unhinged.

"How soon can I move?" I ask, trying to keep my voice steady and even.

She stops writing, sets down her pen, folds her hands and meets my gaze. "Why, as soon as you're wandfasted, Mage Gardner."

Oh, Holy Ancient One. My heart begins to hammer against my chest. Aunt Vyvian...

Everyone has a breaking point, Elloren. Don't force me to find yours.

"I can't wandfast yet," I say, my resolve wavering.

"Well, then," she responds unsympathetically, "I suppose you'll just have to find a way to deal with your situation."

Desperation rises inside me. "I'm going to send word to my uncle."

She eyes me shrewdly. "Your aunt also instructed me to inform you that your uncle has fallen ill. Weak heart, she said."

Shock blasts through me. *"What?"* I can barely get the words out. How could Aunt Vyvian have kept this from me? "Is he all right? How long has he been sick?"

"Oh, it seems he'll recover in time," she says dismissively. "He has a local physician tending to him, but she feels it would be quite stressful for him to get involved in all of this." Her eyes are steady on me, giving her words time to sink in.

I stare back at her as my misery slowly coalesces into a white-hot ball of anger.

"Then I'm going to speak to the High Chancellor," I say, my voice hardening.

She makes a sound of derision. "The High Chancellor doesn't concern himself with petty problems such as these. Besides, your aunt has already spoken to the Vice Chancellor regarding your lodging arrangements. I think you will find that everyone is in complete agreement as to how things stand."

So that's it.

I can't leave Verpax University because I'm at risk of being killed by a demonic, monstrous, wingless Icaral, and I have no alternative but to live with two demonic, monstrous winged Icarals and work in a place where people want to break my arms and legs.

Or I can pressure my sick uncle to let me wandfast, against his wishes, to a man I barely know.

I stand unsteadily, so angry I'm trembling. "Thank you for meeting with me. Everything is clear to me now."

"You're quite welcome," she says, not bothering to get up. "Please let me know if I can be of any further assistance."

My legs unstable, I turn to leave.

"Oh, Mage Gardner," she says mildly, stopping me in my tracks. "What should I tell your aunt if she asks how you are? She can relay your answer to your sick uncle."

I turn to face her again, swallowing back my angry tears. I square my shoulders and look her straight in the eye. "Tell her," I say, my voice gone cold, "that I'm fine, and to tell my uncle not to worry—that sending me to University was the best thing he ever did."

She meets my gaze steadily for a moment then turns her attention back to the lodging book and resumes writing.

I have no idea where to go next, so I begin aimlessly wandering down the University streets, not caring about my disheveled state and numb to the shocked stares of the passing scholars and professors, following the flow of the festive tournament crowd.

I'm soon outside the central grounds, past the buildings, and finally come to a crowded series of tournament fields, a variety of flags flapping in the cool breeze. An archery competition is visible up ahead, a line of Elfin archers frozen in place with arrows set, their field densely rimmed with spectators. Perfectly in sync, their arrows shoot forth toward oval targets placed on thin poles. They hit the targets with a loud *thwap*.

"Cael Eirllyn!" the Match Master calls, a young Elf on a white steed riding forward to claim his prize.

Desperate for my brothers, I turn away from the match, weaving through the boisterous crowds, looking everywhere for a familiar face. And then I find one, but not the one I would have ever wanted to find.

Gardnerian military apprentices are competing in a wand-work contest the next field over. A female in the middle of the line of contestants catches my eye. She's the sole apprentice, the other eight Mages clad in soldier black, Level Five silver stripes on all of their arms.

Fallon Bane.

She's the only female in their group, everyone's wands in hand to take aim at the circular wooden bull's-eye targets that face them across the small field.

I jolt back as fire surges forth from a Mage's wand, the flames streaking toward the target, exploding into the bull's-eye in a small, churning ball of fire.

Applause and cheers rise from the mostly Gardnerian spectators. A grouping of Kelts watch the contest, arms crossed in front of their chests, unsettled looks in their eyes.

The rest of the male Mages take turns sending out fire with similar results.

Fallon is last. She raises her arm and waits for the crowd to quiet to a hush. Then she whips her arm forward and sends a white spear of ice coursing toward the target.

I flinch as her spear knifes into the target with an earsplitting crack, and the target explodes into a giant ball of white, smaller side spears impaling every other target in the row, shattering them to the ground.

There's silence as a cloud of icy snow settles over the destroyed line of targets.

"Called!" the Match Master booms. "For Mage Fallon Bane!"

The Gardnerians erupt into cheers, some military apprentices launching into our national song with boisterous, off-key voices.

The last of my courage seeps out of me. I pull away from the jostling crowd and stumble toward a distant, sheltering tree. I plop down on the damp, shadowed grass, let my sleep-deprived head fall into my hands and cry.

"Elloren."

I startle as a hand makes contact with my shoulder. I look up to find Aislinn and Echo crouched by me, their faces shocked and full of concern.

I don't know what to say. It's just so awful.

"What happened?" Aislinn says. "We've been looking *every-where* for you. When you didn't show up for breakfast, we got worried." She reaches up to gently touch my face, her brow tightly knotted. "Heavens, Elloren. You're bruised. Did someone hit you?"

Sobbing pathetically, I tell them about the Icarals and the kitchen workers as they sit down on the damp grass beside me.

Aislinn shakes her head from side to side. "I can't believe your aunt could be so cruel."

"It's a test, Elloren," Echo informs me gravely.

"I *know* it's a test," I reply, agitatedly pulling at grass with both fists. "To see how much I can take before I back down and get fasted to a man I barely know."

"No," Echo says, her eyes wide and sure. "It's a test sent down by the Ancient One. You are Carnissa Gardner's descendant. There's a reason you look so much like her. You are meant to descend into this pit of Evil. Just like Fain in *The Book*. He was visited upon by every manner of evil and misfortune, remember? But it was all a test. Fain remained true, and in the end, he prevailed and was rewarded by the Ancient One. You, also, are meant to confront the Evil Ones, and you will prevail!"

"I'm not the Black Witch, Echo," I point out, swiping at my tears. "I'm a Level One Mage. Just like you. How exactly am I supposed to prevail against *Icaral demons*?"

"You have the power of the Ancient One on your side," she assures me. "If you remain true to His teachings, you *will* prevail!"

This is of no comfort whatsoever.

Magically, I'm a complete and utter weakling. I need help. Preferably from a Level Five Mage.

I sit bolt upright, struck by inspiration. "Where's Lukas?"

Aislinn's face lights up. "I know where he is, Elloren," she says, getting up and holding out her hand to me. "I saw him earlier. He's here for a few weeks to oversee the Second Division apprentices—that's Randall's division. Come on."

CHAPTER
EIGHT

Weapons

I cling to Aislinn's arm as we wind our way through the tournament fields, my wretched appearance attracting more than a few curious stares.

I spot Lukas up ahead, and a nervous jolt of energy shoots through me.

He's surrounded by a crowd, fencing with an Elfhollen lieutenant, the Gardnerian military apprentices periodically cheering him on. Lukas's eyes are as focused as a hawk bearing down on a small rodent as he points his sword at his opponent, a confident smile on his face.

As we approach, Lukas's eyes flicker to meet mine, causing him to momentarily lose concentration. His opponent mockstabs him with a capped sword tip just above the heart.

Lukas seems oblivious to the sounds of surprise going up around him and the look of shocked triumph on his opponent's face. He cocks his head to the side, takes in my wretched appearance then turns and shakes hands with his victorious opponent, leaning in to say something to the man in the Elfhollen language. The Elfhollen laughs and responds in the strange tongue.

Lukas sheathes his sword and strides over to meet us, another Gardnerian lieutenant taking his place on the field.

"Elloren, what happened to you?" he asks as he approaches. "You're filthy." He pulls his head back sharply. "Did someone strike you?"

"I'm in a really bad situation," I tell him breathlessly. "I don't know what to do."

He narrows his eyes, then glances over at Aislinn and Echo. "Can I speak with her privately?"

"Of course," Echo responds without hesitation. Aislinn gives me a small, encouraging smile.

Echo and Aislinn walk off as Lukas leads me to a nearby bench set under a wide tree. He gestures for me to sit down and I do. I eye his sword—the same sword he used to cut down the Icaral in Valgard. And his wand, attached to his wand belt. I'm glad to see him armed.

"I was attacked," I tell him. "First in the kitchen, when I reported for my labor assignment—"

"Wait," he interrupts, holding up a hand, "why are you working in the kitchen?"

"Aunt Vyvian," I explain. "She won't pay my tithe, so I have to work—"

"Why?" he cuts in, confused.

I hesitate before answering. He's looking at me expectantly. There's no way out. I have to talk about this. I take a deep breath before answering him. "She won't pay my tithe until I'm wandfasted."

He nods with dawning understanding. "But..." he says, in a low, affronted tone, "you don't *want* to be wandfasted."

I hold out my hands to him in supplication. "It's nothing personal. My uncle...he's sick." My voice catches. "And I promised him I'd wait for two years..."

"Two years?" he spits out, incredulous.

"Until I'm done with my University studies."

It's clear from his expression that he thinks my uncle is an idiot, and that I'm an even bigger idiot for agreeing to this.

"Lukas," I say, wanting him to understand, "we barely know each other."

He's quiet for a tense moment, regarding me with no small amount of irritation.

"I really didn't mean to offend you." I grip at the cool Spine-stone of the bench for support. "And I promised my uncle I'd wait to fast before I even met you."

Lukas studies me for a long minute, one eyebrow cocked.

"Will your parents be very upset?" I reluctantly venture.

"Yes," he says.

"I never meant…"

"They don't realize how sheltered you've been. It's becoming common for girls to be wandfasted at thirteen. Were you aware of that?"

"I've only just found out," I reply weakly.

"And most people don't get to meet first. Their parents make all the arrangements, and they meet at the fasting."

"I…I didn't know that." I grip harder at the bench's edge.

"We're older than average, you and I. How old are you? Eighteen?"

"I'll be eighteen in a few weeks," I tell him, realizing something. "But that's just what I'm talking about. I don't even know how old you are. Regardless of how common this is, I've only just met you. I don't even *know* you."

He laughs at this. "Oh, I don't know," he says, his lip curling up at the edge, "we seem to get on pretty well."

I color at this, remembering my aunt's party. His lips on mine. It seems so long ago, but it's only been a few days.

Back before my whole world fell apart.

"How old are you, Lukas?" I ask.

"Twenty."

"Sounds like you've been putting off wandfasting, as well," I point out.

His face grows hard. I can tell he's not used to being challenged.

Why is he so touchy about this? And why isn't he already fasted?

"Who attacked you?" he asks, completely ignoring my last comment.

"A Kelt girl named Iris, and a scary-looking Urisk girl named Bleddyn." I describe everything that happened in the kitchen.

"That's easily managed," he says with a dismissive wave of his hand. "Anything else?"

I'm momentarily silenced by how blasé he is, how confident he is that this impossibly disastrous situation can be rectified.

"I was also attacked by two Icarals," I continue. "Ariel Haven and Wynter Eirllyn. My new lodging mates."

One of his eyebrows goes up at this. "They placed you with the two *Icarals*? After what happened in Valgard?"

I nod my head miserably. "They won't let me move until I'm fasted."

He lets out a short laugh, as if amused and impressed by my aunt's tenacity. "Your aunt *really* wants you wandfasted to me, doesn't she?"

"Apparently."

"You do realize that all of these problems would just disappear if we marched over to Mage Abernathy's office and agreed to be fasted? You wouldn't need to work to pay your tithe. And you'd have your choice of lodging."

The generosity of his offer catches me completely off guard, giving me serious pause. He's made it to twenty unfasted, yet he's willing to drop everything and fast to me. The incredible flattery of this fills me with a heady disbelief.

But it's still much too fast.

"I can't," I say, shaking my head. "Believe me, it's tempting, but I just can't."

He gives me the once-over and sighs. "Well, I guess it's a bit of relief. No offense, but you look truly awful. Is that manure you're covered with?"

I'm suddenly struck by the sheer outrageousness of this situation. I'm covered in barn refuse, and the most eligible man in Gardneria wants to wandfast to me.

A short laugh escapes me, and I shoot Lukas a resigned look. "Yes, it is." I let my head fall into my hands. After a moment I'm aware of him taking a seat next to me, his arm warm against mine.

"Did the Icarals hurt you?" he asks.

I look over at him. "I didn't give them the chance to. I blockaded myself in a storage closet."

Lukas spits out a laugh. He straightens and fingers the hilt of his sword. "They're easily managed, as well."

"Easily managed?" *Is he kidding?* "They're *monsters!*"

"No, they're not."

"They have *wings!* Which means they have their *powers!* They're even worse than the ones in Valgard!"

"No, they're not," he says again.

I'm starting to feel at wits' end. "How can you say that?"

"Well, for starters, Wynter Eirllyn is the daughter of Elfin royalty—"

"I don't care if she's a royal princess," I vehemently counter. "It doesn't change the fact that she wants to *kill* me."

"Wynter Eirllyn is harmless," he calmly disagrees. "She has about as many evil powers as I do." Lukas smirks. "Probably fewer."

This is just too much. "Don't you believe in your own religion?"

"Not really."

Well, that's unexpected. "Does your family know that?" I ask, amazed.

"No."

His candor surprises me. "Why are you telling me this?"

"I don't know, Elloren," he says shortly, seeming exasperated with himself. "I feel a compulsion to be honest with you. I really don't know why." He looks away and leans back against the bench, staring off into the distance, wrestling with some private thought. After a time he turns back to me, a look of resignation on his face.

I knit my brow at him. "If you were here all this time, why didn't you come find me after the wandtesting?" I'm unable to keep a hint of blame out of my tone. "If you'd been with me..."

"I've only just returned," Lukas says, seeming amused by my discomfiture. He leans in close. "*Someone* caused a minor diplomatic crisis. The Elfhollen were not amused by my initial refusal to leave you." His tone takes on a cutting edge. "Neither was my father. There was some talk of imprisonment."

"Oh," I say, feeling contrite. I notice he's in a different military tunic, the silver Level Five bands on his sleeve thinner and close together. "Your uniform. It's different." I trace my finger along one of the silver bands, immediately aware of the intimacy of the gesture. Mortified, I jerk my hand away.

When I venture a look up at him, his smile is slow and seductive, his eyes intent on mine. He raises his wrist slightly, glancing down at the edging. "I've been temporarily demoted, for the usual reason," he says, his voice like velvet.

I gulp. "What's that?"

His smile darkens. "Insubordination." He traces his finger lightly over the back of my hand. "And as further punishment," he goes on, "I'm being forced to spend two months here training Gardneria's most talentless soldier apprentices."

"Sorry," I mumble, distracted by the slow, sultry way he's playing with my hand.

Lukas lets out a short laugh, sits back and eyes me with amused speculation.

I take a deep breath. "So you think Wynter is harmless," I finally say.

"Completely. She's an artist. Spends all her time drawing, sculpting, writing poetry. Hardly ever speaks. Seems afraid of her own shadow. Ariel Haven, on the other hand..."

"The demonic one," I finish for him.

He laughs, but I fail to see the humor in it.

"She's a real nuisance," he continues. "Should have been sent back to the Valgard Sanitorium a long time ago."

"*Back?*" I cut in, horrified.

"She spent most of her childhood there."

"Oh, Ancient One..."

"She was almost expelled last year. Seems she has a penchant for setting fire to things. And to people who annoy her."

I can feel myself blanching.

"Relax, Elloren. No one's going to set you on fire."

I gawk at him, stupefied. "How can you say that? I spent most of last night cowering in a closet while Ariel etched profanities and threats into the door."

"And that was *your* choice. You let her have the upper hand. Ariel is about as weak and harmless as Wynter is. She just makes a big show of being threatening. And you completely fell for it."

"She had a *knife*!"

"Here," he says, pulling his sword out and handing it to me. "Now you have a bigger one."

I push the sword back at him. "I don't have any idea how to use it."

He places his sword back in its sheath with one graceful movement. "You probably have about as much skill with my sword as Ariel does with a knife."

"She's completely demonic!"

"Maybe so, but I doubt she'll do anything to harm any scholar this year. If she does, she'll be arrested, expelled from Verpacia and sent back to the Valgard Sanitorium. Her wings will be cut off and she'll be thrown into a cell, where she'll rot out her days. She'd be as good as dead. Ariel knows this, and it terrifies her. Don't let her fool you."

"I don't understand why the Mage Council hasn't cut her wings off and locked her away already," I grouse.

"Verpacia is bound by international treaty to surrender only *male* Icarals to Gardneria. Because of the Prophecy."

"And she's not male."

Lukas nods resignedly. "Imprisonment of female Icarals is still voluntary, and at the discretion of the Icaral's family. For now. There are some on the Mage Council who hold romantic ideas about Icaral 'rehabilitation,' but they're slowly being voted out."

"Good." I shake my head. "So why didn't Ariel's family have her committed?"

"Her father. He left her wings intact to punish his unfaithful fastmate. So Ariel's mother has to face the fact that she gave birth to a winged demon as a result of her evil."

"Charming." I let out a deep breath. "And the other Icaral? The Elf?"

"If you were to complain to the Elfin hierarchy about Wynter Eirllyn, she'd be cast out of Alfsigr lands and never allowed to return. The Elves hate the Icarals as much as the Gardnerians do. The only reason she hasn't been cast out already is that she has a brother who's fond of her.

"And there's something else. Something you can use to your advantage," Lukas confides. "Ariel is very fond of Wynter Eirllyn. She fancies herself Wynter's protector and doesn't want to leave her. So, you see, you have the upper hand."

I slump down on the bench. "I really don't feel like I have the upper hand."

"Elloren," he cautions, "you can't be weak here. You'll be eaten alive, especially with your appearance, your connections."

"But I *am* weak. I have no magic whatsoever."

A magic-free Level One. But still, there was that feeling of power during my wandtesting. Coming up from the earth.

He's thoughtful for a moment. "I was surprised by the results of your wandtesting." Lukas shrugs. "I have a good sense about these things, and I can sense magic in you. I still think it's there, perhaps dormant."

"You've only just met me," I observe, feeling defeated and not powerful in the least.

"Doesn't matter," he says with a shake of his head. "I can feel it. I can hear it in your music, and..." He hesitates for a moment before continuing, his voice gone low. "I can feel it in your kiss."

Coloring at his words and the memory of his fiery kiss, I lower my eyes. My skirts are filthy. Covered with dirt, and Ancient One knows what else. And my wrist, my head and the side of my face ache.

Now is not the time to be thinking about kissing Lukas again.

I groan and let my head fall into my hands. "So what am I supposed to do, Lukas?"

For a moment he's silent.

"Wands aren't the only tools of power, Elloren," he says, his voice level. "Find your enemies' weaknesses. And become dangerous."

CHAPTER NINE

Balance of Power

Later that afternoon I walk to the kitchen, bolstered by the fact that I'm being escorted by a Level Five Mage in full military regalia whose father is the High Commander of the Gardnerian Mage Guard.

After our talk, Lukas brought me to Aislinn's lodging, so I'm now cleaned up and wearing one of her conservative tunics over a clean, long black skirt. I'm curvier than Aislinn, and my hips and bust strain a bit at the black silk, but the clothes fit me reasonably well.

Lukas walks ahead of me through the small storage foyer leading to the main kitchen. He strides toward the door ahead and throws it open so hard that it slams against a wall, instantly getting everyone's attention. They all grow silent and freeze as we walk in, their expressions of fear more intense, more stark, than those inspired by my arrival the day before.

Only Yvan glares openly at Lukas, slowly rising from where he's just finished loading wood into the cookstove, moving with the slow caution one uses around a predator.

It's clear that they all know *exactly* who Lukas is.

There are no books or maps strewn about today. No small

children running around. The smell of hearty soup hangs thick in the air.

Lukas looks around, taking his time surveying the scene, taking in every last detail with hard, dark green eyes.

"Good afternoon," he finally says, his tone and posture showing his displeasure.

"Good afternoon, Mage Grey," Fernyllia Hawthorne responds. She looks positively stricken.

Lukas glares at her with disdain. "I'd like to speak with Fernyllia Hawthorne, Iris Morgaine and Bleddyn Arterra."

Fernyllia nervously wipes the flour and bread dough from her hands, visibly trying to collect herself before approaching. Iris and Bleddyn march over, shooting threatening glares at me as they do so. I feel myself withering under the force of their combined hatred and glance over at Lukas. He doesn't seem the least bit impressed.

"I don't really believe much in small talk," Lukas states curtly, "so let's just get to the point, shall we? Iris Morgaine. I understand your parents are still farming."

I jerk my gaze toward Lukas, surprised. *Where is he going with this?*

Iris also looks thrown by the unexpected turn of the conversation, her brow knitting tightly as she glares at Lukas with confusion. "Yes," she says warily.

"And their farm is right on the Gardnerian border?" Lukas continues.

"It is."

"Right next to the Essex military encampment, I believe?"

"Yes."

Everyone has the same puzzled expression. Everyone, that is, except for Fernyllia and Yvan, the former looking flat-out scared, and the latter more furious by the second.

"I'm sure you're aware that the location of the border there is a matter of some dispute between your government and ours," Lukas continues.

Iris is silent, her face a picture of dawning horror.

Lukas continues to stare her down. "It would be a shame if our military decided to requisition your parents' farmland. It would also be a shame if something went amiss during military training exercises, and your parents' home was fired upon...by accident, of course. These types of occurrences are, luckily, very rare, but they do happen from time to time."

Iris's mouth opens a few times as if she wants to say something, but no sound comes out. Lukas appears amused by Iris's discomfiture.

A cold unease pricks at the back of my neck.

"I will alert my father, Lachlan Grey, High Commander of the Gardnerian Military Forces, as to the whereabouts of your parents' home, to make sure such an unfortunate event does not occur."

"Thank...thank you," Iris finally manages, her voice shaky now, all defiance shattered. "Thank you, sir."

Lukas nods, pleased with her response, and turns to Bleddyn. "And you, Bleddyn Arterra. You have a mother who labors on the Fae Islands."

Bleddyn narrows her eyes at him, a blood vessel at her temple becoming more pronounced, her face and body growing rigid with tension. It's clear that she wants to lash out at us, that she's struggling to rein in her anger.

"She's been ill, hasn't she?" Lukas prods Bleddyn.

Bleddyn doesn't say anything, but the side of her mouth twitches, her eyes murderous.

"It would be bad for her if it were found that she had been distributing Resistance propaganda amongst the other laborers," Lukas says smoothly. "That could be grounds for getting her transported to the Pyrran Isles. It's difficult to survive there if a person is of a healthy constitution. Your mother might not fare well in a place such as that."

My mind spins, almost dizzy with conflict. The Pyrran Isles—a storm-lashed military prison and war camp—are where we sent our enemies at the end of the Realm War.

Bleddyn's face collapses. Lukas's mouth curls up on one side, like a cat immobilizing a mouse.

"There's no need to look so worried," he assures her. "Even if your mother were found to be dabbling in the Resistance, I'm sure that a lot could be overlooked if her daughter were to exhibit model behavior, having been so generously granted work papers by the Gardnerian government. Am I making myself clear?"

"Yes," Bleddyn croaks out, almost inaudibly.

Lukas cranes his head forward as if he hasn't heard her completely. "Yes, *what*?" he asks.

She seems to be struggling with her jaw for a moment. "Yes, sir," she finally manages.

Lukas smiles. "That's better."

I gape at Lukas, both in awe and troubled by how ruthlessly and efficiently he wields his power over them.

Lukas turns to Fernyllia. "And you, Miss Hawthorne. You have a granddaughter here, don't you?"

As if on cue, the back door swings open, and the little Urisk girl, Fern, runs in, giggling and hugging the big gray kitchen cat in her small arms. Immediately sensing the tension, her smile evaporates. She sets down the cat and half hides behind her grandmother's skirts, nervously peering out at us. Fernyllia seems momentarily devastated.

Guilt pricks at me.

But they hit you, I remind myself. *They beat you and threatened you. And Fernyllia did nothing to stop them.*

"Please, sir," Fernyllia pleads, "the child is only here because her mother's ill. I told her to stay out of the kitchens, not to disturb the laborers..."

Lukas smiles benignly. "Relax, Miss Hawthorne. The child can stay. I'm sure she's useful around the kitchen, and I'm prepared to turn a blind eye to her presence."

Fernyllia lets out a deep breath and bows her head submissively. "Thank you, sir. You're very kind—"

"No, don't make that mistake," Lukas shoots back. "I'm not the least bit kind. A child of her age, with hands as small and nimble as hers, would be a very useful laborer on the Fae Islands."

Little Fern begins to sob, looking up at her grandmother in desperation, pulling at her skirts as she lets loose a stream of panicked pleas in Uriskal.

Fernyllia doesn't take her eyes off Lukas, the way you don't take your eyes off a very dangerous animal. "Fern, be quiet," she snaps.

Fern, possibly shocked by her grandmother's harsh tone, quiets down to a soft whimper.

Lukas glances around at everyone, his expression stern and unforgiving. "I want to make myself *very* clear," he begins. "If Mage Gardner trips again, or bumps her arm on a pot, or accidentally spills boiling water on herself or so much as *scuffs her shoe*, I will see that the child is on the next ship to the Fae Islands. Is there anything about this that is in any way not clear?" He looks back down at Fernyllia, who is regarding him squarely now, but with no small measure of fear.

"No," Fernyllia replies. "No, sir. I think we all understand your meaning."

Lukas nods at her. "Good." He turns to me, his expression softening. "Elloren, I'll meet you here at the end of your shift. I'm sure you'll have a much more pleasant work experience."

"Thank you," I say, my voice stifled. I feel sick as I watch him leave, my mind in tumult.

Fern is crying softly into her grandmother's skirts, clutching them with tiny fists. "Don't let them send me back," she whimpers miserably as Fernyllia, looking stressed and distracted, attempts to calm her, stroking her head with a weathered hand.

"Shhh, now. No one's going to send you anywhere." Fernyllia turns to me, the haze of fear still on her face, showing through her attempt at fake pleasantry. "Mage Gardner, you look tired. Why don't you ice the spice cakes over there?"

I nod mutely, then go over to the sheets of brown cake, my stomach clenched into tight knots as everyone around me silently does the harder, heavier work.

For the rest of my shift, no one meets my eyes.

Except for Yvan.

Every time he brings a load of wood in to fuel the cooking fires, he shoves it into the stove, slams the iron door, then glares at me with a hatred as sharp as the kitchen knives.

I find myself withering under his hostile stare, my shame spiking when little Fern is quickly ushered out of the kitchens, countless worried glances cast my way.

I plop a pile of sticky frosting down on the sheet of cake and begin to slather it around as tears sting at my eyes.

I wish Lukas hadn't threatened everyone so mercilessly—especially the child. I wish he hadn't threatened to harm their families.

My sickening shame stiffens my movements as I work, Fern's terrified sobbing fresh in my mind.

But what's the alternative? To let them bully me? To let them kick me and slap me and threaten me with further violence? No, it's better to make idle threats, if they now fear me.

I may be devoid of magic, but I'm Carnissa Gardner's granddaughter, Vyvian Damon's niece and favored by Lukas Grey.

For the rest of the shift, I try to cling to my roiling fear and anger to bolster myself and justify Lukas's actions, but it's impossible to hold back a fierce wave of sickening guilt. And I'm careful not to meet anyone's eyes for the rest of the shift.

Especially not Yvan's.

CHAPTER TEN

Confrontation

After my shift is over, I leave without saying goodbye to anyone, and no one says goodbye to me.

The large dining hall outside the kitchen is crowded with
scholars and professors and tight groupings of military apprentices sitting at marshwood tables, a steady hum of conversation
reverberating throughout the hall, the clinking and clanking of
silverware and serving spoons creating a noisy din.

Dusk is descending, the stream of pedestrians passing by the
windows fading to dark silhouettes. One of the Urisk laborers
busily lights the wall torches and table lanterns.

I scan the vast room, worriedly searching for Lukas's face.

And that's when I see the Icarals.

They're seated at the far edge of the hall, the tables around
them deserted as if all the other scholars are actively avoiding
them.

My lodging mates—Ariel Haven and Wynter Eirllyn. I didn't
get a very good look at them last night, but I know it *has* to be
them.

Wynter is similar in appearance to every other Elfin maid
in the room. Like them, she has silver eyes and long white hair

decorated with tiny braids, pale skin, gracefully pointed ears and ivory clothing. But unlike them, her graceful clothing is modified in the back to make room for thin, black wings. She sits slumped, her wings wrapped tight around herself like a blanket.

She looks weak and sad.

Ariel, on the other hand, looks like something out of a nightmare. She's dressed in complete, screaming defiance of the Gardnerian dress code. Instead of a tunic, she wears a tight black top, laced haphazardly up and down her back. The lacing makes room for wings that are ragged and torn, making her seem like a crow that has suffered a run-in with a clawed predator. She wears pants like a boy, and large clunky boots, and her hair is chopped very short, standing out at odd angles in greasy-looking black spikes. Her eyes are darkly rimmed with black kohl, making her pale green eyes seem almost as white and soulless as those of the Icarals in Valgard. Unlike Wynter, whose wings are low and now folded discreetly behind her, Ariel seems to be making a show of flapping her wings menacingly. She crouches over, as if dodging a blow, her eyes narrowed and angry, scanning the room darkly.

There they are. My tormentors. Sitting there, eating spice cake.

It all comes flooding back—Ariel's demonic show, the scraping on the door, my terror when I thought I was about to die.

Lukas might have been too harsh with the kitchen workers, but these creatures—they deserve everything they get and more.

I forget about fear as anger rips through me.

My fists balling, I stalk down a side aisle, straight over to their table, and snatch the cake out from under them. They both look up at me with wide-eyed surprise.

"The denizens of hell do *not* get to eat cake!" I snarl, heart racing.

Ariel shoots up to a standing position, her hands supported by rigid, spindly arms crisscrossed with what look like fresh and healing knife marks. She screws up her face into a frightening grimace and lunges at the cake.

I step quickly aside and she loses her footing, crashing down onto the table, plates and food scattering everywhere. Wynter's hands fly up to ward off the stray food and drink as sounds of surprise and shock go up around us.

"What's going on here?" an authoritative male voice says from behind me.

I whirl around and come face-to-face with a green-robed professor—a slightly disheveled Keltic man with messy, short-ish brown hair and spectacles.

The professor's eyes go momentarily wide with shock.

My resemblance to my grandmother. That's what's stunned him so. I can see it in his eyes.

The broad room has gone nearly silent, except for some as-tonished whispering, almost everyone staring at us.

Ariel, now covered in food and drink, pushes herself off the table and points a long finger at me. "She took our food!"

The professor's shock morphs to extreme dismay then barely concealed outrage.

He glares at me. "Give that scholar back her food!"

That "scholar"? Is he kidding?

"No," I refuse, stepping away from him, guarding both slices of cake protectively. "She does *not* get to terrorize me *all night long* and then get to eat the cake that *I* iced!"

The professor turns to Ariel, who's flapping her moth-eaten wings agitatedly. He eyes her suspiciously. "What's this about, Ariel?"

Ariel? He's on a first-name basis with her?

"It's not my fault!" Ariel cries. "She shows up in our room last night, says she can't lodge with filthy Icarals and throws herself into a closet! I tried to get her to come out, but she kept yelling about how she's a Gardnerian and the granddaughter of Carnissa

Gardner and can't mix with Icarals or Elves or Kelts! That we'll pollute her pure blood! She kept going on and on about how the Gardnerians are the superior race, and how everyone else is an inferior Evil One, and how she's the next Black Witch!"

I'm momentarily paralyzed with shock and outrage.

The Keltic teacher turns to me with an odd, pained look before his expression goes hard.

"That's...that's a *lie!*" I sputter as Ariel's face behind him morphs from that of the traumatized victim to a dark, calculating grimace. "She *stalked* me! *Terrorized* me! I had to barricade myself in a *closet!* And then she spent most of the night scratching at the door with a *knife!*"

The professor looks back at Ariel appraisingly then back at me, his eyes cold, his lips set in a tight line.

I've lost. Of course he's on her side. He's a Kelt.

"Mage Elloren Gardner," he orders, his face tensing as if my name pains him. I'm not surprised that he knows my name. Everyone knows my name. "Give those scholars back their food."

The sheer injustice of this roils through me. *"Fine!"* I snarl, throwing the cake down on the table so hard it bounces off the plates, adding to the general mess.

"Thank you, Professor Kristian," Ariel says with wide, puppy-dog eyes.

I want to strike her.

"Elloren," I hear a familiar voice say from behind me, "aren't you done with your shift?"

I turn to see Lukas approaching me.

His eyes flicker over to Professor Kristian and the Icarals disdainfully then back to me again, his sword and wand at his side. I straighten and set my jaw forward defiantly.

Good. I have backup. Real backup. A Level Five Mage. Not some useless Kelt teacher who's too ready to believe lying Icarals instead of me.

I turn to Professor Kristian, who's glaring icily at Lukas, and feel a bitter surge of triumph.

Lukas holds out his arm to me. I take it and walk out without another glance back.

I walk halfway back to the North Tower with Lukas, the two of us pausing near a small grove of trees in the center of a small courtyard.

I lean back against the tree trunk behind me, my hands finding the cool bark. I close my eyes, breathe in deep and let the wood of the tree relax me.

Mmm. Rock Maple.

The wilds rattle me, but lone stands of trees, cut off from the forest, soothe me, rounding out my sharp edges like calming waters.

When I open my eyes, Lukas is watching me closely, his head cocked with curiosity, his hand also on the tree, his fingers languidly rubbing at the bark.

"Can you feel it?" he asks. "The roots?"

I swallow. These odd leanings of mine—I'm not supposed to speak of them. But clearly, Lukas feels them, too. "They run deep," I hesitantly answer.

He smiles at me. "Mmm."

"Thank you," I tell him, rubbing at the bark, the tree strong at my back. "You've...you've been a good friend to me."

He looks me over boldly, then smirks. "Yes, well. I have ulterior motives."

I roll my eyes at this and sigh. He lets out a short laugh, and I can't help but smile.

But a lingering unease tugs at me.

"Lukas?" I hesitantly ask.

Lukas leans into the tree's strong trunk, his sword's hilt reflecting some nearby lamplight.

"Hmm?" He looks down at me, his face unreadable, a faint shimmer to his skin in this dark.

"Was it...was it necessary to threaten the child?"

He narrows his eyes. "I just did them a favor, Elloren." He gives a quick look around to check if we're mostly alone, then, seeing that we are, he turns back to me, his voice going low. "The child's here illegally. They need to do a better job of hiding her."

"Oh," I say, chastened. "I hadn't thought of that."

But what about when he threatened Iris's family and Bleddyn's sick mother? He certainly wasn't doing anyone any favors there.

"Elloren, you have to choose what side you're on," he says, shaking his head. "It's always been that way. It will always be that way. Dominate, or be dominated. Those are your choices. You saw what happened to you when everyone thought you wouldn't fight back, that you couldn't fight back. How much compassion did they show you?"

He's right. Of course he's right. But I just can't shake the image of little Fern crying.

"She was just so scared of being sent back to the Fae Islands."

They've been part of Gardneria since the Realm Wars. We let the Urisk settle there and provide them with homes and work to do. So why was little Fern so scared?

Shame tugs at me over the part I played in her terror. Yvan's sharp, accusatory glare flashes to mind.

Unsettled, I wrap my arms around myself for warmth, the chill of encroaching autumn creeping into the air.

Lukas eyes me thoughtfully. "The Fae Islands are a work colony, Elloren. And the Urisk are expected to work. Quite hard. But you need to keep things in perspective. The Urisk women are better off now than they were when their own men were in charge, or when the Sidhe Fae ruled them, for that matter."

"Still, it seems as if they must be treated...harshly."

Lukas looks slightly irritated by my observation. "And how did the Urisk or the Fae or the Kelts treat *us* when *they* were the major power in the region?"

I already know the answer to that. Worse. They treated us much worse.

The Fae subdued the Urisk, and later, the Kelts subdued the Fae in what seemed like an endless cycle of warfare and violence. And throughout it all, my people were oppressed and abused by all three.

Until recent history.

"Maybe you or I wouldn't want to work in the Fae Islands' labor camps," Lukas goes on, "but believe me, it's a step up for them."

"I guess I don't know enough to make sense of it all," I admit.

I have so much to learn about these different cultures. About how the world works.

"You'll learn," he assures me. "In time." He glances around at the gathering darkness. "It's getting late." He turns back to me. "And *you* need to confront some Icarals."

My stomach clenches at the thought of yet more confrontation. "Lukas?" I ask tentatively, looking up at him.

He raises a brow questioningly.

"Are you still relieved that you don't need to wandfast to me?"

An easy grin spreads over his handsome face. He gives me a once-over. "No, I am not relieved," he says smoothly. "Now that you're no longer covered in dirt, I think it's quite a pity we're not wandfasted."

I swallow, my face warming at his close proximity. My eyes dart down his chest to the sleek wand fastened at his waist. I remember Fallon's ball of ice. "Show me something," I say, gesturing toward his wand. "Show me some of your magic."

His smile is slow as his eyes flick over me. He pulls the wand into his hand in one smooth motion. Holding it loosely, he steps back and points it at me, murmurs words in the Ancient

Tongue, then takes a deep breath and straightens up, as if pulling power up from his feet.

Translucent black lines curl out from the wand tip, fluidly making their way toward me.

I gasp as they flow and curl around my body. At first I feel a gentle pressure from them, tickling at my skin, teasing.

And then they tighten.

It's impossible to resist as the swirling lines pull at my waist, my arms, my legs. I find it both exciting and disconcerting to be so much in his power. My feet skid over the grassy ground as he pulls me closer, until I'm right before him. Once there, he flicks his wrist, and the black lines dissolve as he languidly wraps his arms around me.

"That's amazing," I breathe, in awe of him.

Lukas smiles and brings his lips to mine.

It's late when Lukas finally walks me the rest of the way to the North Tower.

I watch him as he leaves, striding down the sloping field toward the University city's twinkling lights, his cloak flapping behind him like dark wings.

I reach up to absentmindedly touch my mouth, my lips still warm and swollen from his fevered kisses. But my feelings of bliss begin to evaporate like smoke as I watch him disappear from view.

Darkly resolved, I take a deep breath, turn and make my way into the tower.

When I enter my room, it's dark and they're there, waiting for me. I can see Ariel's outline, crouched below the window as she was the night before. Wynter huddles on her bed, appearing as if she wants to be anywhere but where she is, silver eyes peeking out over her wings, wide with fear.

I hesitate, Wynter's terror giving me momentary pause.

Stop it, I tell myself. *These aren't Urisk children. These are Icaral demons.*

I ignore Ariel and walk over to the lamp on one of the desks, lighting it quickly with Bornial flint, the Elvish stones sparking to a small flame when tapped together.

An eerie, reddish glow soon covers the room, making Ariel look even more demonic. She creeps toward me slowly, perhaps expecting the same reaction she got out of me last night. I turn to face her, my hand flat on the desk, eyeing her calmly, trying to control the anger welling up within me and the trembling of my hands.

"It would be a shame if the Gardnerian girl caught fire while she was sleeping," Ariel whispers as she straightens up, unfurling her tattered black wings. She takes another threatening step toward me. "Burning is so painful. I wonder how long she would scream. How long it would take a Gardnerian to die..."

Something snaps within me as Ariel unexpectedly lunges forward. I push her away from me so hard, she falls onto the floor.

It's a shock to see her there. I've never pushed anyone over in my entire life, and my own violence frightens me for a moment.

Ariel hisses up at me, her eyes in tight, evil slits.

"Leave me *alone*!" I warn, bumping against a bedpost as I back away. "If you so much as come near me, I will go straight to the Mage Council. They will throw you back in the sanitorium, where you *belong*, and cut off those foul wings of yours. You'll spend the rest of your life rotting in an empty cell, going even crazier than you already are!"

"Then *do it*, Gardnerian!" she snarls with as much venom as she can muster. "It would be well worth hearing you scream!"

"I'll also go to the Elves!" I cry, pointing at Wynter. "I'll tell them that Wynter Eirllyn attacked me, as well!"

"Wynter won't be the one to attack you!" Ariel screams as Wynter lets out a small cry and cowers on her bed. "*I* will!"

"They won't know that!" I threaten. "Just like that Kelt professor believed *you*, they'll believe *every word I say.*"

As my words register, her attempt to look frightening collapses in on itself, morphing into one of sheer horror, her wings falling to hang limply behind her.

She's afraid of me. Just as Lukas said she'd be.

"I need a bed," I demand, nervously seizing on my advantage, pointing to the bed behind me. Ariel scuttles over to it and hurriedly retrieves her things, taking out her aggression on her belongings, throwing them viciously on the bed next to Wynter's, muttering to herself darkly the whole time.

She turns to glower at me. "You can keep me from hurting you, Gardnerian," she vows, "but you can't keep me from *hating* you!"

"The feeling's mutual!" I snipe back.

I strip the bed of Ariel's sheets, disgusted by the idea of sleeping on anything that's touched an Icaral's skin, and toss them forcefully in her direction. Then I retrieve my things from the downstairs closet and set them by my new bed. I fish out my pen set and some rolled-up parchment, then plop down at my desk and set my writing implements out before me.

I don't feel powerful, even though Lukas says I am. I feel small and scared and intimidated. And I can feel the Icaral demons watching me.

My eyes stinging hot with tears, I begin to write.

Dear Aunt Vyvian,

Please let me move to different lodging. I know you're trying to do what you feel is best for me, and I'm thankful for your good intentions, but the Icarals are frightening and dangerous—more than I think you could have ever imagined.

I agree to be courted by Lukas Grey with the intention of fasting to him. I never closed the door to that possibility. I know that

*is not exactly what you want, but please, Aunt Vyvian, please
don't leave me here with these horrible creatures. I beg of you.*

Your Faithful Niece,
Elloren

I dry the ink, fold the parchment and seal it with wax, then
snuff out the lamp.

That night, after I cry myself to sleep, I dream that I'm far
away from the North Tower. In my dream, I'm strong and fierce
and feared by everyone around me.

My name is Mage Carnissa Gardner.

I'm locking a large metal cage in the bottom of a dark dungeon, a ring of black keys heavy in my hand. The only light
comes from some dim Elfin lumenstone hanging on the walls
at intervals, casting a swampy, greenish glow over the scene.

In the cage are Icarals: Ariel, Wynter and the Icarals from Valgard. Iris from the kitchen is there, too, and Bleddyn Arterra.

I hear a sharp snap as the internal metal hooks engage each
other. I'm just about to turn away, relieved they're all safely
locked up in prison, when I hear a child cry. I squint at the far
corner of the cage. Little Fern and the Valgard Selkie are cowering on the floor. The Selkie looks up at me, her ocean eyes
full of sadness.

I motion for her to approach and put the key back in the lock.
"You two can come out," I tell them, fiddling with the key,
having a hard time with it.

The Selkie doesn't move. She remains there on the ground,
her arms around the sobbing child. "It's too late," she says
mournfully, "you've already locked it."

I break out in a cold sweat, the other creatures in the cage
having disappeared, only the Selkie and Urisk child remaining.
"It can't be too late," I insist, straining with the key.

But the lock won't give.

It's a mistake. It's all a mistake. I hear a noise behind me and turn.

A Watcher, perched on an outcropping of stone, white wings glowing in the green light. Its avian eyes full of sorrow.

I turn back to the Selkie and the child. "It's not too late," I insist. "I'm going to get you out."

For the rest of the night I struggle with the lock, but try as I may, it refuses to give.

CHAPTER ELEVEN

The Gardnerian

I'm awakened the next morning by a knock at the door.

I jolt awake, fear washing over me. Heart thudding, I look around, wildly disoriented. I recoil at the sight of Ariel splayed out on her bed and Wynter curled up in a tight ball, completely buried under her stained bed covering.

"Elloren?"

When I hear Rafe's voice through the door, it's as if the entire world has suddenly righted itself. I spring out of bed, burst out into the hallway and throw my arms around my brother.

Rafe chuckles as he staggers backward. He quickly finds his footing and hugs me tightly. "You sure know how to shake things up, don't you, Ren?" he observes, grinning widely.

I laugh and cry at the same time, overjoyed to be with family again. Suddenly, nothing seems as bad.

His grin fades as he takes in my bruised face. He reaches up to lightly touch my cheek. "Have you seen a healer for this?"

I shake my head against his hand. "I'm okay. It's better than it was." I search past him, down the narrow hall. "Where's Trystan? And Gareth?"

"Downstairs," he says. "Aislinn and Echo are with them."

"They've put me in with Icarals," I tell him in a low, cautioning voice. I gesture toward the door behind me.

He nods grimly. "Aislinn and Echo told us everything."

I wipe at my tears and smile shakily. "I'm so glad you're here."

"Go get dressed," Rafe urges with an affectionate squeeze to my arm. "You look pale. We should get some food into you."

The bleak, gray room is startling in the daylight. It's filthy and smells foul, like the Icarals in Valgard—sour and rotting. And the Icaral demons are awake.

Ariel is now crouching in a corner, still as a gargoyle, watching me carefully through slitted eyes. Wynter's perched on the sill of the large, circular window, her thin, black wings tight around her, only the top of her head poking through like some oversize turtle.

They look rattled and beaten down.

They've been living barely a step above animals. The fireplace is a mess, with ashes spilling out onto the floor. Torn black clothing, books and other ratty belongings are strewn about the room. White bird droppings litter the floor, prompting me to glance upward, squinting at the ceiling and the supporting rafters for signs of avian life, but I can't make anything out.

The bed I've claimed is pressed against the left wall, near the entrance to a small washroom and privy. Ariel's and Wynter's beds lay haphazardly against the opposite wall, bracketing the fireplace. The furniture is a motley mix of old, beat-up pieces. There's no rug on the floor, and no tapestries on the walls to stave off autumn's encroaching cold. Throughout the night, I had to wrap myself in both my woolen winter cloak and my mother's quilt to stay even marginally warm.

It's almost like living in a cave in the woods.

I'm guessing that this old archery post was a convenient place to house the Icarals away from the other scholars, especially the

Gardnerians, who view meeting the gaze of a winged one to be spiritually polluting.

Apparently, my aunt doesn't care how spiritually polluted *I* become, as long as I buckle and wandfast to Lukas Grey.

I search through my travel trunk and pull out some of the fine Gardnerian attire my aunt purchased for me—a shiny onyx silk tunic and long skirt. The resentment I feel toward my aunt does not overshadow the fact that, in one day, I've been forced to learn where my loyalties must lie. I need to be strong and look strong. I've seen firsthand what the Urisk, the Icarals and the Kelts are really like. They consider me an enemy, and I need allies against them—*Gardnerian* allies. And I need to look powerfully Gardnerian.

Lukas's words hang in my mind. *Dominate, or be dominated.*

I wash up quickly, dress in the small washroom, comb my hair and make up my face. I glance at my reflection in the scratched mirror before me. Although my face is bruised and pale, with dark half-moons anchoring my eyes, I'm regal in the elegant clothing.

Just like my grandmother.

I pause in the bedroom, gathering up my books and papers and stuffing them into my book bag. I eye the two Icarals warily as I do so, feeling the weight of Ariel's hostile stare pressing against me. Her gaze shifts to my violin case, and I narrow my eyes at her in suspicion.

I made that violin with my own two hands—there's no way I'm leaving it here with Ariel. I grab the handle of the case, deciding to store it somewhere else for now, and make a hasty exit from the repulsive living quarters and my even more repulsive roommates.

Waiting for me and Rafe outside the door are Trystan, Gareth, Echo and Aislinn. I've gone from being completely on my own to having a supportive crowd around me.

It's a vast improvement.

Cool dew coats the fields, reflecting the morning sun like millions of tiny mirrors, giving the long grass a silvery sheen. The silver in Gareth's hair glints along with the dew as he leans into Trystan for support, his right leg splinted and bandaged.

I rush to Trystan, who's decked out in his gray military tunic, five silver stripes on his sleeve. Trystan gives me a one-armed hug. "Are you okay, Ren?" he asks, quietly searching my eyes.

I nod bravely, my hair lashing about in the chilly wind that's kicking up. I reach over to embrace Gareth, and he pulls me into a warm hug and kisses the top of my head.

"We were so worried about you," he says into my hair.

I laugh against the scratchy wool of his cloak. "I was worried about *you*. How's your leg?"

He smiles, then winces as a strong gust of wind hits us, almost knocking him off-kilter. Trystan redoubles his efforts to brace him. "I won't be dancing a jig anytime soon," Gareth wryly says, "but the healer said I'll be fit for my deportment in a few weeks."

"We would have come up," Echo informs me gravely, her voice raised to compete with the wind, "but we wanted to avoid the Icarals." She glances up at the tower worriedly. "You should go to evening service with Aislinn and me, Elloren. The priest can exorcise their evil."

I shake my head in dismay. "I'm living with them, Echo. I'm going to absorb their evil every single day. I'll need an army of priests at that rate."

I remember the priests exorcising me in Valgard. Their droning chants and pungent incense. How frightened I was.

And Vogel.

I squint up at the North Tower looming over us, bleached almost white by the bright sun. The wind changes direction and a stiff breeze slaps against the unyielding stone as we depart.

★ ★ ★

The dining hall is densely crowded. Urisk laborers dole out a variety of hot porridges, breads and cheese, the food arranged on long wooden tables. The air is thick with the warm smells of strong tea, hot cider, roasted chestnuts and nutty grains.

I throw my cloak over a bench and set down my bag and violin, the heat a relief after being chilled all night, then further chilled by the wind. I warm my hands at one of the many stoves dotting the room, their pipes snaking along the low ceiling rafters. The radiating warmth uncoils my knotted muscles and gradually sinks into my bones.

Most of the hall is heavily segregated, with small groups of Gardnerians, Verpacians, Elfhollen, Elves and Kelts scattered about, some dressed in the military garb of their respective countries. I catch a glimpse of Fernyllia setting out baskets of rolls, and the sight of her causes a tremor of distress to run through me.

Trystan helps Gareth into a seat and props his splinted leg up on the bench as Rafe goes to get food for all of us. I take a seat next to Aislinn, the stove to my back, and am surprised when Echo remains standing.

"Aren't you going to eat with us?" I ask.

She peers over at Gareth uncomfortably, her hands clutching a leather-bound text. "I...can't. I have to go." She glances across the room, toward a group of young Gardnerian women dressed as primly as she is. "I'm glad you found your family, Elloren." Her faint smile evaporates as she casts an unfriendly look at Gareth before leaving.

My heart sinks. I know what Echo's recoiling from.

Gareth's silver-tipped hair.

Echo joins the gaggle of young women, all of them immediately leaning in to whisper to each other and casting furtive, disapproving glances toward Gareth, who seems blessedly distracted by his splinted leg.

Trystan shoots me a jaded, knowing look.

I inwardly rail against Echo's prejudice. Gareth is Gardnerian. So what if his hair has an odd silver glint to it? He's one of us.

"Your friend is here," Aislinn whispers, distracting me from my thoughts. There's warning in her tone.

I follow her gaze and see Fallon entering the rustic hall, flanked by her brothers and four armed Gardnerian soldiers.

Wooden chair legs scrape in unison against the stone floor as every Gardnerian military apprentice in the dining hall, save Trystan, rises to pay her homage, their fists going over their hearts in salute.

I watch her closely through slitted eyes.

Go ahead, Black Witch, I glower. *Try something with my brothers here. Trystan's a Level Five Mage. Just like you.*

Fallon and Sylus Bane have on their slate-gray military apprentice uniforms, in contrast to Damion's full-fledged soldier black.

"Her older brother," I ask Aislinn, "what's he like?"

Aislinn shoots me a look of deep caution. "Damion? He makes Fallon seem like a pussycat." Aislinn regards them warily as she bites at the side of her lip. "He likes...hurting people."

I watch as Damion grabs the arm of a passing Urisk serving girl and jerks her backward. She lets out a startled cry of surprise and nearly drops the large basket of muffins she's carrying. Damion smiles unkindly and leers at her as Fallon and Sylus pick out some muffins, the two of them chatting and ignoring the girl completely. Damion grabs a muffin, releases the girl's arm and pushes her off with a manic smile.

I turn back toward Aislinn with alarm.

"Maybe you should fast to the ship captain's son, Elloren," she whispers, glancing over at Gareth. "Seems the safest course of action. Pursue Lukas Grey, and you set yourself up against the Bane clan. Wait too long to fast, and you could find yourself fasted to someone like Damion."

I'm about to protest when Trystan distracts me.

"His splint's come undone," Trystan remarks from where he kneels by Gareth's leg, fiddling with the bandages.

I look over at Gareth, who seems worse by the minute. I'm about to suggest that we bring him to see the University physician when I notice Wynter shyly making her way into the hall, her black wings pulled in tight around her. It's a shock to see her there in the light of day.

"That's her," I breathe to everyone. "That's one of the Icarals."

Aislinn, Trystan and Gareth all follow my gaze.

Wynter shuffles toward the serving tables, head bent, eyes focused on the floor a few feet in front of her. Groupings of Elves cast disdainful looks in her direction and hide their whispers behind graceful hands. The Gardnerians give her a wide berth, avert their eyes and touch fists to heads then hearts to ward off her evil.

The Icaral-Elf takes a bowl and timidly approaches one of the Urisk kitchen workers. The elderly woman sneers, then slops some bright green porridge into her bowl.

I've seen them preparing this in the kitchen—ground Alfsigr acorn meal. Staple grain of the Elves. There are so many odd foods in the kitchens with foreign smells and exotic spices, each culture partial to certain dishes.

Wynter turns, bowl in hand, searching for a place to sit. Spotting an empty table at the far corner of the room, she starts for it.

Fallon's, Sylus's and Damion's eyes narrow in on Wynter.

Fallon whispers something to Sylus. They both laugh as they munch on their muffins, a cruel glint in their eyes. Fallon reaches over and inconspicuously slides her wand into her hand, flicking it slightly in Wynter's direction.

Wynter trips forward, her porridge spilling all over the floor before she lands, stomach down, on top of it.

I instinctively move to get up, aghast at Fallon's behavior, the memory of how she tripped me stark in my mind. Falling in front of all those people—it was frightening and humiliating.

But…that horrifying night, when Ariel attacked me… Wynter made no move to help…

Rafe, across the room, shows no such hesitation. He strides over to help Wynter as everyone else around her steps away. He kneels down and gently takes hold of her arm to help her up. The moment he touches her, her head jerks up and her eyes fly wide-open.

"Get your hands off my sister, Gardnerian!"

The dining hall grows quiet as an Elfin male pushes through the surrounding scholars and quickly makes his way toward them. He has backup—a younger, willowy Elfin lad, the two of them armed with bows and quivers slung over their shoulders, Elfin blades strapped to their belts.

Two Elfin archers—some of the most dangerous warriors on all of Erthia.

Worry spears through me. Rafe's competent, to be sure, and skilled with a variety of weapons. But he's no match for Elves.

Rafe immediately releases Wynter's arm. She's risen to her knees, green porridge all over her ivory garments. She stares at Rafe, wide-eyed.

"Stay away from my sister!" the older Elf snarls, the words heavily accented as he takes a threatening step toward Rafe and reaches for his knife. "Stay away from our women!"

Rafe holds his hands palms out to the Elf. "Relax, friend, I was only…"

"I am *not* your friend!" the Elf hisses through gritted teeth.

Rafe carefully steps back and bows. "I was only trying to help her. With respect."

"Your kind don't know the *meaning* of respect!"

Rafe takes a deep breath as he warily regards the Elf. He turns back toward Wynter, who's still kneeling on the floor. "Are you okay?" Rafe asks, careful not to touch her this time.

Wynter looks up at him and nods slowly.

Wynter's brother pushes past Rafe and helps Wynter to her feet before turning to glare at my brother. "Don't ever speak to her again. Do you understand?"

"You've made yourself quite clear," Rafe replies calmly.

The Elf shoots Rafe one last, withering glance before leading Wynter out of the dining hall, the two of them trailed by the other Elfin archer.

Fallon is looking at Wynter, a pleased expression on her face, her brothers talking with each other, already having lost interest.

And then she turns her head and looks straight at me.

Her smile is slow and malicious, and it sends a chill down my spine. She leans to say something to her brothers, and they both glance over at me with the same dark smiles. I inwardly recoil as Fallon lightly pats her wand, then laughs and leaves the dining hall with her brothers.

I slump down in relief.

A few moments later Rafe returns to our table. He's carrying a stack of small bowls and a large, steaming bowl of oatmeal coated with a generous helping of roasted chestnuts, honey and sweet butter.

"Stop attacking the Elfin maidens," Trystan wryly advises Rafe as he fusses with Gareth's splint.

Rafe shoots Trystan a look of mock scorn as he sets out the stack of wooden bowls for us and spoons oatmeal into them.

"You're going to get yourself shot," Trystan warns. "With one of those long arrows of theirs."

"I guess that's what you get when you try to help Icarals," I say stiffly as Aislinn accepts a bowl of oatmeal from Rafe.

"The girl's brother is rude," Rafe says as he hands me a full bowl, "but his hostility is not completely unjustified."

"How can you say that?" I snipe. "He should have thanked you. Ancient One knows, she doesn't deserve your help."

Rafe's brow tightens, and he pauses in his serving. "I thought Ariel was the one who attacked you."

"She was, but Wynter made no move to help me, all night long, knowing I was being terrorized." I feel a fresh prick of angry tears.

Aislinn puts a comforting hand on my arm.

"Even so," Rafe says as he pours himself hot cider from a ceramic pitcher, "she's an outcast among Elves and Gardnerians, and Kelts as well, to some extent. That puts her in a dangerous situation. Her brother's just trying to protect her." He sits down and stirs his oatmeal. "I shouldn't have touched her. I forgot that their etiquette is different."

"It's best to stay away from non-Gardnerians," I comment bitterly.

Rafe and Trystan shoot me looks of alarmed censure.

I color. "I don't mean Gareth. Gareth, you know I don't mean *you*. You're *Gardnerian*."

Gareth winces as Trystan tightens the bandage. "It's okay, Ren. I know you're not talking about me."

I look to Trystan for reassurance. My quiet younger brother is always long on listening and slow to judge. Trystan gives me a small, encouraging smile, but Rafe is still blinking at me with concern.

"They *hate* me," I defend myself to him, feeling lost. "They all hate me just because I look like our grandmother."

Rafe takes a deep breath and reaches across the table to put his hand on mine. "I'm sorry about what happened to you. I wish we'd been here."

"I know," I mumble.

Rafe squeezes my hand in solidarity and smiles resignedly. Quiet for a moment, he glances down at the table. When he looks back up at me, his expression has grown strained. "Ren, Uncle Edwin..." His voice trails off.

"I heard," I say sadly. "The Lodging Mistress told me he was ill. Do you have any news? Is he getting better?"

"Aunt Vyvian has him under a physician's care." Rafe is quiet for a moment. "Ren, he's lost use of the left side of his body."

I can feel myself going pale as the weight of this new reality sinks in.

"Will he get it back?" I force out.

"Maybe. A little."

I swallow, my throat gone dry. "Enough to make violins?"

Rafe pauses before answering. "No."

"Oh, no. Oh, Ancient One, no..." I hang my head as the tears come.

Aislinn hastily fishes a handkerchief out of her pockets and I absentmindedly take it. A thousand memories swirl around me. Uncle Edwin teaching a small me to make braided holiday bread with his nimble fingers. Uncle Edwin guiding my tiny hands on my violin. The sweet sound of Uncle Edwin playing by the fire on cold winter nights. A jagged fear rides in close on the heels of these images from my happy childhood.

Uncle Edwin will lose his business. We've never been well-to-do, but now we'll be poor. And beholden to Aunt Vyvian.

Perhaps I've no choice. Perhaps I'll *have* to fast to wealthy Lukas Grey.

"In two years Trystan will be able to earn a wage as a Weapons Mage, and you'll be apprenticed to a physician," Rafe says, as if reading my mind. "You'll make a good wage, as well. And you've work to pay off your tithe."

"Rafe," I say, my voice low. "Lukas Grey...he wants to fast to me."

Rafe's face darkens. "You'd be a fool to fast to Lukas Grey. *Especially* for money."

"I've already told him no." *For now.* I feel a twinge of guilt at not being completely honest with my brother, but it quickly curdles to a defensive frustration with his unasked-for opinions.

Relief washes over his expression. "Good." He pats my arm. "Wait to fast. It's what Uncle Edwin wants. Unless…" Rafe casts a sidelong glance toward Gareth, who's distracted by Trystan's efforts to retie the splint bindings.

I glance over at Gareth, as well.

A mariner's fastmate. Beholden to his pleasant, seafaring family instead of Aunt Vyvian. Gareth once suggested that we fast as friends.

But Gareth and I don't love each other that way.

I do want to fast someday. But not to someone I'll only ever see as a friend. I want to fast to someone I feel strongly about. In every way.

I turn back to Rafe, and I know that he can see my true feelings in my expression.

"Wait to fast," Rafe tells me, squeezing my arm. "Wait until you're sure."

"I'm going to help him to the physician," Trystan says to Rafe, getting up. "I'm making a mess of this splint."

I move to get up, but Rafe gestures for me to stay. "No, Ren. Stay. Eat. We'll tend to Gareth." He smiles at me. "Maybe he'll actually listen to the physician's instructions this time."

"What are *you* going to do?" I ask Rafe, worriedly. "Where will you apprentice?"

"Well," he said, straightening, "I'll finish off the year, and then I'll apprentice myself to the military. I know it's not what Uncle Edwin wants, but it's the only way. We'll go see him in a few weeks. Trystan and I," Rafe tells me reassuringly.

I feel a stab of hurt. "Me, too," I insist.

"No, Ren. You need to stay here, where you'll be safe."

Tears sting at my eyes. The Icaral. I have to stay because of the Valgard Icaral. The one that's stalking me. "All right," I relent miserably.

As I watch Trystan and Rafe leave, Gareth supported between them, anger eats into my sadness.

Icarals.

It's all their fault. If it wasn't for them, I could visit my uncle, and I wouldn't be living in nightmarish lodging.

Aislinn puts her arm around me. "It'll be okay, Elloren. You'll see."

I barely hear her as hatred flares inside me, searing any speck of compassion I might have felt for Wynter Eirllyn and rendering it to ash.

CHAPTER TWELVE

Metallurgie & Mathematics

I unfold my University map and stare at the roughly inked parchment, the layout of Verpax resembling an intricate wheel, the White Hall its center. Mammoth spokes radiate out from the White Hall, lecture halls and laboratories dotting the length of each of them, the spokes alternating above and below ground to make way for Verpax's cobbled street.

Not too difficult to navigate, thank the Ancient One.

Knots of scholars of every race and green-robed professors crowd the White Hall's vast foyer, their conversation and footsteps echoing hollowly off the domed ceiling, morning light streaming down in thick rays from the ring of arching windows necklacing the dome.

I follow the Scientifica spoke, keeping my map in hand as my anchor, quickly locating the correct side hallway marked with Metallurgie Hall engraved on a golden plate.

I've got all my subjects today, back to back, each class abbreviated and jammed together into one orientation day—Metallurgie lecture, then Mathematics, History and Botanicals, Chemistrie, Apothecarium and finally, kitchen labor—no break, no lunch, save the scones and cheese I set aside from breakfast, wrapped in a cloth napkin and tucked into my tunic pocket.

I'm a jangling mass of nerves, my cumbersome black skirts swishing around my ankles.

Three reed-straight Elves in front of me start their descent down a spiraling staircase, and I keep close to their heels, tunneling down through one of the thick underground lines of Spine stone that run beneath Verpacia. I remember poring over geological maps with Trystan when he was home for the summer, marveling at the intricate web of thick Spine stone running under the University, a network of hallways and lecture halls cut right into it.

I gasp as I enter the Metallurgie lecture hall, intricately carved stone arches gracing the entrance, a line of spiraling columns on both sides of the hall.

But the ceiling.

It's curved and made of thick, metallic-violet crystals, as if I've stepped into an enormous geode, the crystals glittering spectacularly with golden stars of reflected lamplight.

My heart lifts.

It's like magic.

To my left, glass-fronted cabinets are cut right into the walls, lined with a rainbow of crystals, stones and metal chunks, all neatly organized. To my right are long tables covered with laboratory equipment, every shape of glass vial and retort, as well as three fully outfitted smith stoves, their chimneys rising straight through the crystal ceiling.

The chalky smell of minerals, as well as the acrid tang of Bornial flint, hang in the air, but it's freshened by the cool, clean scent of Spine stone, and I breathe it all in without reserve.

I've been placed in an odd section of this class to make room for my kitchen labor. I scan the hall and realize I'm the only female here.

Half the hall is filled with Elves, already seated in neat, attentive rows. To the left are a smattering of Kelts, Elfhollen and a much larger grouping of Gardnerian military apprentices. Some of the gray-clad apprentices are seated. A knot of them are standing and notice me right away, shooting me cool, wary looks.

Fallon's friends, I realize, my heart sinking, recognizing them from Aunt Vyvian's dance. Still, I'm begrudgingly impressed by how quickly Fallon's soured things for me here.

I sit down near one of the Gardnerians, a relaxed youth sitting at a casual angle with his arm thrown across the back edge of his chair. He watches me with friendly amusement as I pull out my writing implements, parchment folder and text.

"Hullo, Mage Elloren Gardner." He greets me heartily. The three standing apprentices shoot him a look of annoyance. He grins back at them.

He's attractive, with dancing dark green eyes and a wide, rakish smile. I glance down and take in the fasting lines that mark his hands—that seem to mark most young Gardnerians' hands, with few exceptions.

Aunt Vyvian's right, I think with resignation. *All the good ones are being quickly snatched up.*

Inwardly sighing, I extend my hand to him. "Well met..."

He holds out his own hand and gives mine a cordial shake. "Curran. Mage Curran Dell." He has four silver lines decorating each of his sleeves.

I slump down, my eyes darting toward the unfriendly apprentices. "I suppose Fallon's told you all about me."

He laughs. "Oh, yes. She has. Apparently you're the worst person to ever walk Erthia."

I slump down farther. "Oh, that's just great."

He eyes me with exaggerated displeasure. "*And* you're betraying your grandmother's legacy by having no power."

"My aunt's already given me an earful about that," I comment bitterly.

He laughs again, his gaze full of mischief. "*I* suspect you simply...how shall I put this...*interfered* with Fallon's all-consuming quest for Lukas Grey." He gives me a significant look. "That's like getting between a lion and its prey, that is." He smiles again then grows more serious and looks closely at me. "Seriously, though, you should consider staying away from Lukas. Crossing Fallon Bane..." He takes a deep breath and shakes his head. "That's seriously not good for your health."

An icy chill pricks at the back of my neck, sliding around my throat, working its way under my tunic. I shiver and hug myself tight.

"Drafty in here," I say to Curran. *Of course it is. So much cold stone. So far underground.*

He looks at me quizzically. "I think it's quite warm. There's Verpacian Elm stoves all around us..."

He's cut off by the sound of smart footsteps on stone floor outside, followed by the creak of the door's hinges.

We join the class in sitting at attention, faces turned to the front.

Our green-robed professor sweeps down the center aisle, and I'm thrust into immediate confusion by the long, green hair that flies out behind him like a pennant.

I riffle through my papers, checking.

Professor Xanillir is supposed to be an Elf. A *white-haired* Elf.

The professor swoops around his desk and podium, turns to face us and the entire hall lets out a collective gasp.

He has the long hair and sharp features of an Elf. The gracefully pointed ears and silver eyes.

But he's *scaled*. Completely covered in small, emerald scales that catch the lamplight and reflect back every shade of green, his hair a slightly deeper green than his shimmering skin. And the Elfin-styled tunic that peeks out from under his robe is forest green, covered with sweeping rune-marks that glow as if lit up from behind.

He's one of the Smaragdalfar. A Snake Elf.

I look to Curran with confusion, but he's busy gaping at our professor.

Snake Elves are mine Elves. Deep-earth Elves. Dangerous, criminal Elves. A depraved hoard locked in their underground cities by the Alfsigr and controlled with mine demons and pit dragons.

And I've never seen one. Ever.

How did this one get out? How did a Snake Elf come to stand in front of a lecture hall? In professorial robes?

I reach back and pull my cloak from the back of my chair, over my shoulders. *It's so cold in here.*

"I am Professor Fyon Hawkkyn," the Smaragdalfar says, his voice elegantly accented, his star eyes full of hard, searing light, a row of golden hoops pierced through each ear. "Professor Xanillir has resigned in protest of my appointment by Vice Chancellor Quillen. If any of you wishes to move to another section of this lecture, you may speak with the registrar."

The Elves rise in one gleaming white motion and silently glide out of the hall, the entire left side now emptied.

The Snake Elf's expression remains unflinchingly hard.

The Gardnerians murmur uneasily amongst themselves, shifting about before settling back down to attention.

Professor Hawkkyn's star eyes sweep coldly over our side of the room. They catch on me and bore in. Recognition lights, like Bornial flint catching fire.

"It seems we have a celebrity amongst us," he marvels, his mouth tilting with incredulity, his eyes tight on me with unnerving intensity. "The granddaughter of the Black Witch."

An amorphous dread washes over me, pooling, and I'm overcome by the sense of real danger—something silent, waiting to bare its teeth. I pull my cloak tighter around myself and stare back at the Snake Elf.

"There will be no preferential treatment here, Mage Elloren Gardner." The words are matter-of-fact, but etched in stone.

"I wouldn't expect it," I reply, my voice reedy from the hollowing cold. I glance at the stove closest to me, its red coals glowing hot. I can barely feel its heat.

The feeling of dread grows, like I'm being watched, even after the Snake Elf takes his eyes off me.

"We'll begin with Section Four, gold alloys," he says with efficient grace, opening the text before him as we all follow suit. "Beginning next class, I'll group you according to Guild apprenticeship and tailor your Metallurgie study accordingly. We've groupings of weapons-makers, smiths, jewelers and a single apothecary." His eyes flit coldly to me. "Mage Gardner, you'll work directly with me."

"Yes, Professor Hawkkyn," I say, repressing a shiver, the cold and the dread growing.

He begins to write out a listing of gold alloys on the chalkboard behind him, and I ready myself to take notes, dipping my pen into its inkwell.

My pen clinks hard, the inkwell almost tipping over from the force, like I'm tapping on solid glass instead of thin black ink. Confused, I pull the inkwell toward me then rapidly let go of it, the glass so cold it burns to touch it. Alarm building, I lean forward and tap my pen back into the ink, a subtle rise of cold fogging up from the container in a small, white puff.

Frozen solid.

Curran's watching me sidelong, his head tilted in question. "What's wrong with your—"

The realization hits us both at the same time, Curran's skin visibly paling.

Stomach dropping, going light-headed, I glance around, immediately focusing in on the young woman two rows back with the wide, vicious smile, a patient hatred burning in her stunning eyes.

Fallon Bane.

I quickly turn back to the front, heart racing, as Professor Hawkkyn's chalk taps out a broken rhythm, a new thread of icy cold gently winding its way around my throat.

After class I leave quickly, giving Fallon and her ever-present military guard a wide berth. I notice Curran does the same, the two of us avoiding eye contact with her, treating her as one would treat a rabid animal. I'm uncomfortably aware of her ring of cold still encircling my throat, the icy chill not dissipating until I'm clear out of the Scientifica Wing.

Every step to the Mathematics lecture hall is filled with frustrated, trembling alarm that slowly gives way to a mounting anger.

My first lecture, and already Fallon Bane's set me behind— no notes to study from, only what's in the text and my memory.

Fine, you evil witch, freeze my ink, I seethe. *Chill my throat. I will not cower before you again.*

She can't actually hurt me, I reason with myself. She'd be thrown right out of the University, and out of the military and promptly sent to prison. Using magic against a fellow Gardnerian is a major, major crime.

I grit my teeth and resolve to never slink out of class like a beaten dog ever again.

I'm still fuming as I take a seat in Mathematics, relieved Fallon is nowhere to be seen in the sea of young Gardnerian men, all of them blessedly civilian.

I breathe out a long sigh of relief when no one pays much attention to my arrival. My eyes light on the sole Kelt in the room, a young man two rows in front of me, his brown shirt in sharp contrast to our Gardnerian black.

He turns, and we both flinch as our eyes meet. His posture goes rigid with tight offense as he narrows his green eyes at me with fiery venom.

Oh, wonderful. The icing on the cake.

Yvan turns away and I drop my forehead into my hands, railing against my snowballing bad luck.

First Fallon in Metallurgie, now Yvan Guriel in Mathematics. What next?

I look back up and glower at his strong back, his hand grasping the side of his desk so hard, his tendons stand out in rigid cords.

I can almost feel the simmering heat of his hatred, and it sears through me like a fresh wound, cutting me to the core. Tears sting at my eyes.

Why do I let him rattle me so? I don't care what he thinks of me.

An angry heat rises along my neck, and I silently curse him for his ability to upset me so thoroughly.

CHAPTER
THIRTEEN

Gardnerian History

After Mathematics I doggedly avoid Yvan Guriel's hurtful, scathing looks and scurry away to get to my History class on time, tired of being in class with people who openly despise me.

At least History is clear away from the White Hall complex. It's a relief to be briefly walking outside, the sunlight warming my face.

I'm braced for more hatred when I enter the sunlit lecture hall built just off the Gardnerian Athenaeum—braced for ice magic and eviscerating stares and yet another well that Fallon has preemptively poisoned.

Instead, I'm immediately enveloped by goodwill—solitary scholars and convivial groupings slowly realizing who I am, blinking, murmuring and then blessedly smiling warmly at me.

It's all Gardnerians here, no hateful Kelts. And no Gardnerian military apprentices.

And best of all, no Fallon Bane.

Every muscle in my body relaxes in relief.

The scholars are a mix of male and female, every set of hands marked with swirling fasting lines, most holding steaming cups of tea and snacks on small napkins, a long sidetable overflowing with refreshments interspersed with potted orchids.

It's like I've stumbled off the battlefield and into a genteel party.

"Welcome, Mage Elloren Gardner," a tall young woman says warmly, gesturing toward the table of refreshments, an Erthia orb and a third-year scholar's apothecary pendant hanging from her necklace. "We're thrilled you're joining us. Please, have some food and tea."

I take in the incredible spread set out for us, head spinning over the sudden change in atmosphere and overwhelming luxury. There's a full tea service, several types of cheese, seeded crackers, a bowl of grapes, sliced bread, butter rosettes, a variety of jams and a bowl of oatmeal cookies.

An almost irrepressible laugh bubbles up inside me. I smile back at my fellow scholars.

Everything will be okay, I comfort myself. *Fallon's a paper dragon. She can't hurt me. I'm Carnissa Gardner's granddaughter and Vyvian Damon's niece.*

Immensely grateful for this better turn of events, I set my books down on a desk and pour myself some fragrant vanilla black tea from the elegant porcelain teapot, my hands slowly steadying. The china is decorated with delicate vines, and I can feel my nerves beginning to smooth out the moment the warm, rich tea slides over my lips.

"I'm Elin," the tall woman says warmly as I walk back toward my desk. She makes a string of introductions, drawing me into their pleasant circle, and I nod and smile, struggling to remember names, slowly letting go of the remembrance of cold encircling my neck.

Fallon can't hurt you. Let it go.

I glance around the hall where I'll be taking not only Gardnerian History, but also Botanicals, both taught by Priest Mage Simitri. Rows of exotic orchids are set on long shelves beneath a wall of curving windows. The windows extend to a diamond-paned skylight that forms half the roof, sunlight raining down on us. Pen and watercolor renderings of orchids dot the walls, as well as oil paintings of pivotal moments in the history of my people. One wall is made up entirely of bookshelves lined with weighty history and botany texts. A glass door leads right to a small, domed greenhouse bursting with flowering vegetation.

And the Gardnerian building is wood. All wood. Not the cold, lifeless Spine stone.

I breathe in the rich smell of the Ironwood that surrounds me. Heartened, I glance at the nearest watercolor, drinking in the beautiful depiction of a pale pink river orchid. It's signed *Mage Bartholomew Simitri.*

He's so talented, this new professor of mine. Not just a well-known author of historical and botany texts, he's evidently an accomplished artist, too.

A slim Urisk girl darts in bearing another platter full of art-fully arranged petit fours in a repeating pattern. Elin and the other friendly Gardnerians around me grow quieter and shoot small, wary glances at the pointy-eared, blue-skinned girl.

The girl keeps her head ducked submissively down, works silent as a ghost and barely causes a ripple in the air as she leaves.

The smiles and conversation resume.

Unease pricks at me over the subtle, collective dislike of the girl, but I remember my own harsh treatment in the kitchen and push the feeling away.

As I take my seat, the lecture hall's door opens and our black-haired, hook-nosed, bespectacled professor glides in, his slight portliness and the crinkle of laugh lines fanning out from his eyes giving away his age. He's neatly put together and sets his books down in precise lines on his desk before looking up and beaming at us like we're long-lost and much-beloved relatives.

He's dressed in Gardneria priest vestments, a long black tunic marked with a white bird—one of the Ancient One's many symbols.

His eyes light on me and take on a reverential glow. He sweeps around his desk, makes his way down the aisle and bends down on one knee beside me, his hand resting gently on my arm.

"Mage Elloren Gardner," he says with deep respect. "Your grandmother, may the Ancient One bless Her, saved my entire family." He pauses, as if searching for the right words. "We were being herded up for execution when She swept in and freed us. It was Her, and your father, who liberated us and brought us to Valgard." His eyes glaze over with emotion. "I owe my life to your family. And I am so honored to now have you, Her granddaughter, in my classroom." He pats my hand and smiles at me as he rises, then, as if overcome, pats my shoulder, as well.

I'm deeply touched, tears pricking my own eyes. So relieved to be amongst only Gardnerians and embraced by them.

Priest Simitri looks around, as if overjoyed by the sight of all of us. "Please, Mages, turn to the first section of your history text."

I open the book, the first page bearing the title and the author—*Priest Mage Bartholomew M. Simitri.*

He opens his arms wide, as if embracing all of us. "Let us begin, Mages, with the beginning. With the blessed Ancient One's creation of Erthia, the very ground we stand upon. It is the story of every Gardnerian First Child. A story of Good versus Evil. Of Erthia bequeathed to all of us by the Ancient One above. It is...*your story.*" He speaks with theatrical grace, and a genuine enthusiasm that's contagious.

I feel myself becoming instantly caught up in his grand sweep of Gardnerian history. And liking this professor of mine a great deal.

CHAPTER FOURTEEN

The Lupines

Vastly heartened, I catch up with Aislinn in the White Hall after History.

"Fallon's in my Metallurgie class. And Yvan Guriel's in Math," I breathlessly say to her then relate all that's happened, desperately relieved to be back with my newfound friend. Scholars pass every which way around us on the way to their next classes, sunlight streaming from the dome overhead.

I tell her about Fallon's ice.

Aislinn knits her brow in concern, hugging her books tight, a heavy bag slung over her shoulder. It seems like my archivist friend is always lugging around a small library, enough books to weigh down a sturdy mule.

"You need to stay away from Lukas Grey," she cautions once again.

"Well, that's rather difficult," I counter, "seeing as how Aunt Vyvian has made it her life goal to see us fasted."

Aislinn shakes her head. "Elloren, Fallon's really not to be trifled with."

"She froze my ink," I blurt with outrage. As if that's reason alone to defy her to the wall.

"That's not all she'll freeze if you don't stay away from Lukas," Aislinn warns with deep concern.

I blink at her. How do I explain to this friend of mine who abhors kissing what it's like to kiss Lukas Grey? And that's not the point, really. Why does Fallon get to bully everyone in sight?

"I'm from just as powerful a family as she is," I grouse. "More powerful."

"Not anymore," Aislinn reasons, sighing as if I'm a child who just won't listen and keeps putting her hand in the stove fire. "And she might be the next..."

"Black Witch, yes, I know." I cut her off petulantly, frustrated by my damnable lack of magic. I take a deep breath and look back at Aislinn. "My Metallurgie teacher's a Snake Elf."

Aislinn's eyebrows go up. "How can that possibly be?"

I shake my head. "I don't know, but I'll be studying with him directly." The Snake Elf's bizarre appearance reverberates in my mind. "He's covered in green scales. They look like jewels."

"I'd transfer immediately," Aislinn states emphatically. "The Alfsigr Elves keep the Snake Elves locked underground for good reason." She gives me a significant look.

"Well, I can't transfer," I grumble. "There's no room in my schedule to move. So I'm stuck with a potentially demonic Snake Elf as a professor, and Fallon Bane torturing me through every class."

Aislinn gives me an appropriately pitying look, which makes me feel a tad better.

"How's History?" she finally asks.

"Fantastic," I tell her, fishing a small, napkin-wrapped bundle out of my pocket. "There's an overabundance of cookies. It's the one bright spot in my life right now. That, and new friends." I smile gratefully and hand her an oatmeal cookie.

Aislinn laughs and gives me a sweet smile before taking a dainty bite out of the cookie. "C'mon," she says, hoisting her bag, "we'll be late for class."

★ ★ ★

I follow Aislinn back toward the Scientifica Wing, keeping a close eye out for Fallon as we go down through a series of lamp-lit underground tunnels, up a staircase and through a long, arching hallway toward the Chemistrie Guildhall.

Outside our laboratory classroom, groupings of scholars linger—mostly Gardnerians, with a smattering of Kelts and Verpacians, but no Fallon Bane anywhere.

I breathe a deep sigh of relief.

Some scholars sit on stone hallway benches, some stand in tight clusters. All of them appear agitated, their hushed conversations full of distress. They look to me with some surprise, but my presence is clearly overshadowed by some dark happening.

A conservatively dressed Gardnerian girl passes by, clearly upset.

"What's happened, Sarill?" Aislinn asks, confused. "Where are you going?"

The girl pauses, her eyes lighting briefly with recognition at the sight of me. She attempts a wavering smile, then turns back to Aislinn. "The male Lupine," she says with a flustered wave toward the laboratory entrance. "He's in there."

Aislinn blanches. "He can't be."

"Oh, he's in there, all right," she insists darkly. "And I'm leaving. You should too, Aislinn." She looks to me. "Both of you should."

The girl rushes away, and she isn't alone. Groups of Gardnerians and a few Kelts, most of them female, began to peel off and make their escape from the science hall.

I peer through the laboratory's open door.

They're both there. The blond Lupine twins. Talking to Professor Astrid Volya, the tall, tattooed Amaz professor with the pointed ears. Actually, the female Lupine is doing all the talking, her hand haughtily placed on one hip. The young Lupine male stands by, watching the two of them with his wild eyes.

I turn back toward Aislinn. She's gone even paler and looks about to cry.

"Aislinn?"

"This can't be happening." She stares at the Lupines, her eyes glassing over. "It just can't be happening. I have to take this class. I can't finish my archivist studies without it." She turns to me, her voice gone small and dazed. "I can't take a class with a Lupine male, Elloren. Father'd never allow it. He'll make me leave University." Her eyes dart around as if searching for a way out. "I can't leave before year's end. They'll make me fast to Randall. I *have* to finish my studies before I fast to Randall. If I don't…he'll *never* let me come back." Her lip starts to tremble as she tries to swallow back the tears.

I place a hand on her arm, concerned for her. "Oh, Aislinn…"

Her hand shaky, she fishes a handkerchief from her pocket and dabs at her eyes. "I'm the only female in my family to have ever attended University, Elloren."

"I don't understand why you need Chemistrie to become an archivist," I say, defensive on her behalf. Archivist studies is all literature. Books and more books.

Aislinn sniffs back her tears. "Book preservation. Chemistrie's required. It's useful for us…" She trails off, gazing sadly at the classroom. "Well, at least…it would have been." She turns back to me, her expression full of open longing. "I love books, Elloren. I love them. Sometimes I wish…" Her voice trails off, and her face darkens as if she's admitting to something scandalous. "I wish I didn't have to get fasted."

I'm shocked by her admission. But then I grow sad for her, and this serious dilemma she's in.

"What would you do," I ask her gently, "if you didn't have to?"

A spark flares in her eyes. "I'd work in the University archives. I'd curate the old books collection. Oh, Elloren," she says, a hungry passion in her voice, "the Alfsigr archives are having an exhibit of the Rilynnitryn botany series. It's the most *amazing* work on botany on all of Erthia. The Elves have this painting technique...it allows them to capture light in a three-dimensional way. You *have* to see it." Aislinn makes a gesture with her hand, like a flower blooming. "It's like you can pick the flowers off the page. They're *that real.* They just...*leap* off the page." She stops herself. "Oh, Ancient One," she says, chastened, "don't tell anyone you heard me talking like this."

"Why?" I question, confused.

She stares at me as if it should be obvious. "Because Elves are heathens, of course. It sounds as if I'm...glorifying their culture." She gives me a wan smile. "At least, that's what Father would say."

I'm thrown by the strict rules her family holds her to. Uncle Edwin has never been so narrow-minded with my brothers and me.

"Aislinn, I'm sure we'll be fine if we go in. Professor Volya looks scarier than they do. And the male Lupine, when Fallon set her magic on me...he was so kind."

"You shouldn't let your guard down because of that," Aislinn counters, unmoved. "They're viciously strong. The male alone could take down the entire class. *Easily.*"

She's right. Lupines are supposed to be incredibly strong. And immune to wand magic.

Aislinn peers over at the Lupines through narrowed eyes. "Did you know that Echo and Fallon are being forced to lodge with the female?"

"You're kidding."

Aislinn shakes her head. "Paige, too. Echo told me about her. She said..." Aislinn pauses. She looks toward the Lupines uncomfortably, her cheeks flushing.

"What? What did she say?"

Aislinn leans in, her brow tight. "She told me," she says, her voice low, "that the female walks around...naked."

My mouth falls open. *"Completely?"*

She nods. "They're *wild*, Elloren. Like animals. And the males are immoral and dangerous. I don't know what to do."

I take a deep breath, considering this. "Well, *I* don't have a choice. There's no room in my schedule to take a different section. Not with my kitchen labor. I have to take this class, Lupines or not." I glance over at the laboratory entrance, sure that the Lupines can't be anywhere near as bad as my Icaral lodging mates.

The remaining scholars are filtering in. I turn back to Aislinn. "I think we should just sneak in and take a seat near the back. I doubt the Lupines will even notice us."

Aislinn casts a sidelong glance toward the twins, deliberating.

"My father's away for a few months," she says, staring over at the wolf-shifters as if calculating the risks. "By the time he gets back, the class will be over." She turns back toward me with shaky resolve and wipes the tears from her eyes. "All right, Elloren. Let's go in."

We creep in as unobtrusively as we can, sliding past Professor Volya and the Lupines, making our way toward the back of the room. We're soon approached by a young Elfhollen apprentice, the Chemistrie Guild crest hanging from his neck.

"Names?" he asks with cold formality, his pen poised over a class list. We quietly tell him who we are. He checks us off and moves on, blessedly ignoring my pedigree.

There are a series of distillations on the long tables behind us, the sound of their steady bubbling soothing to the ear, and I find myself instantly fascinated by the equipment. The end product, an oily yellow liquid, is giving off a sour smell that's mildly sulfurous. A set of arching windows on the opposite wall are partially blocked by rows of shelves. They're stocked with vials and bottles filled with substances in every state. Lab tables are set about the room, covered with a kaleidoscope of glassware and burners, the metallic tang of Bornial flint on the chemical-laden air.

By now, most of the scholars are silently standing along the walls, their eyes fixed on the exotic Lupines. The Elfhollen lab assistant walks around the room, quietly directing people to their seats, two to a table.

"This is completely unacceptable," the Lupine female is saying to Professor Volya, her voice all haughty arrogance. "Why can I not partner with my brother?"

Professor Volya is staring daggers at her with coal-black eyes, and I'm sure that look would make most people back down. She's very intimidating—almost a head taller than the Lupines and of a solid, strong build. Her numerous piercings and heavily rune-marked face only add to the effect.

"Diana," she says through gritted teeth, "you and your brother will not become *integrated* here if you only speak with each other."

Diana places one hand on her hip, swings her lustrous blond hair over her shoulder and lifts her chin. "What if he's the only person here worth speaking to?"

Professor Volya pulls herself up to her full height and looms over Diana.

"Miss Ulrich, this is *my* class, and I will run it as I see fit." She grabs the papers from her Elfhollen assistant and scans them, her mouth a tight, unforgiving line. "Well," she announces, "our numbers are reduced, which will allow us to move at a faster pace." She glares over at the Lupines. "Diana Ulrich," she says in a deep tone that brooks no argument. "Your research partner will be Mage Elloren Gardner, and Jarod Ulrich, you will partner with Mage Aislinn Greer."

Aislinn's eyes go wide, her obvious terror dwarfing my own shock. She opens her mouth to say something, but seems unable to speak. Instead, she stands stone-still, her mouth agape as the Elfhollen points toward a pair of adjacent tables in the back row.

Jarod Ulrich is watching Aislinn very closely with fierce eyes, his expression unreadable, and I think I see his nostrils flare. I feel alarmed, but at the same time, I remember how kind he was—how he helped me up when Fallon tripped me.

I walk back to my assigned table, sympathetic stares following me as I go. Diana plops down on the stool next to me with an annoyed huff, like someone forced to entertain fools. I watch Aislinn as Jarod takes his seat next to her. She's gone very pale.

Professor Volya opens a large text and begins to read from it.

Watching him out of the corner of my eye, I see Jarod glance over at Aislinn every now and then, his brow slightly furrowed. Aislinn continues to focus straight ahead, her hands clasped so tight her knuckles are white.

Partnered with a Lupine male. This isn't good.

I turn to my own partner. She's glaring at Professor Volya, her face tight with irritation.

She's arrogant, this girl. But her brother was kind to me. Maybe these Lupines aren't as bad as they're made out to be. It's not ideal to be forced together like this, but perhaps it makes sense to make the best of things and try to get along.

"I'm Elloren Gardner," I whisper to Diana, holding out a hand for her to shake, eager to get the awkward introductions out of the way.

She turns to me, seeming affronted, then glances down at my outstretched hand quizzically, as if she doesn't quite know what to do with it. She flicks her hair proudly over one shoulder and stands up to face me, her chair screeching loudly along the floor as she does so. She clears her throat ceremoniously. "I am Diana Ulrich of the Gerwulf Pack," she announces quite loudly. "Daughter of the Alpha, Gunther Ulrich, and his wife, the healer Daciana Ulrich, sister of Jarod Ulrich and Kendra Ulrich, paternal granddaughter of..."

Professor Volya stops lecturing, one long black eyebrow cocked with surprise. I want to crawl under the table. Diana

Ulrich goes on and on through three generations, like a queen reciting her noble lineage, until her brother interrupts her, his voice low.

"Diana."

She turns to look at him, annoyed at the interruption. *"What?"*

"They don't do that here."

"Do *what?*"

"Establish ancestry as a greeting."

She blinks at him. "Why ever not?" she finally says, clearly appalled.

"It's just not their custom."

She folds her arms in front of her chest and huffs at him.

"Besides," he whispers, gesturing to the front of the room where Professor Volya stands menacingly still as if she's contemplating the most expeditious way to murder Diana. "We should probably pay attention now."

"Why?" Diana asks like a spoiled child.

"Because," he says, raising his eyebrows at her meaningfully, "lecture has *started.*"

Diana frowns at Professor Volya and then at everyone else before finally plopping back down into her seat next to me. Professor Volya shoots her one more stern look before focusing in on the rest of us and resuming her lecture on distillation techniques.

I'm surprised when Diana turns to me and starts whispering. "I have already read this book," she complains stridently. "I do not need to listen to her rehash it. It is a waste of my time!"

I don't know what to say. Besides, it's so hard to resist staring at her flashing amber eyes. The color is mesmerizing.

"The forest is beautiful today, is it not?" she says wistfully, looking toward the line of windows and the orange-and-gold-tipped trees beyond. She sighs longingly. "I love how the trees smell this time of year. And the dried leaves, so sweet. I wish I could be out there now. Such a day for hunting. Do you hunt, Elloren Gardner?"

"No," I reply, still trying to get my mind around the fact that I have a wolf-shifter for a research partner. "But my older brother, Rafe, does."

"Does he?" she asks, seeming curious.

"He's an excellent archer," I whisper. "Do you have a bow?"

Diana laughs at this, a little too loud, causing Professor Volya to shoot her a quick, irritated look. "I don't need a bow," she says, grinning incredulously.

"What do you hunt with, then?" I ask.

She fixes her wild amber eyes on me. "My teeth." She smiles widely, displaying her long, white, glistening canines. The hairs on the back of my neck go up in alarm.

"Oh," I say, swallowing nervously. "You mean when you turn into a wolf?"

"Not necessarily," she says, still smiling dangerously.

Holy Ancient One in the Heavens above.

I gulp and turned back to face the front of the room.

CHAPTER
FIFTEEN

Tierney Calix

I enter the main teaching area of the Apothecary Guildhall breathless, having raced here from Chemistrie. To my dismay, the wooden lab tables filling the long, low-ceilinged room are already populated by pairs of young women hard at work chopping and mashing ingredients, the hiss of steam distillations and the low gurgle of boiling liquid soft on the air.

It reminds me loosely of the Chemistrie laboratory, the walls and tables covered with glass jars, vials and distillation retorts. But here flinty, sulfurous smells do not dominate the room. Instead, there's an all-encompassing, earthy scent, deeply rooted in the forest realm, the containers surrounding me stocked with dried herbs and flowers, powdered bark and wood. My apprehension is tempered as I take in the rich scents, separating them out one by one in my mind—pine sap, birch ashes, cedar shavings. Bunched herbs hang from the ceiling, as well. I breathe deep, detecting nettlewood, briarsweet and black-cherry leaves.

Something inside me settles, contentment washing over me. Unfortunately, that feeling is short-lived, as I catch the eye of a furious-looking young woman storming in my direction.

"You're *late*," she chides me angrily, and I immediately panic at the sight of the gold pendant of a Lead Apprentice dangling from her necklace. Two scholars standing at a nearby lab table mirror her contemptuous glare. Society girls, all three of them, wearing finely embroidered silks under their long black lab aprons.

"I'm so sorry. There was a situation…with a Lupine…"

A low murmur of alarm goes up in the room, young women pausing to look up from their labors. There are no Keltic scholars here, no Elves, no Elfhollen. Gardnerian females dominate the apothecary trade, especially those with a little bit of Magecraft.

"It doesn't *matter*," the apprentice snipes, cutting off my explanation. "It doesn't matter if there's an *army* of Lupines on your tail. Guild Mage Lorel expects you to be on time. As correction, you'll stay after class and scour all the retorts." Her eyes bear down on me, white-hot. There's something vaguely familiar about them.

A sick, sinking feeling pulls me down. This sensation is something new. *Desperation.* Now that Uncle Edwin is ill, I *need* this trade. And I need the Lead Apprentice to like me.

"Yes, Mage…" I shuffle through my papers, searching for her title. "Mage…"

"Bane," she says, with unpleasant emphasis. "Gesine *Bane.*"

The sinking feeling pulls me deeper, weakening my voice as I take note of the wand hanging from her waist. "Might you be related to…"

"I'm Fallon's cousin." She flashes a quick, brittle smile. "We're *quite* close."

All heads turn as the lab door opens and our professor strides in, the smattering of whispering snuffed out. Gesine immediately takes on a studious, deferential manner.

Our professor, Guild Mage Eluthra Lorel, sets her thick stack of well-scuffed botany texts down with a thump, then glances at some papers Gesine holds out to her. She wears conservative attire under her open professorial robe, an Erthia sphere dangling from a silver chain, along with a gold Apothecary Guild Master pendant, and slim, silver glasses set upon a finely chiseled nose.

"Mage Gardner," she says as she reads over the papers, pausing to acknowledge me with a quick glance and nod. "It is a pleasure to have you with us." There's no pleasure in the statement. Only cool formality. She turns to Gesine, a slight hint of reproach in her eyes. "Why isn't Mage Gardner working on her Pertussis Elixir?"

"I was late, Guild Mage," I put in, quickly explaining what happened and how I had to stay late to convince my Chemistrie professor to pair a traumatized Aislinn Greer with a Gardnerian research partner instead of a Lupine.

Professor Lorel's jaw tightens. "I don't tolerate lateness, Mage Gardner," she snaps, then shakes her head as if reconsidering. "But you *were* helping a fellow Gardnerian avoid a potentially dangerous situation. And that *is* commendable. So I will overlook your lateness. *Once.*"

"Thank you, Guild Mage Lorel."

She goes back to looking through her papers. "You will read chapters one through three of your Apothecary text this evening, Mage Gardner, and be ready to present tomorrow."

My stomach drops through the floor. "Present?"

Everything grows still. Guild Mage Lorel raises her head slowly, her eyes gone flinty. When she speaks, her voice is soft and even. "You will recite every medicinal in the first three chapters—their origin, uses and cultivation. Tomorrow morn. From memory."

I swallow uncomfortably as all hope of sleep flits away. "Yes, Guild Mage Lorel."

Guild Mage Lorel waves her hand lightly at her Lead Apprentice. "Gesine, pair her up."

Our professor launches into her lecture as I follow Gesine toward the back of the room.

"There," Gesine says with a flick of her hand as if throwing me toward a refuse bin. "With Tierney Calix. We're arranged by wand level." She shoots me another quick, disdainful smile. "The powerless in the back." Then she turns on her heel and strides away toward the front of the room.

Several young women take turns glancing over at me, some with open dislike, some with wary concern. There's some nasty sniggering, and my heart sinks like a stone. This class is bound to be torture with Fallon's cousin as Lead Apprentice.

I walk around a maze of tables to the very back of the laboratory, self-consciously embarrassed over my lack of power. In wider Gardnerian society, my wand level is a common thing, but not here. These are the best of the best apothecary scholars.

Most of the young women sport military-style silver bands pinned around their arms—almost all of them Level Two.

My lab partner comes into view.

She's hunkered down over her preparations, and I immediately give a start at the sight of her.

Tierney Calix is, by far, the ugliest Gardnerian girl I've ever laid eyes on. Reed-thin, her face is sharp, her nose unevenly hooked, her straight hair oily and uncombed. And she appears bent, her back twisted to the side, trapping her into an odd, unforgiving posture. Like a spider protecting her webby lair, she seems to shrink down at the sight of me, drawing around her experiment protectively as she glares up at me through resentful eyes.

I set my book bag down and force out a perfunctory hello as I adjust to her unpleasant appearance. She ignores me and turns back to the equipment on the table, as if it can form a wall between us, her book open to the formulation of the Pertussis Elixir, her face tight with tension, as if wishing me away. She makes no move to make space for me at the table.

I sit down near the table's edge and push my violin under it. I pull out my Apothecary text and open it to the correct page as anger flares.

"Are you friends with Fallon, too?" I challenge in a tight whisper. I instantly regret how petulant and weak I sound.

She glares at me as she begins to effortlessly milk liquid out of a pile of large glassberries with nimble fingers. "I lodge with her."

"Oh, wonderful," I say darkly. I grab up some berries and a ceramic bowl, push her text over to make some room for myself and attempt to mimic her deft milking. My bowl is quickly filled with a useless, coarse mash.

I glance over in jealous wonder at Tierney's skill, her bowl already topped off with glossy, syrupy liquid, the berry pulp neatly discarded to the side. She'd clearly done this before. Disheartened, I glance around the room. Many of the young women have their wands out and seem to be drawing liquid smoothly out with spells.

In a huff, I pull my book open for guidance and am instantly disheartened by the complexity of the preparation. Clearly, Guild Mage Lorel believes in forcing us to learn on our feet, the elixir involving a cold-water maceration, a complicated distillation and a decoction involving eight different powder ingredients. *Pertussis Negri* is a nasty illness, afflicting mostly infants, and often fatal. It's called the Black Cough because of the dark sputum it produces, and the elixir we're preparing today is its only known cure.

I grab at some nigella tree bark and feel its familiar tingle on my fingers—winding black limbs graced with deep purple leaves sputter into view toward the back of my mind. It can lull you, this tree, its sap rich and slow as warm molasses.

Instinctively aware of its grain, I slice the nigella into strips and began mashing each line into a fine, dark powder. Tierney glances over at my work and I see her do a quick double take. I notice her own nigella powder is badly prepared, lumpy and mottled with strings of gummed-up bark.

Tierney grabs up my fine powder and pours it into a pot of

water she has brought to an even boil. Then she pours her berry liquid into the first of a series of bulbous glass retorts. Eager to keep up with her, I light the flame below the first retort, fiddling with its intensity as the berry juice begins to boil unevenly.

"I know about you and Lukas Grey," Tierney says as she stirs the concoction, watching as the roiling water turns deep purple. The scent of hot, ripe plums fills the air.

"Not surprising, if you live with Fallon," I snipe as I jiggle the distillation flame, increasingly frustrated by everything, hitting at the burner when I can't get the steam to flow in the right direction.

Tierney takes it from me, inches the flame higher and effortlessly positions it in just the right spot. A strong, steady jet of steam bursts through the entire series of retorts.

I slump back, defeated. It's no use. Everyone in the room is more advanced than me. Most have the advantage of magic at their disposal, and everyone seems to be friends with or afraid of Fallon Bane.

I sit there, demoralized, watching Tierney as she works.

"I hope you fast to Lukas," Tierney says as she stirs at the purple liquid, adjusting the flame by a fraction. She speaks so low, I'm sure I've heard her incorrectly.

I lean in toward her, mystified. "I'm sorry. What did you say?"

Tierney measures out some thistle oil and adds it to the liquid, the deep purple quickly morphing to indigo and sending up a sour, lemony scent. "I hope Fallon sees you two together," she whispers as she stirs, "and I hope it rips out whatever shred of a heart she has left in her vile body."

I blink at her, thrown and at a loss for words.

Ignoring me, she keeps working, methodically and efficiently measuring out ingredients and monitoring the flames.

"I never properly introduced myself, and it was rude of me," I tell her, extending my hand, feeling dazed with surprise. "I'm Elloren Gardner. Which, of course, you already know."

She glances over, shooting me an incredulous look. She does not take my hand, but she does move over a fraction, as if deciding to share an edge of her web after all.

"You prepare the powders," she says grudgingly. "I'll keep an eye on the distillate."

I go to work, grinding up burdock root with a stone pestle, quickly and effortlessly rendering it to fine powder.

After class ends, I remain behind, scouring out glass retorts with a thin wire brush, my aching hands quickly caked with oily residue. My stomach rumbles and clenches, adding to the thick knots of tension already there, fatigue beginning to drag me down. I've never gotten so little sleep, and it's making me brittle and edgy.

I look up as a small, corked jar sealed with wax is slid in front of me.

"Goldenseal liniment," Tierney says, pointing to the jar then gesturing along her hollowed-out cheek with a frown. "It will clear up the bruising on your face."

I blink up at her, surprised. "Thank you."

She spits out a laugh, her homely face scrunching up into a grim frown. "It's not because I *like* you," she scoffs. "I just want you to be *pretty*. Prettier than *her*." Tierney's expression grows darker. "I want her to lose. I *hate* her. And I want *you* to win Lukas Grey."

CHAPTER
SIXTEEN

Shards of Ice

After I finish my lab scut work, I leave with a small box of medicinal vials tucked under one arm, under orders from the Lead Apprentice to deliver them to the University infirmary.

As I approach the Physicians' Guildhall, I slow, finding myself transfixed by the sight of the Astronomy Guildhall's domed observatory. It dawns on me that here, at University, I might get the chance to see the moon and constellations close-up. It's enough to lift my bedraggled spirit.

I glance down at the box of vials and back up at the dome, making a split-second decision.

What harm can it do just to have a peek?

The observatory's ceiling is adorned with a breathtaking depiction of the major constellations, highlighted by a blue that swirls so dramatically it almost gives me vertigo. The floor is marked with a giant compass rose, and telescopes encircle the deserted room, evenly spaced in front of huge, arching windows. A panoramic view of the Northern and Southern Spines lit golden by the setting sun takes my breath away.

A tremor of excitement courses through me as I run my hand along the length of one of the smooth, black-lacquered instruments.

My elation is quickly cut short as Fallon Bane sweeps into the observatory, flanked by four Gardnerian military apprentices and, behind them, her military guard.

Former thoughts of bravado instantly forgotten, I shrink back behind the telescope, my heart speeding, praying that Fallon doesn't spot me.

"I can't believe they've got you rooming with the Lupine bitch," a thin-nosed apprentice crows as Fallon claims the next telescope over.

"She won't be here long." Fallon sits down on the windowsill's edge, her ebony wand gleaming at her waist. "She seems easily provoked."

"Are you trying to provoke her, then?" The young man seems amused by Fallon's daring.

"I enjoy provoking anyone who doesn't belong here." Fallon glances at the nails of one hand as if bored. "Lupine bitches, Snake Elves..." She looks straight at me.

Reflexively, I slouch farther behind the scope.

Fallon's mouth turns up in a wicked smirk. "Well, if it isn't *Mage* Elloren Gardner."

I force myself up, struggling not to be cowed by her.

"Enjoying your new roommates?" Fallon jibes.

Anger flares within me. "Not as much as I'm enjoying spending time with Lukas Grey," I reply evenly, surprising myself with my audacity—and my overwhelming stupidity.

The young men surrounding Fallon go quiet and wide-eyed.

There's a flash of murderous rage in her eyes, but Fallon quickly collects herself. She sniffs the air, her lovely nose crinkling. "You smell *vile*," she tells me with a mocking smile. "Like an Icaral."

The young men smirk, a laugh bursting from the thin-nosed

apprentice. One of the other apprentices grimaces and waves the air in front of his face to more chuckling.

I surreptitiously inhale and realize Fallon's right. Some of Ariel's foul odor clings to my clothing.

Not only do I have to live with Icarals, but now I smell like them, too.

My face heats as Fallon revels in my humiliation, and my temper flares, making me reckless. "Well, at least my stench is a temporary situation, unlike Lukas's disinterest in you."

Fallon gapes at me as she coughs out a stunned laugh, her hand grasping her wand.

Stupid. Stupid. Stupid. My heart hammers out. *Have you lost your mind?*

Fallon turns to her companions. "She's a *mouthy* one, isn't she?" She pins me with her gaze, her eyes flicking toward the young men then back to me. "She'd make a nice ice sculpture, don't you think?" A rancid venom is creeping into the edges of her tone. "It would cure both the stink and her...*mouth.*"

Incensed, I glare back at her. "It's against Gardnerian law to threaten another Mage with magic."

She spits out a jeering laugh. "Oh, you're *barely* a Mage." She looks me over with disgust. "Level One, isn't it? Your family must be *so* proud." She's smiling jovially, but there's an off-kilter rage in her eyes that shoots a chill clear up my spine.

I'm starting to wonder if my constant sleep deprivation is seriously compromising my judgment. A Level One mouthing off to a Level Five. With two Level Five brothers.

Smart move, Elloren.

Fallon pointedly turns her back to me, focusing again on the young men vying for her attention. Scholars begin to filter in, followed by the class's long-bearded Gardnerian professor, and I make my escape.

I rush down the stairs and through the building's dim hallways.

In my haste, I take a wrong turn and quickly find myself lost and disoriented in a deserted part of the building, paintings of the night sky on the dark walls illuminated by torchlight. Hearing voices around a bend up ahead, I start forward.

The ground beneath me suddenly becomes unbelievably slick, my feet scrambling until I completely lose my footing. I fall forward against a stone wall, my books and papers scattering everywhere, the box of medicinal vials crashing to the ground in a shower of broken glass and pungent odor. My hands slap the floor with a cold sting, and I find, to my astonishment, that I'm lying on solid ice.

I lift my head and wrench myself around to see Fallon leaning against a wall, regarding me with a satisfied grin as she twirls her ebony wand between dexterous fingers.

"So, that's it?" I spit out foolishly. "Your incredible Level Five powers? Frozen ink and a thousand and one ways to trip people?"

She lifts her wand in the air and murmurs something unintelligible as she watches me like a hawk zeroed in on its prey. Something translucent appears, hovering next to her head on both sides.

Four sharp, icy stakes streak toward my face, catching my hair as they impale themselves through the stone wall behind me with a sickening crack.

Terrified, I tug away from the icicles, some of my hair pulling out of my scalp as I do so.

Fallon twirls her wand, the corner of her mouth turning up. "We don't have to be enemies, Elloren."

"We don't?" I croak out.

"Of course not," she croons.

Her obnoxious, entitled tone kindles my anger. "You know, Fallon, if you want to be friends, you're really going about it the wrong way." I glare at her. "Where I'm from, people generally don't hurl *ice daggers* at people they're trying to be friends with."

Her lips curl with contempt. "It's simple. Just stay away from Lukas, and I'll stay away from you. Understood?"

You mean, bullying witch.

I cough out a sound of disbelief and shake my head at her, anger burning hot at my neck. "You should be thanking me, you know that?"

"Really," she spits out. "How so?"

I find my footing and rise. "Without me on his mind, Lukas might be undistracted enough to see you as you really are. And I think it's safe to say that would make you quite a bit less attractive." I straighten and look her square in the eye. "As if that were *even* possible."

She's on me in a flash, her wand to my neck, and I suck in a tight breath, pressed up against the stone wall.

"Play this game with me, Gardner," she seethes. "See how it ends for you."

The echo of footsteps starts on the stairs and down the hallway, coming in our direction.

Fallon smiles darkly at me and removes her wand from my throat.

Fallon's military guard stops short at the sight of me standing in a large puddle, shattered vials and books scattered all over the wet floor.

"Oh, dear," Fallon croons, shaking her head with a sigh as she glances at the vials. "Guild Master Lorel won't be happy you're so clumsy. Wait until she hears." She looks at me with mock concern. "You might want to clean up the mess you've made."

She shoots me one last evil grin before she turns briskly on her heel and leaves.

CHAPTER
SEVENTEEN

Of Violins

It's dark by the time I finish my kitchen labors, and I'm glad to leave, worn-out by the work and from enduring the hostile silence and forced politeness of the other workers. I go straight to the archives to complete my assignments and pore over Apothecarium texts for several bleary hours, dismay spiking as complicated formulations refuse to stay put in my sleep-deprived head.

Exhausted, I drag my feet toward where Rafe, Gareth and Trystan are lodging. Gareth's only with them until week's end, when he'll travel back to Valgard with the other Maritime apprentices, and from there to the sea.

My brothers' lodging house is a long wood-and-stone building with multiple chimneys that sends up River Maple–scented puffs of smoke into the chilly night air.

I'm enveloped by warmth upon entering. Tapestries adorn the walls of a welcoming common area that houses a roaring fireplace, several benches and a number of chairs. There's wood flooring instead of stone, and it's soothing to my tired feet. The male scholars, most of them Gardnerian, mill about talking, eating and studying. I feel a sting of jealousy.

You could be living somewhere pleasant like this, I can almost hear my aunt say. *You could be with your own kind, in the plushest of lodging houses. If only you would agree to fast to Lukas Grey.*

And get an ice pick through my head? No, thank you. I shake away thoughts of Aunt Vyvian and stifle the memory of Lukas's hot kisses.

I approach the House Master's desk, get permission to meet with my brothers and make my way down a dim hallway. I count down to the correct room and knock briskly on the door.

The door opens, and surprise slams into me.

Yvan Guriel is looming over me, his brown hair tousled and sticking out at odd angles, like he's run his hand through it in irritation one too many times.

I can see from his expression that he's just as surprised to find *me* there.

"What are *you* doing here?" I demand, struggling to keep my composure in the face of his hostility.

"I *live* here," he replies caustically.

Thrown, but undaunted, I try to look around him into the room. "Where are my brothers?"

He doesn't answer, just glares at me hotly.

"Well, if this is where my brothers lodge, I need to drop off my violin," I say testily, lifting the instrument's case.

"Your violin?" he sneers, like I've said something offensive.

"So that the Icarals I'm being forced to live with don't set it on fire," I explain stiffly, trying to ignore how infuriatingly good-looking he is.

He flexes his angular jaw, and his intense green eyes burn into mine.

"Can I please just leave it here?" I finally ask, exasperated.

Reluctantly he opens the door wide, shoots me a look of hatred, then turns his back on me, stalking over to a broad desk lit by a small lamp. Thick physician texts are open on it, along with what must be an essay in progress.

Recognizing Rafe's things, I slide my violin under my brother's bed.

"Thank you for your hospitality," I say to Yvan's back, shooting him an angry look that I know he can't see. Then I walk out and slam the door behind me.

Lukas is leaning against a tree, hidden by the shadows, as I walk out of the lodging house.

"You went in strong last night, I can tell." His voice is silky smooth and warm with approval.

I stop in front of him as I let the startled feeling settle. It's hard to make Lukas out, only the metal hilt of his sword and the gilded edge of his cloak catching the faint moonlight. My eyes adjust, and I can barely make out the subtle shimmer of his skin.

"I did," I reply evenly.

"And? Are the Icarals afraid of you now?"

"Yes."

"Good." He pushes himself away from the tree and strides toward me.

I step back and hold up my hands to ward him off. "Oh, no. I need to stay *far* away from you."

His grin widens. "No, you don't."

I step back farther. "No, I really *do*. Or Fallon's going to kill me."

"She won't kill you. She'll just make your life miserable. But it's worth it, don't you think?"

Before I can comment on his audacity, he flicks his wand, and I'm bound and pulled straight into his arms. The bindings dissolve as he embraces me and kisses my neck. I halfheartedly push at him, and he gives a low chuckle. My resolve weakens, carried away on the cool night air.

"Why is she so obsessed with you?" I ask breathlessly.

He gives me a sly, dark smile. "You have to ask?"

I frown at him and move away a bit. "I thought your affinities clashed."

He cocks his head. "They do. It's like I've told you. She thinks it's exciting. I find it off-putting."

"And *our* affinities?" I wonder, his hand caressing the small of my back.

He pulls me in closer, his breath warm on my ear. "All that fire. And wood. We match up quite nicely, don't you think?"

My breath goes uneven, my palm on his chest. He's so warm.

Lukas grins and steps back, holding out his arm to me.

"Where are you taking me?" I ask with some wariness as he leads me back in the direction from which I came earlier.

"Trust me," he says. "I want to show you there's more to this place than crazy Icarals."

We wind our way through the torch-lit University streets, past lodging houses and crafter's Guildhalls. We finally come to a stop in front of an elegant building adorned with impressive wood carvings, scenes from *The Book of the Ancients* adorning every arch and crevice.

It's a museum of Gardnerian art.

The young military apprentice on guard duty immediately comes to attention when he sees Lukas and hands him a ring of keys without question.

We enter the building, and Lukas leads me through the deserted exhibit hallways, lighting lamps with a tap of his wand as we pass. I follow him past sculptures and paintings and into a circular exhibit hall.

As Lukas illuminates the room, I marvel at the instruments on display here, many protected under thick glass cases. A grand piano stands in the center of the hall, covered in carvings of trees and different species of birds, flying about the dark, ebony branches.

I'm immediately drawn to one of the violins sheltered under protective glass.

"This is a Dellorosa violin," I breathe, amazed. They're the most expensive violins in all of Erthia. Magicked to be perfectly in tune, the bow strings are made from the hair of Asteroth steeds, the swirling decorations wrought from pure gold.

Lukas pulls out his wand, murmurs a spell and points it at the case. A thin green light illuminates the lock before it clicks open. He lifts the glass cover, pulls out the open case and offers the violin to me.

I put my hands up to fend him off. "I...I couldn't..."

He pushes the magical instrument toward me, insisting. "It was meant to be played, not stuck in a glass case."

I relent and take the violin from him, the thrill of doing this forbidden thing coursing through me. I hold the exquisite instrument like a fragile newborn, feeling like I'm a child again and have just been given my most longed-for Yule gift.

Lukas goes to the piano and beckons for me to follow.

"What are we playing?" I ask in breathless anticipation.

He smiles and runs his fingers lightly over the glossy piano keys. "You'll recognize it."

Of course I do. Filyal's *Deep Forest Dream*.

Everyone knows this piece, but played on these instruments, in harmony with each other, it becomes something altogether different. Gone is the nervousness I displayed at my aunt's party. Here, alone with him, I dive into the music and wind the violin part around the piano music sinuously, as if we've played together all our lives. The music is one long, slow kiss, his fingers sliding the deep notes of his song against mine. I lose track of time as we play, his face serious as he moves his fingers deftly over the keys.

Much later, after Lukas brings our final piece to a close and his hands to rest on his knees, I lower the violin and smile at him.

He smiles back and I can feel the heat in his gaze. Flustered, I turn away and lower the instrument gently back into its case.

I'm arranging the bow when Lukas comes up behind me. He wraps his arms around my waist, his breath warm against my cheek. "That was beautiful."

My hands freeze in place on the bow. He begins to nuzzle my neck, untwining one hand from around my waist to gently pull my hair aside so he can kiss me just under it.

That's when I stop breathing.

I release the bow in my hands and turn around, my back resting against the piano.

He twines his arms around me once more and brings his lips to mine. Lulled by the music, I let myself fall into his kiss, into the deep, warm pool of his caresses. As he kisses me, a strange, delicious tingle starts at the soles of my feet and dances around my ankles. I shift my weight, reveling in the sensation as Lukas pulls me closer. He smells wonderful—like pine boughs in deep forest, warm as midnight fire. I sigh and let myself fall deeper.

I run my fingers back through his hair. I can feel his smile on my lips as I lightly trace along the thick hair of his sideburns, the soft, bare skin just behind his ear. Lukas groans and kisses me harder.

Suddenly the sparking around my ankles pulls in tight, and the image of a tree made of dark lightning flashes through my mind, power arcing from the soles of my feet to the tips of my fingers in a fierce, branching wave of pleasure. I shudder and cry out, overwhelmed by the powerful sensation.

I push away from Lukas.

"What was *that*?" I gasp as a dark echo pulsates hot in my core, my legs now unsteady.

Lukas holds on to me, his eyes full of surprise. "I don't know," he says, his voice deep and ragged. "I've never felt anything like that before." His expression shifts from shock to hunger.

He lunges at me, claiming my mouth, and pushes his body hard against mine.

I gasp as the image of the tree flames back to life, dark sinuous branches snaking through my body, his hands all over me.

But it's too much. Too fast. Like being caught in the ocean's undertow.

I try to move away from him, to push away from the black fire, but he tightens his hold on me. I wrench my mouth from his.

"Lukas," I force out. "*Stop.* I want to go."

He pulls back, just barely, and gives me a look so feral that it fills me with serious alarm.

My eyes dart nervously toward the exit.

Abruptly, Lukas steps away, eyes predatory. He holds up his hands in mock surrender as his mouth curls into a slow, dark grin. He bows to me and holds out his hand for me to take.

I hesitate, wary of him now. Wildly conflicted and acutely aware of my vulnerability.

I place my hand in his, unsure of what he'll do. But he simply leads me, wordlessly, back out of the museum, past the young guard and out into the cool night air.

CHAPTER EIGHTEEN

Unforgiving

Two Elves are waiting for me in the hallway outside my room when I return to the North Tower.

Wynter's intimidating brother and the willowy Elfin lad who was with him this morning are leaning against the windowsill. They straighten as I enter, both of them armed with bows and well-stocked quivers.

"Elloren Gardner," Wynter's brother says, his face grave, his words heavily accented. "I am Cael Eirllyn, brother of Wynter Eirllyn, and this is my second, Rhys Thorim." He makes a slight, reluctant bow before continuing. "I need to speak with you."

My heart picks up speed. "You need to leave," I insist as I glance nervously toward the door behind me. "It's not appropriate for you to be here."

Cael makes no move to comply. "My sister told me of the threats you have made against her," he says, stepping forward. "I have come here to respectfully request that you leave my sister alone."

He must be joking.

"Perhaps the Icarals should avoid attacking and abusing people if they wish to be left alone," I counter, pointing an accusing finger at our room.

His eyes widen, incredulous. "My sister? She attacked you? Wynter has never attacked anyone in her entire life. In fact, I've never heard her utter so much as an unkind word, even against those who have treated her ill."

I tense at the injustice of it all. "Ariel Haven attacked me my first night here," I reply. "I cowered in a closet all night long, thinking I was about to be *killed*, and your sister didn't lift a *finger* to stop her."

"My sister..." Cael tries again, softening his tone with what looks like great effort. "If you knew her...she is decent and good. The *Deargdul*, or the Icarals, as you know them, they are as despised by the Elves as they are by the Gardnerians. Our holy book, *The Elliontorin*, speaks about the evil of the winged, demonic ones. Many of our people seek to see my sister exiled forever. Some would like to see her imprisoned...or worse. She is here because she has nowhere else to go. If you make trouble for her, if you decide to spread lies about her, no one will take her side, save myself and Rhys Thorim."

I hesitate, momentarily conflicted. But then I remember where weakness got me. I can't afford to be weak.

Dominate, or be dominated. I can almost hear Lukas whispering in my mind.

I gather my resolve. "Well, that puts me in a very convenient position, don't you think?"

Cael stiffens and anger flashes in his eyes. "I should have known better than to expect compassion from a Gardnerian."

My blood boils at his words. "You should have known better than to expect that I would roll over and play dead when abused by Icarals!"

Cael is clearly furious, but Rhys's eyes fill with such raw hurt that it gives me serious pause.

"You have made your feelings quite clear, Elloren Gardner,"

Cael says with cold formality. "We will not take up any more of your time. Good eve."

He gives me a quick, perfunctory bow, and both Elves depart.

"Why is there a chicken in this room?" I cry as I step into my foul lodging.

A chicken runs around the room, bird feed scattered in a messy pile, droppings littering the floor.

Ariel glares at me with a look of seething hatred, scoops up the chicken and hugs it protectively to her chest.

"Get the chicken out of here now!" I demand.

Ariel springs up, the chicken in her arms. "No! You come near Faiga, Black Witch, and I will set your belongings on fire!"

"It has a *name*? You *named* the chicken? You stole it from the dining hall poultry yard, didn't you?" I take a threatening step toward her.

"I'm warning you, Gardnerian! Get away from my chicken, or your bed goes up in flames!"

"Go ahead, try it," I challenge her. "You'll be expelled!"

Ariel steps toward me, threatening in turn. "I'll be expelled if I set *you* on fire," she rages, "not your things!" A slow, evil grin forms on her face. "And believe me, Black Witch, that's the only thing keeping me from setting you on fire."

I know I should continue the fight. To keep the upper hand, no matter what threats I have to make. But I suddenly feel over-whelmingly tired and beaten down. "Fine!" I relent, shooting her a look of disgust. "Keep your stupid chicken. This room couldn't get any more disgusting anyway. It's like living in a barn."

"With a Gardnerian pig!" Ariel snarls.

"Shut up, *Icaral*."

Wynter winces at the word, her wide, silver eyes now peeking out above her wing wrapping. Shame pricks at me as I watch Wynter cowering, but anger and fatigue override my conscience.

I'll find a way to bring Ariel down. All I need is a few solid nights of sleep.

I'm awakened in the middle of the night by the sound of singing. I open my eyes just enough to see.

It's Ariel.

She's sitting on her bed, singing softly to the chicken and murmuring to it in turn. Gone is her usual evil, slit-eyed look. Her whole face is open, like a child's. The chicken is staring back at her, making a contented, low clucking sound, almost as if it's murmuring back to her.

It's an oddly gentle scene, and it makes me feel unsettled and slightly embarrassed to witness.

Wynter is sitting at the foot of the bed, a large piece of white parchment laid on a thin wooden board in front of her. She's sketching Ariel and the chicken, her thin black wings folded neatly behind her. She has a shiny white stylus in her hand and holds it at angles as she works. Her picture is oddly beautiful, the unusual art tool not only able to draw in multiple colors, but also able to capture the firelight so that it actually flickers on the page. I remember Lukas mentioning that Wynter is an artist.

Stop, I caution myself.

I force myself to remember the terror of my first night here, how Ariel attacked me, how I cowered in the closet, how Wynter never tried to stop her. How the Icarals in Valgard almost killed me.

I push all my thoughts aside and drift back to sleep.

She comes to me again in a dream that night.

The Selkie.

She's following me in the woods, trying to keep up with

my relentless pace. Autumn leaves crackle beneath me with each step.

I look the part of the Black Witch, my long, elegant cloak billowing out behind me.

The Selkie is trying, desperately, to tell me something in a language I don't understand, that I have no interest in understanding. She runs up beside me, only to fall back again as I refuse to slow down for her, refuse to acknowledge her, seeing her only as a flicker in and out of my peripheral vision. Ignoring when she trips and falls back yet again.

As the dream fades to black, I'm left with an uncomfortable gnawing sensation that by refusing to slow down and look at her, *really* look at her, I'm missing something.

Something of vital importance.

CHAPTER
NINETEEN

Spiraling Down

My world spirals down into an ever-worsening ordeal of endless work, extreme sleep deprivation and relentless abuse.

Fallon freezes my ink every Metallurgie class, so I take to carrying a few sharpened pencils. I forget them one day, and Curran Dell quietly slides a pencil to me with a surreptitious look of sympathy, his dislike of Fallon Bane covert but palpable.

No longer able to prevent me from taking notes, Fallon soon decides to move on from freezing inkwells. Instead, she freezes my chair to the floor so I have to struggle to get out of my desk, freezes the back of my cloak to the chair and frequently snuffs out the flames I kindle for my laboratory experiments. She keeps the abuse subtle enough that our professor doesn't notice, and there's absolutely nothing I can do about it.

And she grins all the while, like it's one big, fun game.

The workload for an ordinary apothecary apprentice is staggering in and of itself, with countless hours of rote memorization and preparation of medicines. *I* have the added burden of laboring in the hostile kitchen, enduring Yvan Guriel's green-eyed glare, as well as the extra tasks piled on daily by Fallon's cousin.

"I'm staying away from Lukas," I blearily tell Gesine one afternoon as she watches me scrub down charcoal-encrusted vials.

She looks up from her papers, unimpressed, and narrows her eyes at me. "Well, we'll just have to keep you busy, to make absolutely sure of that."

On top of everything else, my Icaral roommates continue to be a trial to live with.

Every night Ariel hovers protectively about her chicken. If I even get near the animal, she screams something unintelligible about cages and setting me on fire. She's completely unhinged, and I catch her doing mad, confusing things, like listlessly taking a knife to herself, slowly pushing the blade into her flesh until blood comes, adding to the rows of long scars up and down her arms. If she catches me looking, she hisses and screws her face up into a frightening scowl before throwing the knife on the floor and turning herself over to face the wall, her rancid wings lying on the bed like rotting, wilted leaves.

Under her bed, she keeps a stash of foul-smelling black berries. They're foreign to me, and I make a mental note to find out what they are once I have the time. Ariel chews them for hours on end, staring at the ceiling apathetically. At other times, she seems to lose herself in studying thick animal husbandry texts, most of them detailing how to care for birds.

Wynter remains an unsettling ghost, often perched on the windowsill, hiding in her wings. She never says a word in my presence, and I'm beginning to wonder if she'll ever speak to me at all.

The two of them don't seem to get cold and never bother to make a fire. Even being as frozen as I am, I avoid going over to the filthy fireplace, since it's on their side of the room and I don't want to provoke Ariel's wrath. But as fall settles in, the room grows colder and colder, and I'm running out of layers of winter clothes to wear under my quilt.

Almost every night the Selkie from Valgard haunts my dreams, and I wake up in a cold sweat, feeling lost and alone and scared. At such times the only thing that can calm down my racing heart is the warmth of my quilt and the memory of being wrapped safe in my mother's arms.

And the wand. The white wand.

I've hidden it in my pillowcase, and I'm strangely compelled by it. It's become like a talisman, my hands drawn to it through the fabric. Initially a blank page, the wand is gradually revealing its source wood to me more and more. Every night now, I surrender and let the wood of the wand send snow-white branches into the back of my mind. They unfold within, smoothing out my worry and fear, lulling me as white birds nestle deep in the wand's secret hollows.

And sometimes I fancifully muse—what if this truly is the White Wand of legend?

A letter from Aunt Vyvian comes.

To my niece,

I received your correspondence, and it has become clear to me that you are in a situation that is quite horrifying.

I have arranged to have you moved to lovely housing in Bathe Hall. You'll have a private room waiting for you there, and will only need to share the spacious common area with a quiet Gardnerian scholar and one Elfin girl (to fulfill the University's ridiculous integration rules).

Both the room and the common area boast a beautiful view of Verpax's Central Gardens. You'll have your own lady's maid, as well as a private dining area with the menu of your choice. It's warm and comfortable in Bathe Hall—nothing like the North Tower with winter fast approaching, I would imagine.

After you move, I will promptly take over your University tithe, which will relieve you of any need to work in the kitchens.

All you need to do is fast to Lukas Grey.

Once you are safely fasted to Lukas, you can put this unfortunate and frightening chapter behind you as a harsh but necessary lesson in the realities of the world we Gardnerians are faced with.

Please do not write again until that felicitous occurrence has taken place. Once it does, the Lodging Mistress has instructions to move you to your new lodging immediately.

Your attentive aunt,
Vyvian

I crumple the letter in my fist and toss it out the North Tower's hallway window.

Stubbornly set on the harder path, I shoulder on.

One evening I spot Lukas with Fallon Bane outside the main dining hall, her military guard hanging back a bit. I feel a stab of jealousy so strong, I almost drop the basket of warfrin root I'm lugging.

You've no reason to be jealous, I chastise myself. *You've no claim on him.*

Quickly spotting me, Fallon gives me a once-over as she takes in my mussed appearance—my flyaway, sweat-soaked hair and hands stained warfrin green right up to the wrists. She shoots me a gloating, triumphant look and makes a point of putting her hand on Lukas's shoulder.

Maybe he's decided to view her magical affinities as exciting after all, I bitterly consider. It's been over two weeks since I last saw him and vowed to stay away, intimidated by his aggression and his fiery magic, as well as Fallon's territorial claim on him.

Lukas turns and catches my eye.

My stomach clenches into a tight knot as I remember the

warm, seductive feel of his kiss, the overwhelming power of his magic. I force my gaze from his before he can detect any of the hurt in my expression and hurry away.

A few nights later I find a bundle of violin music waiting for me on the stone bench in the North Tower's hallway. It's by a composer Lukas knows I admire, written out in the composer's own hand and signed with a flourish. I feel a sharp pang of regret as I hold Lukas's gift in my medicine-encrusted hands.

We fit together, Lukas and I. Fire to fire. Branches twining tight.

I think back to Aunt Vyvian's letter and how much my situation would improve if I gave in and fasted to Lukas.

But that black fire of his. It's too much.

I shake my head as I flip through the music ruefully.

It's no use. Rafe is right about Lukas Grey. Affinity match or no, he's too powerful, too unpredictable. And too worldly for me.

He belongs with Fallon Bane.

CHAPTER
TWENTY

Revenge

"It is the nature of Icarals to draw evil and tribulation into the world," Priest Simitri gently tells me as I wipe away tears, once again lingering behind after his lecture has ended.

I love Priest Simitri's classes. Unlike Guild Mage Lorel, who is fair but dauntingly stern, Priest Simitri is refreshingly full of smiling excitement for both his subjects, ecstatic over all things flora as well as the grand sweep of Gardnerian history.

And he's not only an enthusiastic and patient teacher, he's become my supportive confidant, as well—as kind to me as Uncle Edwin.

Sniffling, I look past Priest Simitri's shoulder to the oil painting that dominates the lecture hall—two Gardnerian soldiers, wands drawn, boldly facing off against four red-eyed Icarals with black wings unfurled. *Outnumbered by Icarals. Just like me.*

I sniff again and nod, keenly aware of how exhausted I am, like an anchor sunk to the ocean's great depths. "The Icarals frighten me," I tell him. "I'm...I'm not sleeping well."

He nods in grave understanding and squeezes my arm. "Stay strong, Elloren. The Golden Age is coming. The Black Witch will rise, and she will smite them all. The Icarals, the Kelts, the shapeshifters—*all* the infidel races."

Yes, but if it's Fallon Bane, she might smite me, too.

His eyes are fixed on me, intent on my absorbing the full weight of the Prophecy. I want to take solace in his words as I rub at the scar encircling my wrist. I want to believe that there's another Black Witch on her way to usher in a world without cruelty and evil. But I can feel myself succumbing to doubt and a darker and darker melancholy.

Reluctant as I am to go against my uncle's wishes, I know that if nothing changes, I will eventually buckle and fast to Lukas Grey—or practically anyone my aunt wants—just to get out of my North Tower dungeon.

That evening I find myself passed out in the kitchen, the side of my face down on a blueberry tart I'm supposed to be assembling. The sticky berry jam is all over my cheek, temple and hair as my eyes flutter open. I've no idea how long I've been lying there. Everyone is long gone, save Iris Morgaine. Yvan enters the kitchen from outside, a load of wood in his arm for tomorrow morning's fires. I freeze, not wanting to alert them to my presence.

Iris bounds over to Yvan as he drops the firewood onto the kitchen's wood rack. "Here, taste this," she playfully flirts, offering up a piece of pastry to him.

"My hands are filthy," he says with a slight smile.

"Just open your mouth," she cajoles, her voice sultry. She leans into him and holds the food up to his lips.

He awkwardly complies, and she slides the food into his mouth, letting her thumb linger on his lower lip to wipe away a small smear of berry.

He's so attractive when he's not busy glaring at me, his full lips so at odds with the sharp lines of his face, his eyes like sunlight through green glass. I'm momentarily overwhelmed by how handsome he is.

I remind myself that he's a Kelt, likely no different from the boy who seduced Sage into breaking her wandfasting. There's also the undeniable fact that he can't stand the sight of me.

"What do you think?" Iris asks, still leaning into him.

"It's good," he mumbles through the food, his eyes intense on her.

"Would you like more?" It's clear from her tone that she's not only offering up the pastry.

Yvan swallows as if mesmerized.

"Oh, I got some on your chin," she purrs.

He steps back a fraction. "It's okay."

Undaunted, she reaches up with one hand to stroke pastry crumbs off his chin, then leans in to playfully nuzzle his neck.

He freezes uncomfortably and looks to be fighting off a whole range of powerful emotions. "Iris..."

A surge of hateful jealousy courses over me, seeing them like this.

Here I am, with a whole pan of berry tart stuck to my head and my tongue stained blue from boswillin tincture to ward off a persistent chest cold from sleeping in an icy tower. My general appearance is a shambles these days—even the fine clothes Aunt Vyvian bought me can't disguise the sorry state I'm in. Watching Iris Morgaine, the girl who once attacked me, having so much *fun* with absurdly gorgeous Yvan Guriel adds a spark to a resentment so raw, its force surprises me. I want to burst into tears and throw the bowl of jam at them all at the same time.

As if sensing my rancid thoughts, Yvan's gaze shifts to rest hard on me. A mortified flush sears my face.

I pull my head off the tart, humiliated by the indentation my face has left in the jam and dough.

Iris spots me as well, every trace of playfulness erased from her expression. She whispers something into Yvan's ear.

"No, I didn't know she was here," he says, his eyes still riveted hard on mine.

Iris hisses something else at him and then storms out, slamming the door behind her.

Yvan is still glaring at me hotly, reveling in my wretched state, no doubt—the powerless granddaughter of Carnissa Gardner, brought so terribly low.

I glare back at him, tears pooling in my eyes, my lips trembling, suddenly unable to disguise my naked hurt.

Yvan's expression turns momentarily conflicted then unexpectedly concerned.

The softening of his vivid green eyes sparks a powerful ache deep inside me, and then a sudden, fierce resentment of him and Iris and how they all belong.

Feeling shaky and struggling to fight off my humiliating, angry tears, I avert my eyes from him, grab up a damp cloth and roughly wipe the jam from my face.

I will not give him the satisfaction of seeing me cry.

Everything around me beginning to blur, I throw down the rag and flee. I run all the way back to the freezing North Tower, throw myself into bed, shut my eyes tight to block out the hateful Icarals and cry myself to sleep.

A crash wakes me up the next morning. I'm shivering and mentally reeling from yet another Selkie nightmare. Disoriented, I look around. Ariel and Wynter are gone, but Ariel's chicken is on my desk, pecking at my pens and papers, haphazardly pushing things down onto the desk chair and floor. My eyes slide down to find the ceramic portrait of my parents cracked to smithereens on the floor.

My only likeness of my parents.

Anger crashes through me like an avalanche long straining for release. I launch myself from my bed, rush toward my desk, stoop down and pick up a small slice of the portrait, my mother's eye still visible on the tiny sliver as tears streak down my face.

I'll never see my mother and father's faces again.

My anger grows and grows, until it becomes a vicious tide.

That's it. It's time to fight back. Let Ariel try to set me on fire. It will be well worth it. Then I can go to the High Chancellor's office and get her sent back to the insane asylum she grew up in.

I get up and throw on some clothes.

Then I pick up Ariel's chicken, bring it outside and set it roughly down on the blue-frosted grass.

I know her chicken probably won't survive long on the University grounds. It's likely someone will pick it up and return it to the poultry yard. Or it will be eaten by some predator.

I beat down a small stab of guilt and go to class.

My classes grind by slowly. And through all the lectures and laboratory work, I find it impossible to fight a mounting unease.

She deserves it, I angrily remind myself as I grind roots and help Tierney prepare a new distillation. *And it's just a chicken. Stolen from the poultry yard. It should have long ago graced a supper plate or been served up as soup.*

Late that afternoon I make my way back to the North Tower, wanting to drop off my heavy shoulder sack before going to my kitchen labor. I push through the blustery, gray day as I trudge up the long hill, a light, icy rain pricking at my skin, anger at Ariel spiking with every step.

When I finally reach the North Tower, I'm mentally girded for battle, ready to take her on.

I march up the tower steps, each stomp smashing away at my guilt.

She deserved it. She deserved it. Over and over on each new stair.

As I reach the upper floor and make my way through the oddly quiet hallway, I notice a strange smell—something charred, like an old cook fire. With nervous trepidation, I grasp the cold handle of our lodging's door and pull it open.

All the blood drains from my face when I see what she's done.

My quilt. My most beloved possession.

It lays in the middle of the deserted room, reduced to a charred heap, only a small portion still on fire, the flames crackling and disintegrating the dry fabric.

I run to it, a cry tearing from my throat. I stomp at the flames and burn my fingers as I grab at the last remaining scrap, feeling faint when the piece falls apart in my hand.

She's destroyed it.

I fall to my knees in front of the smoking ashes of my only remaining link to my mother and sob.

"I want her gone."

Lukas turns from where he stands watching a long row of military apprentices shoot arrows through the cool, damp air toward circular targets. Twilight is descending, torches being lit around the range. Lukas does a double take when he sees my expression.

"Who?" he asks, eyes narrowing.

"Ariel."

He searches my face for a long moment, then takes my arm and leads me away from the archery range. "What happened?" he asks.

"It doesn't matter," I tell him, my voice unforgiving. "I just want her gone. I don't care what you have to do."

I expect him to tell me to fight my own battles. At that moment I'm ready to hate him forever if he does. But instead, his expression turns calculating.

"The only way to get her out is to get her to attack you," he cautions.

"I don't care."

He draws a deep breath and motions toward a nearby bench.

"Well, then," he says, a dark smile pulling at the corner of his mouth. "Sit down. Tell me everything you know about Ariel Haven."

I'm bolstered after a long talk with Lukas, sure he'll find a way to help me get Ariel kicked out of University and sent far away from me. But almost as soon as I'm alone again, I think of my destroyed quilt and quickly descend back into misery.

I go to my kitchen labor in a fog of despair, distracted and unable to focus even on the simple task Fernyllia Hawthorne gives me of stirring a pot of gravy, unable to hold back the tears as I stand beside the large cast-iron stove.

Iris and Bleddyn find it hard to hide their pleasure at seeing me so beaten down, the two of them shooting each other smiles full of dark satisfaction.

"Oh, the Roach is *sad*," Bleddyn mockingly remarks to Iris in a low voice, the two of them increasingly bold, as if testing the waters.

"Awww." Iris glances sidelong at Bleddyn, her face screwed up in a mimicry of sympathy, as she plucks hot biscuits off large trays and arranges them in a series of wide baskets.

Bleddyn brings her cleaver down harder than necessary onto the cooked chicken carcass she's dismembering. I jump at the sound, and the huge Urisk girl smirks, her eyes narrowed caustically at me.

Iris spits out a laugh.

Yvan comes into the kitchen carrying a load of wood. He pauses in annoyed surprise when he catches sight of me, green eyes piercing. "Why are you crying?" he asks harshly.

"My quilt," I choke out as I watch my tears plop down into the gravy. "It's been destroyed." I have no idea why I've bothered to confess this to him—it's not as if he truly cares about why I'm upset.

His face screws up with disgust. "You're crying over a *blanket?*"

"Yes!" I sob, hating him, hating Iris and Bleddyn, hating all of them.

"It must be nice to be Gardnerian," Yvan sneers as he smacks down the stove's iron lever and throws in some logs. "It must be nice to live such a charmed life that the loss of a quilt constitutes a major tragedy."

"That's us," I counter, my voice stuffy. "We Gardnerians live such charmed lives."

His lips curl up into an obnoxious sneer. "I am *so* sorry for your loss."

"Leave me alone, Kelt!" I snarl.

Iris's eyes flit toward Yvan with a knowing look that he briefly returns.

"Gladly," Yvan replies, glaring at me. He loads more wood into the cookstove and slams the iron door shut.

CHAPTER
TWENTY-ONE

Kindred

That evening I trudge back to the North Tower, lugging books and notes. A rancid, churning hatred fuels my every step. I picture hurling Ariel across the room, ripping at those foul wings of hers.

My hands balled into tight fists, I storm up the tower's spiraling staircase, enter the hall and freeze.

Ariel is lying passed out on the floor, her wings limp behind her. Wynter is cradling her, frantically murmuring in Elvish. She looks up at me, wide-eyed and horrified.

Ariel's chicken is dead.

Lukas found it somehow.

It hangs from the door, two stakes driven through its breast, its head dangling. Its severed wings are staked on either side of the animal's body. Blood streaks down the door and pools on the floor below.

"Oh, no," I breathe. "Oh, Ancient One."

"She passed out," Wynter tells me, her heavily accented voice strange to my ears. "It was too much to bear. The winged...it was a kindred."

I'm reeling in confusion. "A kindred?"

"The wingeds. We can speak to them. With our minds." Silent tears begin to streak down Wynter's pale face. "Ariel loved this one," she says, crying now. "Elloren Gardner...why did you do this?"

My throat goes dry. "I...I never meant for this to happen."

"This could break her. Make her turn."

My head is spinning. "Make her turn?"

Ariel suddenly convulses in Wynter's arms, her body writhing, her face contorted with misery. Then Ariel's eyes fly open, and she swivels to face me. She recoils at the sight of me at first, but quickly recovers, her eyes taking on a frightening glow. She slowly pushes herself away from Wynter, her gaze fixed tight on mine as Wynter frantically murmurs to her in Elvish.

Wings slowly unfurling, Ariel rises.

My heart pounds as I back away.

"I. Will. Kill. You!" She pushes Wynter aside and leaps at me.

My world descends into chaos as Ariel slams me to the ground. Her fists, her nails, her kicking feet are everywhere all at once, punching me, scratching me, beating me as I frantically try to fight her off. The metallic taste of blood fills my mouth as fear courses through my system. Wynter frantically yells something at Ariel as she tries, unsuccessfully, to pry Ariel off me. But Ariel is strong and scrappy. My flailing, grasping arms are only able to slightly lessen her blows, not stop even one of them.

And then, as she kneels on top of me, my hands tight around her wrists, Ariel abruptly weakens. Her lips curl back into a terrifying hiss as her green eyes mist over like frost forming on water, until they're nothing but opaque windows into nothing. Her eyes flash back to green, then white, back and forth as I watch, horrified.

And then Wynter's arms are around Ariel, struggling to haul her backward, dragging her across the cold stone floor, away from me. Ariel's body stiffens and her eyes roll back into her head. She seems to be unconscious again, lost in some private hell. As Wynter pulls her past the door, Ariel's eyes snap open.

"Get her *down!*" she screams as her butchered kindred comes into view. She wrenches herself away from Wynter and hurls herself at the door. She slides to her knees, her hands clawing at the trails of blood streaking the wood.

"My sweet one!" she shrieks. "What have they *done* to you?"

Wynter moves toward me, her eyes wide. "You should leave, Elloren Gardner."

I teeter from side to side as I rise, dizzy from so many blows to the head. Wynter reaches out to steady me.

The minute her hand makes contact with my arm, Wynter's mouth flies open, her eyes roll back in her head and she falls backward onto the floor, grasping at her hand as if it's been burned.

"What's the matter?" I cry.

"When I touch people…" Her thin voice trails off, her eyes fixed on me with an expression of sheer terror.

I gasp. "You're an Empath, aren't you?" I remember the Icaral in Valgard, the one who could read people's minds just by touching them.

So that's why Wynter's brother was so angered when Rafe touched her.

She nods slowly, her expression one of awful shock.

Why is she so scared of me? What did she see?

Wynter's horrified daze is broken by the sound of Ariel screaming. "You need to leave," she pleads as she forces herself up.

I find my bearings and flee.

I stumble blindly down the staircase, my heart beating wildly. I steady myself against the wall, legs quivering, my vision blurry. I slide down the cold stone to the floor, dazed. I can feel my eye beginning to swell where Ariel repeatedly punched me. I reach up to touch the wound. When I lower my hand, there's blood all over it.

This is my chance. The one I asked Lukas for.

If I go to the High Chancellor's office now, Ariel will be removed from the University, sent back to the Valgard asylum and stripped of her wings. People will thank me for getting rid of her, and the North Tower will become a much more pleasant place to live.

I'm distracted from this train of thought by the soft rustling of wings and give a start when I look up.

A Watcher.

On the sill of the arching window.

It's like falling into a crystal clear pool, staring into the serene, sad eyes of the Watcher. Memories come rushing in, visions of things I've tried to ignore.

Ariel singing to her kindred at night, petting it lovingly. Ariel being laughed at and ridiculed wherever she goes. People everywhere turning their heads away, refusing to look at her.

In a month's time, unlike me and even unlike Wynter, Ariel has never received a letter or a visit from a family member, never heard a kind word from anyone save Wynter and Professor Kristian.

She's an Evil One, a voice inside me insists shrilly. *There is nothing good in her.*

But the way she cared for her bird, the bird that's now dead and staked to the door. She was so tender with it; so loving.

The question forces itself to the surface, even as I struggle to keep it down.

Is she really completely evil?

I realize I don't know the answer, and staring into the sad, soulful eyes of the Watcher, it suddenly seems vitally important to find that answer before sealing Ariel's fate.

"How could you torture her pet like that?"

I find Lukas in the dining hall supping with some other Gardnerian soldiers. I try to ignore the gasps and shocked murmuring of the soldiers and other scholars as they take in my battered appearance. The murmuring grows as kitchen laborers begin to notice me, as professors look up from their long table by the windows to see what all the commotion is about.

A slow grin forms on Lukas's face as he gets up and looks me up and down. "Worked, didn't it?"

"It was *cruel!*"

I can see by his expression that he's thrown by my reaction. He takes my arm and roughly pulls me off to the side.

"You asked for my help," he reminds me.

I jerk my arm away from him. "It was *too much!*"

He leans in close. "You told me you wanted her out," he says. "Now look at you. Here's your chance. Go to the professor of your choice. Tell them who attacked you. Get her out. No one here will miss her."

I don't even need to seek out a professor. To my dismay, a number of them have already risen from where they're sitting and are making their way toward us, Vice Chancellor Quillen among them.

"Holy Ancient One!" Priest Simitri exclaims, his black robes flapping behind him. "Elloren...who did this to you?"

I glance around wildly. Yvan, Fernyllia, Iris, Bleddyn and several other kitchen laborers have streamed out of the kitchen to gawk at the beat-up Gardnerian.

"Who attacked you, Mage Gardner?" Vice Chancellor Quillen asks.

I look into her unflinching green eyes and bite at the inside of my cheek to steady myself, feeling as if the room is closing in on me. Everyone grows silent as they wait for my answer. I have to say something. Anything, before Lukas does.

"I tripped."

Priest Simitri's face screws up in confusion. "You...*tripped?*"

I nod. "Down the North Tower's staircase. I'm terribly

clumsy. I even tripped *here* my first day." I motion toward the kitchen staff and narrow my eyes in their direction. "Ask them."

Yvan's eyes fly open with surprise. Iris and Bleddyn both gape at me in confusion.

"You need a healer." Priest Simitri steps forward to gently take my arm. "I'll bring you there."

As the priest leads me away, I turn to face Lukas.

Something irretrievable has broken between us. It was too much, what he did. I don't think I can ever forgive him.

As if reading my thoughts, Lukas shoots me a look of disgust and strides off.

Late that evening I'm out by the chicken shed, fumbling in the darkness to find the latch on one of the cages, a burlap sack in hand. Even after a healer's care, my left eye is still slightly swollen, and it throbs along with my head.

"What are you doing?"

Yvan's stern voice makes me jump. I can just make out the silhouette of his tall, lanky form, a large scrap bucket in each of his hands.

"I'm stealing a chicken," I snap, my heart thumping against my chest. "For Ariel."

"The Icaral," he says flatly, disbelieving.

"She can speak to them with her mind."

His black shape stands there for a long minute, and I can begin to make out those intense green eyes of his.

"Are you going to turn me in for theft, or are you going to leave me alone?" I demand in challenge. "Because I'd really like you to choose one or the other."

His brow goes tight as if deeply troubled, and he opens his mouth to say something but then closes it again in a tight, uncertain line.

My bravado collapses in on itself.

"I made a mistake," I tell him, my voice breaking. My anger

is gone, only raw shame remaining, leaving me suddenly un-guarded. "I was wrong. I never meant…"

I stop, afraid I'll burst into tears. My face tensed tight, I look away.

When I turn back to him, his eyes have gone wide, un-guarded as well, and I feel a warm rush of shock, so strong is this brief sense of inexplicable kinship.

Yvan tenses and shakes his head as if to ward me off. But he stares at me for a moment longer, conflict raging in his eyes, before abruptly turning and stalking away.

When I return to the North Tower, Wynter is sitting on Ariel's bed, murmuring to her and gently stroking her head. Ariel lies there limply, her back to me.

The dead kindred is gone, but the blood stains on the door remain as dark reminders of what happened.

I release the chicken from the burlap sack. The animal im-mediately makes its way over to Wynter and Ariel and flies up to roost against Ariel's side.

Wynter views the bird with surprise. She looks up at me, her face softening.

I sit down on my bed, chastened by guilt. "I never meant for this to happen."

"I know," Wynter says, her expression pained. She sighs and looks down at Ariel. "It is my curse to know." She turns to face me once more. "This is not all on your shoulders, Elloren Gardner. This is but one terrible cruelty in an endless string of terrible cruelties stretched out over all her years." She goes back to stroking Ariel's hair. "Her mother had her committed to the Valgard asylum when she was but a young child. She was so horrified that she had given birth to one of the *Deargdul*… an 'Icaral,' as you call us. The asylum kept Ariel in a cage. She was two years old."

I swallow hard, my throat going dry. The desire to avert my eyes is gone. I need to see this for what it is.

"It there anything I can do?" I ask hoarsely.

Wynter looks back down at Ariel and mournfully shakes her head from side to side.

And so I do the only thing I can do.

I sit in silence as Wynter sings to Ariel in High Elvish, standing vigil with her, the room softly lit by a single, guttering lamp, a Watcher briefly appearing on the rafter above.

We remain by Ariel's side all through the night, waiting for her to come back to herself. Wynter sings, and I silently pray. And we wait.

Until a few hours before dawn, when Ariel's green eyes finally flicker open, dazed, but whole once more.

Poetry

I'm more aware of the changing season this year than in years past. My breath now puffs out in small clouds as I scurry over the fields from the North Tower to the University grounds, knuckles smarting from the icy air.

Perhaps it's the furious pace of production in our apothecary lab—autumn is prime time for apothecaries. The Black Cough, lung fever, chilblains, suffocative catarrh, the Red Grippe—they all creep in with the cold, reveling in the stale air of crowded, stuffy rooms with windows shut tight.

In Metallurgie, the Snake Elf forces me to work at a break-neck speed, allowing me scant time and inconvenient hours to prepare metal powders for chelation agents in medicines, grading my papers (barely passing) with a stern hand. The dislike for all of the Gardnerians in his class is subtle, but quite evident in his star eyes—and his dislike for me is the most intense of all. Only Curran's small kindnesses—sliding notes toward me, quietly sharing lab results—make the class semibearable. Especially with Fallon's continuous, low-grade bullying.

Mathematics and Chemistrie are also demanding, although Professor Volya is uniformly fair. Only Professor Simitri remains magnanimous and forgiving in his approach, my classmates in his lectures reserved, but blessedly cordial.

And regular letters continue to come from Aunt Vyvian, describing how easy, luxurious and happy my life at University could be if I would just agree to wandfast to Lukas. My cloak pulled tight in my constantly chilled lodging, I take each letter and throw it into our messy fireplace, taking advantage of the fire's brief flare to warm my hands.

Early morning has a strange stillness to it now, as if the entire world is holding its breath, waiting for something. Only the great Vs of geese break the silence, sounding out their distant call.

Flee while you can. Winter is looming.

"How are things with the Icarals?" Aislinn asks one day in Chemistrie lecture.

About a week has passed since Ariel's kindred was killed, and my North Tower lodging remains a tense but newly silent place. My bruises and cuts are mostly healed, thanks to the ministrations of Priest Simitri's personal physician and a strong healing liniment I mixed up in the apothecary workroom.

"I only go back there to sleep," I tell Aislinn. "And Ariel's gotten very quiet. Mostly she just lies around. She never speaks to me. Never looks at me." I glance furtively around the mostly deserted Chemistrie lab, my voice low, scholars slowly filtering in. "Seems to like the chicken I stole for her, though."

"Do you think she's safe to be around?" Aislinn asks, concerned.

"I don't know." I pull out some parchment and my pen and ink. "Wynter stays close to her. She seems to be able to keep her relatively calm."

Wynter and I are increasingly on speaking terms, although I try to give her space, not wanting to have my mind read. She is, in turn, extraordinarily careful not to touch me. We exist in a polite, wary orbit of each other. I'm becoming increasingly curious about her, however, finding excuses to wander past as she draws. She no longer waits until I'm asleep to work on her art, and I steal glances of her beautiful sketches, which are mostly of Ariel and the chicken or of Elfin archers.

"I hardly ever see Ariel anywhere but in the North Tower," I tell Aislinn. "But she turned up in Mathematics a few days ago."

Aislinn's eyes widen at this. "You're kidding."

I shake my head. "It was a huge surprise."

"What happened?" she asks, and I launch into the story.

I was quietly taking my seat as Professor Mage Klinmann's chalk clicked out a staccato rhythm on the wall slate, a steady rain pelting the long, arching windows. He's a Gardnerian, my Mathematics professor, and pleasant enough to me. But it's hard to warm up to such a rigid man. I'm always uncomfortably aware of the glint of cruel bitterness ever present in his cool green eyes when he looks at anyone of another race.

I had just finished setting out my pen, ink and notepaper when a collective gasp went up from the Gardnerian scholars around me. I glanced up from my desk.

To my great surprise, Ariel was standing in the doorway, her wings flapping around herself agitatedly.

Mage Klinmann turned his head to look at her, then quickly jerked it away, as if the sight of Ariel burned his eyes. All of the scholars looked away as well, murmuring to each other unhappily.

Everyone except Yvan, the only non-Gardnerian in the class.

"For what reason do you interrupt my class, Ariel Haven?" Mage Klinmann questioned. His voice was calm when he said it, but he wasn't looking at her. He was looking out at his fellow Gardnerians, catching their sympathetic glances as they, also, pointedly tried to avoid looking at Ariel.

"They said I'm too smart for the class I was in," Ariel spit out, self-consciously, her eyes darting around as she fidgeted from one foot to the other. I could see her fighting off the urge to cower, her posture that of someone braced for an attack. She thrust out a piece of parchment at Mage Klinmann. He must have seen it out of the corner of his eye—his lip twitched and he turned farther away from her.

"And how do I know you did not fool your professor in some way, Icaral?" he asked, almost sounding bored. "I'm told that your kind are very crafty." He smiled at this, still not looking at her.

I'd seen people avert their eyes from Ariel and Wynter before, but only as they passed, never during conversation. It was strange and demeaning and filled me with an intense discomfort.

"You should *look* at me!" Ariel cried, her pockmarked face reddening, her hands balling into tight fists.

"Excuse me?"

"I'm *talking* to you! You should *look* at me!"

Professor Klinmann sniggered lightly. "And why, exactly, is it so important that I look at you?" He eyed the other scholars, as if they all shared an inside joke she was excluded from.

"Because I'm *talking* to you!" she cried, her eyes blazing with humiliation.

This prompted outright, incredulous laughter from some of the Gardnerian scholars.

Professor Klinmann seemed to be valiantly trying to ward off a smile. "Now, now, Icaral. To look at you would be against my religious beliefs. You're well aware of that. It's not a personal slight, and it would be foolish of you to take it as such. So you shouldn't let your feathers get all...ruffled." His eyes shot up to the Gardnerians before him, twinkling, and the scholars obliged him by breaking out into polite laughter, everyone studiously continuing to avert their eyes from Ariel.

Ariel flinched back as if struck, then turned and stormed out of the room.

I half rose, almost ready to go after her, then remembered that she hates me, and slowly sank back down.

I'd never seen anything like this.

I listened to the laughter of the scholars surrounding me in horror, suddenly nauseated. I turned to Yvan, who was seated across the aisle from me. He was the only other person in the classroom not smirking or outright laughing. He looked just as horrified as I felt.

Perhaps sensing my stare, Yvan turned to me, his eyebrows knit tightly together in anger. The moment his intense green eyes met mine, he gave a start, possibly surprised that I wasn't laughing like the others, the two of us instantly united in this sickening outrage. We held each other's gaze for a long moment as the anger in his face gave way to something akin to astonishment.

As if he was seeing me for the first time.

"It seems like it would be terrible to always have people looking away," Aislinn considers as I finish telling her my story. Her brow tenses. "I never really thought about it before."

"And now," I tell her, "Yvan doesn't flat-out hate me anymore. He still won't speak to me, but the other day during my kitchen labor, when no one else was looking, I was having trouble picking up a large bucket of water, and he helped me. He grabbed the bucket out of my hand and walked off with it, cursing under his breath and acting like he was angry at himself for even doing it, but he helped me nonetheless."

"Strange."

"I know."

The other scholars in Professor Volya's class are trickling in, including our rune-marked professor herself, so we cease our conversation and turn our attention toward the front of the room.

Aislinn and I are not only fast friends by now, but research partners, as well. Not able to partner with a Lupine, on the second day of class Aislinn simply took a seat next to me, sitting as far away from Jarod Ulrich as possible. Diana smugly and wordlessly took the seat next to her brother, shooting a triumphant look at Professor Volya. Professor Volya pursed her lips unhappily, but decided to ignore the slight. Jarod's face, however, remained tense and troubled for the rest of the class.

Aislinn, for her part, doesn't spend much class time taking notes, as I'm generous in sharing mine. Instead, Aislinn hides classic novels and poetry books in her Chemistrie text and reads discreetly through every lecture. The class we're currently sitting in is no different from any other, and after Professor Volya begins her lecture, Aislinn plasters a studious expression on her face and dives into her secret book.

I, in turn, dive into furiously scribbling notes on the distillation of essential oils. We're about half an hour into the lecture when a neatly folded piece of parchment is tossed onto my papers from the direction of the Lupines. I look at it curiously.

It reads *Aislinn*, in neat, attractive script.

Confused, I glance over at the Lupines. Diana seems clearly annoyed about something, and Jarod appears to be concentrating on the lecture.

I hand Aislinn the note, needing to elbow her to break her reading haze. Her brow furrows in puzzlement as I give it to her.

Aislinn quickly opens the neatly folded note. It reads:

What are you reading?
Jarod Ulrich

We both give a start, Aislinn's eyes flying open wide. We glance over at the Lupines in unison. Jarod is focusing straight ahead at Professor Volya with an expression of unbroken concentration. I turn back to Aislinn. She's now staring sideways at Jarod uneasily.

I can't imagine that she'll respond. After all, she's afraid of him. He tried to help her twice, once when she dropped her books, another time when she spilled a vial of Ornithellon powder. Both times, he appeared wordlessly by her side, and both times, his attentions made Aislinn obviously fearful and uncomfortable.

But this time she surprises me.

Aislinn quickly writes the name of the poetry book on the paper, as if she has to act fast before she loses her nerve, then places the note firmly before me. I gape at her, dumbfounded, wondering if she's taken complete leave of her senses. She gestures sharply toward the Lupines with her chin to spur me on, her brow knit hard with tension. For a few seconds we silently argue, but she remains resolute. I sigh deeply in reluctant surrender, shooting her a look of utter disbelief. The next time Professor Volya turns her broad back to us, I pick up the note and toss it onto Diana's papers.

Diana glares at me, rolling her eyes disapprovingly, then hands the note to her brother.

Jarod takes it nonchalantly, his eyes never leaving the front of the room. He opens the note without looking at it, then lets his eyes flicker down briefly, his expression neutral. He pulls out a fresh piece of paper and begins to write as if he's taking notes from the lecture. Aislinn and I watch him out of the corners of our eyes as he folds the note and places it in front of his sister, ignoring Diana's irritated huffing as she defiantly folds her arms in front of herself, letting the note just sit there, unmoved. She shoots her twin repeated, hostile looks, but he calmly keeps his eyes straight ahead. Finally, when I think I'll die from curiosity, Diana gives in, picks up the note and throws it at me.

I immediately pass the note to Aislinn and she eagerly unfolds the paper. "What is it?" I whisper.

A look of amazement spreads across her face. "Poetry!" she gasps.

I glance over at Jarod. He's still pretending to be engrossed in the lecture.

Aislinn impatiently flips through her poetry book, biting on her lip in consternation, until she finds what she's looking for. Then she places the note on the open book and moves them both toward me for my perusal.

The poem Jarod has written, an ode to the beauty of autumn, is identical to the one on the printed page. I look over at Jarod again, and there's a small smirk playing at the corner of his mouth. Aislinn carefully refolds Jarod's note, places it as a pagemarker in her book and pretends to focus in on the lecture, her eyes glazed over with surprise.

I turn to Aislinn at the end of class, dumbfounded. "I cannot believe you are passing notes with a Lupine male." I stare at her, amazed. "I thought you were terrified of them."

Aislinn turns to me, her silver Erthia sphere necklace catching the light, her expression riddled with conflict, as if faced with a world suddenly turned clear on its head. "There's been a mistake. There has to be some mistake." Her eyes flicker to where Jarod stands with his sister. She looks back to me and shakes her head, but her gaze is full of certainty. "Elloren, it's impossible to be evil and uncivilized *and* love the poetry of Fleming. I'm sure of this."

I look toward Jarod just in time to see him briefly and discreetly meet Aislinn's gaze and smile. Aislinn returns his smile shyly, colors then quickly turns away, hugging her poetry book close to her heart.

Stick Magic

"There's something strange about you and wood."

I pause, my hands coated with esmin bark powder.

Only the *drip, drip, drip* of condensation from a distillation tube breaks the silence of the deserted lab. Tierney and I are the last scholars here at this late hour, finishing up work that takes twice as long without wand magic.

I've known for some time that Tierney's noticed. It's like something in me is waking up, and it's more than just the echo of my grandmother's power in my blood. I've always had fanciful imaginings about source trees, but the more time I spend in the apothecary laboratory, and especially in the attached greenhouse, the stronger my strange leanings have become.

And Tierney's noticed.

She noticed when the small, potted Gorthan trees from the inaccessible northwestern forests opened their flowers at the brush of my hand. How a fiddlehead fern once reached up to curl lovingly around my finger, the small plant's waves of adoration washing over me. She knows that I don't have to label any ingredients that come from trees now. That I've learned to read mixtures intuitively, and can easily and effectively stray from the stated formulas more and more.

I level my gaze at Tierney. "Yes, well, there's something strange about you and water."

A flash of fear crosses Tierney's face.

Whereas I know Tierney has been surreptitiously watching me, I also know she hasn't realized that I've been doing the same. On several occasions, I've peered into the lab, late at night, and have caught sight of odd things. Things that left me blinking and wondering if my ongoing sleep deprivation is playing tricks on my mind. Tierney absentmindedly playing with water rivulets, the streams and balls of water following her swirling finger like playful kittens. Tierney directing steam with her fingers. Tierney holding a ball of water in her hand.

I've been forced to come face-to-face with the truth of it—like Gareth, there's no doubt that Tierney and I have tainted blood.

Fae blood.

For a long moment Tierney and I stare at each other in edgy silence.

"Have you noticed," Tierney ventures, "that we're the only two people in class without white armbands?"

More and more Gardnerian scholars have begun wearing these armbands, showing their support for Marcus Vogel's rise to High Mage in the spring referendum, Fallon Bane being one of the first. I can't bring myself to wear one, no matter how important it is to fit in. The thought of Vogel as our next High Mage fills me with a powerful dread I can't explain.

"Oh, I don't get involved in politics," I tell her with forced lightness. "That's my aunt's domain."

Tierney shoots me a look of hard appraisal, her mouth inching up in a coldly sardonic smile.

It makes me uncomfortable, her look. Like I'm being harshly judged and found lacking.

"I'll need your help with the vials," Tierney uneasily blurts out. "Carrying them, I mean. With this crook in my back—I can only carry a little."

I nod, eager to let all these threads of conversation drop into oblivion. I take my bowl of powder and shake it into the viscous syrup that's simmering before us. The rich scent of cedar and cloves flavors the air.

"They're in my room," she adds.

I cough out a sound of disbelief as I wipe the bark powder from my hands. "I can't go to your room. What if Fallon sees me there?"

"She won't," Tierney says with a shake of her head. "She has military drills most evenings." She shoots me a significant look. "Weapons training."

A dark laugh wells up. "Oh. *Weapons*. Is that all? So she'll be well practiced when she walks in and slays me."

Tierney cocks a shrewd eyebrow and regards me evenly. As if waiting for me to get this humor out of my system.

I let out a long sigh. "I cannot run into her, Tierney."

"Fallon's a fanatic about her schedule," Tierney states evenly. "She won't be there for a few more hours. I'm sure of it."

I stare at Diana Ulrich, blinking.

She's dozing on one of the four beds in Tierney's crowded room, belly down, one arm dangling listlessly off the bed, snoring loudly.

Completely naked.

Tierney notices me gaping at Diana as she packs soft cloths around each vial in the first of two long, partitioned wooden boxes. She shrugs. "It's shocking at first. But I've gotten used to it."

Diana makes a snarfling sound and rolls over, her legs splayed apart. I blush and turn away.

Tierney sends me a thin smile. "I'm almost done."

I glance around the room as Tierney works, curious. "So which bed is Fallon's?"

Tierney snorts and gives me an incredulous look. "You think she'd sleep out *here*? With all of *us*?" Tierney jabs her thumb in the direction of a side room. "Her bed's in there."

I cautiously step into the adjacent room as Tierney begins loading the second tray of vials. It's dramatic, as I expected it would be—done up in deep red and hard black, an expansive four-poster bed in its center, expensive sheets thrown about, a half-eaten plate of fruit spilling onto the white undersheet.

I note, with some petty satisfaction, that Fallon Bane is a slob.

I guiltily pad into the room, feeling like a thief in the night, curiosity getting the better of me. She has an impressive spell-book collection. Rows of brand-new grimoires, leather-bound with crisp gold-embossed titles, are housed in a locked book-shelf, its diamond-paned glass reinforced with iron latticework. Silver knives and swords with bejeweled handles and a cunning bow hang from the walls. An expansive fireplace with a grate of wrought iron worked into the shape of dragons' claws cranks out a delicious warmth. And to top it all off, a real-life dragon skull hangs over the mantel.

I walk over to her bed and run my hand over the silky down comforter, feeling a stab of jealousy over the luxury she basks in every night. The jealousy digs its claws deeper when I spot a small ceramic portrait on her night table.

Lukas Grey.

It's a good likeness—handsome as sin.

I hear a terrified squeak behind me and jump, the portrait falling from my hands, landing on the tile flooring with a sharp crack that sets me wincing.

It's Olilly, one of the Urisk workers from the kitchens. Like green-skinned Bleddyn, her coloration stands out there, as she's not the usual rose-white, but lavender. She's framed by the door-way, hugging a pile of clean, folded sheets to her chest.

"Beg your pardon, Mage," she forces out, ducking her head as if I might swipe it off.

"It's all right," I stammer, heart racing. "It's fine."

She's a fragile slip of a girl with a sweet, easily frightened nature, barely a day over fourteen, if I had to guess. I notice her amethyst eyes are a sickly red around the edges.

My eyes flick to Lukas's portrait, which is now split right down the middle.

Oh, Ancient One. Fallon cannot come back to find this broken.

I pick up the cracked portrait of Lukas, smile at Olilly as if nothing is amiss and stuff the pieces into my cloak pocket.

There's the jostling click and small creak of a door being opened, a flurry of troubled murmuring and then a familiar voice rises above the others.

"Holy Ancient One! She is such a filthy *animal!*"

My heart drops through my feet and straight to the ground.

Fallon.

I recoil back behind the door, my legs quickly rendered to jelly, the breath sucked clear out of my lungs.

What will she do to me? My heart feels as though it will pound straight through my chest. I glance through the slit by the door frame to see Echo, Paige and Fallon standing in the room, and another spasm of fear shoots through me. Tierney is frozen by her desk, regarding them with barely concealed panic.

Olilly eyes me with abject horror, quickly realizing that I'm not supposed to be here.

"I can't do this anymore!" Echo cries with a morally outraged wave of her hand toward the naked Diana. "She's *disgusting.* Look at her! We can't be expected…we're *Gardnerians!* Not filthy, heathen *whores!*"

Fallon throws a blanket roughly over Diana. Diana snorts a few times, turns over and resumes snoring. "There," Fallon says to Echo. "Better?"

"No, Fallon. No," Echo rejoins. "Only her leaving here for *good* would make it better."

Fallon laughs and throws her cloak onto a nearby chair. "She sounds like a snuffling pig." Fallon's smile disappears as she takes in Tierney's frozen expression.

"What are *you* looking at?" she demands. "Ancient One, you're like a ghoul."

I shrink farther back behind the door.

Fallon glances around, as if sensing something amiss, her eyes lighting on Olilly. Her face goes hard. "What are *you* doing here?"

Eyes wide with terror, Olilly opens her mouth but no sound emerges.

Fallon sighs as if she's dealing with an unruly dog. "Get over here," she demands, straightening and pointing to a spot on the floor before her.

Olilly rushes to her, head down, hugging at the sheets.

Fallon narrows her eyes at the girl, slides out her wand and lets it rest in the palm of her hand. "What did I ask you to be?" she asks calmly.

The girl mumbles something, her eyes on the floor.

"I can't hear you," Fallon says.

"Invisible," the girl mumbles.

"What's that?" Fallon asks, holding a hand to her ear.

"Invisible," Olilly mumbles a hair louder, her voice choked with fear. "I beg your pardon, Mage Bane, I didn't expect you..."

"No, no, no," Fallon grinds out slowly. "To *be* invisible, you have to *sound* invisible. Do you sound invisible?"

"Y...yes, Mage Bane. I mean, no, Mage Bane," the girl stammers.

"Well, which is it?"

The girl just stands there, mired in confusion.

"Get out," says Fallon, sounding bored.

Fuming, I glower at Fallon, watching her through slitted eyes. Wishing I had a wand and the power to use it.

Hugging the clean sheets, the girl flees.

Fallon blows out a sound of disgust and leans back against a desk. She lifts her wand, murmurs a spell and absentmindedly creates a roiling, blue ball of smoke that whooshes to life over the wand's tip.

I cringe at her casual showing of power. The ball morphs into a sapphire swirl and then into a puff of gray smoke.

Fallon turns to Echo with a sly smile. "Did you hear about Grasine Pelthier?"

"No," Echo replies.

Fallon's grin turns malicious. "She's to be fasted. To Leander Starke."

Tierney's hands freeze on the vials.

Who's Leander?

"The glassmaker?" Paige chimes in. "He apprentices with Tierney's father, doesn't he?"

Pain slices across Tierney's features, the soft rain outside hardening into a pelting downpour.

"Oh, that's *right*," Fallon says to Tierney with mock concern. "I heard something about your fancying him."

My neck burns with frustrated outrage.

Tierney doesn't move, doesn't look up at Fallon. Muted thunder rumbles and the heavens open up, a sheet of rain now obscuring the window's view.

"He kissed her," Fallon crows to Paige and Echo.

Tierney's head rises, hatred burning in her eyes. Lightning flashes, and the rain beats down harder.

Fallon sighs. "She said he has lips soft as silk."

Lightning flashes again, the windows rattling as if they'll blow in. Tierney grasps at the desk's edge, her eyes as dark as the storm. I worriedly look toward the window and wonder if Tierney's distress is somehow influencing the weather.

"Don't worry, Tierney," Fallon croons. "Fasting's soon to be mandatory. I'm sure the Council will even find someone for you." Fallon turns to Echo and Paige, fighting back the laughter. "Someone they want to punish." Fallon can't help herself; she laughs openly and glances sideways at Paige, who's fighting back a giggle. Echo shakes her head as if they're being impossibly childish.

Disgust wars with surprise inside me.

Fasting soon to be mandatory? When was that decided?

Losing interest in Tierney and ignoring the storm that's blown up out of nowhere, Fallon grabs up the package she's come in with. "Look what I've got," she crows. She pulls off the wrapping paper and brown string.

A new military uniform spills out. The darker gray of a Lead Apprentice; no more lower apprentice gray. Five wide stripes of silver are embroidered around the sleeve.

"Oh, Fallon," Paige gushes. "You've got your new uniform! The cloak, too?"

Fallon hangs her uniform on a wall hook, then unfurls a new cloak edged with another five stripes of silver.

Fallon throws the cloak on and swirls around.

Envy jabs at me as I take her in.

She looks dramatic and powerful and beautiful—the image of everything the Black Witch should be.

Fallon grins smugly. "And they're promoting me to full soldier at year's end. Twelfth Division."

"Oh, and that's Lukas's division!" Paige giddily enthuses. "You'll be together again!"

Of course they will be, I think bitterly. *A perfect match in both power and cruelty.*

"I'm not surprised they're promoting you early," Echo says with approval. "We need our Black Witch. And you're our best hope. Someone needs to put down that awful Resistance movement before it gets any more out of hand."

Out of hand? I wasn't aware the fight against the weak and shadowy Resistance had escalated.

"They attacked the Sixth Division Base only last week," Echo continues. "Dressed as our soldiers!"

Fallon spits out a dismissive laugh. "Oh, we'll take care of the heathens' little Resistance," she boasts, her hand jauntily on her hip. "We'll roast a few Keltic villages if they keep it up. The Resistance will be routed out and struck down soon enough."

My heart thuds high and hard in my chest.

Fallon swirls again, then grows petulant and plops down on Paige's bed. "He left today."

"Oh, how can you *bear* it?" Paige cries.

"You'll be fasted in no time," Echo assures her. "All that worry about Elloren Gardner for nothing. I told you to ignore the rumors."

Fallon glares at Echo accusingly. "Well, you were certainly friendly with her for a time."

Echo purses her lips at Fallon. "Yes, well, that was before I realized she was intent on being friends with a half-breed."

A spike of outrage over the slight to Gareth cuts into my debilitating fear.

Fallon pulls out her wand and sends up a puff of ice crystals from it. "What I would give for an excuse to freeze her blood."

Fear renewed, I shrink back against the wall.

"Fallon!" Echo chastises her sharply. "Don't joke so. She's a *Gardnerian*."

"She smells like an Icaral," Fallon snipes back with a smirk.

Diana snorts, still asleep, and kicks off her blanket.

Echo eyes Diana with horror. "She's so…disgusting! And *arrogant!*"

"And the way she tosses her hair!" Paige puts in, eager to be included.

Fallon rises, picks up a set of shears from the desk and grins at Echo. "I think it's time to teach the Lupine bitch a lesson."

Paige chews at her lip nervously. "Oh, I don't think that's such a good idea…"

Grinning widely and moving as stealthily as a cat, Fallon slides off her cloak and creeps toward Diana. I hold my breath as she kneels down on one knee, takes a thick bunch of Diana's hair and places the shears around it…

Fast as a blur, Diana leaps out of bed and slams Fallon to the ground. Paige lets out a scream, and Tierney and I fall back.

The next thing I know, Fallon is belly down on the floor and Diana is astride her, grasping both of Fallon's wrists in one hand, the shears in the other. Fallon cries out as Diana wrenches her arms behind her back and throws the shears toward the wall to impale Fallon's new uniform with a sharp *thwack*.

"You *dare* attack the daughter of an alpha?" Diana snarls. "You *fool*! Do you not think I can sense your attack? Even in my *sleep*?"

Diana holds her free hand in front of Fallon's face, and we all watch in complete horror as her hand morphs into a wild, hairy appendage with curved claws.

"If you ever try to attack me again, I will mark you. To remind you what happens to those who challenge the daughter of an alpha." Diana morphs her hand back, reaches under Fallon and grabs hold of her wand. "And your attempts to use your pathetic stick magic bore me!" She takes the wand in hand, snaps it in two and tosses it aside.

Fallon cries out as Diana gives her arms a final wrench, then, in another blur, Diana is off Fallon and looming over her. Fallon forces herself quickly to her feet, her face red and furious. She grasps at her forearms, wincing in pain.

Fallon shoots Diana a murderous look. "I'll be back for you!" she cries before fleeing from the room with Echo and Paige.

Diana tosses her blond mane over one shoulder and pads over to her bed. She grimaces at the blanket, throws it to the floor, then plops down onto the bed and curls up, her naked back to us.

Tierney turns toward my hiding place, her voice hoarse. "She's gone."

"Of course she's gone," Diana mumbles into her pillow. "She's a coward without her stick. You can come out now, Elloren Gardner."

My head jerks back with surprise. I look to Diana with dumbfounded awe.

"Elloren." Tierney pushes a box of vials toward me as I come back into the room. She gestures at the door with her chin, her eyes urgent.

Legs unsteady, I take the vials and let Tierney tug me out of the room.

"Who's Leander?" I ask Tierney once we're back in the deserted lab.

Tierney's work is uncharacteristically sloppy and slipshod as we rush to finish our project, topping off each vial with warm syrup.

It's full dark now, the apothecary lab's arching windows black as slate.

"Nobody," she says testily, not looking at me.

I wait, unmoving, until she finally relents.

"He works for my father." She shrugs, her mouth trembling. "He's…nothing to me." Her mouth turns down and she begins to cry, then sob, shoulders heaving, her head bent low. "He's *nothing*. I don't care… I don't care what happens to him…" Her arm comes up to cover her eyes, and she's momentarily unable to speak coherently through her tears. "Why did they do it?" she moans. "Why did they have to make me so *ugly*?"

Suddenly, water explodes from the few open containers in the room, flying to Tierney, swirling around her in a great rush.

My hands fly up to ward off the liquid. The swirling lines abruptly fizz into a great cloud, obscuring the view before me.

I can just make out Tierney's ghostly face in the white haze. She's staring at me, wide-eyed and terrified.

Fae. She's full-blooded Water Fae. That's the only explanation.

And someone "made" her ugly. Which means someone glamoured her. Her real hair is probably blue. Her skin, too.

And I'm bound by Gardnerian and Verpacian law to turn her in. Sheltering Fae is punishable by imprisonment.

I force the idea from my mind as the cloud falls to the ground in a thin puddle.

Maybe she isn't Fae. Maybe she's like me. Like Gareth. All of us Gardnerian, but with tainted blood, maybe. That's all. Hers is just...*extraordinarily* tainted.

No, I finally admit to myself, the crushing truth settling in. She's Fae. She'll be sent to the Pyrran Isles if she's discovered.

And she's done *nothing* to deserve any of this.

"Elloren..." Tierney starts, her throat hoarse. Gone is her usual guarded cynicism. She looks small and lost and afraid.

"No." I cut her off, bringing my hand up to stop her. "You don't have to explain yourself to me. Let's just not speak of it. Whatever it is."

I meet her eyes, and her face is an open book, filled with overwhelming, stunned gratitude.

Something shifts between us in that moment, and I can feel the beginnings of real friendship start to take root.

"Here," I say, grabbing a rag. "Let me help you clean this up."

Tierney nods stiffly, and I can see her fighting back more tears. She wordlessly picks up a rag, stoops down and together we clean up the floor.

Outside the rain has stopped, and a cold mist hangs in the air. As we start to walk away from the lab complex, we're approached by a young Gardnerian military apprentice with the tree insignia of the Twelfth Division.

He bows and hands me a letter. "I'm to give this to you, Mage," he says. He bows again stiffly and takes his leave.

I look down at the letter. My name is written on it in clean, elegant script. I break the wax seal, the Twelfth Division's River Oak, and pull the letter open as Tierney looks on over my shoulder.

I'm to rejoin my division at Essex.
I'll be back for you. At Yule.

Lukas

My heart speeds up, warmth flushing my face, then indignation.

The sheer arrogance of him.

How could he possibly think, after what happened with Ariel, that we could still go to this dance together? And yet…it's flattering that we could be so at odds, and *still* he's trying to pursue me.

"At Yule?" Tierney queries, pulling my thoughts back to the present.

"There's a dance," I explain, conflicted. "I promised to go with him."

Tierney's brows fly up in amazed surprise. "Oh, ho!" she crows, wickedly delighted. "Looks like Fallon Bane's going to wish she'd frozen your blood after all."

CHAPTER
TWENTY-FOUR

Diana Ulrich

Diana Ulrich slams her books down on the Chemistrie lab table, and Aislinn and I both jump, our eyes snapping up.

It's early the next morning, class about to start, two sleepy Kelt scholars shuffling in, followed by a straight-backed Elf.

Diana falls into her seat with a loud huff. Her brother looks over at her, raising his eyebrows.

"You would not believe what I had to deal with this morning!" she cries to him, her voice as loud as usual.

The Kelts turn and blink at her, the Elf shooting her a quick look of annoyance.

"What happened?" Diana's brother asks her calmly.

"I've been put on warning!"

"But why?"

Diana snorts indignantly. "Because of Fallon Bane, that stupid Gardnerian I am being forced to live with against my will!"

Aislinn and I shoot each other quick looks of surprise.

"I don't understand," Jarod says.

"Last night," Diana snipes, "Fallon Bane thought she would amuse herself by cutting my hair off while I slept."

Jarod whistles to himself and laughs softly. "Poor Fallon."

Diana's whole posture stiffens. "Poor *Fallon*?" she exclaims self-righteously. "She's a bully!"

Jarod makes a valiant attempt to rein in his amusement and look serious. "And I can just about imagine how you reacted," he says, suppressing a smile.

"I reacted with extraordinary restraint!" Diana proclaims, clearly annoyed that her brother isn't taking this more seriously.

"Does she still have four limbs?" he asks, not completely in jest, it seems.

"I simply gave her a warning."

"That was very diplomatic of you."

"And I broke her wand."

"Oh."

"And now I'm on academic warning! For 'interfering with the peaceful integration of cultures.' After that fool Mage tried to attack me in my sleep!" Jarod opens his mouth to say something, but Diana cuts him off. "I think Father was mistaken about these Gardnerians. There is no way to learn to live with them! They are pathetic and worthless and weak!"

Aislinn uncomfortably averts her eyes as I gape at Diana.

Jarod clears his throat and glares at his sister, his eyes flickering meaningfully over at Aislinn and me.

"What?" Diana snaps in annoyance.

Jarod sighs and rubs his forehead, gesturing toward us. "We happen to be sitting right by some Gardnerians," he points out.

Diana glances over at us, undaunted. "I don't mean Elloren and Aislinn. You two aren't the least bit pathetic and worthless. You're both somewhat pleasant. Unlike the vast majority of your race."

Jarod stops rubbing his forehead and just lets his head fall into his hands.

I'm surprised and oddly amused by Diana's reluctant compliment and Jarod's futile attempt to rein his sister in. I turn to Aislinn, who's regarding Diana and Jarod with equal amazement.

Jarod glances over and shoots us an apologetic look. He's been nothing but kind and diplomatic for weeks now. It seems foolish to keep our distance any longer.

"It's all right," I say, more to Jarod than to Diana, who doesn't seem the least bit sorry for the slight. "I'd be careful about Fallon, though. She's pretty vindictive."

Jarod looks over at me, clearly surprised that I'm addressing him directly.

"She's a bully," Diana says with a dismissive wave of her hand, "but she's too weak to be an effective one. With *me*, at least." She pauses to narrow her amber eyes at me. "She does seem to be obsessed with *you*, though, Elloren Gardner."

"Oh?" I say, trying to sound innocent.

"She doesn't like the fact that you look like your grandmother. It threatens her. She's also territorial about Lukas Grey. She wants him as her mate, but is afraid you will claim him first."

I color at her blunt statement. "I... I've only known Lukas for a couple of months," I stammer defensively.

"What does that matter?" Diana says with a snort. "My parents knew they were destined for each other when they first inhaled each other's scent. They took each other to mate that same day."

"They did?" I'm shocked by her bluntness.

Diana nods matter-of-factly. "That was twenty-five years ago."

That brings me up short. "That's a long time," I concede, chastened.

"Mmm," she agrees. "Well, Elloren Gardner," she says, "I hope you are the one to claim this Lukas Grey. Fallon Bane is a fool, and even though you are a Gardnerian, you seem nice. Aislinn, too. Nicer than the others."

I swallow uncomfortably, thinking of Ariel's dead kindred. A situation I caused.

No, Diana's mistaken. I'm not nice. And even if I did want Lukas Grey, claiming him seems akin to playing with dragons.

I ponder Diana's precarious lodging situation as I walk back from my kitchen labor the next night. A full moon shines overhead, and the air is crisp and clear. Pulling my cloak tight to fight off the chill, I walk alongside a small, scrubby side field that borders the wilds. The field lies near a long series of men's lodging houses, and I can hear men's voices up ahead. Small knots of dark figures linger outside a half-open doorway, talking and laughing, most windows of the low, thatched-roof lodging houses warmed by the deep golden glow of lamplight. Squinting over at the men, I strain to see if I can make out one of my brothers.

A rustling from the forest catches my ear, and I turn to see Diana emerging from the trees.

Completely naked.

Seeing me, Diana breaks into a wide, exhilarated grin. She strides toward me, oblivious to the two Gardnerian men down the path who halt to gawk at her.

The moonlight shines on Diana's bare skin, rendering her almost blue-white. Her body is long and slender, all lean muscle, but curvaceous enough to interest any man. She isn't the slightest bit self-conscious as she approaches.

"Hello, Elloren," she says casually.

I am absolutely mortified on her behalf, my mouth agape. "Why...why are you naked...*out here*?" I stammer.

She looks down at herself as if she hadn't noticed, her face registering some confusion at the question. "I just came back from a run in the woods." As if her reasoning should be obvious.

"Without *clothes*?" My voice comes out high-pitched.

Diana laughs and looks at me as if I'm a child who just babbled something very silly. "Of course without clothes," she replies, smiling. "I can't very well Change in my clothes. They'd be destroyed."

I'm stunned by her outrageous nudity.

My eyes dart to the men. I hurriedly pull my cloak off. "Here," I urgently offer, "put my cloak on. I'll walk back with you."

"I don't need a cloak," she says, refusing it, perplexed by my stridency. "Anyway, my clothes are right over there on the bench."

"You mean you undressed *here*? In full view of the men's lodging?"

Now she's regarding me like I'm mentally unhinged. "Really, Elloren, it's as good a place as any." Diana's face takes on a rapturous look. She lifts her head into the cool night air and inhales deeply. "You should have seen the forest tonight. It was *so* beautiful! The moon is so bright. There's a lake about an hour's run in." She motions happily in the direction from which she came. "The moon's reflection on the lake was dazzling, like liquid silver on water. And the hunting here…it's glorious!" Diana grins widely, her strong, white teeth glistening in the moonlight like a set of dangerous pearls. She regards me for a moment as if she feels a little sorry for me. "It's a pity you can't see the forest like we can."

The small knot of men by the lodging house has stopped talking and are now focused in on Diana, one of the men gesturing for someone inside to come out and see. My panic for her rises.

"Please put my cloak on. Those men are staring at you."

Diana glances around as if noticing them for the first time. "I don't care," she says dismissively, swatting the air with the back of her hand. "Besides, I'm hot from my run. I want to cool off first."

"You can't… Diana, you've *got* to put some clothes on!" *Ancient One, she's stubborn.*

She's beginning to look irritated. "Why? Really, *why*? It's ridiculous that this means so much to you people."

"Because being unclothed is not allowed. You could seriously get kicked out for this. I think…it means something here that maybe you're not aware of."

"What?"

"They'll think you want to sleep with them!" I blurt out, mortified by my own scandalous words.

She looks over at them, irritated. "I am not tired. I always feel energized after I hunt."

"No, no. That's not what I mean. I meant that they might think you want to…to *be* with them."

She stares at me blankly. "I do not understand."

"They'll think you want to have relations with them!" I can feel my face burning. Gardnerians just don't *speak* about these things.

"Are you saying—" she puts a hand on one of her hips and motions to the growing audience "—that they'll think I want to take one of them as my *mate*?"

"Yes! Exactly!" I cry.

"Oh, *please*, Elloren, you must be *kidding*! Not one of them is worthy to be my mate." She shoots the watching men a look of utter contempt. "They are weak. I am strong and magnificent. I need an equally strong mate, one of my kind. Besides, your men have too many strange ideas. I don't understand them."

"*Please* take my cloak!" I'm growing desperate.

Ignoring me, Diana starts for the bench just as Echo and some other young Gardnerian women round the corner and look over to see what all the men are staring at. They spot me, then gasp in horror when they catch sight of Diana. They hide their eyes and quickly hurry away.

I open my mouth as if to call out something in my defense, embarrassed over being caught near a buck-naked Lupine.

I catch up with Diana, who's now standing near the bench

stretching, her hands high above her head, bending this way and that as she stares contentedly at the moon.

Just then, my brother Rafe comes around the bend, his bow and quiver and hunting bag thrown over his shoulder. He does a complete double take when he sees Diana, his eyes going wide, then narrowing as he looks around, taking in the entire situation, his brow furrowing in concern. As he walks quickly over to us, I feel my face growing even hotter, not knowing which way to look.

"Hello, Elloren," he says, greeting me, his expression devoid of the usual grin.

"Hi, Rafe," I say weakly, at a complete loss.

He turns to Diana, who's regarding him with some curiosity. I motion to Rafe weakly. "Diana, this is my brother, Rafe."

"You must be the Lupine girl," he states matter-of-factly, like there isn't a stark-naked female in front of him. This really is completely surreal, and the most wildly mortifying thing that has ever happened to me.

Diana inhales deeply, closing her eyes for a moment. She opens them and looks at Rafe intently. "You smell nice. Like the forest."

"Yes, well… I spent the last few days as a hunting guide around the Verpacian range." Rafe motions toward the mountains behind him.

"Did you see the lake tonight? The one to the east, about an hour's run in?" Diana enthuses.

I listen, completely dumbfounded as they launch into a conversation about the beauty of the forest, the abundance and health of the game, the best hunting areas. My brother is speaking to her as if he's completely oblivious to her lack of attire, keeping his gaze militantly focused on her eyes.

Rafe glances over at our audience.

Diana follows his gaze, a look of annoyance crossing her features. "Why are they still staring at me?"

"I don't think you realize it," says Rafe politely, "but it's *really* not acceptable to go without clothing here."

"Oh, I'm just about to put them on," she says unhurriedly. "I'm just cooling off from my run."

"I understand that," he says. "I've read about your people, so I'm familiar with some of your ways, but it is *really* important, Diana, that you put on some clothing. *Now.*"

Diana narrows her eyes at him and seems, at last, to infer that there could be something serious at stake here, as ridiculous as it seems to her. "All right," she says warily, still looking closely at Rafe.

I quickly wrap my cloak around her, hearing some murmurs of disappointment from a few of the men. At my urging, Diana gives in and goes back into the forest to throw on her clothes before emerging once more, only fully clothed this time. The young men shoot her dark looks, then quickly disperse.

"I'm thirsty," Diana announces imperiously.

"Well, then," says Rafe, "why don't we all go over to the dining hall and get something to drink?"

"It is not our custom to be unclothed," Rafe explains as I bring over a tray with hot tea and dried fruit from the kitchens.

"Yes, yes, I know, but it's ridiculous," Diana counters. "How do you bathe? You don't smell bad, so you must bathe. My ridiculous roommates are very crazed about no one walking in on them in the washroom, but I assume there is bathing going on."

Rafe smirks at this. "Yes, we bathe, but it's unacceptable for us to be unclothed around other people."

"Even little children? Even babies? Do they always need to be clothed?"

"Yes. Everyone needs to be clothed. Especially older children and adults. And they can't *ever* be unclothed around people of the opposite sex."

"Ever?" Diana screws her face up in wry disbelief. "How do

you mate? There are quite a lot of you, so you must mate at some point."

Rafe lets out a surprised laugh, spitting out some of his tea as he does so. Diana smiles at him smugly.

"I would assume...there is, in fact...the removal of cloth- ing," Rafe concedes, his eyes swimming with amusement as he stumbles over his response. "But in all seriousness, Diana, I know it seems ludicrous to you, but there are...religious beliefs that condemn it."

"What?"

"Nudity."

"*Religious* beliefs?"

"Yes," he tells her. "There are people who would assume that because you're comfortable being naked, that you have no mor- als...and that you would...mate with any man."

"That's ridiculous," Diana says, waving her hand in the air. "We mate for life."

"I know. But *here*, there are men who would mate with you who have no desire for a life bond. They wouldn't even have to like you."

Diana pauses and stares at Rafe for a long moment, her mouth agape. "That is very shocking. This is extremely immoral." Diana purses her lips in disapproval, glowering at my brother. "You are a strange people." Someone across the room catches Diana's eye, and she holds up a hand to get his attention. "Jarod," she calls to her brother.

Jarod sees her, smiles and approaches our table.

"What we heard about their people is true," Diana says to him, with no lead-in. She motions to us with a wave of her hand. "These people will mate with people they *don't even like*." She's clearly appalled.

Rafe holds up both hands at Diana, as if warding off this ac- cusation. "I meant that *some* Gardnerians and Kelts are like this, not *all*," he vehemently clarifies.

Jarod's face takes on a shocked expression as he sits on a chair next to Diana, straddling it backward. "Really?" he asks his sister in a low voice, ashamed on our behalf. "I thought that was just a nasty rumor."

"As did I," Diana agrees. "I thought Father was exaggerating." She turns to me censoriously. "Have you mated in this way, Elloren?"

I nearly spit out all the tea in my mouth. "*Me? No!* I've never..." My voice gets smaller and tighter with each word.

"And you." Diana jabs a finger at Rafe. "Have you mated in this way? With someone you don't even care for?"

"No!" Rafe says defensively, his hands flying up again. "Like my sister, I haven't..." He trails off.

Diana relaxes her accusatory posture, sits back in her chair and sighs deeply. "I have not yet taken a mate, either, although I am greatly looking forward to it." She smiles happily at the prospect, then points to Jarod with her thumb. "My brother has also not yet taken someone to mate."

Jarod grins brightly at us. "I, too, greatly look forward to it."

"You must be looking forward to taking a mate, Elloren," said Diana, her tone conversational. "You're almost of age." She and her brother smile at me expectantly, and I begin to wonder how hot my face can get before it causes some type of physical problem. I desperately want to crawl under the table and disappear.

"Listen," says Rafe, leaning forward toward Diana, grasping his mug with both hands. "I happen to agree with you that it is morally wrong to...*be* with someone you don't care for. I just want to clarify that."

"You know," I say to Jarod and Diana, "I've heard quite a few rumors about Lupines, as well."

They both lean forward with interest.

"Really?" asks Diana. "What type of rumors?"

I instantly regret saying it. There's no way out now. I take

a deep breath and spit it out. "I heard you sometimes mate...
as wolves."

Neither one of them so much as bats an eyelash.

"That's true," Diana brags. "My parents conceived my brother
and me as wolves." She smiles thinking about it. "*That's* why
I'm such a good hunter!"

"It's true," agrees Jarod. "She's one of the best hunters in the
pack." Diana's smile brightens at her brother's praise.

I'm speechless for a moment, then manage to collect myself
enough to continue. I can't get any more embarrassed than I
already am, so I figure I might as well lay all the cards out on
the table. "I also heard," I continue, hesitantly, "that sometimes
you mate when...your men are in wolf form...and your women
are in...human form."

They both stare at me blankly, their mouths agape.

Finally, Jarod turns to Diana, an incredulous look on his face.
"Would that even be physically possible?"

Diana continues to stare at me. "That's ridiculous," she spits
out, her tone clipped.

"Some interesting conversations you've been having with the
morally upstanding girls of Gardneria," muses Rafe, grinning
widely at me. I shoot him an annoyed look.

"Let me guess," he speculates. "Did that one come from
Echo Flood?"

"Fallon Bane," I admit.

"Figures," he says, chuckling to himself.

"What other rumors have you heard about us?" asks Diana.
"That last one was very creative."

"I really don't want to offend you," I say.

Diana waves her hand in the air dismissively. "Your people's
ignorance reflects badly on them, not on us."

"I was told you mate in front of your entire pack."

Again the blank stares.

"That's just simply untrue," said Diana, sounding truly offended for the first time.

"Mating is a *private* thing," Jarod adds, looking at us like we're foolish to need this explained.

"Where would they get such ideas about us?" Diana asks, perplexed.

"I think nudity gets our people's minds going off in all sorts of strange directions," offers Rafe.

"Well," says Diana with a sigh, "I've heard lots of fantastic rumors about your people, as well."

"Like what?" I ask, curious if hers are as colorful as ours.

She leans forward, her voice low. "I heard that you force girls as young as thirteen to choose a mate."

"That's actually true," I say, thinking of Paige Snowden. "It's called wandfasting. It's a magical way of binding people together as future mates. It creates the marks that you see on the hands of most of the Gardnerian women here. Sometimes the girls are quite young."

Jarod and Diana stare at me gravely.

"But you can't possibly be old enough at thirteen to choose your life mate," counters Diana, shaking her head.

"They're chosen *for* you, usually," I clarify, thinking of Aislinn.

Jarod and Diana glance at each other, disapproval written all over their faces.

"But what if you don't *love* the person? What if you don't care for their scent?" Diana seems greatly upset by the prospect of such a thing. "Do you still have to mate with them?"

"Well, yes," I say, realizing how awful this must sound to her. It *is* awful.

"That is truly terrible," murmurs Diana. She glances at my hands then Rafe's. "Yet neither of you are fasted."

I share a quick glance with my brother. "My uncle wants us to wait," I tell Diana. "He thinks we should be older."

"You absolutely should," Diana states with an emphatic nod.

"I heard that your men mate with seals...even if they have life mates," Jarod blurts out.

Diana turns to her brother, a mortified expression on her face. *"Jarod!"*

"That's what I heard," he says, shrugging his shoulders defensively at her.

Rafe sighs. "Some of our men do this. The seals are called Selkies, and they can take human form."

"What?" I choke out, really shocked. "Aunt Vyvian told me people kept them as *pets*."

Rafe cocks an eyebrow and shoots me an uncomfortable look. "They're not pets, Ren."

Disgust washes over me as the obscene truth of things falls into place.

"This is very sordid," mutters Diana, embarrassed for us. "Perhaps these shocking things would not come about if you mated at a reasonable age with people you care deeply for, like we do. This is very unnatural, the way you mate."

"There are happy Gardnerian couples," I counter defensively. "My parents loved each other very much."

"Which is why you and your brother have good morals, unlike the others of your kind," Diana states emphatically.

"What happened to your parents?" Jarod asks softly, catching my past tense where Diana did not.

"They died when we were very young," I reply, staring down at my tea. When I glance up, Diana's face is filled with sadness.

"I am so sorry to hear this," she says.

I just shrug, momentarily at a loss for words and suddenly aware of how late it is and how tired I feel. I think about my quilt and how much I wish it was still here so that I could wrap myself up in it. Diana's hand gently touches my arm.

"You must come home with us the next time we visit our

pack," she says, her voice kind. "They would like you very much. I think you would find many friends there."

I'm startled to find my eyes filling with tears. Blinking them back, I struggle to maintain my composure. "Thank you," I say, my voice cracking as I keep my eyes focused on my mug. "That's very kind of you to offer."

Diana gives my arm a warm squeeze before releasing it. I look up at her, her face an open book like her brother's, devoid of guile. Aside from the uncomfortably blunt questions about mating, I have a sudden feeling that I would actually like Diana's people.

"It seems as if we may have been mistaken about them," Aislinn tells me a few evenings later as we sit on a bench outside, staring up at the waning moon and discussing the Lupines. We pull our cloaks tight around us as a cold breeze rustles the dry autumn leaves clinging to the tree above us, our heavy book bags on the ground next to us.

"I know," I agree.

"But really, Elloren," she says, "some of their behavior. It's still...*really* shocking."

"But not evil, really."

Aislinn is silent for a moment, considering this before speaking again. "But I just don't understand. I overheard my father telling my mother about the Lupines once. The Mage Council sent him on a diplomatic mission to the Northern packs. While he was there, a male Lupine suddenly announced to the entire pack that he was going to mate with one of the females, and then he just...well, he dragged her out into the woods. Why would my father say something so shocking if it wasn't true?"

"I don't know," I admit, my face tensing at the puzzle.

"Maybe the Northern packs are different," Aislinn says hopefully. "Maybe Jarod and Diana's pack is more moral."

"Perhaps."

"I just can't imagine Jarod doing something so shocking."

I look back up at the moon, small gray clouds drifting lazily around it.

"You know," Aislinn furtively admits, "Jarod gave me a poem today. About the moon."

I'm not surprised by this. What began as a small trickle of stealth correspondence in Chemistrie lab has quickly become a steady stream, so much so that Diana flat-out refused to be a courier. Instead, she and I rearranged ourselves so that Jarod and Aislinn could have the aisle seats.

Aislinn opens one of her stealth books, fishes a neatly folded piece of paper out of it and hands it to me. I open it and read Jarod's flowing script by the thin lamplight.

It's a poem about loneliness and yearning, the moon a bright witness to it.

"It's beautiful," I tell her as I refold it, feeling as if I'm intruding on something private.

"I know," she acknowledges, her voice dreamy, far away.

"Aislinn," I venture with some hesitation, "I saw you and Jarod together. In the archives last night."

They were sitting, a book open before them as they huddled together, their heads and hands almost touching. They seemed oblivious to the rest of the world, enthralled with each other, both of their faces lit up as they talked in animated, hushed tones. Unable to hold back their shy smiles.

Aislinn blushes and looks down at her lap. She shrugs. "I guess we're becoming...friends of sorts. Strange, isn't it? Me. Friends with a Lupine." She looks up at me. "It's all perfectly innocent, you know. Jarod's family is bringing him to visit the Northern packs this summer so he can look for a mate, and he knows I'm about to be fasted to Randall. We're just...friends."

"I know," I said. "I just worry."

Aislinn's brow knits tight. "If my family knew I was on speaking terms with him...my father would pull me out of University.

That's why we only meet late in the evenings. It's just that we both love books so much. It's so nice to have someone to discuss literature with who's so…insightful. He's incredibly well-read."

"Seems he's as well-read as you," I concur.

"You know, Elloren," Aislinn says, her voice tentative, "talking to Jarod…it just makes me wonder if…if our people might be mistaken about some things."

I settle back, catching sight of a familiar constellation through the branches. "I know what you mean."

We're quiet for a moment, looking up at the stars.

Chilled, I slide my hands into my cloak pockets. My hand scrapes against hard, jagged pieces.

Lukas's broken portrait. I'd completely forgotten about it.

I fish it out of my pocket and hold it in my opened palm. I push the two pieces together to form his ridiculously handsome visage.

Aislinn gapes. "You have a portrait? Of *Lukas Grey?*"

I nod, resigned. "I broke it by accident and lifted it from Fallon's room." I fill Aislinn in on everything that happened, including Diana's outrageous nudity and how effectively she dealt with Fallon Bane.

Aislinn struggles to keep down the incredulous laughter that's bubbling up, and I start to laugh, too.

Aislinn shakes her head as she fights back her grin, gesturing toward the portrait. "Fallon will freeze you if she finds out."

I slide the pieces back into my pocket and pat the side of my cloak. "Not if it's safely hidden away, she won't."

My fingers worry the portrait pieces through my cloak as trepidation pricks at me.

She'll never find out. How could she?

It's later that same evening when Ariel finally speaks to me again.

The room is a completely different place than it used to be.

Wynter and I have cleaned it up, and the majority of the room, except for Ariel's third of it, is now neatly swept and organized. A small rookery that Rafe has thrown together now sits by Ariel's bed. It houses two stolen chickens and an owl with a broken wing that Ariel has been nursing back to health.

I have to admit, I'm a bit fascinated by the owl and enjoy watching the smooth way it can rotate its head almost completely around, as well as looking into its beautiful, wide eyes. I've never been so close to one before.

Ariel is an apprentice in animal husbandry, her desk a haphazard jumble of books devoted mainly to avian medicine. As unfocused and unhinged as she is around people, with animals, she's calm and skillful. She loves birds especially, even to the point where she refuses to eat them.

I lie on my bed in the warm room, studying, a mountain of books and notes surrounding me, a fire roaring in the fireplace and casting a soft glow over everything. The owl and the chickens are perched on Ariel's bed next to her, and Wynter is sitting on the floor, sketching the owl, while Ariel pats it gently.

Ariel unexpectedly looks over at me, eyes narrowed, her head resting on a pillow. "You could have had me sent away."

The sound of her rough voice startles me, and Wynter's sketching hand freezes in place.

It takes me a moment to find my voice. "I know."

"I hurt you," she insists. "You were bloody and covered in bruises. You could have had me sent to...to that place."

"I know," I say again, ashamed and uncomfortable. "I decided not to."

"But," she presses, becoming angry, "you were bloody..."

"I told everyone that I tripped down the stairs."

She continues to stare at me as her eyes take on a glazed, pained expression. "I still hate you, you know."

I swallow and nod. Of course she does. I deserve it. She destroyed a precious belonging, but I caused the death of something living, something she loved.

"I don't expect you to ever stop hating me," I finally say with effort. "But I want you to know… I'm sorry for what happened to your kindred. I didn't know Lukas would do that… I didn't think… I was so angry at you. I'm sorry."

"It doesn't matter," she says flatly, cutting me off and rolling onto her back, staring blankly at the ceiling. "She's better off dead than here. I wish I was dead."

I'm shocked. "Don't say that."

"All right," Ariel amends, her mouth curling up into an angry sneer. "I wish you were dead instead. And every other scholar here. Except for Wynter."

It's a fair enough sentiment, and I let it hang in the air unchallenged as Wynter regards Ariel with sad understanding and then turns to me, her expression softening to a warm look of approval.

I turn my attention back to my text, unexpectedly touched. And, oddly enough, I feel, for the first time since I've come to the University, a small sense of peace blooming inside me.

CHAPTER
TWENTY-FIVE

Trystan

"Where's Rafe?"

"Rafe's out," Trystan says absently as he lies on his bed, not bothering to look up from the large Physiks text he's engrossed in.

The eleventh month has come, and with it a killing frost, the trees suddenly laid bare, the fire in the North Tower now a necessity.

It's late, the end of another week, and I've spent the last hour wrestling with my *History of Gardneria* text, new questions clamoring for my attention as I read and reread parts of the large volume. Things aren't adding up, and I want to talk to Rafe about it.

We're supposed to be Gardnerians, the Blessed Ones, the First Children, blameless and pure. And all of the other races are supposed to be the Evil Ones, the Cursed Ones. But more and more it seems as if life has the disturbing habit of refusing to align itself into such neat columns.

It's all extremely confusing.

"What's Rafe doing?" I ask as Trystan continues to read.

"Hiking. As usual," he says absently.

"Oh." That's disappointing. Rafe's always out and unavailable lately.

"He's hiking with Diana Ulrich," Trystan says as an after-thought. "He's been out hiking with her every night this week."

My eyes widen. "He has?"

Trystan glances up at me, perplexed by my surprise.

"She's the Lupine girl," I point out.

"I know," he says calmly, looking back down at his book, as if the idea of Rafe spending so much time with a shapeshifter is somehow normal.

I think back to that night in the dining hall, to the way Rafe and Diana seemed to instantly fall in with each other. The look on her face when she glanced back at him, just before leaving.

"Don't you think that's a little...strange?" I prod.

Trystan shrugs. "Life is strange."

My worry spikes. Rafe can't become interested in a Lupine. He'll bring the wrath of two powerful races straight onto his head. And hers, too.

"Do you think they...like each other?"

"Maybe," Trystan says flatly.

I blink at him, really concerned now. "She's a *shapeshifter*."

Both his eyebrows go up. "Translation: 'she's an Evil One'?"

"Sweet Ancient One, no," I sputter, sounding shrill and de-fensive to my own ears. "Of course I don't think she's evil, but... but Rafe can't like her that way. Our people aren't exactly on good terms with each other."

Trystan smirks, his tone bitter. "So you think affection re-spects diplomatic pettiness?"

I fume at his sarcasm. "Perhaps it should. When it's hazard-ous to your future."

Trystan rolls his eyes and goes back to reading.

"How can you be so calm?" I don't know why I'm asking him that. Trystan is always calm. And right now it's driving me up the wall.

"Ren, maybe they're just friends."

I snort derisively at this. "Have you even met her?"

"No," Trystan replies, his tone clipped. "I haven't."

"Well, she can be infuriating. And arrogant." *And brave. And kind. But she's placing our brother in potentially serious danger.* "And she runs around naked half the time!" I insist. "And now she's trying to steal our brother away from us."

There are things I'm growing to truly like about Diana, admire even, but I push them roughly to the back of my mind. I know I'm being wrongheaded, and I'm ashamed of my words even as I say them, but this is a road that could lead to disaster. There's just no way around that fact.

Trystan's eyes flicker up briefly from his book. He looks at me like I'm becoming mentally unhinged. "Do you honestly think someone could steal...*Rafe?*"

"She has bewitched him with her beauty."

Trystan rolls his eyes at me. "They're probably just walking around in the woods, Ren."

How can he be so infuriatingly blind? "No. She's trying to sink her claws, and I do mean *claws*, into him."

Trystan smiles slightly at this.

I plop down on the bed behind me and glare at him in consternation, my arms crossed tightly in front of me. He goes back to reading his text, doing his best to ignore me as I sit there stupidly fuming.

Just then Yvan barges in, a bag slung over his shoulder, a pile of large texts under one arm. He stops dead in his tracks when he sees me and freezes, his expression rearranging itself into the familiar intense appearance he always wears when I'm around.

"What?" I snap at him, stung by his persistent unfriendly behavior.

He doesn't answer me, just stands there looking mortified, spots of color lighting both his cheeks. I suddenly realize, in complete embarrassment, that I'm sitting on his bed.

"Oh, I'm so sorry," I quickly apologize, grabbing my books and bag as I shoot up, my face also coloring deeply. Gardnerian and Keltic girls do *not* sit on men's beds, not unless the man is a brother. This is a huge breach of etiquette.

Yvan stiffly pulls off his dark woolen cloak and throws it on the bed, along with his bag and books, as if marking his territory, and fixes me with another intense, green-eyed glare. Then he grabs some texts and stalks over to the desk near his bed.

I, in turn, take a seat at the foot of Trystan's bed, my back slumped down against the wall behind me, my face hot and uncomfortable. The room has become claustrophobic, but I'm determined to stay so that I can confront Rafe about all this gallivanting with Diana. I pull my own books out, and the three of us retreat into the transient escape of study.

Every now and then I glance over at Trystan, and am surprised to catch him peering at Yvan's back, his expression a bit odd, almost liquid, like he's slipping into a dream state.

Feeling my stare, Trystan quickly looks back down at his book, and I nonchalantly peek at Yvan out of the corner of my eye to try and figure out what, exactly, Trystan is seeing.

Yvan is resting his forehead on his hand as he reads, his body stiff and ill at ease. It's a Physicians' Guild text, and I can make out surgical diagrams on the pages he's open to.

Yvan cuts a nice figure, I reluctantly admit. He's long and lean, and when his piercing green eyes aren't tense, they're stunning. My eyes are increasingly drawn to him in the kitchens, his strength and lithe grace tangling my thoughts and setting my heart thudding harder. I can't help but remember how he looked when he smiled at Fern on my first day in the kitchens—how dazzling that smile was, how devastatingly handsome I found him to be.

I bite the inside of my cheek in annoyance.

Why does he have to be so distractingly good-looking? And why do

I have to find him so attractive when he clearly doesn't like me at all? And besides—he's a Kelt!

But I can't help but notice that his hostility toward me has lessened lately. I catch him in the kitchens, sometimes, eyeing me back with those intense green eyes of his. As if he's trying to figure me out. It always sends an unsettling warmth prickling through me. But soon after our eyes meet, there's always that searing flash of anger as he glares at me, then looks sharply away.

After about an hour of tension-filled silence, Yvan abruptly shuts his book, gets up, grabs the bag on his bed and storms out of the room, slamming the door behind him. The thick, uncomfortable tension in the room leaves with him, and I breathe a deep sigh of relief at his going.

"I don't know how you can stand living with him," I tell Trystan. "He's so intense."

Trystan doesn't say anything. His eyes flicker up to meet mine for a brief second before making their way back down to his book.

"Hey," I say suspiciously, "why were you staring at him?"

Trystan doesn't say anything for a moment, continuing to focus on his book as I wait impatiently for his response.

"Because he's beautiful," Trystan finally says, his voice so low it's almost a whisper.

The words hang in the air between us, and I can feel the weight of them pressing down on me. I have a sudden, uncomfortable feeling that things I've long been ignoring are becoming undeniable.

"What do you mean?" I ask slowly.

He doesn't answer me, only stiffens and continues to stare at his book.

I'm misinterpreting him. I have to be. Yvan *is* beautiful. Achingly so. Trystan's just stating an obvious fact. But the *way* he said it.

Unwelcome thoughts begin to assert themselves. Whereas

I've often seen Rafe flirting with girls and noticing the pretty ones walking when we'd travel to the large, open-air winter markets, I've never once seen Trystan notice a girl. He's always been happy to just spend time with Gareth.

Trystan's eyes flicker up to meet mine again, his expression sad and defiant at the same time. I'm barely breathing, my mouth agape.

"Oh, Trystan. Please tell me you're not saying…"

His mouth tightens into a hard line, his expression pained.

"You can't really think he's…beautiful. You can't think that way. Trystan, tell me you don't mean it that way."

He doesn't respond and plasters his eyes to a spot on his book as panic rears up inside me.

"Holy Ancient One, Trystan, does Yvan know?"

Yvan can't know. No one can know this.

"I think so," Trystan says stiffly. "Maybe that's why he's so careful not to undress around me."

"Oh, Trystan," I breathe, panic clamoring at the edges of my thoughts, "this is really bad."

"I know," he admits tightly.

"The Mage Council…they throw people in prison who…"

"I know, Ren."

"You can't be this way. You just *can't*. You have to change."

Trystan continues to stare rigidly at the book. "I don't think I can," he says softly.

"Then you can't tell anyone," I insist, shaking my head for emphasis. "No one can know."

"Don't you think I know that?" His voice is still calm, but I can hear pain breaking through. And an edge of anger.

"Who else knows?" I ask, my thoughts spinning out in all directions.

"I think Rafe's figured it out."

"And what does he think?"

Trystan lets out a deep breath. "You know Rafe. He goes

351

his own way on practically everything. And lets others do the same."

"What about Uncle Edwin?"

"I don't know."

"And Gareth?"

"Gareth knows," he says succinctly.

"You told him?"

Why did he tell Gareth and not me? I feel a sharp pang of hurt.

"He figured it out."

"How?"

Trystan finally abandons the pretense of reading and closes his book. "He knows because I tried to kiss him."

My face flies open in shock. "You tried to kiss...*Gareth*?" For a moment I just gape at him. "What...what did he do? When you tried to..."

"When I tried to *kiss* him?" he cuts in sharply. "He told me he was sorry, but he was only attracted to women."

We stare at each other for a long moment, the ramifications of his being this way like a dark storm brewing.

I rub at my aching head. "Oh, Trystan," I say, stunned. My religion has just been turned into a weapon. Aimed straight at my brother. "They'll see you as one of the Evil Ones. If anyone finds out..."

"I know."

I shake my head, feeling dazed. "I seem to be collecting them these days, you know."

"Evil Ones?"

"Icarals, Lupines—" *A hidden Water Fae.* "—and now you."

Trystan shrugs slightly in response, suddenly looking very tired.

I gently nudge his foot. "I know you're not evil, you know," I softly tell him.

He nods back at me, seeming momentarily at a loss for words.

I sigh deeply, pressing my head back hard against the wall,

staring up at the play of shadows on the ceiling rafters from the flickering fireplace and lamplight.

"I'm beginning to think it's all hogwash anyway," I tell him. "All this stuff about Evil Ones. But that doesn't change the fact that everyone else seems to believe it." I swivel my head on the wall to look at him with concern. "Trystan, I'm really worried about you now. I can't..." Tears prick at my eyes as an unbidden image forms of Trystan being taken away, thrown into prison somewhere. A fierce urgency wells up inside me, accompanied by a very justified fear for my brother's safety. "You've got to keep this secret."

"I know, Ren," he says softly.

"I'm not kidding. This is very dangerous. Promise me. Promise me you won't tell anyone."

"I promise. I'll be careful," he assures me, and I know he's being serious and humoring me at the same time. But it will have to be enough for now.

CHAPTER TWENTY-SIX

History

Over the next few days Yvan's intense and aloof manner toward me begins to seriously chafe at my nerves, made worse by my sharp fear that Yvan knows Trystan's secret. I take to nervously carrying on one-sided conversations with Yvan, desperate to engage him and win his favor.

This particular evening, we're both cutting up a large pile of turnips, just about my least favorite kitchen task. Iris is kneading bread dough on the next table over, her flaxen hair tied up into pretty braids. I can feel her territorial attention on me, her eyes flitting up to glower at me every so often—a Gardnerian so unforgivably close to *her* Yvan.

It stings to see Iris and Yvan together sometimes. To hear them laughing in a corner, to witness their easy camaraderie, her casual touches on his shoulder, his arm, his hand. It's clear they're old friends, but is there more?

Do they kiss in the shadows? Sneak off late at night to the barn's dark loft?

I immediately chastise myself for having such thoughts.

Yvan's a Kelt, and one who dislikes me intensely. I need to ignore how just the sight of him can set my blood racing. Being attracted to a Kelt is pointless enough. In this case, it's more than a little bit dangerous.

Thoughts of Lukas suddenly come to mind, and I flush, wondering what he'd make of me privately mooning over a Kelt.

Ignoring Iris's nasty looks, I lever my knife down on the hard root before me with a loud *thwap*. I find dealing with these starchy vegetables to be as enjoyable as trying to slice through rocks.

I'm relieved a few minutes later, when Iris finally wipes off her hands and steps out. Now is my chance to talk to Yvan, to try to win him to our side—to convince him not to reveal my brother's secret.

My eyes flit toward him. "So, how are you this evening?" I ask in the most pleasant, honey-coated voice I can muster. Predictably, he just glowers at me briefly before focusing militantly on chopping up the turnips in front of him.

In desperation, I babble on and on about the weather, what I had for lunch, anything inane I can think of to spark his interest as Urisk kitchen workers come and go around us in the flurry of activity almost always present here.

"...And my aunt Vyvian just sent me some new dresses. I think she feels guilty about lodging me with Icarals." I throw waxy turnip peels into a large, wooden bowl. "It was quite a surprise to get her gift," I prattle on. "I think she's trying to win me over via pleasant means, since punishment isn't working. I'm wearing one of the dresses now. Isn't it lovely?"

The dress *is* lovely, with delicate Ironflowers embroidered in deep blue all over the midnight-black silk.

Yvan stops slicing turnips and pauses, stone-still, the newly sharpened knife clenched tight in his hand. *"What?"* he asks, his eyes two furious slits.

An actual response. Amazing. Though his tone isn't exactly what I'd hoped it would be. "My dress," I repeat congenially. "Isn't the embroidery lovely?"

Yvan sets the knife carefully down on the table and swivels around in his chair to face me. "No," he says, his voice heavy with disgust. "I think it's revolting."

I blink at Yvan in shock. Angry hurt pricks at my insides like tiny pins, and my face starts to flush. My eyes go hard on him. "You overwhelm me with your charm sometimes, do you know that?"

"Those clothes," he continues caustically, gesturing sharply at my dress, "were made from the blood and sweat of slaves."

"What are you talking about?" I counter. "Aunt Vyvian got them from a dress shop in Valgard."

"Do you have any idea who actually *makes* your fancy silks?"

"No...no, I don't...but..."

He leans in toward me confrontationally, and I shrink back slightly, intimidated. "Embroidery that intricate? It was done by Urisk workers. On the Fae Islands. Many of them children. Working for practically nothing, beaten if they try to protest."

He's lying. He has to be. He's just trying to be mean.

I glower at him, nervously biting at my lip, but his steady glare doesn't waver, and I have the overwhelmingly uncomfortable feeling that he's telling me the truth.

"I... I didn't know..." I croak out defensively.

"You don't *want* to know. None of you want to know," he spits back. "So, *no*, I don't like your dress. I think both you and your dress are revolting."

A sharp pain stabs at my temple, and my stomach clenches as his words cut through me to the core, tears stinging at my eyes. He's so mean and unforgiving. Why does he have to go out of his way to be so awful to me? And why do I even let him bother me?

Stupid, idiotic Kelt.

But what if he's right? Could it be true? My mind is a troubled whirl, and I fight back the tears.

No, I won't let him make me cry.

I grab at my knife, desperate to shut him and his disturbing words out, and turn my full attention to the rhythmic motion of slicing through the turnips' thick, unyielding flesh.

"Priest Simitri," I venture the next day as I tentatively approach him. It's the end of class, and Gardnerian scholars are filtering out of the stately lecture hall.

"Mage Gardner." He greets me warmly, his robes smelling pleasantly of incense, a white Vogel band around his arm. "I have something for you." He reaches down behind his desk and draws out a beautiful Ironwood tree seedling in a glazed black pot, handing it to me.

"Thank you," I say, touched by his thoughtfulness.

"It will cleanse your room of the demon stain," he tells me paternally. He leans in as if we share an unfortunate secret. "The Icarals may not love this, but I think you will find it soothing."

I inwardly stiffen. *They have names*, I think. *Ariel and Wynter.* But I don't voice anything to indicate my newfound change of heart. "Thank you," I say instead, taking the small tree from him. It's heavy in my hands. But as much as I love seedlings, I don't want it. Not if it will make Wynter—or even Ariel—uncomfortable.

"I'll help you repot it when it gets a little larger," he tells me brightly. "The roots are delicate. They need room to spread out."

"Thank you," I say again.

Perhaps sensing my unease, he smiles encouragingly. "What can I do for you, Mage Gardner, on this fine day the Ancient One has blessed us with?"

"I was wondering, Priest Simitri," I say hesitantly, shifting my weight from foot to foot, "if you could tell me if there's any truth to a rumor I've heard."

He leans back against his desk, clasps his hands together on his lap and gives me his full attention. "The world is full of rumors, Mage Gardner. It is wise to seek out the truth of the matter."

I smile, feeling bolstered. "Is it true," I begin cautiously, "that the fabric my clothes are made of might have been made by Urisk on the Fae Islands? Workers who are treated like slaves?"

His expression turns solemn. "It *is* true that your dress's fabric may have been made by Urisk workers. It is *not* true that they are treated like slaves. What *is* true is that before the Gardnerians took over the Urisk lands, by the grace of the Ancient One, the Urisk were living like savages, worshipping stone statues of false gods, the men taking multiple wives. They waged war on each other almost as much as they waged war on others. They were uncivilized and very dangerous. Now, because of our intervention, the Urisk women lead quiet lives of morality. Are their lives full of hard work? The answer would be yes, but hard work, especially if it can help keep a people from devolving into savagery...well, it can only be a help to them." He smiles encouragingly at me.

"So," I press, uncomfortably, "there aren't any children working there?"

Priest Simitri turns thoughtful. "If there *are*, I'm sure it's out of the goodwill of their overseers—so that their mothers can keep an eye on them. Don't let yourself be sentimental, Elloren. Urisk children are not like Gardnerian children. They are not First Children. They need structure and hard work to rein in their baser instincts. They lack the intelligence, the sensibility... the *soul* of our people."

My mind immediately wanders to an image of Fern laughing and blowing bubbles in the kitchen.

No, she's just like any other child. Just like a Gardnerian child, in fact.

Priest Simitri points to the history book tucked under my arm. "Why don't you go read the history of the Urisk race in your text. I'm sure what you find there will enlighten you."

But *he* wrote the history text. And I've already read it. *No. I'm not getting the whole story.*

I bid Priest Simitri goodbye and depart the lecture hall in search of answers.

There's only one history professor that I know of who isn't a Gardnerian. Professor Kristian. The Keltic professor who defended Ariel when I took her spice cake.

Professor Kristian sits at a small, battered-looking desk in his disheveled office, its door wide-open. Equally worn wooden shelves line the walls, stuffed to the brim with books and papers, some shelves containing double rows of books crammed into them every which way. There are still more piles of large, well-read volumes stacked on his desk and on the floor by the walls.

He sits, engrossed in writing, several books open in front of him. He pushes up at his wire-rimmed glasses every now and then as they repeatedly slip down his nose.

The gesture and the office make me think of Uncle Edwin. My uncle has the same habit of always having to push his glasses up, and a similar tendency to attract clutter, especially books and stacks of violin music.

I cough uncomfortably to get his attention.

He looks up and does a double take.

There's a brief storm of emotion in his eyes, there and gone again as he regards me with wary caution. He pushes his glasses up and blinks at me several times before saying anything. "Mage Elloren Gardner."

I try to smile, but it comes off more like some bizarre, crooked lip tightening.

He continues to blink at me as I stand there in the door frame.

"I...I have a question," I stammer awkwardly.

More blinking.

The words come out in a tangled rush. "I was told...that my clothing, or the cloth anyway...might have been made by slaves. Is there any truth to that?"

He inclines his head to one side, looking perplexed. "Why are you coming to me with this question, Elloren Gardner?"

"I thought you might give me an honest answer. I went to Priest Simitri, but his answer seemed...biased."

Professor Kristian makes a contemptuous sound and removes his glasses. He grabs a cloth on his desk and peers up at me as he cleans the lenses, eyes narrowing. Replacing the glasses on his nose, he sits back, folds his arms in front of himself and considers me squarely as I hover in the door frame.

"Your clothes, Elloren Gardner," he begins, "were most likely made by Urisk women on the Fae Islands. Some of these workers may have been children, but all were most certainly paid barely enough to survive and are laboring in conditions akin to out-and-out-slavery. They have no freedom of movement, no means of leaving the Islands for a better life, as they are heavily guarded. They can get off the Islands via pirates who will smuggle them out for a steep price, often delivering them to a worse master who will forever hold deportment or time in prison over their heads. Or they can get off the island by becoming indentured servants to the Gardnerians, which is, again, little more than glorified slavery with the threat of deportment always hanging over them. So, Elloren Gardner, if you are asking me whether your dress is made not of the finest silk, but of the oppression and misery of countless others, the answer would be a firm yes."

I swallow hard. *He certainly doesn't mince words.* His blunt manner of speaking makes me uncomfortable, and I have to remind myself that I haven't come here looking for more dancing around the truth.

"Thank you for being honest with me," I tell him, feeling ashamed, thinking of little Fern and her fear of returning to the Fae Islands.

The hard edge of his expression softens a little. His brow knits together, his eyes full of questions. "You're welcome."

Having heard more than enough for today, I turn and walk away.

★ ★ ★

The next day in the kitchen, I take my place lugging piles of dirty plates and trays from the open dining hall counter to the sinks. I'm in my old, comfortable clothing from home—the brown woolen garb dark enough to pass muster as Garnderian clothing, but just barely. I look more like a Kelt than a Gardnerian. But I feel like myself again. My old tunic and skirt are a far cry from elegant, much too loose to show off even a hint of my figure, but I'm finally able to move and breathe.

My new attire has attracted a good many confused and disapproving stares from my fellow Gardnerians, and even more disapproval from non-Gardnerians.

"You must be kidding," Iris snaps when she enters the kitchens, her eyes immediately lighting on me as I transfer a pile of plates.

Heat stings the back of my neck, but I attempt to ignore her and keep working.

Bleddyn almost drops the sack of flour she's lugging when she comes in. "So she's a Kelt now, is that it?" She spits at the floor, her mouth twisted into a disgusted sneer, her eyes hot on me. She looks to Fernyllia, outraged.

Fernyllia shrugs and glances at me, then gestures discreetly with flour-dusted hands for Iris and Bleddyn to stop.

Olilly, the sickly waif of a serving girl with the lavender skin, eyes me with fearful confusion, looking to Fernyllia for reassurance. The Kitchen Mistress gives the small Urisk maid a comforting smile before her eyes dart warily back to me.

"No matter," Iris whispers loudly as she takes the flour from Bleddyn, glaring at me with courageous swagger. "You could dress a Roach like a princess, but she's still a Roach."

Fernyllia shoots Iris a sharp look of censure, which only partially dampens the dark smiles now on Iris's and Bleddyn's lips. The two young women leave for the storeroom, and I can hear them burst into laughter the moment they step out.

Neck burning now, I settle in to vigorously scrubbing plates in the broad sink.

When he finally arrives, Yvan ignores me completely, not even looking over as he takes his place by my side to scrub dishes and pots with a coarse, bristled brush. Eventually he glances over at me, then quickly glances again, a brief flash of surprise in his eyes, before he focuses back on scrubbing pots.

I'm aware of my face going red, imagining what he probably thinks. Braced for more abuse.

"I didn't stop wearing my other clothes for you," I awkwardly explain, sounding irritable, the sting from the harsh words he had for me the day before still smarting. "I really couldn't care less what you think of me."

He glances over at me again with his usual silent intensity as he scrubs the pot in front of him vigorously.

"I asked Professor Kristian if what you said was true," I explain defensively, really not wanting Yvan to think that he has any influence over me whatsoever. "He said it was, so I decided I liked my own clothes better, the clothes I grew up wearing. I'm more comfortable this way anyway. That's the real reason I changed."

Yvan stops scrubbing for a moment as he stares at the wall in front of us, the muscles in his face and neck tensing. With a sigh, he returns to his work and says, "You look better this way."

I give a start. *A compliment from Yvan?*

I'm unexpectedly touched by his words, a warm flush washing over me. His voice, when he's not angry or irritated, is deep and surprisingly kind.

I stare at him sidelong as he continues to focus only on the pot in front of him.

I go to visit Professor Kristian's office again a few days later, questions multiplying like shadowy rabbits in my mind. I'm hungry for answers, wanting to know the truth about things.

Professor Kristian blinks a few times as I enter the room, raising his eyebrows in what looks like surprise at my seeking him out again. He leans forward and peers out into the hallway from which I've come, perhaps expecting to see someone else out there. Then, seeing no one, he sits back in his desk chair and eyes me thoughtfully.

A shadow crosses his expression, there and gone again, his brow tensing. "You look just like your father," he muses. He clears his throat, stiffening. "And your grandmother, of course."

I blink at him in amazed surprise. "You knew my father?"

His eyes become guarded. "I knew *of* him. Many people did."

"Oh," I say, disappointed.

"What brings you here, Mage Gardner?" he inquires, his tone now suspicious. "More questions?"

I nod, and after a long, tense moment, he resignedly gestures to the wooden chair in front of his desk.

I close his door and sit down, feeling awkward and nervous.

"I notice you've changed your dress since our last discussion," he notes, and I think I detect a small glimmer of approval in his eyes.

"Yes, well...um..." I stammer. "I prefer my old clothing anyway."

He raises his eyebrows at this, releases the papers he's holding and folds his hands in front of himself, giving me his full attention. "What would you like to know?" he asks.

I bite my lip and let out a long breath before answering. "I want to know about the history of Gardneria." I hold up my history book. "The *real* history of Gardneria. Not this."

The side of his mouth twitches. "That is considered a well-respected text—"

"It's the *Gardnerian* history of Gardneria," I clarify.

He nods. "You are, perhaps, looking for a Keltic history of Gardneria instead?" he asks, wry amusement in his tone.

"No, I'm looking for a *factual* history."

He purses his lips and gives me an appraising look. "History is a tricky thing, Mage Gardner. What is written about it is usually subjective, and it's often very difficult to find the truth of the matter."

"Well, then," I persist, "what's *your* history of Gardneria?"

He coughs out an uncomfortable laugh in response. "Professors aren't supposed to teach that way, Mage Gardner. My opinion hardly matters."

"Please, Professor Kristian," I press with some vehemence. "It's important to me. Please just tell me what you know."

He looks down at his desk for a moment, his brow knits as if deliberating with himself how best to answer me before meeting my stubborn gaze once more.

"It could take some time," he cautions.

"I have the time," I reply, undaunted. I settle back against the chair.

He stares at me for a long, uncomfortable minute, perhaps waiting to see if I'll give up and go away. "Very well, Mage Gardner," he finally says, leaning toward me. "The story of Gardneria rightfully begins with Styvius Gardner, your people's first Great Mage. He was your grandfather...about six generations back, I believe?"

I nod in assent.

"That's quite the bloodline you have," he observes, eyeing me shrewdly. "Not only Carnissa Gardner, The Black Witch, but Styvius Gardner, as well—both of Gardneria's Great Mages in one family."

I consider this. "I didn't really know just how revered my family is. And hated. Not until I left Halfix anyway."

"And I'm sure you know that Styvius was born to a Mage mother back when the Kelts were the region's ruling power?"

I inwardly stiffen, aware of Professor Kristian's Keltic ethnicity. "I know that the Kelts hated my people and were horrible to them."

"And do you know *why* your people were hated?" Professor Kristian asks.

I eye him squarely. "Prejudice."

"Quite so," he says, sitting back and nodding. "They were treated very badly. Abused in every way. Treated like slaves. Sometimes even killed at birth. The Kelts saw them as half-breeds polluted by Fae blood."

I bristle at the slur, then think uncomfortably about Gareth, Tierney and my own hidden attraction to wood.

He tilts his head. "Haven't you ever wondered where you get that slight shimmer to your skin?"

"It's the mark of the First Children," I tell him. "Set down on us by the Ancient One in blessing."

He lets out a short, unsurprised laugh. "A lofty notion, indeed. And complete fiction. It's more likely your people are descended from the union of Kelts settled at the Northern Forest border and Fae Dryads."

I gape at him, stunned. "What? The Tree Fae?" That's ridiculous. We're a pure-blooded race.

"It would explain why your kind possess some weak branch magic, and the Dryads were said to have skin that glimmered in the night," he says.

I arch my brow at him, eyeing him with deep skepticism. There's no telling what the Tree Fae looked like—they were killed off by the Kelts long ago. And Gardnerians have *wand* magic. Not crass *branch* magic. I clutch at the wooden chair under my hands.

River Maple.

I pull my hands away from the smooth wood and set them in my lap.

"The ancient Kelts had good reason to despise the Fae," Professor Kristian continues. "When they first set foot on this land, around the year 2000 D, the Fae attacked and enslaved them.

But the Kelts quickly discovered that they could gain the upper hand with iron weapons."

This I already know. The Kelts came here fleeing a war, the distant Keltic lands now impossible to return to, a thick band of kracken-infested sea making it treacherous to travel there. The Kelts came, jammed onto ships, half starved, to the shores of the Western Realm. They were immediately set upon and promptly enslaved by the Fae. Until the Kelts realized that the iron they are impervious to is death to the Fae.

I know that iron-wielding Kelts then annihilated most of the Fae and took over a large chunk of the Western Realm.

An unbidden image of Tierney enters my mind—her ever-present lab gloves, her careful, focused expression when handling iron lab equipment. I push the thought to the back of my mind.

Professor Kristian leans forward. "Styvius Gardner was born a half-breed into Keltic society, one of the despised Kelt-Dryad Mages."

I blanch. Professor Kristian could be imprisoned if he uttered such outrageous blasphemy in Gardneria. "It's dangerous to talk like that," I warn him sharply.

He smiles, his eyes steely. "Perhaps, then, it's good that my door is *shut*."

I stare back at him, amazed by his boldness.

"Shall we continue?"

I swallow and nod.

"The Dryad Fae had been killed off long ago, but Dryad blood lived on in the Mage line, giving the Mages their characteristic black hair, and shimmering skin. And branch magic lived on as well, although at a very weak level—only intricately laminated wooden wands could bring forth a fraction of the same magic Dryads could access through simple branches.

"Styvius Gardner was a different sort of Mage, however. His magic wasn't weak. From early on, it was apparent that the magic in his veins was much stronger than any Mage who had ever been born. He could summon fire with a ferocity never before seen and create tornadoes out of small breezes."

I settle back in my chair. This is not new to me. This I've heard.

"When Styvius was only eight years old," Professor Kristian goes on, "he came upon a Kelt overseer viciously beating his Mage mother."

"I know," I tell him flatly.

Professor Kristian nods. "Horrified at the sight of his bloodied mother, Styvius killed the overseer, setting him ablaze with wand magic. The Kelts responded by sending out soldiers to kill young Styvius. They murdered his beloved mother as she needlessly tried to shield the boy. The Kelts planned on killing every Mage in the village to teach them a lesson in obedience.

"But Styvius stopped them. Driven mad by the death of his mother, he killed every soldier in sight."

This I also know. The priests speak of it in church. I know the story of how Styvius took his vengeance on the Evil Kelts, slaying his mother's cruel tormentors.

"Then he set out and killed every Kelt in his village and all the surrounding villages," Professor Kristian continues.

This part catches me off guard. "Wait. What?"

Professor Kristian nods gravely. "*Everyone*. Men. Women. Children. And then he slaughtered everyone in the village next to that one. And the next. And the next." Professor Kristian pauses, his expression darkening. "He quickly developed a predilection for torture."

I tense my face at him in disbelief. "What? No. That can't be right..." My voice trails off as I try to make sense of what he's saying.

"The Kelts repeatedly tried to kill Styvius," Professor Kristian goes on, "but he was invincible, able to summon shields to protect himself and throw huge balls of fire. Eventually, the Kelts fled from northern Keltania, sending the beleaguered Mages to settle there in an effort to placate the child. The half-breed Mages, of course, loved Styvius. He liberated them, gave them a homeland and exacted vengeance on their Keltic tormentors. *That* was the beginning of Gardneria."

I sit there, dumbfounded. It's bizarre to hear this familiar story told so starkly, stripped of its religious underpinnings. And in my people's story, they were not half-breeds at all, but pure-blooded Mages created by the Ancient One from the seeds of the sacred Ironflowers and gathered up as His First Children.

"When he reached adulthood," Professor Kristian continues, "Styvius became a religious zealot. He took the Kelts' *Book of the Ancients* and decided that the Mages weren't Kelt/Dryad half-breeds after all, but the First Children talked about in *The Book*, the rightful owners of Erthia. The Mages, beaten down and abused for generations, were eager to hear this new take on the old religion. Styvius began to claim that he was the Ancient One's prophet, and that the Ancient One was speaking directly to him. He wrote a new last chapter to *The Book* and called it 'The Blessed Mages.' Then he renamed his people 'Gardnerian Mages,' declared northern Keltania to be 'The Republic of Gardneria' and installed himself as High Mage."

I'm inwardly drawing away from him, my people's cherished history being roughly stabbed at and picked apart by his words.

"So, you don't believe Styvius was actually a prophet?" I inquire, acutely aware of how blasphemous the question is.

Professor Kristian doesn't blink. "I think he was a madman."

I sit there, struggling to make sense of it all.

"Styvius set out to populate the entirety of Erthia with nothing but Mages," Professor Kristian continues. "He set down in 'The Blessed Mages' the commandment that Gardnerian Mage women are to wandfast to Gardnerian men at an early age to keep their magic affinity lines pure and their Mage blood untainted. Styvius himself created the highly protected spells that are still used for the Gardnerian sacrament of wandfasting.

Women who broke their wandfasting commitment with non-Gardnerians were to be struck down as brutally as possible, along with their non-Gardnerian lovers. The men's families were also killed, as a lesson to all. A Banishment ceremony was required to exorcise the Evil of the woman from her family."

"My neighbor, Sage Gaffney, was Banished," I tell him, inwardly cringing at the thought.

"And how did you feel about that?" he asks.

I remember Sage's bloodied hands, her terrified appearance and Shane's stories of how her fastmate had beaten her.

"I'm very troubled by it," I reply.

"Shall I continue?" he asks gently, perhaps noticing my discomfort.

I nod in assent.

"For a number of years, the Gardnerians kept to themselves, quietly increasing their numbers—"

"And then the Keltic War came."

A shadow falls over his expression. "Yes. Styvius's power had grown. And magic was becoming stronger in a number of your men, more prevalent with each passing generation. Styvius led his Mages to invade Keltania, taking over half of the Keltish lands and ruthlessly annihilating the population of those lands. Styvius planned to continue his conquest until the entire Western Realm was claimed for the Mages."

"But then Styvius was killed."

"By a Vu Trin sorceress."

"And the war ended."

"After a drawn-out battle." Professor Kristian pauses to pour himself some tea, asking with a hand gesture if I want some, as well. I nod, and he pours me a cup. I sit back and sip at the bitter tea. "The Gardnerians had to cede some of the land they had annexed," he tells me, "and my people reclaimed about half of what had been taken from them."

His people, I note smugly. This has to be a biased account.

"What happened next?" I ask, wanting to catch him in a blatant half-truth.

He sips at his tea. "Many years of peace ensued. It was a time of growth for the Guilds, for trade. Verpacia once again became a major trade crossroads. The University was formally established. And Keltic society became more open to the point where even Icarals were tolerated."

I stop him here. "Where did the Icarals come from?"

He tilts his head, considering. "No one knows for sure. They've popped up in virtually every race as far back as can be remembered, and are hated by almost everyone in the Western Realm."

It's true. It seems that practically everyone's religious traditions cast the Icarals as demonic beings.

"Why are they hated so?" I wonder.

He shrugs. "Like the Fae, they can be full of unpredictable power. They're often dangerous as children. It's probably because they have wyvern blood."

"Wyvern? You mean dragon-shifters?" I try to wrap my head around this. Are Ariel and Wynter part...dragon?

"Well, they do share the western wyverns' feathered, black wings," he says, his mouth tilting up. "And their fire power and fire magic."

Wyverns. Not demons at all. It makes sense. "So...the Icarals are hated because of their wyvern blood?"

Professor Kristian spits out a disdainful breath. "I would postulate that they're hated because you can't hide wings."

I scrunch my face up in confusion.

"All that wyvern blood floating around," he explains, "interferes rather inconveniently with cherished ideas of racial purity. Which, in and of itself, is probably the greatest myth of all time." His eyes gleam with mischief. "Gardnerians are touchy about racial lines not being clearly drawn. The Elves are even touchier. It's easier to cast the Icarals as evil and shun them at birth than it is to admit that every race is a mix."

I grasp at my mug, thoughts swirling as he stirs some honey into his tea and glances sidelong at me, giving his words ample time to sink in.

He sits back, a question in his eyes. "Shall we continue?"

I nod.

"Where were we, then?" His brow knits tight as he focuses into the middle distance.

"It was a time of peace."

"Ah, yes," he says, taking another sip and eyeing me poignantly. "So...enter Carnissa Gardner onto our historical stage."

"My grandmother."

"Yes, your grandmother. She was the long-awaited one. The powerful Great Mage of Prophecy, born with magic more powerful than Styvius's. At a time when Mages saw their borders shrinking as the Kelts reclaimed lost land, purging that land of any Mages they could find."

"You mean murdering them," I flatly state.

He gives me a sober look. "Yes, Elloren. Rounding them up and murdering them."

I sit back, cross my arms and wait for him to continue.

"Your grandmother, Carnissa, set out not only to avenge the Mages, but also to finish what Styvius had started. As she honed her power, the Mages secretly built a dragon army to rival the Urisk and Keltish forces—the Gardnerians were aided in this by the despised Urisk underclass, the Uuril."

"The light-colored Urisk?" I question. "Like some of the kitchen workers? They have pinkish hair."

"They would be part of the Uuril underclass," Professor Kristian affirms.

I think of little Fern and her bubbles, troubled by her low-class status.

"Carnissa invaded Keltania and quickly annexed it," Professor Kristian continues. "Then she aligned herself with the Alf-sigr Elves, shipped the remaining Fae—as well as anyone with even a drop of Fae blood—to the Pyrran Isles and took over the Fae Islands. Like Styvius, she didn't plan on stopping there. By that point she had turned into a cruel, religious zealot who wanted to wipe out every race in the Western Realm, save the Gardnerian Mages."

This isn't how I know this story. "She was protecting my people," I protest. "The Kelts wanted their land back so they could enslave my people again."

"It may have started out that way," he counters, "but it certainly didn't end that way. Your people wanted revenge. And they needed more farmland. They didn't want just some of the land, they wanted *all* of it." He pauses, perhaps seeing how much this is upsetting me.

He's wrong. He has to be. My grandmother wasn't some bloodthirsty, land-grabbing monster. She was a great warrior. She saved and protected us all.

"Elloren," he says, his expression conflicted. "Your grandmother wanted to kill everyone who wasn't Gardnerian."

"Because they wanted to attack us," I say, my voice tight and strained. *My parents fought with her. They died fighting for her. Fighting for all of my people. They were heroes.*

Professor Kristian tightens his lips as if holding back a counterargument. After a short pause he speaks again. "An Icaral rose up during your grandmother's push east. He killed her and died doing it. The Icaral was a Keltic healer who gave his life to save Keltania, a society that still harbored lingering prejudice against his kind." He sets down his tea. "So, here we are."

Here we are. A Kelt and a Gardnerian, calmly discussing the whole thing. Calm enough on the surface at least. My mind is a tumult of warring emotions.

"Your people and the Alfsigr Elves are currently the major powers in the region," he continues. "With only a few very fragile checks on their power. There's the Vu Trin guard at the Western and Eastern passes, positioned to keep Gardnerian and Alfsigr power confined to the Western Realm. There's also the loose threat that war could force an alliance between the Lupines and the Amaz. And both groups are formidable opponents on their own."

"And there's the Resistance," I add.

He narrows his eyes at me. "Yes, there's a scattered Resistance movement. The Resistance being the only group willing to defy the Gardnerians and Alfsigr Elves at the moment."

I hold his level stare. "You think opposition will grow?"

He tilts his head in consideration. "Perhaps. Especially with Priest Marcus Vogel poised to take control of the Gardnerian Mage Council."

A thread of fear tightens in my gut at the mention of Vogel.

"I've met him," I tell Professor Kristian.

He eyes me appraisingly. "And did you like him?"

I remember the dark tree, the feel of the black void. "He scared me," I admit.

"He should," Professor Kristian warns. "And you should start paying attention to what your own Mage Council is doing." He rubs at his temple, then looks back at me. "Vogel's a Level Five Mage, but he lacks the power of Styvius and Carnissa."

"So he's no Great Mage."

Professor Kristian shakes his head. "No. But something is working in his favor—another Prophecy, echoed by the seers of several races, making everyone fearful and reactionary. It speaks of the imminent arrival of another Black Witch, the greatest Gardnerian Mage yet. It also speaks of the rising of another Icaral—a male—who will challenge her. According to this Prophecy, this new Black Witch will need to kill the Icaral, or an age of darkness will descend on Gardneria.

"Of course, the enemies of Gardneria see darkness for Gardneria as a good thing, so there are already assassins roaming the lands, desperate to locate the Black Witch of Prophecy. And, of course, the Gardnerians are desperate to locate both the Black Witch and the Icaral who is supposed to rise up and challenge Her. There have been some rumors that an Icaral baby boy was recently born to a Gardnerian girl, and that both the baby and the mother are on the run from the Gardnerian Mage Council."

Sage's baby. The Icaral of Prophecy—an unbroken Icaral who could come into his full powers. An Icaral who might keep his wings and possess unspeakable magic. And a new Black Witch—Fallon Bane.

For a moment we're both silent as I digest all this new information.

"So...the next Black Witch," I venture. "What if it's true? What if she comes?"

He grows quiet, his eyes grave with foreboding. "The Gardnerians have built the most powerful army they have ever had, with more dragons at their command than ever before. If another Black Witch rises, it is likely that the Gardnerians will succeed in taking over every land that exists on our maps, crushing the Resistance and making everyone who is not a Mage into a slave, with the exception, perhaps, of the Lupines." He leans toward me, his voice low. "Is that what you want, Elloren Gardner?"

I think of Fern and her bubbles. I swallow hard, feeling off-kilter and troubled. "I'm a Level One Mage," I say, struggling to keep my tone light. "It hardly matters what I want."

"Perhaps, but I'm still curious."

"I don't know," I say, my worldview like shifting sand unsteady beneath my feet. "Lukas Grey told me that you have to dominate or be dominated. That all of history is like this."

He considers this, nodding with a look of sad resignation. "Much of history *is* like that," he agrees. "But perhaps there is another way."

"Like what?"

"I don't know, Elloren Gardner. I don't know," he says sadly, shaking his head. "But for me, life would not be worth living without at least having faith in that one thing—that there is another way, a path of justice, if you will. And that there is at least a very small sliver of hope that this path will one day be discovered."

"So you think there's hope for something better than all of this fighting? Some other future that's possible?"

"A future of fairness? A future of justice? A future where resources are shared by all peoples instead of fought over? Yes, I think it's possible, but I think it will all come down to the choices of individuals."

"Even powerless individuals?"

"I like to think so, yes."

I sigh and slump down. "It all seems very confusing." I eye him piercingly. "And I'm not sure if I even believe everything you say."

Unexpectedly, Professor Kristian stands up and pulls several books from the shelves lining his small office. I read the front covers as he hands them to me one by one.

The Annotated History of Keltania, by the Keltic historian Mikael Noallan

A History of the Alfsigr Realm, translated from High Elvish by Ital'lyr Ciarnyllir

A Comprehensive History of the Faekin, translated from Asrai Fae by Elfhollen historian Connor Haldash

The Amazakaran Worldview, by the Keltic historian Mikael Noallan

Lupine Societies: A History, by Lupine historian Dolf Boarg

"But these will all be from different points of view," I say as he once again takes his seat. "I'll be even more confused than I already am."

He smiles slightly. "Who said confusion is a bad thing? I have found that confusion can be a very good thing. Often you have to fall into the blackness of utter confusion before you can emerge to see even the smallest glimmer of the truth. My heartfelt wish is that you read these books and are thrown into a complete tailspin of befuddlement."

I frown at him. "I came here for answers."

He laughs at this, pushing up his spectacles. "Good history professors have only questions. You will have to find your own answers, Elloren Gardner."

I stand up, my arms wrapped around the heavy volumes. "Thank you," I say to him, my voice uncertain as I look down at the thick books he's given me.

"Don't thank me," he says, all amusement gone. "Real education doesn't make your life easy. It complicates things and makes everything messy and disturbing. But the alternative, Elloren Gardner, is to live your life based on injustice and lies."

I bite at my lower lip, not liking what he's saying. Hating some of it.

He abruptly glances back down at the papers on his desk and begins to write on them, making it clear that it's time for me to leave.

I hug the heavy books tight under both arms and walk out.

CHAPTER
TWENTY-SEVEN

Damion Bane

Late that night, after spending about two hours peeling potatoes and a few more toiling in the apothecary lab, I start back to the North Tower. Halfway across the cold, windy field, I realize I've left Professor Kristian's books in the kitchen.

It's well past midnight when I return to the kitchen to fetch the books. I've never been out so late, and it's strange to find the University so quiet and deserted, only a few stray scholars walking here and there, some scattered lamplight visible through windows.

I push open the door that leads to the kitchen's storage room, hearing some muffled voices in the otherwise quiet kitchen up ahead. I hesitate near the second door, curious as to who could be here at such a late hour.

"Please...please let me go," a young woman pleads, crying softly.

"Now, why would I do that?" a velvety voice answers.

I creep up to the door in front of me and peer through its window. My gut clenches when I see who it is.

Fallon's older brother, Lieutenant Damion Bane, decked out in his black military garb, silver-striped cloak and white armband. He's grabbing at Olilly, the shy, violet-skinned Urisk girl who cleans the floors at night. The girl Fallon chased away.

"I have to go. Please let me go," Olilly begs, trying to pull away from the hand firmly clenched around her thin arm.

Anger courses through me, making my heart race. *Trystan.* I should get Trystan. He's a Level Five like Damion. He doesn't have as much training, but still...

"*You* have something that belongs to my sister," Damion says with a smile. "So you're going to do exactly what I want, or I'm going to report you for theft and get you sent back to the Islands."

"I didn't take anything. I swear it." Her words are muffled by crying.

"There, there," he purrs, reaching up to finger the buttons of her tunic. "What Fallon doesn't know won't hurt her. You're going to come with me, and we'll have a little talk. We're going to take a walk in the woods."

Anger boils over inside me. *Level Five be damned.*

I grab up the biggest iron skillet I can find, swinging it by its wooden handle, and make for the kitchen door.

I burst into the kitchen wielding my makeshift weapon. As Damion turns to look at me in surprise, there's a crash, and a blur streaks through the kitchen, colliding with Damion.

He falls backward away from the girl and onto a table with a groan.

Yvan Guriel is now standing over him, Damion's wand in his hand. Yvan deftly casts it into the bread stove's fire. Cold air rushes in from the still-open back door, the logs Yvan had been carrying lying all over the floor near the door in disarray.

I blink, momentarily thrown off balance. How did Yvan move so *fast*? Impossibly so.

Yvan's fists are clenched, his body tightly coiled as if he's ready to spring at Damion at any moment, green eyes blazing.

Damion looks at him, then me, ignoring Olilly as she cries

and huddles against the spice shelf. He smiles and pushes himself off the table, then pauses to brush off his fine clothes.

"Doing some late-night cooking?" he asks me, amused.

My arm hurts from holding the heavy skillet, but I don't care. I want to throw it straight at his head.

"Stay away from the kitchen girls," I tell him, my voice steely.

I've heard all about him, and some of the other soldiers. Preying on any Urisk girl unlucky enough to find herself alone with them. The kitchen workers don't talk to me directly, but they talk *around* me, and I've ears to hear.

"She's a thief," Damion tells me conversationally, flicking his fingers in the direction of the girl without looking at her. "She's coming with me. She stole something from my sister. A picture."

Oh, Ancient One. Guilt lashes through me. *Lukas's cracked portrait at the bottom of my cloak pocket. Olilly's predicament is all my fault.*

I hoist the skillet a little higher on the handle, fearing I may drop it. "She didn't take Fallon's picture," I tell him, heart pounding. "*I* did."

His eyebrows fly up, then his gaze turns malevolent and he lets out a short laugh. "So *you* have my sister's picture of Lukas Grey?"

"Yes. Yes, I do."

"Interesting rivalry you two have going," he says, shooting me a dark look.

I fish the broken portrait pieces from my cloak pocket, walk over to him, the skillet hanging heavily from my other hand, and drop the pieces into his outstretched palm.

He smiles chillingly. "I don't suppose she'll laugh this off."

"No, I'd imagine not," I reply flatly.

I let out a long breath as he takes his leave, then turn to find Olilly and Yvan staring at me, Olilly terrified and frozen in place, Yvan's eyes a storm of emotion.

"I left my books here," I explain weakly, mind spinning with the many ways Fallon will soon be devising to kill me. And still reeling over Yvan's otherworldly speed.

I awkwardly set the skillet down on a table. The kitchen is now quiet as a tomb, and my gaze is drawn to Olilly's bloodshot eyes, the telltale spots around the corners of her lips.

The Red Grippe.

I've noticed that a few of the kitchen workers have been ill with this for some time. It's easy, but expensive, to cure. I've tried to sneak medicine to them, but none of them have been able to get past their fear of me.

But maybe she'll take it with Yvan here.

I pause, pull a medicinal vial out of my tunic pocket and hold it out to her. "Olilly, I made this for you."

Olilly recoils and shakes her head stiffly from side to side. She looks to Yvan, terror stark in her eyes.

Yvan turns his back to me, puts his hand on Olilly's arm and murmurs something, his words too low to decipher. He's so gentle with her, his long fingers brushing her hair back so kindly, his voice so deep and resonant as he reassures her. It sets off the usual unsettling, warm thrum deep inside me.

Olilly starts to sob, lifting a slender, shaking hand to wipe at her eyes. She looks up at Yvan imploringly. "He could follow me. What if he follows me?"

"I'll walk you back," Yvan assures her, his voice low and soothing. "All right?"

Olilly sniffs back her tears and nods.

"Go on," he tells her, his voice barely audible. "Gather your things."

Olilly nods again, some of the tension loosening from her stance. She shoots me another fearful look, then disappears into the back storeroom.

I sigh and glance worriedly toward where Olilly exited. "Maybe *you* can give this to her," I say, holding the medicine out to Yvan, my emotions pulsing through me in a tangled mess. "She's much too afraid to take it from me."

His severe expression doesn't budge.

"It's *Norfure* tincture," I press. "I've seen what she's taking. You know as well as I do that it won't cure her. *This* will." It's medicine that works. Expensive Gardnerian medicine. Medicine she'll never be able to afford.

Yvan stands, blinking at me. But then he walks over and takes it, his warm fingers brushing against my own, sparks lighting on my skin as my pulse quickens. His green eyes lock onto mine as he slides the vial into his pants pocket.

Feeling wildly self-conscious, I go and fish my books out from under a nearby table and straighten to find Yvan still watching me, his brow tensed as if he's trying to figure something out.

"That was…brave, what you just did," I tell him awkwardly, clutching at Professor Kristian's books, hesitant to compliment him.

"You were going to attack a Level Five Gardnerian Mage," he says, more a statement than a question. "With a skillet."

I lift my chin defensively. "Why, yes. I was." Heart thudding, I fight the urge to break eye contact with his intense, unwavering stare.

For a moment it looks as if he wants to say something. Instead he turns and picks up his own books, laid on a shelf with the spice jars.

Olilly emerges from the storeroom, cloaked and with a bag slung over her shoulder. Averting her eyes from me, she hurries out the back door and holds it open for Yvan to follow.

Yvan glances over at her, pausing. He looks back to me, his hard expression now conflicted. "Good night, Elloren," he says stiffly, but not unpleasantly, before following Olilly out into the night.

His use of my name stuns me into openmouthed silence.

I watch him leave, his back broad and straight, deeply warmed by his thawing demeanor.

And still wondering how he could possibly be so fast.

I know I should put in an hour or so memorizing cough remedies. Especially after spending so much time with Professor Kristian—time that should have been spent studying.

I sit in my dim North Tower room, my Apothecarium text open on the desk before me, dawn soon approaching. I need to get at least a few hours of sleep, and I'm running out of time for study. But I can't seem to focus. Professor Kristian's tower of history books seems to be quietly waiting for me, and I find it hard to resist their forbidden pull.

Simply possessing these books feels like a traitorous thing. Especially the Keltic history. The Kelts oppressed my people for generations. How can I read a history book written by one of them?

But then I look to Ariel, passed out with one of her chickens. And to Wynter, asleep with threadbare wings wrapped tight around her thin frame. I think of Olilly—how poor she is, and how afraid of me. And of Yvan's use of my first name, for the first time.

I decide to do the dangerous thing, not the smart thing.

I push my Apothecarium text to the side, pick up Professor Kristian's history text and begin to read.

✳

PART THREE

✳

PROLOGUE

Vyvian Damon can't take her eyes off him.

Marcus Vogel owns the Council Chamber. His piercing eyes are like green fire and send rippling waves of excitement through her.

And fear through everyone who's not aligned with him. She's sure of that.

He's going to win in the spring.

The Council members' seats are set between sanded Ironwood trees that rise up to either side of Vyvian, a tangle of branches flowing out over the ceiling. The arcing Council platform looks out over rows of seating, and today the Council Hall is filled with Mages—almost all of them with white bands around their arms.

Vogel bands.

"Where is the male Icaral?" Vogel inquires with terrible calm, his shattering stare pinned on Council Mage Phinneas Callnan, the traitors' favorite for the spring High Mage referendum and Council envoy to the military.

Mage Callnan glares back at Vogel, jaw set tight. "Not found, as of yet."

A troubled murmur sweeps through the crowded room.

"The Ancient One has set the Prophecy ringing in our ears," Vogel states, the words burning with a zealous fire that shudders heat through Vyvian. "Louder and louder and louder." Vogel holds up *The Book of the Ancients*. "Yet you ignore His Holy Voice."

Mage Callnan rises to his feet, outrage smoldering in his eyes. "How dare you question my faith!" He jabs his finger toward the heavens. "No one is ignoring His Holy Voice!"

Vogel goes still as a snake, and when he speaks, his voice is low and frighteningly hard. "You ignore Him when you allow the Icaral demon of Prophecy to escape. You ignore Him when you let heathen races procreate like *wild beasts* on land that belongs to the *Holy Magedom*. You ignore Him when you dismiss *His Holy Charge* to claim Erthia for the *Mages*. You ignore Him when you allow Keltic spirits to be smuggled through our borders and for Selkies to be sold right here in Valgard! You ignore Him when you support a depraved University where races mix and *Icaral demons roam free!*"

The Council Chamber erupts into angry cries that slowly morph into a thundering chant that shakes the very floor.

"Vogel! Vogel! Vogel! Vogel!"

Giddy with vengeful fire, Vyvian scans the other Mage Council members. All twelve of them are there, the doddering High Mage Aldus Worthin seated in the center. Vyvian narrows her eyes at the white-bearded High Mage. He's peering out over the frenzied crowd with a look of shocked befuddlement. Vyvian sneers.

The old relic.

Vyvian does the math. Five white-banded Council Mages are aligned with Marcus—herself, Mage Gaffney, Mage Greer, Mage Flood and Mage Snowden. Six heathen Mages are aligned with High Mage Worthin and his increasingly profane ideas— static borders that allow infidel races and shapeshifters to hold on to Mage land, a relaxation of the ban on intermarriage, trade with the perverse Amazakaran, support of the race-polluted University. And perhaps the most heinous of all—the allowance of Icaral demons to even exist!

Vyvian looks to the side of the room where bald Priest Alfex waits in the wings, a white band around the arm of his priestly robe.

The favorite for the next vacancy on the Council.

Vyvian smiles.

If Vogel wins, and Priest Alfex slides into his Council seat, Vogel will hold a majority on the Council. Seven to six.

And just like that, the world will change.

CHAPTER ONE

Mage Council Papers

I read history every spare minute, but there aren't many minutes to spare, the fear of imminent death by Fallon's ice scratching at the back of my mind.

I read Urisk history while cough syrup simmers before me, poring over accounts of how the cruel Fae set the elements on the Urisk people, blowing whole villages to bits with great, funneling winds, crushing the Urisk fishing fleets with shattering storms.

I read Fae history when I should be memorizing medicinal formulas, with its tales of the barbarian Urisk and how their vicious wyvern allies rained fire down on Fae cities, the great dragons using long talons to rip Fae children to shreds. And later, how the cruel Keltic invaders were quickly subdued before they could wreak havoc on the Fae with their iron weapons.

I read Keltic history as I stir molasses pudding, the text propped up on a shelf just above the stove, half ignoring the thick bubbles popping up to the pudding's surface like hungry fish mouths. I learn that the ancient Kelts' ships were met by Fae aggressors, who forced them to their knees, separating families and shackling them all into servitude.

It's enough conflicting information to make me want to scream.

"You're reading Mikael Noallan," Yvan observes flatly, pausing after dropping an armful of logs onto the growing pile beside my stove, his green eyes flashing.

I eye him with defiance. *I can read Keltic history if I want to.* "Professor Kristian lent me some books."

Yvan meets my defiant stare full-on, and my pulse quickens.

"Ignore the Roach," Iris sounds out from across the kitchen, and my muscles go tight with offense.

Let it go. Just let it go.

Yvan's head whips around. "Don't call her that."

The entire kitchen goes silent and motionless. I gape at him in shocked surprise.

Iris glares hard at Yvan, her eyes catching fire, her lip curling with overwhelming, trembling disgust. "You're defending...a *Roach*?" She can barely get the words out.

There's danger in his eyes. "I said, *don't call her that.*"

Iris's eyes glaze over with tears as her eyes flit from me to Yvan, her fury collapsing into raw hurt.

"Iris." Yvan relents, holding out a conciliatory hand.

Shaking her head violently from side to side, Iris bursts into tears, throws down the rag in her hands and runs out of the kitchen.

Yvan shoots me a brief, storming look, then strides out after her.

My heart is racing fast as a hare, the kitchen workers slowly and carefully launching back into their respective tasks, their eyes darting warily toward me.

Completely astonished by this turn of events, I absent-mindedly notice that one of the pots is starting to boil over and reach for its iron handle without remembering to use a mitt.

Heat sears my palm, and I cry out and lurch back, pulling my hand protectively in. Pain streaks up my arm, and I dare a look at my palm, a red half-moon already rising up.

Everyone ignores me, going about their tasks with silent deliberation. I blink back tears and turn toward the stove, grasping my wrist, raw from the pain and from their pointed indifference.

There's a gentle tug at my tunic arm.

I turn to find Olilly staring up at me with wide, amethyst eyes. Clear eyes. And skin free of red spots.

She used the medicine after all.

"Here, Mage," she says softly, fishing a small glass container of salve out of her tunic pocket, opening it and holding it out to me. "For burns."

I blink back more tears as an overwhelming gratitude washes over me.

"Thank you, Olilly," I say, my voice breaking as I rub the creamy salve into my already blistering burn, the pain quickly dampening.

She ignores the subtle looks of censure thrown her way and gives me a small, tentative smile.

"I'd like a copy of this week's *Mage Council Motions & Rulings*," I tell the Gardnerian Archivist.

It's late that same evening, my left hand wrapped with a thin bandage, the burn tamped down to an annoying sting by Olilly's healing salve.

I think about Olilly's debilitating fear of Gardnerians the whole walk over here. Her enforced servitude. Her shy doe eyes and gentle ways. *And she's so young—too young to be facing the rest of her life as a virtual slave.*

Professor Kristian is right, I think. *It's time to start paying attention to what my own government is doing.* And the Gardnerian Archives are a prime place to begin.

The archivist is bespectacled and has gray hair tied up in a loose bun, her eyes set on me with awed approval. There's a white ribbon neatly tied around her arm.

"I'm so sorry, Mage Gardner," she says with an apologetic smile. "They're all checked out." She motions with a subtle flick of her finger toward the crooked, taciturn Mage hunched over the papers at a table clear across the room.

Tierney.

I thank the archivist and make my way to Tierney's table. The Gardnerian Archives are thinly populated at this late hour, the lighting dimmed to a soft amber glow.

"Can I see those when you're done?" I say with no preamble.

Tierney looks up at me, her expression full of its usual grim sarcasm. "I thought politics wasn't your domain."

"Well, I've changed my mind."

Her sharp eyes flick toward my arm. "Still no armband."

I throw a pointed look at her arm, as well. "You, either."

Her eyes narrow to slits. "I hope Marcus Vogel rots in a fiery hell," she whispers scathingly.

I stand there blinking at her for a moment. "Well, I might not phrase it quite like that, but I certainly don't want him to be High Mage."

Now she's blinking at me like she doesn't quite know what to make of me.

Without a word, she slides over and makes room for me next to her so we can read the papers together.

The *Mage Council Motions & Rulings* are deeply boring reading, and I have to bite my tongue more than once to keep from nodding off. Mind-numbing details regarding Council building, shipping and military contracts, tax figures and land disputes make up the vast majority of the tiny print.

But then my eye catches on a motion presented by Marcus Vogel and struck down by Phinneas Callnan's majority.

"Look at this," I whisper, pointing. "Vogel wants to make wandfasting mandatory by the age of eighteen."

There's tight strain around Tierney's eyes, her mouth twisting into a grimace. "He's been pushing for that for months. Refuse to fast, and the Council will pick someone for you."

I bet Aunt Vyvian would love it if this motion passed.

"How old are you, Tierney?" I hesitantly whisper.

She takes a shuddering breath, her expression haunted. "Eighteen." Her tone is the fall of an ax, final and inescapable.

I swallow, an uneasy chill working its way down my spine. I pull one arm protectively around myself and look back down at the papers.

There's another motion, again presented by Marcus Vogel, to iron-test every Mage seeking admittance to the Guilds.

I look to Tierney. She's sitting back, watching me read now with dark patience as if waiting for the full catastrophe that is Vogel to completely sink into my mind.

Wide-awake now, I follow the print down the page with the tip of my index finger.

There's a motion presented by Marcus Vogel—and struck down—to execute any Urisk found to be in Gardneria without work papers. And a motion presented by Marcus Vogel, passed as a ruling, to execute a band of Keltic Resistance fighters for setting fire to the Sixth Division's military barracks. Another passed motion to execute two Resistance workers found to be smuggling Urisk east.

A slim thread of fear pulls at my insides. *Vogel seems fond of executions.*

There's one last motion passed to ruling, also presented by Marcus Vogel—to block trade with the Amazakaran in retaliation for their offer to give amnesty to Urisk women, even those here illegally. The Amaz leader, Queen Alkaia, is quoted as saying, "The Amazakaran Free Peoples of the Caledonian Mountains will not recognize any bindings of servitude placed on any woman." In addition, the Amaz have made the "incendiary and outrageous" decision to also give amnesty to any women with mixed or even full Fae blood.

I look to Tierney, my finger resting discreetly and hopefully on the ruling.

Her face tenses, and she looks carefully around the empty archives, the archivist filing papers clear across the room, her back to us. Tierney glances sidelong at me. "The Amaz won't give amnesty to males," she whispers, the sound constricted and almost inaudible.

Tierney's father. And brother. Are they Fae, too?

"At least we're in Verpacia." I reassure her. "Your family could come here, maybe?"

Tierney shoots me a deeply incredulous glare. "You don't follow any politics, do you?"

"No... I haven't in the past," I stammer, worry rising.

She lets out a jaded breath. "The Verpacian Council's elections were held just last month. There's now a Gardnerian majority on it. For the first time ever."

"But it's still Verpacia," I counter. "There's a mix of cultures here. There are too many different races living here for any one race to have too much influence..."

"You haven't followed politics because you haven't had to," she snipes, raw resentment breaking through. "And it shows. You're incredibly naive." She leans closer, confrontation burning in her eyes. "Your people have huge families. Because you're supposed to take over the entire world."

"*Our* people," I hastily caution her, my eyes darting carefully around, relieved to find no one in earshot or seemingly paying attention to us.

Tierney hunches down, her voice lowered to a rough whisper. "The number of Gardnerians living and settling here in Verpacia—it's rising every year. That's why they've gained a majority on the Verpacian Council. If Vogel wins in the spring..." She stops, swallows and goes pale. All fire is gone from her eyes now—only pure dread remains. "If he wins, the Verpacian Council will fall right in line behind him. The Gardnerian members will out of true allegiance. The rest, out of well-founded fear."

"So, if Vogel wins," I venture worriedly, "it affects much more than just Gardneria." I run Vogel's motions over in my mind, all of them uniformly and disastrously harsh. The feel of his dark void that day I met him, his eyes pinned tight on mine, creeps into my mind. And the startling image of the dead tree.

It's like his black void has spread to this room and beyond. Gathering patiently at the edges of everything.

Chilled, I rub at my arms, trying to warm myself.

There's stark fear in Tierney's eyes. "Elloren, if Vogel wins, the world changes."

The entire Western Realm quickly becoming one giant trap for everyone who isn't Gardnerian.

"They'll hunt down the Icarals first," she whispers, her tone deadened. "Then the Urisk and the Kelts..." She stops, her voice breaking.

Stricken, I finish for her. "And then they'll come for the Fae."

CHAPTER TWO

Randall Greyson

The following morning I arrive at apothecary lab to find Tierney waiting for me at our lab table with a look of profound alarm.

We're early for class today. Gesine is quietly talking to a group of white-arm-banded apothecary apprentices, all four of the young women shooting me a troublingly smug look as I pass them.

I glance at our lab table as I near Tierney.

My violin is sitting right in the middle of the table, case open.

"Tierney," I question, deeply thrown, "why…"

"I didn't put it there," she quickly points out, her eyes full of warning.

My stomach lurches, my whole body tensing.

Fallon. How on Erthia did she get it out of my brothers' lodging?

I quickly pull myself together, assessing the situation with a wary eye. "That's her big revenge?" I scoff, loud enough for Gesine and the other apprentices to hear. "Moving my violin from one place to another?"

I give them a defiant smile and reach out to pick my violin

up. As I lift the instrument, it falls apart into two neat halves, cleanly split down the middle.

Just like Lukas's portrait.

My center drops, and I can feel myself blanching.

"I'm sorry, Elloren," Tierney says, pained, keeping her voice low. "It's important to you, I'm sure." She glances darkly toward Gesine and the other young women, her eyes narrowing to slits. "Or else she wouldn't have bothered with it."

Tears sting at my eyes, and I can barely choke the words out. "It was important, yes." *And I'll never be able to make another violin with Uncle Edwin again.*

I can't say any more than that without bursting into pathetic sobbing, my mouth trembling.

Gesine and the other women's eyes dart toward me, the four of them barely able to suppress their gloating smiles, waiting for me to fall apart.

No. I will not give them the satisfaction.

"What will you do?" Tierney asks me worriedly.

"Nothing," I say, my fury pulling me firmly together, searing the tears to oblivion. "I imagine, in Fallon's warped mind, that we're about even at the moment." I pick up my violin, force a trembling, defiant smile and look right at Gesine and her cohorts as I calmly slide my precious, broken-beyond-repair violin back into its case.

I dust off my hands, sit down next to Tierney and turn to see her blinking at me with unwavering concern.

I give her a wide, chilling smile. "You know, I just might go to that Yule Dance after all."

It's early evening, two days later, and I'm sitting with Jarod Ulrich in an out-of-the-way alcove of the main University archives. Chemistrie notes, paper, pens and ink are spread out on the rough wooden table in front of Jarod and me, my mounting hatred of Fallon Bane having to get in line behind the need to buckle down and study, but I can't seem to let it go.

Soon after I found my destroyed violin, I marched straight to my brothers' lodging. Only Trystan was there, his face lighting with concern the moment he opened the door and took in my expression—my whole body practically vibrating with hot fury.

She'd wounded me, Fallon. Hit me where the blow would truly hurt. I was increasingly finding that this was her specialty.

Trystan quietly stepped back, opening the door wider in welcome. I stepped inside and pulled out the remains of my violin for him to peruse.

His eyes widened as he took it into his hands, strings dangling.

"Fallon Bane's work." I spat out each word.

He shot me a quick look of surprise before turning his attention back to the violin. "That's quite a clean cut," he marveled as he ran his finger along the perfectly straight edge, studying it. "She must have used a jigsaw."

"Or some evil spell," I ground out under my breath, abhorrence coursing over me in waves.

"I knew something wasn't right," Trystan said, shaking his head. "When I got back here last night, our doorknob was so cold it hurt to touch it."

Of course it was. Compliments of the Ice Witch.

"How could she know I kept it in here?" I wondered.

Trystan shrugged. "The cleaning women? They're in and out—and the case *is* marked with your name."

And Fallon's got every servant girl in Verpax terrified of her wrath. It's not a great leap of logic to assume I'm storing things here, with Ariel Haven as my lodging mate.

"She should be thankful," I told him, voice menacingly low, "that I have no magic whatsoever."

Trystan eyed me soberly and set down the violin halves on

his desk. "Do you want me to go to the Vice Chancellor with you? To file a complaint?"

"No," I spat out. "I want you to freeze Fallon's head. Or set it on fire. Can you do that for me?"

Trystan took a deep breath and looked at me with his usual measured calm. "Um...yes. I could, Elloren. Followed by my immediate expulsion from University. Minor detail."

I glowered at him petulantly and plopped down on his bed, defeated.

Trystan quietly took a seat beside me. "You know, you might be able to enlist Diana Ulrich to your cause."

I looked to him questioningly.

Trystan's lip lifted with a trace of amusement. "Apparently Diana's been going on and on about putting Fallon's head on a spike and posting it at the city gates. 'For the crows to devour.' Her words, not mine."

I can't suppress a smirk at this, both heartened and darkly gratified by Diana's bloodthirsty sentiment.

The *tap, tap, tap* of Jarod's pen draws me back to the present.

He's bent over the table transcribing my Chemistrie notes, his script neat and compact. My notes are now a necessity for him, since Diana won't share hers anymore.

Initially contemptuous of Professor Volya, Diana has reversed course entirely now that she's realized how knowledgeable our professor is. As a result, Diana has taken a very hard line against sharing notes with her inattentive twin brother, who, in Diana's words, should "put away the ridiculous poetry books and concentrate on the lecture." So, in a wildly improbable turn of events, I've become the note-taker for both Aislinn and Jarod, who continue their written dialogue about great literature throughout every class now.

Jarod's head suddenly lifts, nostrils flaring. He turns just as

Aislinn rounds a long bookshelf and comes into view. She hurries toward us, her expression strained.

"I'm so glad I found you two." She's flustered and out of breath.

"Randall was looking for you earlier," I inform Aislinn, confused by her troubled demeanor.

"I'm trying to avoid him, actually," she admits, her eyes darting around the bookcases and shadowy halls.

I let out a small, rueful laugh. "You won't be able to avoid him forever. Not if you plan on wandfasting to him."

Her face tenses, and she looks down at the floor, hands clutched at her skirts. "I know."

Jarod, who's been quietly watching Aislinn, straightens and looks past us, his nostrils flaring.

"Aislinn, I've been looking all over for you!"

She turns around to where Randall has just emerged, and her face falls. "Well, now you've found me," she says, her voice flat, her body language unwelcoming.

Randall turns a critical eye on Jarod and me. "Elloren," he says guardedly. He shoots Jarod a look of disgust and pointedly turns back toward Aislinn.

I find myself bristling at this, while Jarod calmly regards Randall, his face neutral.

"You told me you'd be in your room," Randall complains, the well-pressed slate-gray silk of his military apprentice uniform stiff and new, a white ribbon neatly pinned around his arm. "I don't like having to search for you."

Aislinn stares back at him, emotionless. "I'm sorry, Randall. I didn't mean to inconvenience you."

"Yes, well." He sniffs. He casts another sidelong glance at Jarod, then takes hold of Aislinn's arm. "You need to come with me."

A look of reluctance crosses Aislinn's face. "Why? Where are you taking me?"

Randall narrows his eyes at Jarod. "Out of here."

Aislinn's expression turns deeply conflicted, and I notice that she has the same book of poetry tucked under her arm that Jarod has sitting underneath his Chemistrie notes.

"Maybe I'll see you later?" she asks me hopefully, her eyes flickering toward Jarod and then to me again.

"Of course," I says encouragingly. "I'll be around."

We watch as Randall pulls her away. Aislinn glances back longingly before she's led from our sight.

I turn to Jarod. He's staring after them, his face newly tense.

"Is that who she's wandfasting to?" he asks me, incredulous. "Please tell me that's not him."

"That's him."

"But…she's repulsed by his touch."

"Yes, well…" I pause, frowning at him. "How do you know that?"

Jarod shrugs as he gathers some papers together. "I can smell it on her." He looks off in the direction they've gone, his blond brow furrowing. "He's not repulsed by *her*, though," he grinds out, surprising me with the level of disgust in his tone.

"No, unfortunately." I stare hard at Jarod. "Can you tell that, too?"

He nods.

"That's an interesting skill to have."

"What? To sense attraction?"

"Mmm. But it must complicate life in your societies, everyone knowing everyone else's romantic secrets. Everything completely out in the open."

"On the contrary," he replies thoughtfully, "I think it simplifies things. It makes it easier to find the right life mate. Your people have to go around guessing how you feel about each other."

"It is a bit frustrating," I agree.

"I can't imagine."

"So, what do you do if you fall in love with someone and they aren't interested in you?"

"Well, it's immediately apparent, so you back off before chasing after a lost cause."

"But what if you really like someone?"

"If they didn't reciprocate, it would all feel...wrong. Their scent, their emotions, their body language. It would just be too off-putting."

"So if Randall and Aislinn were Lupine, he would stop chasing after her?"

"No," Jarod says after considering this for a moment. "He seems...special. I think if he were Lupine, he'd still be an idiot."

I laugh at this, and he smiles at me.

Jarod resumes transcribing where he had left off, but I'm having a hard time concentrating. "I wonder where he took her," I say, thinking out loud.

Jarod doesn't look up from his writing. "They're still in the archives. I can hear him lecturing her."

I listen closely, straining my ears for sound. *Nothing.* "You can hear them?" I say, disbelieving.

Jarod continues to write. "He's warning her about staying away from me. Thinks I'll attack her, do what he wants to do..."

My mouth falls open, and I gape at him.

After a moment he looks up at me. "Our hearing is vastly superior to yours."

"Another interesting skill to have," I say, amazed.

"It's a horrible skill to have here," he replies, exasperated. "I've been privy to countless conversations regarding the Gardnerian females' worries that I will abduct them at any moment, which is absurd."

"There might be a reason why they're so concerned," I point out. "The Northern Lupine packs may be different from yours. Aislinn's father visited them and came back with some very disturbing tales."

"Really. What exactly did he see?" Jarod asks with deep skepticism. He lays his pen down and gives me his full attention.

"Aislinn said that he saw one of the men get up in front of the entire pack, grab a young woman and drag her off into the woods to..." I gesture vaguely with my hand to fill in the blanks.

"And you believe this?"

"Jarod, he saw it with his own eyes."

"People see what they expect to see," he says sharply. "Through a filter of their own hatred and prejudice. You should realize this by now, rooming with two Icarals."

"Couldn't a different pack have different ways?" I rejoin defensively.

Jarod shakes his head tersely. "Our pack is no different from the Northern packs."

"But, Jarod, he *saw* it—"

"Here's what Aislinn's father saw," he says, cutting me off. "When two Lupines decide to take each other as life mates, one of them stands up and announces his or her desire to be with each other to the whole pack. The two then go off *privately* into the woods, and when they return, there is a joyful gathering to celebrate their union. Now, correct me if I'm mistaken, but this doesn't seem to be all that different from your people's traditions. Don't you have some type of religious ceremony where couples who wish to be life mates announce their intentions before friends and family? And then the couple goes off to mate with each other afterward?"

I bite at my lip, my face coloring. It's embarrassing to hear him talking about mating the way he and his sister do, so bluntly. But...he's essentially right. "I guess...it's similar, yes," I admit.

"Except for just a few details, perhaps," he continues, his tone clipped. "The mutual love and affection of the couple is an absolute given, or the pack would never approve of the match." He leans back in his chair, his glowing amber eyes full of disapproval. "Aislinn's father saw something beautiful, and twisted it into something sick and ugly, reinforcing his own unfair prejudices against us."

I think about everything I was told about the Lupines before I got to know Jarod and Diana. How much of it was blatant lies? How much of it was twisted truth?

"That may be a fair assessment," I finally agree.

"Hmm," is all he says before returning to his studies.

"Elloren, can I speak with you?"

It's later that same evening, and I'm still ensconced in the back of the main archives.

I look up from my pile of books and notes as Aislinn sits down across from me, her face pale and strained, her book bag slung over one shoulder.

"What's the matter?" My table sits near a window with a strong draft, but I'm blessedly next to a large iron stove that pumps out warmth.

"It's Randall." Aislinn glances around furtively before continuing, her voice low. "He doesn't want to wait. He wants to fast to me as soon as possible."

"Can't you put him off a little longer?"

"I've already put him off for over a year. He wants to wandfast over Yule and then have the sealing ceremony as soon as I graduate."

"How long would *you* like to wait?"

Her face goes tight with anxiety. "Forever."

I set down my pen and level my eyes at her. "Well, then, why don't you just do that?"

"You *know* that's not an option for me." She's quiet for a long moment. "He insisted on bringing me to this secluded spot behind the history buildings so he could kiss me and…" She looks away, blushing.

"And what?" I press, concern spiking. "Did he hurt you?"

"No, no. He's not like that. He's just gotten very…insistent.

Kissing used to be enough. Now he...grabs at me. I *hate* it. It's embarrassing."

"What do you mean, grabs at you?"

She slumps, her face coloring. "He...he grabbed at my chest."

I shake my head, angered on her behalf. "Aislinn, they need to find someone else for you."

"It doesn't matter who it is!" she cries. "I wouldn't like these things with anyone! I just don't like it. I don't like *any* of it."

"Have you told your parents how you feel about all this?" I ask, trying to find a solution.

Aislinn wrings her hands together. "I spoke to my mother about it."

"And...what did she say?"

"She said that all virtuous Gardnerian women dislike the type of...attentions wandfasting and sealing bring. But that it's something that has to be endured so we can have the joy of children. I love children, Elloren, you know that. I've always wanted to be a mother someday. But I'm shy. I don't want any man to touch me...not like that. I wish there was some other way to have children."

I let out a short laugh and grin at her. "What, like laying eggs?"

Aislinn breaks into a small smile at the ludicrous thought, and I'm glad for it. "Laying eggs would be good," she agrees.

Aislinn stares out the window, over the barren fields pressed down under a cold, dark sky. Another freezing rain seems imminent. Her smile grows shaky, as if she's apologizing for her thoughts.

"I just feel so miserable lately," she laments.

"We could walk over to the dining hall. Get some tea," I offer.

She shakes her head. "No. No, thank you. I'm going to go back to my lodging. I'm tired. I'm going to study for a while, try to get my mind off...everything."

I get up, embrace her and bid her good-night, and she leaves, shoulders slumped in defeat. I stare after her, troubled and perplexed. Wishing there was some way to get my friend out of this mess.

CHAPTER THREE

Elfin Art

A few nights later I return from my kitchen shift to find Jarod and Aislinn waiting for me in the North Tower's upstairs hallway, Wynter perched lightly on the windowsill behind them. Wynter is watching us all with a look of curiosity, her dark wings loosely wrapped around herself.

"You're visiting me!" I cry, made inexplicably happy by the sight of a Lupine, a conservative Gardnerian and an Elfin Icaral bunched together in such a calm and peaceful way.

Aislinn shrugs. "I'm finding that I like meeting new people," she says quietly. "People different from me. I'm tired of being afraid of everyone." She looks up at Jarod shyly, and he smiles warmly down at her.

"We're going to see the Elfin art exhibit," Jarod tells me, his arm wrapped around a few books. "Your roommate expressed an interest in accompanying us. We hoped you'd join us, as well."

"We've just discovered that we all share an interest in art," Aislinn tells me, clarifying this strange trio that has sprung up out of nowhere.

"And poetry," Jarod adds. He gestures to the books with his chin.

They look at me expectantly.

I'm way behind in my Apothecary and Metallurgie studies, I have a Mathematics exam in two days and I'm supposed to have drawings of virtually every species of Verpacian cornflower done by tomorrow.

And I don't care.

"Just let me throw my books on my bed," I tell them, unable to contain my excitement at the thought of so many new friends coming together.

We reach the Elfin gallery after a long and winding walk, Jarod swinging a lamp in front of us.

I'm surprised to see how different the Elfin architecture is from what I'm used to, the gallery nestled just inside the wilds. The buildings are bone white and all curves, like great seashells, and are topped by wavy, spiraling turrets that remind me of candle flames. They stretch toward the pinnacles of the tall pine trees and are joined to each other by cobbled walkways made of thousands of flat, silvery stones.

Wynter leads us into the largest of the buildings, down a twisting route through multiple doors with strange, curving symbols carved into them.

A large exhibit hall opens up before us, the floor's inlaid tiles of polished gray and blue stone set in flowing lines that make me feel as if I'm walking on water. The cathedral-like walls are curved and sloping and lit by the green-tinged light of Elfin lumenstone.

There are statues and paintings of Elfin kings and queens on horseback, landscapes depicting strange ivory dwellings built on steep mountainsides and nature studies in which the images of plants and stones appear as if they're floating above the paper.

And there are things I didn't even know could exist.

Statues made of swirling mist, tapestries depicting scenes that seem to come to life as you move in front of them, sculptures formed from moving water.

Wynter perches on one of the gallery's oval windowsills, still as stone, and follows us with her eyes.

I moved from piece to piece as Aislinn and Jarod talk about the art, engrossed in their conversation with each other. I can't help but notice how happy and animated Aislinn seems, and how bright Jarod's eyes glow.

"Where is *your* art?" Jarod asks Wynter.

Wynter cocks her head and considers his question. "My art cannot be displayed here," she explains in her softly accented voice. "It is infected with my darkness."

I frown at Wynter, saddened by her harsh statement and casual acceptance of her exclusion.

Aislinn and Jarod are both looking at her as well, Aislinn's eyes gone wide, Jarod's face tense and troubled.

"Show us," I find myself saying.

Wynter hesitates, then reluctantly hops down from her perch and leads us out of the museum and toward an out-of-the-way storage barn built in the Keltic style.

It's cold inside the large structure, and it smells slightly of mildew. Old furniture and battered frames line the walls, along with abandoned canvas, intricate weaving looms and a variety of worn art tools.

But in the center of this unattractive space, spiraling upward toward the rafters, is a large statue carved in white stone that glows as if illuminated from within.

It's an Elfin archer on horseback, the horse rearing high, the archer's bow and arrow pointed into the sky. It's slightly larger than life, and so real I'm almost afraid to step in front of it, lest the horse's hooves come crashing down on my head.

Jarod, Aislinn and I circle around it as Wynter trails quietly behind, hugging the shadows.

"You *made* this?" I breathe.

"Yes," she says softly.

I turn to her. "It's your brother, Cael. Isn't it?"

Wynter dips her head shyly. "Yes."

"Has he seen this?" Aislinn wonders, her tone one of awe.

Wynter nods.

"What did he say?" Aislinn asks.

"He was very touched," Wynter answers, almost in a whisper. "He liked it a great deal." Wynter reaches up to reverently run her hand along the cool white stone of the statue's base.

"It's beautiful," Jarod tells her. "Is there more?"

Wynter nods and gestures all around.

I'm like someone who has just been sent on a treasure hunt. We all are. Aislinn, Jarod and I immediately begin rummaging around, pulling old canvas sheets off sculptures and paintings, each new discovery bringing forth delighted gasps.

"Oh, look at the tapestries!" Aislinn's voice rings out as she lifts some canvas to expose four loosely rolled works. She turns to Wynter. "Did you weave these?"

Wynter nods as Jarod and I join Aislinn. The intricacy of what Wynter has done is evident even from a quick glimpse of the fabric's edging.

Wynter watches us modestly from where she sits, now perched on the base of her statue of her brother, her hand resting on the horse's smooth leg.

Aislinn pulls at one of the tapestries unsuccessfully. "They're terribly heavy..."

Jarod reaches around her with long, sinewy arms and effortlessly pulls one out.

Aislinn turns to him, amazed.

"Pretty handy to have a Lupine around," I observe, beaming at him, and he shoots me a small smile.

Jarod lowers the tapestry down on the floor and carefully unrolls it. It's large, able to cover a sizable wall, and pictures ethereal white birds flying across a summer field. I move my head and am fascinated to find the birds move as I do so, their wings flapping gracefully up and down.

Watchers.

Aislinn and Jarod enthusiastically move on to unfurling more tapestries as I stare at the ivory birds.

Wynter quietly approaches my side.

"I've seen them," I tell her, my voice low.

"I know this," she says. She looks to me with concern. "It is not good to see them, Elloren Gardner."

"Why?"

"The Shining Ones of the Inner Sanctum have deemed it so. They are messengers of the Shining Ones. Only the most holy may look upon them. For the impure to gaze upon them is blasphemy."

I'm thrown by how foreign her faith is to me, and how odd it all sounds. "And they think you impure?"

Wynter hangs her head, sorrowful. "All Icarals are impure. Cast out for their evil."

A spark of outrage rises deep inside me. "But how did all of this start? Why are Icarals viewed as evil?" I'm dismayed that her religion echoes this prejudice of ours.

Wynter is staring at me evenly, as if the truth of this is written in stone. "Because they seek to fly away from the Inner Sanctum into the realm of the Dark Ones. It is written in our sacred texts." Wynter's shoulders drop, and she looks to the birds in the tapestry with open longing. "I know that I should not sculpt these messengers, or paint them...but I find them to be so beautiful. I know it is blasphemy to say it, but they call to me." Wynter's voice grows stifled and faint. "They are my muse." She says it as if she's confessing some heinous, unforgivable crime.

I glance around at the unrolled tapestries, suddenly filled with stubborn purpose. "We should hang these up."

Wynter gives a start. She shakes her head in shocked disagreement. "No, Elloren Gardner. My work can never be hung in the gallery."

"Not in the gallery. In the North Tower."

She peers at me with deep concern. "My work would pollute any dwelling. Curse it—"

"No, Wynter." I cut her off gently. "This artwork was not meant to be thrown in the corner of some storeroom. Besides, we need the tapestries to keep out the drafts. I've noticed the cold doesn't seem to affect you and Ariel, but it sure affects me."

"You can hang the paintings all along the staircase," Jarod amiably suggests.

"And the flower series in the upstairs hallway," Aislinn chimes in.

"Surely some of the smaller sculptures could be brought up," Jarod adds.

We all turn to look at Wynter.

"Very well," she quietly agrees, a small smile lighting her face.

We make our way back to the North Tower, Jarod effortlessly carrying several tapestries. Aislinn, Wynter and I lug paintings.

"So, Black Witch, collecting freaks, are we?" Ariel asks as we walk in, her words slurred. She's lying on her bed, slumped down against the wall behind her, her eyes hooded, her lips stained black.

By now I recognize this state of hers. She's been eating those berries.

"You're the biggest freak of us all, you know," she goes on, attempting a look of hatred. "And you better keep the wild dog away from my chickens."

"He's *Lupine*," I clarify, irritated by her continual insistence on using racist language when talking to anyone but Wynter. But then I remember—it wasn't too long ago that I harbored quite a few prejudices of my own.

Jarod sets the four tapestries down on the floor and glances at Ariel.

"I mean it, wolf-boy," she snarls. "Touch my chickens, and I'll singe your mangy hide."

"Jarod's not interested in your chickens, Ariel," I tell her as I prop paintings up against the walls.

"*It* has a name?"

"It's best to just ignore her when she gets like this," I tell Jarod.

Jarod nods, seeming to understand.

Ariel sinks down against the wall, apathy finally settling in, her eyes going blank.

Aislinn and Jarod stand over the tapestries, discussing the best way to hang them. Aislinn fishes the hooks she's collected from the gallery out of her tunic pockets and holds them up for Jarod's perusal.

I sit down on my bed next to Wynter. "What are the berries that Ariel chews on?" I ask her, my voice low. I've been meaning to research them, but have had so little free time.

Wynter glances over at Ariel, who's now passed out on her bed. She sighs deeply. "They are nilantyr, a very powerful sedative," she says.

I inhale sharply, hearing this. "Ancient One, Wynter. It's illegal to possess. How on Erthia did she get it?"

Wynter shakes her head sadly. "I do not know. All I know is that when she was thrown in the Valgard asylum, they had a hard time controlling her. So they fed her the nilantyr to keep her calm."

I look to Ariel, sober understanding washing over me. "And she'll get the craving sickness if she stops taking it. They turned her into a craven."

Wynter nods.

"She told you all this? About being forced to take nilantyr?"

"Oh, no. She never speaks of it. When I touch her, I am

shown these memories." Wynter hesitates before continuing. "When she takes the nilantyr, the memories disappear. It all goes blank and empty. It is a cold peace, but peace nonetheless."

"It must be hard for you to see all this."

"It is very painful," she agrees, pulling her wings more tightly around herself.

I think of how often Ariel lies wrapped in Wynter's arms. All of those times, Ariel's memories were flooding into Wynter, and yet I've never seen Wynter pull away.

"You're a good friend to her," I say, moved.

"I love her," Wynter says softly. "She has become a sister to me. I want her to be at peace. But I fear that the nilantyr is a dark path. It is like a parasite, slowly breaking her. It has brought her to a point where she cannot fly, although she could when she was younger, and it robs her of her fire. She could once summon a large flame, but every day it grows smaller and smaller. And the drug, it has an odor that seeps through her skin. Even when she does not take it for a time, it lingers."

I think of the Icarals in Valgard, of their foul smell.

Were they fed this drug? Thrown in a cage when they were small children? Were they truly demons, or slowly driven mad from the cruelty inflicted on them?

"Can you fly?" I ask Wynter. I've never seen her use her wings for anything other than a flimsy shawl. I wonder if she's partaken of this nilantyr, as well—though I doubt it as she doesn't have Ariel's rancid smell.

Wynter shakes her head resignedly and lifts her wings. "My wings, they are too thin."

I turn back to glance at Aislinn and Jarod. They've finished organizing the hardware Aislinn pilfered and look about ready to start hanging the tapestries.

"We don't have any tools," Aislinn laments, looking around.

"I have tools," Jarod informs her.

"You do?" she asks, looking confused.

Jarod hesitates. "I…don't want to shock you."

"What do you mean?" Aislinn inquires.

"My claws. They're…useful."

Aislinn swallows and looks at him, wide-eyed. "I…I won't be afraid."

Jarod rolls up the right sleeve of his tunic and lifts his hand, keeping his eyes on Aislinn. We all watch, mesmerized, as it morphs and grows furred, with curving claws for nails.

Jarod walks over to the wall and uses a claw to quickly hollow out multiple areas in the stone, then morphs his hand back to normal and screws the hooks in. He turns to gauge Aislinn's reaction.

"That's very…useful," she observes, her understated words at odds with the stunned expression on her face.

Jarod studies her reaction for a moment longer before repeating the process, Aislinn's shock softening as he works.

Well past midnight, we all rest on the floor by the fire.

The room is completely transformed. Warm tapestries now hang on every wall, and a series of sculptures and paintings line the upstairs hallway and spiraling staircase. The North Tower has become a small but impressive private gallery of fine art.

I make tea and pour it for everyone. Everyone except for Ariel, who's still passed out on her messy bed.

Jarod and Aislinn are taking turns reading from Jarod's poetry books as Wynter sits on the windowsill listening.

After a time, Aislinn's lids grow heavier, and she keeps interrupting herself with yawns when it's her turn to read, so Jarod takes over the reading in its entirety, his deep, steady voice pleasant to listen to as I drink my tea.

I watch, amused, as Aislinn's eyes close, little by little, until, like a flower folding its petals in for the night, she eventually gives in, lets her eyes fall shut and leans into Jarod.

Jarod pauses in his reading. He gently puts his arm around

Aislinn to steady her. She breathes deeply and snuggles in close to him, her hand finding his waist.

Jarod raises his eyebrows in surprise, frozen in place, the poetry book now lying forgotten in his lap. Wynter has retreated under her wings, perhaps asleep, as well.

Jarod's eyes dart toward mine warily. And his wariness is not unfounded.

My heart speeds up slightly at the sight of them so close, so intimate, and I suddenly feel worried about my friend. It's one thing to wish Jarod was Gardnerian in the abstract. But he isn't. He's the son of his people's alpha, and Aislinn's from one of the most conservative families in Gardneria. Our people hate each other.

No, this isn't good. This is a road best not traveled down—a road leading straight off a cliff.

"Jarod," I say, a cautionary note to my tone, "Aislinn's become a good friend to me."

He cocks one eyebrow and regards me coolly. "I know, Elloren," he says slowly. "To me, as well."

"I can see that," I reply as I glance pointedly at the arm he has wrapped loosely around her. "I just don't want to see her get hurt." The atmosphere between us grows chilled, the tension palpable.

"And you think wandfasting to Randall is the best way for Aislinn to not get hurt?"

I don't know what to say to that, and am momentarily unnerved by those glowing amber eyes of his boring into me.

Of course it's probably the best way for her not to get hurt. She and Jarod are good friends, but a romance between them would tear Aislinn from a family she loves more than anything. Maybe Randall isn't Aislinn's idea of the best person to spend time with, but he won't be around much, and she has many other interests and people who love her to make her life complete. Besides, she finds romantic attentions of a physical nature to be very off-putting—although I have to admit that she looks pretty comfortable nestled in Jarod's arm. I can't for the life of me imagine her looking like that lying against Randall.

A flicker of disgust passes over Jarod's face, and he turns to look at the fire. "Don't worry, Elloren. I don't plan on dragging her off into the woods anytime soon."

His words sting, and I feel immediately guilty for interfering in something that is really none of my business. "I'm not worried about that, Jarod," I clarify anxiously.

He turns his Lupine eyes back to mine. "I know what you're getting at. We're just friends." Bitterness gives way to a flash of quiet devastation in his eyes before he looks away. "I know that…anything else between us would be impossible."

My eyes catch on Jarod's fingers. He's stroking Aislinn's hair absently with a tenderness that's heartbreaking to witness. I turn away from them both, tears filling my eyes over their hopeless situation.

CHAPTER FOUR

Lupine Eyes

Aislinn and I are having breakfast a few days later. It's week's end, the dining hall almost empty at this early hour, pale streaks of sunlight spearing down through the arching windows. Aislinn stirs honey into her wheatberries, chatting gaily about her family. She's been happily anticipating the arrival of her sisters for weeks now, and they're due to arrive anytime now.

I glance up to catch Yvan staring at me as he sets a basket of rolls out on one of the long serving tables. His green eyes flash through me and set off a restless longing that's becoming harder and harder to ignore.

Things have changed between us since that day he defended me in the kitchens. I now catch him staring at me throughout my shifts, and we're always incredibly aware of each other's physical presence. If he's loading wood at my stove and I shift, he immediately compensates, like a dance. It's hard in those moments, when he's so close and so aware of me, to fight off an intense, irrational urge to touch his hand, his chestnut hair, his shoulder.

I wonder what's wrong with me. How can I be so drawn to a Kelt? I imagine Aunt Vyvian's reaction and can't stifle the smile that quavers on my lips just as Yvan's eyes settle back on me. My pulse quickens, and I dampen my smile, but can't pull my eyes away from him, the air suddenly charged between us. Even from this far distance, his gaze is hot on me, a ruddy flush coloring his cheeks.

Iris bursts from the kitchen, jauntily balancing a tray of smoked meat, and the moment abruptly shatters. She has a flirtatious smile dancing on her face as she sets down her tray and sidles up to Yvan, one hand on her cocked hip, her golden hair loose today and cascading down her back.

Yvan launches into conversation with her, but he's holding himself rigidly, as if he's as distracted and unsettled as I am.

"Oh, Elloren, they're here!" Aislinn enthuses, breaking my heated focus.

I turn, cheeks uncomfortably flushed, to find Aislinn's sisters making a boisterous entrance, children swirling around them like a swarm of busy bees, a baby in the arms of each sister.

"Linnie!" they call out to her.

Aislinn springs from her seat, overjoyed. She rushes to them and is quickly enveloped in a tangle of hugs and kisses.

I rise and briefly look toward where Yvan was. I note, with a spike of envy, that both he and Iris have gone back into the kitchen.

Let it go, Elloren, I tell myself. *You're a Gardnerian. He's a Kelt. These thoughts need to stop.* I sigh and turn back to Aislinn's family.

Both her sisters are wearing white armbands, the children surprisingly banded as well, unlike Aislinn and me. I wonder what Aislinn's sisters will make of her lack of Vogel fervor.

"Oh, how we've missed you!" the taller of her two sisters exclaims, beaming at Aislinn.

"Look at how big everyone's grown!" Aislinn gushes over her nieces and nephews, the children hugging her legs. "Elloren!" She beckons for me to join them, her face full of happiness. "These are my sisters and some of their children."

Some of them? Gardnerians, as a rule, usually have large families, but Aislinn's sisters don't look much older than her.

"How many more nieces and nephews do you have?" I ask Aislinn, trying to keep my tone friendly instead of incredulous.

Aislinn smiles. "Auralie has two more boys. They're back in Valgard with Mother."

There are twin boys about three years of age, one clinging to the leg of Aislinn's shorter sister, another energetically running around making horse noises. An older girl of about five years stands calmly, beaming up at Aislinn, and a four-year-old boy runs over to hug Aislinn. She affectionately ruffles his hair.

The sisters are plain like Aislinn, their hair swept back into neat, unstylish buns. They wear the layered, shapeless clothing of the most conservative Gardnerian families, Erthia orbs on chains around their necks.

"Elloren Gardner! Heavens, you *do* look like your grandmother!" The taller sister, Liesbeth, approaches me and introduces herself. She embraces me warmly as we kiss on both cheeks. "Aislinn's told us all about you in her letters. We're so happy she's found such a good friend."

The shorter sister, Auralie, smiles awkwardly in my direction, then looks back down at the floor, her baby fussing in her arms.

What a contrast these two sisters are. Liesbeth is well put together, not a hair out of place and comfortable in her surroundings, her baby plump and neatly swaddled.

Auralie, a heavyset girl with hair escaping her bun at odd angles, has a look in her eyes similar to Ariel—not quite there. And her baby looks stressed and too thin.

It's easy to match the other children with their mothers. I pick out the neatly attired, well-behaved children and mentally match them to Liesbeth. To Auralie, I match the disheveled twin boys with tense faces.

"We know your aunt quite well," Liesbeth tells me, beaming.

"She's a great ally to our father on the Mage Council—they're of one mind about practically *everything*."

I stiffen at the mention of Aunt Vyvian, wondering when my aunt will finally tire of sending a steady stream of letters and sporadic gifts to get me to wandfast. I fear it's only a matter of time before she shifts tactics once more.

"Aunt Linnie!" the little girl cuts in, tugging at Aislinn's skirts. "When are you coming to visit? We got a kitten!"

Aislinn sets her hand on the child's shoulder and smiles down at her. "That's wonderful, Erin. I love kittens, you know that."

"I baked your favorite cookies, Linnie." Liesbeth pulls back the blue cloth that covers a woven basket she's carrying. "You're welcome to have some, too, Elloren."

Aislinn's smile instantly becomes as strained as mine as we glance down at the traditional Gardnerian harvest cookies. They're in the shape of Icaral wings. Before eating them, it's customary to first break the wings in two, symbolic of the breaking of the wings of the Evil Ones by the Gardnerian First Children. I've eaten these cookies hundreds of times and performed the breaking ritual mindlessly. Now all I can think about is Wynter. And Ariel, too—thrown into a cage when she was only a child.

The children grab at the cookies and snap them noisily.

"I can do it louder than you," little Erin taunts one of the boys good-naturedly. She breaks the wings with a deft snap.

Aislinn flinches at the sound of it. She shoots me a troubled look, and then her eyes go wide. She's staring at something past me, her face gone chalk white.

Curious, I turn to follow her gaze.

It's Jarod, leaning against a far wall, watching us.

Aislinn's sisters immediately notice Aislinn's rattled expression, stop smiling and follow her gaze, as well.

"Is that…" Liesbeth whispers, horrified, "…the *Lupine male*?"

Auralie gasps, and both sisters touch their heads, then their hearts, as they murmur the familiar prayer:

Oh, Most Holy Ancient One, purify our minds, purify our hearts, purify Erthia. Protect us from the stain of the Evil Ones.

Liesbeth turns to Aislinn, concerned. "Has he been bothering you, Linnie?"

"No," Aislinn protests, her brow furrowing tightly. "No, he stays away from me."

"Is he still in that class you're taking?" Liesbeth presses worriedly. "I remember how scared you were to have him there."

"He leaves me alone," Aislinn insists, her voice strained. "It turns out he hasn't the slightest interest in me."

"But he's quite wild-looking, isn't he?" Auralie breathes, peering over at Jarod, who hasn't moved.

"Look at his eyes," Liesbeth exclaims. "They're positively inhuman!"

Aislinn glances over at me, horrified, knowing as well as I do that Jarod can hear every word of this conversation. He's turned away, his face expressionless.

"Take great care, Linnie," Auralie warns Aislinn, her tone hushed. "Lupine males...they have no respect for women. Father says they're like animals. All they can think about is dragging women off into the woods and..."

Jarod abruptly walks out.

"Oh, good, he's leaving," Auralie says, breathing a heavy sigh of relief. She pats Aislinn on the shoulder comfortingly. "There, Linnie, he's gone. You can relax now."

"Thank the Ancient One," Liesbeth says, echoing the sentiment.

"Mommy, who was the man with the strange eyes?" Aislinn's niece asks.

"A very bad man," Liesbeth says, hugging the child soothingly. "But he's gone now, sweetheart, so you needn't worry."

"Is he like my toy, Momma?" one of the boys asks with morbid enthusiasm. He pulls a wooden figurine out of a little sack he's carrying. It's a scowling Lupine with glowing eyes painted bright amber, his hands morphed into hairy wolf hands with long claws.

"That's him, all right," Auralie agrees, nodding.

Aislinn's nephew dumps out the rest of his toys onto a nearby table, and all the familiar wooden figures spill out: evil Icarals, flames in their palms; sinister Vu Trin sorceresses; an evil-looking Fae queen; and the valiant Gardnerian soldiers, some on horseback.

"I'm gonna have the soldiers kill him!" the boy announces as he begins to set the Gardnerian soldiers up in a circle around the Lupine.

"That sounds like a good idea," Liesbeth says, pleased.

The little girl, Erin, looks worriedly toward the door. "Will he come back?" she asks Liesbeth, clinging to her skirts.

"Oh, honey, he won't bother you." Her mother reassures her. "Look at all the Gardnerian soldiers here. You're quite safe. And when Marcus Vogel takes over as High Mage, the brave soldiers like Poppa will get rid of them someday. Then no one will have to worry about them ever again."

And we can all live happily-ever-after, I think sarcastically. It's becoming unbearable to remain silent, yet neither one of us can say anything. If we do, Aislinn's sisters will become suspicious about our intermingling with Lupines, and those suspicions will surely find their way back to Aislinn's father.

"The Lupine...he hasn't bothered me," Aislinn ventures weakly. "He and his sister leave everyone alone. They keep to themselves."

"Nonetheless," Liesbeth says as she deftly restrains the toddler who's running in circles around her legs. "I wish you'd hurry up and fast to Randall. Lupine men see an unfasted woman and think she's easy prey. Plus, once you're fasted and married, we can all be together again."

"We miss you, Linnie," Auralie laments, a deep sadness in her eyes.

"I miss you, too," Aislinn admits, her voice tight with longing. Aislinn is looking at her sisters the way you stare at a boat that's sailing off, leaving you behind.

"Aunt Linnie, you promised in your letter that you'd play with me when I saw you," Aislinn's niece entreats, pouting up at her aunt. "I brought my new marbles to show you!"

"Oh, show her, Erin!" Liesbeth enthuses. "They're from the Valgard glassworks, Tierney's father's shop."

Little Erin opens up a black velvet bag with a red, tasseled pull string, and we all reach in to pull out the large marbles. We hold them each up in turn so we can peer through them at the swirling colors that catch the surrounding light.

Aislinn holds one up, studying it closely. "Look at this one, Elloren," she breathes. "It's so beautiful. It reminds me of something...but I don't know what."

She hands it to me, and I look through it with her as she leans close, studying the bright amber globe with me.

"Oh, I know," she says, smiling with sudden realization. "It's just like..." She catches herself, colors deeply and looks away, her smile disappearing.

I turn back to view the swirling orb in my hand. It *is* beautiful, just like she said.

The exact color of Lupine eyes.

CHAPTER
FIVE

Howl

A few days later I hear the howling.

Aislinn and I are eating lunch in the dining hall. I look up from my food to see what the commotion is.

It's coming from a group of Gardnerian military apprentices, all with white armbands.

Fallon Bane sits imperiously in their center, her military guard nearby.

Other young Gardnerian men soon join in, and the dining hall begins to sound like there's a wolf pack running around in it.

In the center of all the animal noises stands Diana Ulrich. She strides down a center aisle toward us, chin raised, a large plate of food cradled in both hands, a bag slung over her shoulder.

As she passes, young men laugh and proposition her.

"Hey, wolf-girl!"

"Strip for us!"

They're all leering at her shamelessly. The scattered Gardnerian women seated with the men avert their eyes and studiously ignore this display, but not Fallon. She scandalously laughs right along with the men.

Diana flicks her long, luxurious hair over one shoulder dismissively, like a goddess forced to spend time with some very distasteful mortals.

"Hello, Elloren, Aislinn," she says as she sits down at our table and flashes us a dazzling smile. Without further ado, she picks up a large piece of chicken and begins to gnaw on it with relish.

I can't believe the amount of meat on her plate. Practically a whole chicken.

The howling dies down, only a few of the men now glancing in our direction as they laugh and nudge each other suggestively.

"Doesn't that bother you?" I ask as Diana unconcernedly chomps down on some gristle. I throw a resentful glance toward Fallon, who's laughing and having a grand old time being the center of the Gardnerian universe.

Diana looks up, confused, and glances over at the Gardnerians. "Why should that bother me?" she asks, her mouth full of meat. She swallows in one loud gulp. "They are as insignificant as that fool of a Mage, Fallon Bane."

"They were *howling* at you."

Diana shrugs and rolls her eyes. "They can't help themselves," she says rather arrogantly. "They all wish they could mate with me. It's not surprising in the least." She straightens as she chews and tosses her golden mane. "Look at me. I am *magnificent*. Every male wants me." She picks up another hunk of meat and tears at it with her long, white teeth as Aislinn and I stare at her, dumbfounded.

"Of course I have no interest in them," she continues loftily. "They are weak and pathetic. I really don't understand how you can tolerate men such as these. Like this Randall you're to be wandfasted to, Aislinn." She gestures toward Aislinn with a bone. "Jarod says he's an idiot who doesn't deserve you."

Aislinn goes white and sits frozen in place, staring at her.

Completely oblivious, Diana continues to chew, her teeth making an unnatural grinding noise. Her eyes light up. "You should become Lupine, Aislinn! Then you could mate with

one of *our* men. They are completely superior. Strong and vir-
ile. Lupine men are excellent lovers, not like these sense-blind
Gardnerian idiots must be. I'm not surprised that they have to
run off to be with seal women. Their own women must refuse
to mate with them, and really, it's quite understandable." Diana
chuckles to herself and then points a bone at me. "You, too, Elloren. You should also become one of us."

I almost choke on my food. Eyes watering, I take a drink of
water as I eye Diana with incredulity.

I turn to Aislinn. She's still shocked into silence by Diana's
screaming lack of tact.

"Diana," I venture, my voice hoarse from choking. I take
another drink of water. "You're not going to make any friends
talking like this."

"Talking like what?" she asks as she chews loudly.

"You're insulting Gardnerian men. I do have two brothers,
you know, and they happen to be Gardnerians."

Diana waves a bone in the air as if chasing away the idea.
"Rafe is different. He should become Lupine as soon as possible. He is *seriously* out of place here."

She's infuriating. Hands down, the most arrogant person I
have ever met. "I *have* noticed that you've been spending a good
deal of time with my brother," I observe, bristling as Diana pulls
a leg off her chicken carcass with a loud *snap*.

"We share a love of the woods," she replies, concentrating
more on her meat than on me.

"Diana," I probe testily, "what's going on with you and my
brother?"

She looks up at me, a large piece of meat half in her mouth,
half still attached to the bone in her hand. She appears genuinely surprised by the question. "We've been hiking," she replies, her words muffled around the meat.

"Hasn't anyone ever told you not to talk with your mouth
full?" I ask snidely, growing increasingly irritated.

"Why?" she asks.

"Because it's *rude!*" I cry.

Diana puts down her chicken bone, finishes chewing, swallows and calmly clasps her long, grease-coated fingers in front of herself, humoring me like one would humor a very silly child. "Your people have many ridiculous rules."

"It's a relief to hear you talk without meat hanging out of your mouth!"

"I am *hungry.* This is a *stupid* conversation!"

"Don't you lead my brother on!" I jab a finger at her accusingly. "I think he likes you!"

"I like Rafe as well, and haven't the foggiest idea what you are talking about!"

"Are you romantically involved with my brother?" If she can be blunt and tactless, so can I.

She snorts haughtily. "Of course not. He's not Lupine."

"Then why do you spend so much time with him?"

"He likes the woods. I like the woods. We both like to hunt. We both like to hike," she says, exasperated. "We go *hiking!*"

"And that's *it?*"

"What, exactly, are you asking me? I keep *trying* to answer you!"

"Are you running around naked?"

"No, I am not," she replies, glowering at me. "Not since you and your brother informed me of how offensive my magnificent form is to Gardnerian eyes."

"Have you kissed him?"

"That is mating behavior. Your brother is not Lupine." Now she's talking to me like I'm three years old. "I will not mate with a man who is not Lupine, so *no,* I have not kissed your brother! Can I go back to eating my chicken, please? Or is there some stupid rule about that, too?"

"Go ahead! *Eat!*"

"Thank you," she says, her tone clipped.

"Randall's not so bad," Aislinn says weakly, finally finding her voice.

"Jarod said Randall's an idiot," Diana repeats around another mouthful of meat.

I grind my own teeth in deep irritation.

"Well," says Aislinn defensively, "you can tell Jarod that I could do a lot worse!"

Diana laughs derisively at this, spitting out some pieces of meat in the process. I have to make sure Rafe sees her eat. If there is any attraction on his part, watching her destroy a chicken with her teeth will surely kill it dead.

"That," Diana says, grinning widely, meat sticking out between her teeth, "I find *completely* believable."

"You tell Jarod that Randall's not so bad!" Aislinn insists.

Diana points a rib cage at a spot behind Aislinn. "Tell him yourself."

Jarod has just come in. He quickly spots us, smiles warmly and makes his way over to our table. "Hello," he says as he reaches us. "Are we eating together now?"

Aislinn turns to glare at him with open hostility.

"What's the matter?" he asks, concerned.

"I told Aislinn what you said about Randall being an idiot," Diana explains nonchalantly.

Jarod blanches and swallows hard. Diana doesn't seem to notice this as she tears a wing off the rapidly disappearing carcass in front of her, her hands and lips slick with chicken fat. Apparently, complete tactlessness isn't a Lupine trait. It's a Diana trait.

"That wasn't really something I wanted repeated," Jarod tells his sister, his voice weak.

"Why?" asks Diana. "She should know this. Before she does this awful wandfasting thing."

"He's not an idiot," Aislinn says as she stares at her plate, sounding hurt and as if she's trying to convince herself that the sentence is true.

"I'm sorry, Aislinn," Jarod apologizes, his voice low and kind. "I didn't mean to offend you. I...I think highly of you and would not think most men were good enough for you."

Diana snorts. "That's because most Gardnerian men are fools."

Jarod tries to ignore his sister, his eyes focused on my Gardnerian friend. "Aislinn," he says, his voice sincere, "I really am sorry."

She looks away from him, her face strained.

"Sit down, Jarod." I invite him with a sigh. "Join us. It's all water under the bridge."

"Thank you," he says. He sets his meat-laden plate down and ventures a worried look in Aislinn's direction. She picks absently at her muffin, eyes on her plate, her expression vacant.

Jarod picks up a knife and fork and begins to cut his chicken into neat little bites.

Diana stops eating and stares at him, incredulous. "Since when do you use utensils?" she asks, a note of accusation in her voice.

"Since we've been living in Verpacia," he shoots back. "Unlike you, I'm trying to fit in here."

Diana shrugs and gives the meat her full attention once more. "Suit yourself."

Jarod turns back to Aislinn. "Is it still all right if we meet later?"

Aislinn frowns at her muffin. "Yes, Jarod," she agrees, her voice tentative.

"Perhaps at nineteenth hour? I'll meet you in the archives?"

Aislinn nods at her plate, still not looking at him.

"Okay, then," Jarod says. He ventures a small smile in her direction, then goes back to cutting his chicken into tiny pieces.

CHAPTER SIX

Jarod

Later that evening I sit at my desk, alone except for the slumbering chickens, staring at a list of metal powders recently given to me by Professor Hawkkyn.

I'm passing Metallurgie now instead of barely passing, my Snake Elf professor turned into an unlikely ally, making me suddenly wonder if I've been told nothing but lies about his kind.

A few weeks ago Professor Hawkkyn called me aside, curious and thrown by my newly casual attire.

"You're dressed like a Kelt," he observed flatly as if I was plotting some dark scheme, the silvery glinting of his star eyes distracting me.

I straightened and held his silvered gaze. "Professor Kristian told me my clothes were made by Urisk slaves, so I decided not to wear them anymore." I shrugged defensively. "Anyway, these are more comfortable."

He stared at me for a long moment, and I was suddenly struck by how beautiful he is, each flat scale reflecting a kaleidoscope of stunning greens. "You know Jules Kristian?" he asked.

"Yes," I replied, then knit my brow in question. "You...as well?"

Professor Hawkkyn broke into a dazzling, incredulous smile, his teeth snow white in contrast to his deep green scales. "Jules is...a good friend." He considered me for another long moment, then spit out a short laugh, shook his head and expeditiously went back to correcting papers. "I rescind your second assignment, Elloren Gardner," he said without looking up. "Just complete the first section." He paused from his corrections, gave me a long, appraising look, then pulled a paper out from one of his folders and handed it to me.

I glanced at the list of metal powders as I took it from him, confused. "Are these...what we're going to test the chelating agents on?"

He narrowed his star eyes at me. "No. It's a list of metal powders that block ice magic. I thought that might be of some interest to you."

I gaped at the list then at him, dark delight and overwhelming gratitude bubbling up. "I...I never knew about this. Does it really work?"

"Wand magic's not the only power," he replied in a low voice, his teeth set in another dazzling, dangerous grin.

I stare at the list in the quiet of my room, thinking of all the ways that I can now make myself impervious to Fallon's low-level, yet still-constant bullying.

I'm interrupted by a tentative knock at my door.

Setting down my pen, I get up and open the door to find Aislinn, her eyes red and puffy.

"Aislinn, what's the matter?" I ask, surprised.

"I—I need to talk to you," she stammers.

I let her in and close the door behind us. She plops down onto my bed, her arms clasped protectively around herself, and begins to sob.

I sit down and put a comforting hand on her heaving back. "Aislinn, what's wrong?"

"Jarod kissed me!" she blurts out, her tone deeply anguished.

My eyes fly open in surprise. I know how much Aislinn dislikes kissing.

"Did he force you?" I ask, a protective edge rearing up, along with strident disbelief that Jarod could be capable of such a thing.

"No," she says, shaking her head. "No. It just...*happened.*"

Relief washes over me. "Then why are you so upset?"

"Because...I..." She doubles over as if in pain. I try to calm her down by shushing her and rubbing her back. She turns to me, her face soaked with tears. "I *liked* it!"

I blink at her, baffled. "*That's* why you're crying?"

"No," she sobs, her voice stuffy. "That's a lie. I didn't just like it. I *loved* it. We kissed for over an hour," she chokes out. "It was like heaven. I never knew. I've never felt that way before! I thought it was all made up. All those silly romantic ideas. I thought no one ever really felt that way. Oh, Elloren, my life is ruined!"

I shake my head vehemently. "It's not ruined—"

"How can I ever be happy with Randall now? Now that I know what it's like with Jarod? Why can't Jarod be a Gardnerian? He's *Lupine*, Elloren! Do you know what my family would do to me if they knew I'd spent the last hour kissing a Lupine? They'd disown me! I'd never see my mother again! My sisters! My nieces and nephews! I'd be all alone! I'm going to hell, Elloren! I'm an abomination!"

"You are not going to hell. You don't really believe Jarod is evil, do you?"

"No!" she cries. "I just... My whole world is upside down. I should *never* have taken that class with him. Oh, Elloren, what am I going to *do?*"

"What happened," I ask, "after he kissed you?" *Ancient One, this is a complicated mess.*

"I started crying," she sobs. "And I ran away."

I let out a long breath, dismayed. "Oh. Poor Jarod."

That only makes her cry harder.

"What if your parents actually met him?" I venture, grasping for some hope. "Remember how *we* were scared of Jarod and Diana? Maybe if they saw how nice he is..."

"You don't *understand*! You have no idea how strict they are! My father is Gardneria's ambassador to the Lupines. He *hates* them. He has all sorts of...*ideas* about them!" She shakes her head vehemently. "I can't be around Jarod anymore. I'll just stay as far away from him as I possibly can." Her head falls into her hands, her slender body racked with violent sobbing.

A knock at my door pulls my attention away. I get up and open the door to find Jarod standing in the hallway, not in tears, but still looking distraught.

"I need to talk to Aislinn," he says.

I step out into the hallway and close the door. "I don't think she wants to talk to you right now."

"Can I talk to you, then?" he asks, his brow deeply furrowed. "She probably told you what happened."

"She did. Jarod, she can't be with a Lupine. She'd be disowned."

"I'm in love with her, Elloren."

My breath catches tight in my throat. *Oh, Ancient One.* There's nothing but the deepest of sincerity in his amber eyes, his expression one of raw anguish.

I let out a deep sigh. "I respect that. I know your people don't say that lightly."

"No. We don't," he says. "I want to mate with her, Elloren. For life."

Oh, Sweet Ancient One. "But you're Lupine, Jarod, and she's Gardnerian. Her family is incredibly conservative."

"I don't care," he says. "I don't care what she is. I don't care who her family is. I love her. I can't help it. I just do."

He places one hand on his hip and brings the other to his temples, like he's massaging a headache. He looks around blankly, then takes a seat on the hallway bench and drops his head into his hands. "This complicates my life as well, you know. My pack will accept outsiders, but they *must* become Lupine. If I were to take a Gardnerian female to mate before she became Lupine, I would cease to be a member of my pack. My family wouldn't cut off contact with me like hers would, but I would not be allowed to return home until my mate became Lupine."

I sit down next to him. "Aislinn doesn't want to be Lupine, Jarod. She loves being a Gardnerian. And she loves her family very much."

"I know." He's quiet for a moment, Aislinn's muffled sobs audible through the door.

"Jarod," I say, placing my hand on his shoulder. "Give her some time. She didn't expect to like kissing you so much. It came as a bit of a shock. She always thought of kissing as a rather unpleasant chore, actually."

"Randall's an idiot," Jarod snarls, exposing his gleaming canines. "When I think of him taking Aislinn to mate, I feel physically ill."

I let out a long sigh. "I think she feels the same way."

He gives me an imploring look. "Do you think she'll speak to me again? Before she wandfasts to that fool?"

"I think so. But you might have to give her some time. I think she loves you, too, and it's scaring her."

"She's the last person on Erthia I want to frighten."

"I know that."

"You'll speak to her? You'll tell her all this?"

I hesitate, but the devastation in his eyes softens me toward him. "I will."

He breathes a long sigh of relief. "Thank you."

When I return to my room, Aislinn has stopped crying and is sitting on the bed, staring straight ahead at nothing, a traumatized look in her glassy eyes.

"What did he say?" she asks, her voice flat and emotionless.

I sit down in my desk chair and lean forward to face her. "He says that he loves you. That he doesn't care who your family is. That he still loves you. That he doesn't care if his own pack disowns him. That he only wants you. For life. And that he never meant to cause you any pain."

Aislinn begins to sob again. She closes her eyes tight as if her thoughts hurt, turns slowly and lies down on the bed, curling herself into a tight ball, her back to me.

I sit and watch her for a long moment, not sure what to do, heartbroken for the both of them. I blink back tears.

There's nothing I can do. There's no easy way out for either of them.

I wipe away my tears, blow out the lamp on my desk, pull a blanket over Aislinn, then lie down next to her and put my arm around her. Aislinn grasps hold of my arm with a firm, desperate grip.

I hold her for a long time, until she finally cries herself to sleep.

CHAPTER
SEVEN

Trapped

"I'm worried about you, Aislinn."

It's early morning, and she's sitting against a tree listlessly, dark circles anchored beneath her eyes. Looking like she hasn't slept at all.

A week has passed, and Aislinn has made an uneasy peace with Jarod. He's taken my advice, giving Aislinn space to think, although I can see it takes a great effort on his part to do so. Aislinn doesn't stop coming to Chemistrie, but their note passing ceases.

Aislinn stares at me despondently. "I'm trapped."

The words hang in the air, a wintry breeze swirling around them. It's been a strange year—colder every day, but still we wait for snow.

I try to think of something to distract her. "You know, Diana Ulrich is living with me now."

I've chosen my subject well.

Aislinn's pained expression becomes more muted as her eyebrows arch up in surprise. "Really?"

★ ★ ★

The previous night Diana appeared at my door, two large travel bags in hand.

"I will hurt her if I stay," Diana announced as she swept into the room and threw her things on my bed.

"Who?" I asked, looking up from my studies, as mystified as Ariel and Wynter by Diana's sudden presence here.

"Echo Flood…all of them," Diana informed us imperiously. "I will live with you now. Ah, good, chickens. A snack. I'm famished."

Incensed, Ariel leaped in front of her chickens and thrust out her palms. A small circle of fire erupted around Diana. This surprised me. I'd seen Ariel start the fireplace fire on numerous occasions, but she never seemed able to summon more than a very small flame.

Diana looked down and viewed the rapidly disappearing ring of fire with disdain. "Why is she so protective of these chickens?"

"Get out!" Ariel hissed.

"No!" Diana replied, indignant as she crossed her arms in front of herself.

"Diana," I said firmly, "promise Ariel you won't eat the chickens!"

"But…"

"Just promise her! You cannot stay here unless you leave any birds that make their way into this room alone."

Diana looked back and forth from Ariel to me like we were both completely unhinged. "All right," she relented, humoring us. "I promise. I will not eat these chickens. I would just like to know one simple thing."

I raised my eyebrows at her.

"Are there no normal people in this University?"

I glanced over at Ariel, who was crouched in front of her chickens, eyeing Diana murderously, the terrified chickens glued to her ankles. Then I looked over at Wynter, who was hiding under her wings, and finally at Diana's glowing eyes. And then there was me, the magic-free Black Witch look-alike.

Laughter at the sheer absurdity of it all bubbled up inside me. "I don't know about the whole University, Diana, but there are definitely no normal people in this room."

Diana stared at me for a moment, one eyebrow arched as if mildly affronted. But I caught Wynter's eye, and she gave me a small, tentative smile.

"I'm going out!" Diana abruptly announced with a dissatisfied huff.

"Where?" I asked.

"To find some rabbits!" she snapped. "Since you are all so protective of these chickens!"

"What did she do next?" Aislinn asks, enthralled despite her dark mood.

"She came back about an hour later with a rabbit, proceeded to strip naked and sat glowering by the fireplace eating it."

Aislinn swallows, mortified. "Naked?"

"Naked," I confirm, matter-of-factly. "I finally had a chance to speak to Rafe about her, too. He stopped by my room earlier, looking for her."

"What did he say?"

"He thought the story about her moving in is pretty funny. He thinks everything's funny. I told him that I'm worried about how much time he's been spending with Diana. I mean, she's the daughter of an alpha, and our people aren't on the best terms with each other." I hesitate before continuing.

"Go on," Aislinn prods.

"I told him I didn't want to see him do something incredibly dangerous...for love." I glance sidelong at Aislinn, watching for her reaction.

"And what did he say?" she asks, her voice now muted.

"Oh, you know. Typical Rafe. He told me not to worry so much—that he'd be careful. But then he laughed and said that if he was going to do something incredibly dangerous, he really couldn't think of a better reason to."

"That's not very encouraging, is it?" Aislinn says, looking away uncomfortably.

I follow Aislinn's gaze down the long, sloping field before us, the wilds just beyond.

In the distance a lone figure catches my attention. It takes a moment for me to recognize who it is.

Yvan, walking toward the forest at a fast clip.

It's not the first time I've seen him heading into the wilds. I've spotted him a number of times from the North Tower window, striding purposefully toward the forest, always curiously alone.

I watch Yvan's long, powerful stride and think about how things between us have continued to change. His overt hostility is gone. I catch him watching me in both the kitchen and Mathematics now. His expression is often difficult to read, and he quickly looks away as soon as I catch his eye. Against my better judgment, I continue to do a fair bit of discreet watching, too. It's thrilling to look at him; he's so absurdly handsome.

And I can't stop thinking about the mystery of him—how fast and strong he was when going up against Damion Bane. Unnaturally so. And I notice, more and more, how he's able to pick up heavy things around the kitchen as though they weigh nothing. Just like Jarod.

I dwell on other things, as well.

How he always leaves the top button of his shirt undone, the shadows of the kitchen playing over his elegant neck and throat. The sinuous grace of his movements, never a clumsy, false step, his reflexes razor-sharp. The sharp line of his jaw. The perfect bow of his upper lip, his mouth so distractingly sensual.

A warm flush rises in my cheeks just thinking about it.

"Where does he go?" I wonder as I watch him, thinking out loud.

Aislinn turns to me. "Where does *who* go?"

"Yvan Guriel. He's always going off into the woods like Rafe, but not hunting. He never carries anything with him. He just goes. It's like he's Lupine or something."

"So follow him," Aislinn says despondently.

"That's bold advice," I laugh.

Aislinn shrugs listlessly.

I get up and brush dried leaves off my tunic.

"Where are you going?" Aislinn asks.

"I'm taking your advice," I tell her. "I'm going to follow him."

Rescue

"Why are you following me, Elloren?" Yvan's tone is exasperated, but not angry. He doesn't bother to turn around.

My face grows hot at being discovered, and from the ridiculous thrill of hearing his deep voice say my name. "I'm curious about you," I reply, my tone self-conscious and stilted.

"About what, exactly?" he asks, not slowing, not looking back.

About so many things. "About why you're always going off into the woods. I'm wondering if you're secretly Lupine."

He stops abruptly, and I stop, too, a nervous rush of energy coupled with my efforts to keep up making my heart race in my chest.

He puts his hands on his hips and looks down as if collecting himself, and then turns to me, his emerald gaze disconcerting.

My thoughts scatter like marbles, overcome by his severe beauty.

Our eyes lock tight, the woods quieting around us, save for the dry rustling of the remaining autumn leaves and intermittent birdsong. The silence between us grows charged, vibrating with suppressed emotion, an unsettling heat taking hold deep inside me. I search his eyes and wonder if he feels it, too.

"All right, then," he finally says, his voice low, his eyes darkening, as if with challenge. "Try to keep up."

"Where's the University's border?" I ask after what seems like an eternity of hiking.

He pauses and turns to me, brow furrowed in question.

My breath hitches in my throat. It would be easier to talk to his back. I stare at him for a split second like a complete idiot, distracted by the way a shaft of sunlight illuminates his handsome face.

He cocks one perfectly arched brow, his expression hardening with what seems like discomfited annoyance. Like he can read my thoughts.

"It's dangerous for me...to cross the University border," I testily clarify.

The furrow of his brow deepens. "Why?"

"There's an Icaral trying to kill me."

His eyes light with surprise.

"It thinks I'm the next Black Witch," I try to explain. "Of course, I'm *not*. I've no magic at all, but it doesn't know that."

Yvan's face darkens. "You look exactly like Her, Elloren."

I bristle, stung by the accusation in his tone. Hurt by it. "*Really*, Yvan?" I snap, my traitorous voice breaking. "I had absolutely no idea."

His eyes widen a fraction, then he gives me a close look as if taking my measure.

I inwardly slump, the impenetrable wall between us laid bare. I suddenly and fiercely wish I could be on the other side of it. Somewhere I could truly belong.

If only I looked like Iris.

I immediately regret the thought. I harshly remind myself that I'm not a Kelt. And I can't be having these thoughts about a Kelt. He shouldn't be so focused on me, either. It's a stretch for Yvan and me to even be friends, and it would be impossible for us to be anything more. But I suddenly wish with surprising force that we could at least be friends.

There's frustration and hurt in my eyes, and I'm too exhausted to hide it.

Yvan swallows and blinks at me, his expression losing its edge.

"I won't let anyone hurt you," he says with firm certainty, like it's an unassailable fact.

Warmth spreads through me, some of the anxiety melting from my shoulders. I take a deep breath and nod, believing him and bolstered by his steadiness. Somehow, I know I'll be safe with him.

Yvan stands there for a moment longer, considering. "Did the Vu Trin magic the border? To keep the Icaral out?"

"They put some type of protective ward along Verpacia's western border, and an even stronger ward around the University's border." I gesture around loosely with my hand. "The Icaral escaped from the sanitorium, so I guess it's ward-marked."

Yvan frowns and spends a long moment studying me through narrowed eyes. "I'm going well past the border."

Fear slashes through me, and I see the Valgard Icarals' hideous faces in the back of my mind. I force the image away, grit my teeth and decide to be brave.

"You said you'll protect me," I say grimly. *And I know you're stronger and faster than a broken Icaral.* "I'll take my chances."

After what seems like another hour, we come to the northwestern edge of the Verpacian Spine.

Yvan circles a tree near a jutting behemoth of Spine stone then, bends to lift a tangle of brush that covers the entrance to an underground tunnel. He steps inside and turns to me. "Coming?"

"Where? What is this?"

"A way into Gardneria." He points up toward the vertical mountain of stone and gives me a wry look. "Unless you want to go over the Spine, that is."

I frown and follow him through the thin brush and down into a hidden, cavernous tunnel as he fishes some Elfin lumenstone from his pocket to light our way.

I wonder how on Erthia he found this tunnel. And how many people know about it?

We travel through a series of caves, not much to see but the dripping of water and the occasional resting bat, all of it cast in the lumenstone's green glow. We ascend through more brush, pushing through a veil of dry branches to the outside.

I wordlessly follow him on. Soon the forest starts to slope upward. I struggle to keep up with his fast clip, a sharp cramp in my side. Sounds ahead begin to assert themselves. Commands being shouted. Horses. And something strange, something that makes the hairs on the back of my neck stand up on end—a low-pitched shriek that sets the forest floor vibrating.

Yvan pauses, then turns to me and holds a finger to his lips in unspoken warning. He motions for me to stay still, then climbs swiftly up a steep hill before us.

I watch him, amazed by his speed and silent ability to fluidly wind around the trees without even needing to grasp onto anything for balance.

He's now at the top of the wooded hill, crouched down behind some thick brush and peering over it. He motions for me to follow.

I labor up, skidding a few times on the dry leaves, grabbing onto small trees for leverage. Breathing hard, I finally catch up with him. I gasp when I see what lies ahead.

A vast Gardnerian military base stretches out over the entire valley. It's surrounded by the wilds and framed by the imposing Spine and the Caledonian mountain range. Huge blocks of Gardnerian soldiers move in formation, a cacophony of commands ringing out. They're surrounded by a city of black military tents, wooden barracks and Spine-stone structures cut into the imposing rock.

And there are dragons.

Scores of them. Moving in formation. Gardnerian soldiers astride them, whips in hand.

I fall back as close to twenty dragons rise into the sky with one unified shriek, my hands flying up to cover my ears. The dragons fly in formation behind a lead dragon.

Without warning, they soar up and swoop directly toward us.

I hit the ground as Yvan pulls me back, and the dragons zoom in close, then arc away toward the middle of the valley.

My heart pounds, and I feel light-headed. I've seen artists' renderings of military dragons, like dignified horses with wings. But these dragons are terrifying—black as night, with emaciated bodies that hint at their underlying skeletons. And their wings—jagged, jutting things with sharp feathers that resemble dull blades.

"Oh, Sweet Ancient One," I breathe, an icy chill coursing down my spine. "Do they breathe fire?"

Yvan frowns and shakes his head. "No. They lose the ability when they're broken. But as you can see, they can still fly. And they're strong, with sharp teeth and large talons."

"Are they getting ready to attack the Keltic military?"

"And anyone else in their path. Just like last time. Villages. Families. You won't hear about *that*, of course. You'll hear about one glorious military victory after another." He grimaces. "You won't read about whole families being torn to pieces by soulless dragons."

I imagine one of those creatures landing in a village. It's too terrible to fathom.

"Can't anyone stop this?" I ask him, horrified.

He gives a tight shake to his head. "The Resistance is no match for the Gardnerian Guard. The most they can do is slow them down. Get as many people out as they can." His expression turns bitter. "I imagine," he says, his voice thick with disgust, "when the inevitable happens, you'll be enjoying a party somewhere, celebrating your victory over the Evil Ones."

His words sting. I'm genuinely hurt by them. "You're so... you're *wrong* about me." I defend myself, grasping for words. "You don't know *anything* about me. I'm living with two chickens, did you know that? Do you have any idea how messy two chickens are?"

Yvan glares at me, furious. "They're called *Icarals*, not *chickens!*"

"*What?*" I'm momentarily thrown, but quickly figure out where the confusion lies. "I'm not talking about Ariel and Wynter. I'm talking about Ariel's *pets*. It used to be just one chicken; now it's two. So please, stop judging me so harshly. Have you ever spent any time with Ariel Haven? I should be given some type of medal for living with her!"

"Yes, Icarals are such vile, disgusting creatures," he snipes.

"Actually," I counter, "Wynter's quite pleasant, now that she's stopped acting so spooky, and Ariel's not quite as homicidal as she used to be. I know I look a lot like my grandmother, but I'm really not what you think I am, and neither are my brothers, for that matter."

An unfriendly grin plays at the corners of Yvan's mouth. "Yes, your brother Trystan does present a bit of a dilemma for your illustrious family, doesn't he?"

A cold dread twists itself around me as all of my bravado evaporates. "Trystan's a good person," I say, my voice low. "Please...please don't make trouble for him."

The anger in Yvan's face dissipates as he takes in how deeply his words have affected me. "I won't," he says, his voice uncharacteristically kind. He studies me for a long moment. "Come on," he says, then abruptly gets up as if deciding on a spur-of-the-moment course of action. He glides down the hill and turns to wait for me at its base.

I follow him into denser forest, thick with evergreens and brush. When we reach a small ridge, Yvan crouches down, then motions for me to follow.

There are cages up ahead, just around the ridge—a great number of them scattered throughout the woods, their bars black and curving.

All of them holding dragons.

I swallow nervously as we creep by the cages. The sight of the dragons' horrible faces startles me—thin drool falling from long mouths, lips pulled back to reveal killing teeth. But worst of all...

Their eyes. Milky opaque and soulless. *Like the Icarals in Valgard.*

Were these dragons tortured like those Icarals in Valgard were? Turned into broken monsters?

The dragons watch me pass, and I feel like I'm being watched by demons.

Yvan grabs my arm and pulls me behind the back wall of a cage.

Two Gardnerian soldiers pass, chatting amiably. Yvan fishes a watch out of his pocket and glances at it as their voices fade. "The changing of the guard," he whispers.

Heart racing, I follow him around a small hillock to an isolated cage that's surrounded by a wide swath of charred forest.

It holds a single dragon, but it might as well be a completely different creature, for how much it resembles the others.

It's black, but not a dull tar black. Each scale shimmers like an opal. And its wings aren't rancid and jagged, but strong and sleek, the feathers stiff and shiny like polished obsidian. The dragon paces back and forth on the far side of the cage, its movements strong and fluid as we walk up to the bars.

The dragon stops, slowly swivels its muscular head and sets its emerald green eyes on me.

I stare back at the dragon, frozen in place.

Suddenly, the dragon lunges toward me at incredible speed. Yvan thrusts me back and throws himself in front of me.

I fall backward as the dragon crashes against the cage's bars, sharp talons thrust through the gaps around Yvan. The dragon and Yvan stare at each other for a long moment, both of them stock-still as if facing each other down.

"It...it tried to kill me!" I stammer, my breath coming in great gasps.

"She," he corrects.

He cannot honestly be arguing semantics. "Okay, *she*," I breathlessly amend. "*She* seems like she wants to kill me!"

"She won't hurt you," Yvan says, his eyes locked on the dragon's as if he's convincing the dragon that this is true instead of attempting to reassure me.

The dragon snorts derisively, falls back then fluidly turns and stalks to the other side of the cage. She shoots Yvan a look of misery, draws herself down and turns away. I notice that her body is covered with bloody lash marks.

"She seems like she understands what we're saying." I gulp as I find my bearings.

The corner of Yvan's mouth twitches. "Dragons are...very observant."

"So *this* is where you go when you walk off by yourself?"

Yvan stares at me for a moment, then nods.

I take a deep breath, my heart slowly falling into a more normal rhythm.

"She's been beaten," I observe, my brow knitting as I take in the crisscrossing lash marks.

Yvan tenses, and he looks toward the dragon. "They're trying to break her." An anguished expression crosses his face.

"Will they keep beating her?" I ask.

He swallows, then glances back at the dragon, his eyes dark with worry. "They'll place her with another dragon," he says. "A young one. They'll wait for her to become attached to the child…and then…they'll torture it to death in front of her. I've seen it done. To another dragon here."

He's quiet for a moment. When he looks back at me, I can see the pain etched deep in his mind, his voice breaking. "I still have nightmares about it." His brow tightens, and he looks away.

"I have nightmares, too," I confide in him. "About Selkies."

He glances back at me, surprised. "Selkies?"

"I saw one once. In a cage, in Valgard. She was screaming." I wince at the memory. "It was *awful*. I've dreamed about her almost every night since."

For a long moment he just stares at me. "I've never seen one," he finally says. "I've heard about them, though." He turns back to the dragon, his eyes darting to every last part of the cage, like he's trying to work out a complicated puzzle. "The bars," he says absently, "they're made of Elfin steel. She's tried to melt it, but it's not possible. And they don't use keys to open the cage. They use wand magic."

"You've given this a lot of thought, haven't you?" I observe with dawning suspicion.

He doesn't answer, his attention still riveted to the dragon's cage.

My eyes fly open with stunned realization. "You want to rescue her, don't you?"

His entire face constricts, as if suddenly caught in a vise.

"You do!" I marvel. "You want to steal a dragon. From a Gardnerian military base!"

Yvan shoots me an angry look, turns and starts back into the woods.

I run after him, struggling to keep up. "You're going to get yourself shot—you know that?"

He doesn't answer, only walks faster as if attempting to put as much distance between us as possible.

The dragon's low, keening moan of despair resonates on the air, snagging my heart. Yvan and I both halt. Yvan's back has gone rigidly straight, but he quickly gathers himself and resumes stalking rapidly away from me.

By the time we're back on the Verpacian side of the border, the tension between us has become unbearably thick. It distracts me from keeping my footing, and I silently blame Yvan for every stubbed toe and scratched arm.

After a time a weathered cottage becomes visible through the trees. It's unkempt, with tools scattered about, a weedy garden and unhealthy livestock in cramped pens.

"Who lives there?" I ask Yvan's back as he walks well ahead of me, keeping the same unfriendly distance between us as he did on the walk out.

"The University's groundskeeper," he answers curtly as a flash of white darts through the trees.

A Watcher.

I follow its curving flight around the trees with my eyes. It lands on a branch just before the cottage's clearing and turns to face me. And then it disappears.

The hairs on the back of my neck stand on end.

There's something there. Something in the cottage it wants me to see.

I don't know why these Watchers came to me with Sage's wand. I don't know why they've taken such an interest in me to begin with. But I've come to realize that when they appear, it's because they need to show me important things.

I start for the clearing.

"Elloren," Yvan says, "where are you going?"

"Just give me a moment."

Geese sound in the distance as I near the cottage.

I hear a crash and jump back in fright. Then an angry male voice.

More shouting. Another crash.

Then a strange shriek, a sound both exotic and heart-wrenchingly familiar.

No, it can't be.

The door to the cottage flies open, and a young woman runs out, her eyes wild, her face a mask of pure, unadulterated terror. Her movements are unfocused, panicked, as she trips over a stone and falls flat on her face.

My breath catches in my throat. It's the Selkie from Valgard. The Selkie we were just speaking of.

A beefy, bearded man with stained clothing and an unwashed appearance storms out of the cottage, following close at the Selkie's heels. He quickly catches up with her, his face red with fury. Before she can get up, he kicks her hard in the side with his heavy black boot.

Fury rocks through me. Fists balled, I start forward, but reason quickly reins me in. I'm no match for the huge groundskeeper. I fall back behind a tree instead, my heart slamming against my chest.

The Selkie lets out a bloodcurdling scream and curls herself into a protective ball, cradling the side where she's been kicked.

The man grabs her roughly by the arm and wrenches her up into a standing position. "Shut up!" he thunders, shaking her violently as she continues her unearthly shrieking. "I said *shut up, you bitch*!" He pulls his free hand back above his head and strikes her so hard that she cries out and falls backward to the ground.

The Selkie cups the side of her head with her hands and rolls onto her side on the ground, her whimper high-pitched and strange.

I turn in desperation to Yvan, quivering with outrage. He stands, frozen in place, mouth agape.

The man is now standing over her, his large hands on his broad hips as the Selkie cowers below him.

"The next time I tell you to do something, you stupid animal," he bellows as he jabs a sausagy finger in her direction, "you better damn well do it!" He grabs up a ring of keys hanging from a wall hook and storms over to the Selkie, then wrenches her up by her hair.

She gasps as the groundskeeper swipes up a metal collar secured by a heavy chain to a long post. He forces his knee into the Selkie's back, throws the collar around her neck, locks it into place and pushes her headfirst onto the dusty ground. Then he storms back toward the cottage, throws the ring of keys onto the hook, mutters something about the "damn Selkies" and disappears inside, slamming the door behind him.

The Selkie lies there, whimpering, her eyes closed, her face twisted in despair, a large, bloody red welt now encompassing the side of her face, her lovely silver hair caked with dirt and mud.

Tears of outrage sting at my eyes. *Animal or not, how can he be so cruel?*

I'm suddenly filled with a wild, desperate idea.

I turn to Yvan, my anger solidifying. "I'm going to rescue the Selkie," I say, my heart pounding.

His eyebrows fly up. *"What?"*

I crouch down and make my way toward the Selkie as stealthily as I can, my legs trembling beneath me. "Selkie girl!" I call out in a rough whisper.

Her eyes fly open wide, like two terrified moons, a low moan catching in her throat. She focuses in on me, and her expression abruptly changes as if she remembers me just as well as I remember her.

I retrieve the keys and rush to the Selkie as heavy boot heels sound inside the cottage. Pushing her silver hair aside, I force the key into the lock with shaking hands. I feel a warm flush of surprise when her metal collar opens and falls to the ground with a clank. I motion frantically toward the woods as I pull at her arm.

We make a run for it, scrambling across the clearing and into the woods.

Upon spotting Yvan, she lets out a terrified shriek and falls backward, her feet frantically skidding against the forest floor as she holds up her arms to ward him off.

"Back up, Yvan!" I push my hand out toward him.

Yvan falls back and crouches low, his palms up.

I clasp the Selkie's trembling shoulders. She flinches as I touch her. I reach a hand up to gently stroke her hair. "Shhhh," I croon. "We're not going to hurt you."

Her hair is a strange and wonderful consistency, soft as warm water. "We've got to get you out of here," I say, wishing I could speak Seal. Her mouth opens slightly, but no sound comes out, the gills on her neck flapping open and closed.

I manage to pull her into a crouch as her eyes dart around in panic. We slowly start away from the cottage, both the Selkie and I tripping repeatedly over our feet, made clumsy by fear. Yvan keeps his distance off to the side, always keeping us within sight, his face tense.

Soon we find our courage, along with our footing, and break into a run, leaping over logs, swerving around trees, the forest whizzing by, listening desperately for the sound of heavy foot-steps behind us. I keep my hand tight on the Selkie's wrist as we run for what seems like forever. We run until my breath starts to feel like sharp glass, my sides cramping up.

A clearing appears just ahead. The blessed University grounds.

I never imagined I'd be so overjoyed to see the North Tower.

We slow, the Selkie and I panting heavily, her gills ruffled open, her thin wrist weak and fragile in my hand. She stumbles, and I throw an arm around her before she can fall. We're a few paces away from the University grounds, barely hidden by the thinning trees.

"Elloren." I hear Yvan's calm voice from a few feet away. The Selkie flinches at the sound of it. "Have you thought through where you're going to hide her?" Yvan is leaning calmly against the trunk of a large tree, studying me, looking like he hasn't even broken a sweat.

"No," I reply defensively as I reach up with my free hand to stroke the trembling Selkie's strange hair.

"This is a little reckless, you know that, right?"

I glare at him as I catch my breath. "Oh, and rescuing dragons from the Gardnerian military isn't?" I *really* don't need this from him right now.

The corners of his mouth lift into a wry smile.

"It was the right thing to do, Yvan," I say.

He nods, serious again. "I know it was."

There's something new in his expression. Something that catches me completely off guard.

Respect.

We're both startled by the sound of a horse whinnying nearby.

I whip my head around and see Andras Volya, the young, heavily rune-marked Amaz man—Professor Volya's son. He's a short distance away from us, across the wide field astride a large, black mare.

He's staring straight at us.

The horror of being discovered presses down on me.

Andras pulls hard on the horse's mane. The animal rears and turns sharply around before galloping away toward the University stables.

"Oh, Sweet Ancient One," I breathe. "You don't think he saw us, do you?"

"I think he did," Yvan says, his voice low.

"What do you think he'll do?"

Yvan narrows his gaze and looks toward Andras's receding figure. "I don't know." He sets his green eyes on me. "But we need to get her inside. Before anyone else sees her."

CHAPTER
NINE

Refuge

Diana crouches down next to me and peers under the bed.

The Selkie is lying listlessly on her side, a glazed look in her eyes.

"I can smell her fear," Diana observes. "She's in shock. And she's soiled herself." Diana stands up and crosses her arms in front of herself authoritatively. "Elloren, go get your new violin."

I'm deeply rattled and thrown by how *un*rattled Diana is. Yvan's gone to get food for the Selkie. It's best that he left, as the seal-girl was in such a panic to get away from him, she scrunched herself up far under my bed. She's obviously terrified of men.

I peer up at Diana, my brow knitting together in puzzlement. "Why?"

"Selkies love music. I read it somewhere once. It may calm her."

I get up and shoot a skeptical look at Diana. Trystan and Rafe recently gifted me with a second-hand violin, the only instrument they could afford. It was a touching gesture and deeply appreciated, but the instrument's wood is slightly warped and it can barely hold a tuning.

Initially, I sent word to Uncle Edwin, asking him if there was a spare violin that could be sent, since mine was destroyed. I received a prompt response from Aunt Vyvian, who has taken over my uncle's care and evidently his affairs as well, his mail now rerouted directly to her.

My Dear Niece,

I would be happy to send you the finest violin Valgard has to offer. I have friends who play in the Valgard Symphony, and I'm sure they could procure a brand-new Maelorian violin lacquered in the color of your choice. How does that sound?

You have great musical talent, just like your blessed grand-mother, and I want nothing more than to help foster it once you are fasted to Lukas Grey.

Please let me know when that happy event has transpired.

With Affection,
Vyvian

Resigned to a substandard instrument, but bolstered by the fraternal affection it represents, I fetch the coarsely-made violin.

After what the Selkie's been through, I doubt a little off-key music will make it all better. Still, it's worth a try.

I sit down on the floor and begin to play, the music enveloping the room. Ariel watches us suspiciously from her bed. Wynter hops down from her usual perch on the windowsill to the surface of my desk.

"Keep playing," Diana directs. "Her fear is lessening."

After an hour my fingers are beginning to hurt, my neck starting to ache, but the Selkie remains decidedly under the bed. "It's not working," I say, turning to Diana.

Wynter unexpectedly opens up her wings and hops down from my desk to land lightly on her feet. She crouches down, then closes her eyes as if deep in meditation. Finally, she raises her head and begins to sing. She sings in High Elvish, the words smooth and graceful as flowing water, winding around the room.

"Elloren," Diana breathes.

The Selkie's blue-white arm appears from beneath the bed and reaches out toward Wynter. Wynter continues to sing as she takes the Selkie's hand and leads her slowly out until the seal-girl curls into a ball and hides in the shelter of Wynter's wings.

Wynter strokes the Selkie's hair as she continues to sing her mournful song, a wet trail of urine now streaking the floor.

"We should get her cleaned up," observes Diana, wrinkling her nose. "Ariel," she orders, "go heat up the bathwater."

"Do I look like your servant?" Ariel snaps.

"No," replies Diana, "but we *could* make use of your abilities. Don't you *like* starting fires?"

Unable to resist playing with fire, Ariel stomps off toward the washroom, muttering to herself darkly.

Wynter and I manage to get the exhausted Selkie into the washroom as Diana goes downstairs to fetch a bucket and mop. Wynter cradles the Selkie and sings to her as I gently help her out of her clothes. The Selkie doesn't struggle. She just looks at us with wide, sad eyes, her body limp as a rag doll. As I pull her tunic over her head, I gasp, my hand involuntarily flying up to cover my mouth in horror. Wynter stops singing.

The Selkie's entire body is bruised and beaten. Bright red lash marks crisscross her blue-white skin.

Diana walks in, swinging a large, wooden bucket full of soapy water in one hand, a mop in the other. When she sees the Selkie, she freezes, her mouth falling open. She quickly collects herself and sets the bucket neatly on the floor and the mop carefully against the wall.

"I'll be right back," she says, her voice pleasant. "I'm going to go kill him now."

Her tone is so nonchalant it takes my mind a few seconds to process the meaning of her words.

"Wha...*what?*" I stutter as Diana turns on her heel to leave.

She stops and turns to look at me like I'm daft. "The man who did this to her," she explains slowly, as if I'm a child. "I'm going to snap his neck. He deserves to die."

I spring up, my hands flying out to caution her. "Wait, no, you can't!"

"Of course I can," she says, annoyed. Her expression turns thoughtful. "No, of course you're right, Elloren." I breathe a sigh of relief. "Snapping his neck would be much too quick and painless." She nods matter-of-factly. "He deserves to suffer for this. I will beat him first. And I will mark him like he marked her." Diana's eyes momentarily take on a wicked gleam. "Then I will tear his throat out."

Panic mushrooms inside me. "You...you can't kill him!"

"Why do you keep saying that?" She looks offended. "Of *course* I can kill him."

"You'll get in *serious* trouble!"

She shoots me an incredulous, disgusted look. "With *who?* Not with *my* people. If my mother was here, she would have already torn this man to pieces."

"At least wait until we've spoken to Rafe," I plead.

She places a hand on her hip and glares at me with exasperation. "Oh, fine," she relents. "I can smell your fear. It is completely unwarranted, but if it will set your mind at ease, we will speak with Rafe first."

Diana directs Wynter to go and fetch Rafe, and to my surprise, Wynter leaves to get him without hesitation.

"Your brother will agree with me," Diana assures me as she kneels to wash the wounds on the Selkie's back with a soft cloth. "And then I will kill this man. And after I kill him, I will rip his head off and bring it back to the Selkie. It will bring her much comfort to know he is dead."

★ ★ ★

A few minutes later Rafe and I sit on the stone bench in the hall, watching Diana pace angrily back and forth, Wynter having taken over the Selkie's care.

"Diana, quit pacing and sit down." Rafe's voice is quiet, but there's an undercurrent of authority that's unmistakable.

Diana stops moving and faces him, hands on her hips. She shoots him a defiant look, which he calmly meets.

"You can't kill him," Rafe says, keeping his tone neutral.

"Of course I can," she snaps. "Your people are weak."

"Yes, I know you could kill him quite easily and effortlessly," he replies, his voice firm. "But you shouldn't."

"Why?" she demands, raising her chin.

"Okay, Diana," Rafe says. "Let's say you go out and kill him. Then what?"

"Then I bring his head to the Selkie woman so that she can see that she is now safe."

"All right, then what?"

She huffs at him impatiently. "Then I toss it back into the woods for the scavengers to eat."

"And what happens when the University investigates and finds out what happened? They *will* notice that their grounds-keeper is missing."

"They can hire someone new."

Rafe sighs and rubs the bridge of his nose. "They'll arrest you, is what they'll do."

Diana snorts. "I'd like to see them try!"

"They'll fine Elloren for theft and they'll throw you in prison for murder. And they'll send the Selkie back to the dealer he bought her from and sell her to someone else, potentially someone worse."

"You are being absurd. Once we explain what happened, how he was treating her, they will understand. The proof is all over her body!"

Rafe shakes his head in disagreement. "You're wrong, Diana. According to them, this man did nothing unlawful. Repugnant, maybe, but not unlawful. You two, on the other hand, have already broken multiple laws. Do you really want to throw murder on top of that?"

"So we keep her hidden," Diana says stubbornly. "No one has to know who killed him."

Rafe screws up his face in disbelief. "Diana, your kind are seen by my people as uncivilized, violent savages. You and your brother would be immediately suspect. And, if, by some miracle, they didn't figure out that you were the culprits, they would assume the Selkie found her skin and killed him. There's talk of shooting all of the Selkies in captivity. Were you aware of that? The Council is pretty evenly divided on this. The murder of the University's groundskeeper would easily tip the balance in favor of a mass execution. Do you really want to be responsible for that?"

Diana leans toward Rafe, undaunted. "Then I'll kill him and take her with me. To my pack. They'll know what to do. They'll save all the Selkies."

"So you'll leave the University?"

"Yes, if necessary!"

"And Jarod? He'd have no choice but to leave, as well."

"He'd leave," she says with smug assurance. "*He'd* understand."

"So, let's say you and Jarod take her back to your pack," Rafe calmly postulates. "You do realize you'd be plunging your entire pack into a potentially dangerous political situation."

Diana snorts at this. "Dangerous for *your* people, maybe. Not for ours."

Rafe exhales sharply and shakes his head. "Things are very tense between your people and the Mage Council right now, Diana. Our government considers your land rightfully ours. There's talk of sending the military out to force your people—"

Diana huffs impatiently, cutting him off. "Your military is no match for my pack. You know that as well as I do. Your magic is useless against us, and the weakest of our kind is stronger than your strongest soldier. If your people were stronger, they would have stolen our land long ago, just as you've stolen land from everyone else around you."

"Think how this would be written up in the arrest warrant," Rafe continues. *"Lupine Girl Kills University Groundskeeper…"*

"…Who Horribly Abused Seal Woman!" Diana finishes for him.

"That part won't make it in, Diana. Selkies are like a dirty little secret no one wants to talk about. No. It will be seen as proof that Lupines are dangerous, bloodthirsty monsters who should be eradicated. Do you really want to be responsible for throwing your pack into this?"

Diana throws up her hands like she's throwing sand into Rafe's face. "This is nonsense!"

"No, Diana, it's not! Do you really want to be the one to make this decision? Without speaking to your pack first? Without speaking to your alpha?"

Diana freezes.

There, he's done it, I realize with relief. He's finally found an argument that registers with a Lupine.

She stands, staring at Rafe with a fiery glare.

Finally, she lurches forward toward Rafe, fists clenched. "I'm going out!" she snarls. She whirls around and heads for the door.

Rafe is on his feet in a flash. He strides forward and grabs Diana by the arm.

"To do *what*, Diana?" he demands.

Diana's arm tenses and her fist clenches sharply like his hand on her is a challenge. She shoots him an incredulous look and glances down at the hand that attempts to restrain her, staring at it like she can't quite believe that he would dare to be so bold. I wonder myself if Rafe has temporarily taken leave of his senses.

The tension in the room has suddenly become unbearable—and dangerous. Very slowly, Diana raises her head, her lips pulling back into a threatening grimace, a deep growl starting at the base of her throat as her amber eyes take on a ferocious glow. She takes a sudden, threatening step toward Rafe, and I flinch. He knows as well as I do, as well as Diana does, that she could rip his arm clear off without so much as breaking a sweat, and there'd be nothing Rafe or I could do about it. I've never thought of Diana as frightening before, but I realize now, for the first time, that she's truly dangerous.

"I asked you where you're going," Rafe repeats, his jaw tensing, his tone unyielding, as he ignores her threatening posture completely.

Diana's lips pull back farther into a full-blown snarl. "I'm going deep into the woods," she growls, her voice low, her eyes two enraged slits, "where no one can see me. Where I can strip naked without offending the very *delicate* sensibilities of your most *morally upstanding* people. Then I will *Change*. And I will *run*. For a *very long time*. Because if I stay here, I will ignore all reason, and I *will* kill him."

Rafe nods and abruptly releases her arm. She shoots him one last vicious look before storming out.

I start to breathe again as Rafe stares off in the direction she's exited.

"Do you think she'll kill him?" I ask, my voice almost a whisper.

Rafe places a hand on one hip and turns to me. "No," he says, his lips tensing. "She just needs to blow off some steam."

"She's right, you know. He deserves to die. He'll probably just buy another Selkie girl to abuse."

"Probably," Rafe agrees. He walks over to the window that overlooks the large open field leading to the edge of the wilds. I follow and can see Diana stalking toward the wilderness at an angry pace, the late-afternoon sun sending a soft, gentle glow over everything, making her golden hair appear as if it's on fire.

Later, after leaving the sleeping Selkie under Wynter's care, I set out to find Andras Volya, ready to beg, if necessary, to convince him to keep our secret.

As I walk along the upstairs hallway, I hear my brother downstairs talking to someone and pause.

"Hello, Diana," Rafe's voice is low and wary.

For a moment there's silence, and I feel a tremor of nervousness for my brother's safety.

"You were right," Diana blurts out, her voice uncharacteristically strained. "You were right about everything. Everything you said was true."

"I'm glad you've calmed down," Rafe says patiently.

"I'm sorry. I'm sorry I got so angry at you."

"It's okay, Diana. Apology accepted."

There's another uncomfortable silence.

"And I'm sorry I thought about tearing your arm off," she says.

I creep to the doorway and peer through the slit where the door swings away from the wall.

Rafe stands facing Diana, his arm on the stone wall next to them. He looks down, collecting his thoughts. Then he glances back up at her, a small smile on his face. "Thank you, Diana. Thank you for not ripping my arm off."

"It's just that... I...I have no experience with...with this level of cruelty," Diana explains haltingly. "I've just never seen anything like it." Diana looks up at Rafe, her face distraught. "Rafe, her whole body...he must have beaten her *repeatedly*..."

"I know."

"She's so *scared*. So *broken*. And her eyes...her *eyes*..." Diana's voice breaks, and she begins to sob.

My brow flies up in surprise. Diana is so strong and sure,

never ruffled by anything. My own sadness for the Selkie wells up inside me, hearing Diana cry so.

"Shhh…" I hear Rafe say. "Come here."

Diana's sobs become muffled as Rafe pulls her into a tight embrace.

"I'm *so* sorry!" Diana cries. "I wasn't thinking! I could have caused so much trouble! My first real test…and I *failed*!" Her words come out in a tangled rush. "I'm a disgrace to my pack!"

"Shhh, Diana…you're not," Rafe whispers into her hair. "They'd understand. You're not a disgrace."

"Yes, I *am*!"

"*No*, you're *not*. Stop. Look at me."

Diana raises her tear-soaked face, amber eyes now red and puffy.

"You are *not* a disgrace," Rafe insists, his voice full of kindness. "You are brave and kind. You're just a little…impetuous." He smiles and reaches up to gently wipe away some of her tears.

Diana nods and manages a reluctant smile in return. "You're just being nice to me because I let you keep your arm."

Rafe laughs. "Maybe so."

They're both quiet for a moment, their arms loose around each other.

"Rafe," Diana finally says, her voice uncharacteristically soft. "I'm falling in love with you."

Rafe's face immediately grows serious, and he inhales sharply. "Oh, Diana," he breathes as he reaches up to cup the side of her face, "I've already fallen…" He pulls her toward him and kisses her hair, her arms twining around him. He brings his mouth to hers and they kiss, gently at first. Then Diana moans and presses herself into him, their kissing quickly becoming passionate.

I pull away from the door, heart thumping, a pang of distress spreading through my chest.

My brother, the Gardnerian, and a shapeshifter. All my suspicions about them completely on the mark.

THE BLACK WITCH

Sweet Ancient One in the Heavens Above, what a mess we're all in.

I've stolen a Selkie. Yvan's plotting to steal a military dragon. Both Rafe and Aislinn are in love with Lupines, and I'm becoming increasingly close friends with a shunned Elfin Icaral.

This has actually gone way beyond a mess. We're all treading on increasingly dangerous ground.

What on Erthia are we all going to do from here?

CHAPTER TEN

Andras Volya

After Diana and Rafe leave together, I step out and find Andras Volya in the University stables.

Andras is crouched down on one knee as he tends to the front leg of a black mare, gently massaging herbal paste into the animal's leg. If he sees me, he gives no indication, as he continues to focus entirely on the horse. The horse, on the other hand, turns to eye me with calm curiosity.

I walk slowly over to where he kneels. "Andras?" My voice is tentative, and he doesn't look up. "I...I need to speak with you," I persist.

"I won't say anything about the Selkie," he says, "if that's what you've come to ask." He stops massaging the horse's leg, stands and murmurs softly to her as she nuzzles him, the crimson rune-marks all over his red tunic glimmering in the light. "His treatment of her bothered me greatly," he says. His brow tenses as if he's remembering something disturbing. He turns to look at me. "You were right to rescue her. I should have done so myself."

"How long was she there?" I ask him.

He considers this, staring off into the wilds, in the direction of the groundskeeper's cottage. "A month's time, I'd say." Andras cocks his head to one side and studies me as if I'm a puzzle to him. "The granddaughter of Carnissa Gardner. Rescuing Selkies." He sets the paste jar down and wipes his hands with a rag. "Doesn't your aunt want the Selkies shot?"

Stunned, I stare at him blankly.

He lifts his chin and considers me closely. "She introduced the motion. On your Mage Council. Earlier this year. To have them shot as soon as they come to shore."

There are better ways to deal with Selkies that are far more humane than keeping them in cages, forcing them to…act human.

She meant…*killing* them!

He must read the shock in my expression. "You didn't know?"

I shake my head and let out a long sigh of disgust. *Just when I think Aunt Vyvian can't get any worse.* I sit down on the hay bale behind me, momentarily reaching up to massage my aching temples. The world is so much worse than I ever imagined. And Aunt Vyvian is so devastatingly cruel.

The mare's tail makes a swishing sound as she flicks it from side to side, a chilly breeze flowing into the stable from the outside. My eyes are drawn to the rolling, violet-tinged hills, their base carpeted with a line of bright yellow larch trees.

"It's beautiful here," I observe.

Andras looks out over the landscape and nods.

"It's like another world," I muse. "It reminds me of my home." I hold up my hand, covering up the University city, which is rendered small by our distance from it. "It's like you can almost pretend the University doesn't exist."

"I try to do that sometimes," he admits.

I turn to look at him. "You don't like it here?"

He shakes his head. "My mother and I used to live on the outskirts of Western Keltania. I much prefer it."

"Oh," I say softly, momentarily at a loss for what else to say.

Then my eyes alight on the intricate designs on his tunic. "Your runes," I observe hesitantly. "They glow."

He glances down at the marks and nods. "Amaz runes. They're crafted from a melding of several runic systems. They enhance our power—"

Andras breaks off suddenly, eyes darting to look at something behind me, and his whole body stiffens.

I turn to see Andras's mother, Professor Volya, standing in the stable's back entranceway. Fear swamps over me. *How long has she been standing there? Did she hear us?*

I can see it in her shrewd gaze—she did hear us. My heart hammers out my dire concern.

"Mother," Andras says, his deep voice guarded.

"My son," she replies tersely.

We all stare at each other for a long moment, the silence thick and uncomfortable.

"Mage Gardner," Professor Volya finally says, her black eyes sharp on me. "I just had the most intriguing visit from the area's Vu Trin commander and the Verpax groundskeeper. It seems as if the groundskeeper's Selkie has gone missing."

I stare back at her like a deer caught in the torchlight.

Her eyes tight on mine, she takes a seat on a hay bale. She sits like a man. Legs spread apart, arms crossed.

"Relax, Mage Gardner," she tells me. "I, too, will keep your secret."

I let out a heavy breath, relief washing over me.

"So," Professor Volya says, peering at me, "Carnissa Gardner's granddaughter has rescued a Selkie."

"Her body," I tell them, my voice low. "It's covered in lash marks. He must have whipped her over and over again."

Andras makes a sound of disgust and looks away.

Professor Volya doesn't look the least bit surprised. "It is the nature of men."

Andras's head jerks toward his mother, his brow tight with offense.

"To beat women senseless?" I question, incredulous.

"To be cruel," she replies. "To attempt to dominate women in any way possible."

Andras's jaw tenses, and his face takes on a hard look. He throws down his cloth and stalks out.

His mother ignores him. "It has been this way since the beginning of time," she continues, her eyes steady on me.

I shift uncomfortably on the prickly hay bale beneath me. "I don't understand what you mean."

"It is not surprising," she observes, "that you are ignorant of your own history. Sad, but not surprising." Professor Volya regards me coolly for a moment. "This world," she says, leaning forward, "and everything in it, was made by the Great Mother. And the first people she made were the Three Sisters. *This* is your history." She waits a moment for this to sink in as I stare back at her. "After they were created, *Ama*, the Great Mother, saw that the Sisters were lonely, so she took a bone from each of their fists and made the First Men." She holds her fist straight up as she tells me this, then lowers it again. "The First Men were not grateful for all the Goddess had done for them. Instead, they tried to convince the Three Sisters to join them and slay the Great Mother, so that they could rule over all of Erthia." Again she pauses.

I'm amazed at how different this creation story is from the one I've grown up knowing.

"One of the Sisters refused to betray the Goddess. She went to her and warned her of the terrible plan. The Great Mother renamed this First Sister Amaz, and set down a curse on the others."

"How did she curse them?"

"The two Sisters who betrayed the Goddess were sent to live with the First Men, who were strengthened by the extra bone in their fists and emboldened. They sought to enslave these two Sisters and abused them in every way. But the loyal Daughter was greatly blessed by the Goddess and remained strong and free. So you see," Professor Volya says, sitting back again on the hay bale, "from the beginnings of time, men have been untrustworthy and only interested in cruelty and domination."

"But your own son," I say, "he seems a decent sort..."

Her eyes take on a faraway look. "He is kind and good because we perform every ritual the Goddess requires. In return, She has taken pity on him and blessed him greatly." She's quiet for a moment, considering me as a nearby mare snuffles and pulls at some hay. "You should be going," she says, getting up. "It would not be good for the Vu Trin to find you here."

I get up and brush the hay off my tunic.

"Good luck with your Selkie, Elloren Gardner," she says to me. "You have done a brave thing. May the Goddess help and protect you."

Andras is standing next to a large Keltic workhorse, stroking its neck, speaking to it softly. He keeps his eyes on the horse as I approach.

"So," he says, "did my mother tell you the story of my cursed fist?" The disdain in his voice is surprisingly sharp.

"She did."

Andras makes a disgusted sound as he continues to stroke the horse's neck. "It's a powerful story," he admits, a hard edge to his tone.

"I'd never heard it before."

Andras shakes his head in bitter disapproval. "She never stops recruiting for her tribe, my mother. Shunned for more than eighteen years, and still she's loyal to them. The ironic thing is, my mother's a brilliant scientist." He holds his hand up for my inspection. "She knows that I have exactly the same number of bones in my fist as she does in hers, and yet, she believes."

Andras peers off into the distance, where his mother is astride a white Elfin mare, riding away from us, her tunic's rune-marks streaking red trails in their wake. "If she'd had a daughter, instead of me, she'd be with them still." He turns to me, his brow tight. "I ruined my mother's life." He reaches up and strokes the horse's neck. "And so," he continues, his face full of resignation, "I go with her every full moon to perform the rituals the Goddess requires. Every morning we leave offerings and pray to Her. We follow every last Amaz tradition to the letter of the law. All except one."

"What would that be?" I ask hesitantly.

He turns to me, his hand still on the horse. "My mother refused to abandon me at birth because I'm male, as Amaz tradition dictates. And she's spent every single day of her life trying to atone for it." He shakes his head and lets out a deep sigh. "Do you know what else is ironic about all this?"

I hold his gaze, waiting.

"I've never once had the slightest urge to raise my fist against a woman, contrary to what the Amaz creation myth says about men. The only person I've ever wanted to seriously hurt is the University groundskeeper, but I'm sure I'm in complete agreement with my mother in that regard. She may wind up killing him before I get a chance to."

"Actually," I say, "I think Diana Ulrich is first in line."

He looks surprised. "The Lupine girl?"

I nod. "We had to talk her out of ripping his head off earlier."

Andras stares at me for a moment, then laughs. He has a nice smile, wide and open. "I think I would like this Diana Ulrich."

CHAPTER ELEVEN

Safety

When I return to the North Tower, the sun newly set, I find Yvan waiting for me in the upstairs hallway.

He's sitting on the stone bench, a sack propped next to him. He snaps to vivid attention when I enter and rises.

My steps halt as I catch sight of him, the breath momentarily hitching in my throat. Our eyes lock, and I stare at him, blinking. His larger-than-life presence fills the narrow hallway, the low ceiling making him seem taller than he already is.

"Dried cod," he says, not taking his eyes off me as he lifts the sack a fraction and sets it back down on the bench. "For the Selkie."

My eyes flit to the sack then back up to him. I clutch at the sides of my cloak and close the distance between us, feeling self-conscious and flustered. There's a gentleness about him that's unexpected, his green eyes intense, but newly open and unguarded.

"I met your lodging mate," he tells me, his tone significant. "Diana Ulrich." His brow rises in unspoken disbelief.

His voice is always deeper than I expect it to be, smooth and alluring.

I let out a deep breath and shrug. "Yes, well, Diana's been living here for a while now."

"You're living with two Icarals *and* a Lupine," he states as if I'm not already aware of this fact.

"And a Selkie," I remind him, fully comprehending how surreal this is. And increasingly risky.

And now there's a disconcertingly attractive Kelt in my hallway.

But even with a stolen Selkie sitting in my room, it's impossible not to have my thoughts completely scattered by how disarmingly handsome Yvan is.

He blinks at me, clearly surprised, the color of his eyes deepened by the dim lamplight, warm gold flecking the bright green, his gaze full of sharp intelligence. He holds himself in a long, stiff column, so formal, as if reining his emotions tightly in.

I ignore my fluttering pulse and eye him with arch amusement. "I never imagined you of all people would be standing in this hallway, Yvan."

His lip twitches up. "About as unexpected as having a Selkie here, I'm sure."

I let out a short laugh. "Actually, it's stranger having *you* here. *By far.*" I shoot him a pointed look.

He stares at me, his lips parting slightly as if in question then closing again. He takes a deep breath, then glances sidelong at my bedroom. His face tenses, and he steps back a fraction, clears his throat and averts his gaze from me, suddenly ill at ease.

I'm abruptly uncomfortable, too, both of us clearly aware of how inappropriate this is in both of our staid cultures—a single male, unchaperoned, here, so close to my bed. The two of us alone.

I've been in his bedroom, and that was pushing the limits of scandal, but it was always in the presence of one or both of my brothers. Except that one time, back when Yvan and I hated each other.

Yvan's eyes catch on Wynter's white bird tapestry, and his unease seems to drop away. He focuses in on it as if noticing for the first time that he's surrounded by artwork.

"That's beautiful." He exhales, taking it in.

A flock of Watchers. Gliding above a summer field.

"Wynter made it," I tell him. "It's my favorite of all her work."

He nods, still staring at the woven scene as if entranced.

His eyes occupied, my own gaze inadvertently slips over him, first tentatively then freely, surreptitiously drinking him in. His long, lean body. His exquisite profile. The long lines of his neck. His hair a tousled mess, grazing his neck in uneven spikes, curling around the back of his ear. I imagine it would be soft to the touch. Soft, where the rest of him is hard.

Except for his lips.

I wonder, suddenly, what it would be like to kiss him…to feel his full lips against mine.

Yvan's head snaps up, color lighting his cheeks, his mouth open in surprise.

I look quickly away, heart thudding, flushed and mortified, scared that he can see clear into my mind and view these wildly improper thoughts.

He can't read your mind, I insist to myself. *Of course he can't. But…how else to explain his reaction?*

I glance back up at him, deeply embarrassed.

The color on his cheeks has deepened, and he's now staring at me with an ardent intensity that sets me reeling even more.

He swallows audibly, his eyes riveted on mine. "I should… be going."

I nod disjointedly, his green eyes playing havoc with my heartbeat.

He hands me the sack, his warm fingers brushing mine, and steps back, constrained and formal once again.

I grip the sack tight. "Good night, Yvan," I force out, heat burning at my neck and cheeks. "Thank you for the food."

We're silent for a few tension-fraught heartbeats.

"Good night, Elloren." His voice is low and warm as dark honey.

His eyes flit down my form in one languid line. Then his face grows uneasy and his head gives a small jerk up, his eyes gone a fraction wider like he's startled himself. His gaze turns deeply conflicted.

He shoots me his familiar intense, fiery look and strides out.

My heartbeat is still erratic when I slip into my lodging, wildly flustered.

The fire is fully stoked, the room cast in a warm, comforting glow that instantly begins to soothe my troubled emotions.

Diana is lying on my bed, her arm around the sleeping Selkie. Ariel is lying on her own disastrous bed, her angry eyes hard on the Selkie as if she's trying to mentally drive her away, and Wynter is kneeling in front of Ariel's bed, talking to her in a low voice, her thin hand gentle on Ariel's scarred arm.

Diana's eyes, very much awake and alert, follow me as I take off my woolen cloak, hang it on a hook Jarod placed for us and sit down on the floor by my bed, resting my shoulder against the mattress. I realize we're going to have to get more beds, with so many people now living here.

"How is she?" I notice how pained the Selkie's expression is, even in sleep.

"She seems very tired, but not as scared," Diana replies. "I think she's beginning to realize that she is safe, and that I am dangerous and on her side." Diana grins at me, her intimidating *I am the daughter of an alpha* grin that never fails to raise the hairs on the back of my neck.

"Yvan Guriel brought her some food." I lift the bag. "Dried fish."

Diana wrinkles her nose. "I knew *that* before you set foot in the room," she says, affronted by my continual underestimation of her superior Lupine senses. "I smelled him out there," she tells me, cocking her head and watching me closely. "Waiting for you."

Her words hang in the air between us, my flush heating again.

Lupine senses. I realize she heard my entire conversation with Yvan and can sense our pointless attraction. Diana stares levelly back at me, remaining uncharacteristically and blessedly silent on the matter.

I'm quiet for a moment, Wynter's murmuring to Ariel and the crackling of the fire the only sounds in the tranquil room.

I'm grateful that Diana refrains from commenting about me and Yvan, but I'm not able to remain silent when it comes to my brother.

"Diana," I say hesitantly. "I...I saw you kissing my brother earlier, you know."

Diana blinks at me, expressionless. "I wish to mate with him," she finally says.

My worry spikes. "But you told me you wouldn't because he's not Lupine, so I'm a little confused on that point..."

"I would not mate with him at present," she clarifies with a wave of her hand as if this should be obvious. "Only *after* he becomes Lupine."

"My brother's a Gardnerian, Diana," I point out, growing even more worried.

"What is your point, exactly?"

"Gardnerians don't become Lupine."

"Oh, he will," she says with complete confidence, "to mate with *me*."

"Become Lupine?" My brother, a *shapeshifter*?

"Yes."

I sigh in surrender and rest my head on the bed, facing Diana and the sleeping Selkie, a fierce melancholy overtaking me.

Here she is—Rafe's choice. What little family I have is beginning to fracture and fall away. Rafe will become a Lupine and leave us. And Trystan... Ancient One knows what will happen to him.

And me—I don't fit in anywhere. Least of all with Yvan. A bitter pang of hurt and regret courses through me.

"How does someone become Lupine?" I ask, my voice low and sad, curious about how exactly Rafe will be taken away.

She hesitates before answering. "A bite to the base of the throat that draws blood, on the night of the full moon."

"What will your father do?" I ask, worriedly. "When he finds out about Rafe?"

"My father will like Rafe a great deal," she assures me. "I am sure of it."

The two of us are silent for a moment as I fight back stinging tears.

"You know, Elloren Gardner," Diana finally says, her voice kind, "when I take your brother to mate, we will become sisters."

I turn my head to look at her, surprised.

"You will be part of my family, then," she goes on, "whether you become Lupine or not."

The loneliness, the fear, not being able to go home and be with my uncle, the loss of my quilt, the risks we're taking, the intense conflict in Yvan's eyes—all of a sudden, these things wash over me, and I close my eyes tightly, embarrassed to be openly crying into the blanket beneath me. I feel Diana's hand on my head, which makes me cry even harder.

"It's not natural, how you people live," she says as she strokes my hair. "Cut off from each other, so alone. My family will like you very much, Elloren Gardner."

"They won't," I counter, my nose stuffing up. "They'll see

who I look like, and they'll hate me. Just like everyone else who's not Gardnerian."

"No, they will trust my opinion of you, and I like you, El-loren Gardner, even though you are so strange to me. What you did…freeing this Selkie girl, weak as you are. It was very brave."

Her compliment catches me off guard. I inwardly straighten up at her praise, my embarrassment fading. Diana always seems to be merely suffering through the company of all us non-Lupines, so her good opinion seems all the more valuable and well earned.

"I don't fit in anywhere," I tell her.

"You will find a place with my pack," Diana insists. "I am quite sure of it. I think you should spend next summer with us."

My tears subside at the improbable thought of spending the summer with Diana.

What if she's right? What if her people do accept me? Would I truly be gaining family when Diana and Rafe become a mated pair?

Diana and Jarod have mentioned their little sister, Kendra, on more than one occasion. Would she become part of my family, too? And Diana's mother? Maybe she would become my friend.

A little bit of hope takes hold inside me.

Her hand on my head is so comforting, so kind. It's so good to be touched, and I feel myself letting go of some of the stress roiling inside me.

"You didn't hesitate to help me," I tell her. "You didn't hesi-tate to help the Selkie. Thank you."

Diana nods slightly in acknowledgment.

"I'd be very happy," I tell her, "to have you as a sister someday."

I realize, with warm surprise, how deeply and genuinely I mean it.

Diana's lips curve into a small, satisfied smile, and a few min-utes later I let my eyes fall shut like the Selkie's, the rhythm of Diana's fingers soothing on my hair, a blessedly dreamless sleep quickly overtaking me.

★ ★ ★

"Elloren, wake up."

Diana's insistent voice pulls my eyes open the next morning. The strange expression on her face, her gaze focused on the door, drives out whatever sleepiness remains.

She's off the bed and in a defensive crouch. Ariel and Wynter are gone. The Selkie is awake and backed up against the headboard of my bed, motionless except for her terrified ocean-gray eyes, which dart wildly around.

I push myself up and into a straighter position, my back stiff from sleeping all night propped up against the bed.

"What's the matter?"

Diana's finger flies up to her lips. "Someone's coming. I don't recognize their scent. Two people." Diana cocks her head to one side, listening, her face grim. "They're coming for her, Elloren. The groundskeeper. And someone else."

"What will we do?" I breathe, my throat clenching with fear.

Diana falls farther into her protective crouch. Her eyes take on a scary glow as her lips pull back into a threatening snarl. "If they try to take her," she says, showing all her teeth to the door, "I will kill them."

I can hear three things. A terrifying growl starting at the base of Diana's throat, the sound of footsteps in the hallway and my own heart slamming against my chest.

The door swings open, and Diana's growl morphs into a full-blown death threat.

Standing in the doorway is a Vu Trin sorceress.

She's young and dressed in uniform—black garb marked with glowing blue runes and silver weaponry strapped all over her body. I notice that she resembles Commander Kam Vin, their leader. She has the same dark eyes and hair, deep brown skin and similar facial features. But she's also very different from Kam Vin.

She's scarred. Horribly so. A good half of her face is covered in burn scars, the hair on one side of her head gone, covered partially by a long, black scarf. One ear is completely melted away, the scars extending down her neck and disappearing inside her clothing, only to reappear in the disfigured stump that must have, at one time, been a hand, but now looks as if all the fingers have melted together. It's a strange effect—one side of her strong and lovely, the other mutilated.

Diana slowly raises one hand and rapidly morphs it into a clawed weapon.

The young sorceress narrows her eyes at Diana, amazingly serene in the face of such a formidable threat. "I am Ni Vin," she announces formally, "younger sister to Commander Kam Vin. Under auspices of the Verpacian Guard, I have jurisdiction over this area of the University. And, I have a search warrant."

"Make one move for the Selkie, Sorceress," Diana warns, her voice frighteningly calm, "and I will tear you limb from limb."

A small smirk plays at the corners of the sorceress's mouth. "What Selkie?" she asks.

Diana's head jerks back, her eyebrows knitting in confusion.

"It seems the groundskeeper's Selkie has gone missing," the sorceress informs us. "Pity. I have been asked to accompany him on a thorough search of the University grounds."

"Where is he?" Diana growls as she exposes her canines, her eyes glowing furiously.

Ni Vin gestures with her head toward the door. "He would not come up." A calculating glint lights her eyes. "I warned him that Icarals live in these quarters. Being a Gardnerian, he feels a very strong aversion to their kind. He considers the entire tower to be unclean."

Diana slowly straightens as the realization dawns on both of us that we've gained an unexpected ally. Diana's hand morphs back to its human shape.

"I am glad to find that your lodging is free of the Selkie,"

Ni Vin informs us. "I am sure that you would not object to my searching the tower quite thoroughly."

"No," Diana says, clearly as surprised as I am by this unexpected turn of events. "You are free to search and have our full cooperation."

"Thank you," the sorceress replies stiffly. She stands there for what seems like a long time as the Selkie cowers on the bed, eyes darting from person to person.

"It is as I thought," Ni Vin finally announces. "The Selkie is nowhere to be found. Perhaps she was stolen by a Gardnerian soldier seeking some amusement."

"A likely scenario," Diana agrees.

"Thank you again for your cooperation," Ni Vin says with a quick bow. "Good day." She turns on her boot heels and leaves.

"Distract her," Diana orders, gesturing toward the terrified Selkie, who is crouched down low on the bed.

I sit down next to the trembling Selkie and stroke her hair as Diana stalks out into the hallway. The Selkie looks up at me, a desperate plea in her otherworldly gaze.

"Shh." I try to reassure her, putting my arm around her thin body, fierce resolve growing within me. "We won't let them take you."

She closes her eyes tight as if deeply pained, then presses her head down against my shoulder, hiding her face from view.

After a few minutes Diana comes back into the room, a serious expression on her face.

"Do you trust the sorceress?" I ask her.

She cocks an eyebrow at me. "We don't really have a choice."

I shoot her a worried look.

"Relax, Elloren Gardner," she assures me. "I believe she was telling the truth. I did not smell a threat in her words."

"I think I need more help with this situation than I realized," I admit, my heart racing. "And what if Aunt Vyvian decides to pay me a visit?" I worry, dread rising. "She's sent a constant stream of letters to pressure me to wandfast. There's no way she'll stay away forever—she likes getting her way."

"Perhaps," Diana agrees. Her amber eyes dart to the quivering Selkie. "It might be wise to call a meeting of everyone who would be willing to help us find a safer place for this Selkie."

CHAPTER TWELVE

Allies

It's startling to be staring into Elfin eyes. Like liquid metal mixed with starlight.

It's even more startling to have Wynter's brother, Cael, his second, Rhys Thorim, Wynter and my brother Rafe grouped together in the North Tower's upper hallway this evening.

Along with the Lupines, Andras and Yvan.

We've quickly pulled together a meeting of everyone who could help the Selkie, but I never expected we'd be joined by two Alfsigr Elves.

I hold straight-backed Cael's disconcerting, glittering stare. "Last time you were with my brother, you were threatening him."

Cael's stare is unwavering, his words heavily accented. "The last time I saw you, Elloren Gardner, you were threatening my sister."

I blink at him, chastened. "Yes, well... I'm sorry about that."

"I was wrong about your brother." His accent is lilting. He says "wrong" with a gentle trill to the "wr."

"I don't understand," I say, looking to Wynter, who is perched on the North Tower's upper hallway windowsill, her wings neatly folded behind her.

"My sister told me what you have done," Cael explains. "Rhys Thorim and myself, we were concerned that this rescue is unsafe for my sister to be involved in. But then when we saw this Selkie and heard what was done to her..." Cael's silver eyes go tense with conflict, his voice lowering. "It is terrible how she has been treated." Resolve steels his gaze. "There are many who believe that my sister is little more than an animal, as well. We support you in your decision to rescue this Selkie, Elloren Gardner."

I glance around at everyone, amazed, then back to Cael. "So, you're all...friendly now?"

Cael's mouth lifts. "Yes, Elloren Gardner. We are friendly."

Shaking my head, I look to Wynter, who seems tired and drawn. "How's she doing?" I ask.

"Aislinn is with her," Wynter tells me. "She's sleeping."

I glance worriedly at Jarod, his face tensing at the mention of Aislinn's name. I sit down on the hallway's stone bench between Jarod and Trystan, giving Jarod a small, encouraging bump to his arm with mine.

Jarod looks down at me and attempts a weary smile.

I look to Yvan. He's leaning back against the stone wall, his gaze trained on me. My cheeks warm from his attention, and I turn away, suddenly lit up by the silent, heated intensity that exists between us. It's like a forbidden, thrilling secret.

Rafe glances around at all of us and steps forward. "So, as you all know, we need to figure out what to do about the stolen Selkie."

"*Freed* Selkie," Diana corrects him.

"An important distinction," Rafe agrees.

"She was being held prisoner by a cruel man," Diana continues, "who I volunteer to kill at the appropriate time."

Rafe turns to Diana. I can tell he's trying to suppress a look of amusement. "Thank you, Diana."

Diana lifts her chin in acknowledgment.

"I'm assuming everyone here supports Elloren's decision," Rafe continues.

"I've seen the Selkies brought into the docks in Valgard," Trystan comments quietly. "They were stacked inside of crates. It bothered me a great deal."

"I often rode past the groundskeeper's cottage," Andras interjects. "He kept her chained to a post. I also volunteer to kill this man."

"Thank you, Andras," Rafe says, "but we need to wait on killing him for the time being." He looks around again. "Does everyone here understand that to help Elloren is to be in violation of the law, Verpacian and Gardnerian, and could result in fines for theft and possible suspension or dismissal from the University?"

Everyone nods.

"Well, all right, then. If that's understood, we can think about where to go from here."

"Perhaps it would be good if we introduce ourselves," I suggest. "Not everyone here knows each other."

"I don't know, Ren," Rafe points out. "Yvan here has been so annoyingly chatty from day one, I feel like I know everything there is to know about him."

Rafe raises his eyebrows at Yvan pointedly, and Yvan steps forward, hands in his pockets, and coolly meets Rafe's gaze before glancing around at all of us.

"I'm Yvan Guriel, from the Lyndon region of Keltania, and I was shocked to see the groundskeeper's treatment of the Selkie." He turns to look at me. "I believe Elloren did the right thing."

Flustered, I look away, only to find Jarod staring at me, his brow raised in momentary surprise.

Like Diana, no doubt he can sense my mortifyingly strong attraction to Yvan. The realization makes me want to crawl clear under the bench. My flush deepening, I stiffen, sit up straighter and fruitlessly try to ignore Yvan.

Jarod's, Andras's, Trystan's and Diana's introductions follow, Diana shooting me a self-satisfied glance when she only lists her ancestry back two generations instead of the usual five. But I can barely focus on her, my attention continuously pulled back to Yvan like a compass needle to true north. Out of the corner of my eye, I see he's distracted as well, his eyes repeatedly drawing back to me.

Finally, there's only one introduction left, and all eyes turn to the figure perched on the windowsill.

Wynter lets her wings drop to her sides. "I am Wynter Eirllyn," she says very softly, "cursed daughter of Feonir and Avalyn, sister to Cael. I am one of the Foul Ones. One who brings great shame to all of Elfinkin, and who is shunned by the Shining Ones." Wynter slumps back down and wraps her wings around herself.

"What are you speaking of?" Diana demands. "Who are these Shining Ones who are being so cruel to you?"

"They are the Keepers of the Inner Sanctum," Wynter explains. "The creators of our world."

"This is foolishness," Diana protests indignantly. "Maiya, The Great Mother, created the world. And you seem perfectly pleasant, and not foul at all. Why are you insulting yourself?" Diana turns to all of us. "She has been very kind to the Selkie woman. She is not the least bit foul."

Cael and Rhys look at Diana, surprised.

Rafe leans in toward Diana. "The Elfin religion differs from yours, Diana."

"My sister believes very strongly in Elfin ways," Cael explains.

Diana snorts at him disdainfully. "Well, these ways of yours are ridiculous, and just not true. Maiya created the world and placed the shapeshifters in it as her special children. Then she made all of you as an afterthought, but no one is despised or shunned or any of this nonsense she is speaking of. No one, except for people who act like that groundskeeper, who should be killed as soon as possible."

"Different cultures have different ideas about things," Rafe interjects.

"They are deluded," Diana counters. "The Lupines are correct."

Rafe arches an eyebrow at her. "Because you are the superior race?"

"You are mocking me. Yes, we are superior. It is easy to see. We do not beat seal women and force people to mate with people they dislike and take everyone's land..."

"The Gardnerians would say that their military successes are proof that the Ancient One is real and most powerful," Rafe counters. "And the Elves would perhaps point to their rich art, music and culture as proof of their being especially blessed by the Shining Ones."

"You are not making any sense!"

"My apologies. I forgot that your religion is the only correct one."

"You are mocking me again. He is mocking me, isn't he?" she asks all of us. Jarod, Andras and Trystan are attempting to stifle grins.

"No, Diana, I'm not," Rafe laughs. "I'm trying to make a point."

"I really don't want to interrupt this rather fascinating theological debate you two seem to be having," Trystan interjects wryly, "but can we get back to the topic at hand?"

Diana crosses her arms in front of herself, visibly fuming at Rafe. "You will feel differently when you become one of us," she insists.

"Wait a minute," Trystan interrupts, eyes flying open. He shoots Rafe an incredulous look. *"One of us?"*

"I'm thinking about becoming Lupine," Rafe explains off-handedly.

"Thank you for informing your siblings," I put in with some censure. Of course, I know this already, but I'm still vexed that Rafe hasn't bothered to talk to Trystan and me about it.

"You're going to become...*Lupine*," Trystan repeats, as if in a momentary daze.

Rafe shoots Trystan a level stare. "I don't particularly enjoy being a Gardnerian, you know that." His mouth tilts into a cagey grin, his tone gaining an edge. "I'd rather be out in the woods. Not hating everyone on Erthia."

Trystan is blinking at him, disbelieving. "Can I be there when you tell Aunt Vyvian?"

Rafe laughs.

I reach up to massage my temple, a headache beginning to throb.

Everyone is silent for a long moment.

"All right, then," Trystan finally says with a respectful nod toward Diana. He glances around at all of us, his usual calm restored as if everything is all settled.

Cael, Rhys, Andras and Yvan are looking at my brothers and me as if we've all sprouted horns.

"How did the three of you become this way?" Cael wonders. "How is it that you have sprung up from the same family as Carnissa Gardner and Vyvian Damon?"

My brothers and I glance at each other, at a loss over how to answer.

"Our uncle," Rafe replies. "He's somewhat eccentric. He raised us."

"He's going to get himself killed," Cael observes, half in jest, but with an undertone of real warning.

I swallow apprehensively, not liking such teasing. "Uncle Edwin keeps to himself," I say. "No one would want to hurt him..."

"You three are as close to Gardnerian royalty as you can get," Cael points out. "And this uncle of yours, he raised you to be so...subversive. It's amazing he's still alive. He must be a very clever man."

It's an odd choice of words to describe our bumbling, bookish uncle Edwin, who spends his free time making herbal teas, hunting for mushrooms and playing with my cat. Who often goes looking for his glasses when they're sitting on his head.

"Seems to me you two are bucking tradition a little yourselves," Rafe says to Cael, "with your support of your sister."

"Maybe we should get back to talking about the Selkie?" Jarod suggests diplomatically.

"She needs to be named," Diana points out. "We can't keep referring to her as 'the Selkie.' It's insulting. She deserves to be named."

Rafe's look of amusement disappears as he studies Diana. "You're right."

"Marina," says Wynter quietly. "It means ocean. It's where she wants to go. Where her family is. I think that should be her name."

"It's beautiful," I tell Wynter as she wraps her wings tightly around herself.

Rafe is looking around, gauging everyone's response. "Well, if we're all in agreement," he says, "Marina it is. Now, my understanding is that Yvan has brought us some books from the archives that contain information about Selkies."

Yvan leans over to pull two leather-bound volumes from a sack next to him.

"It's not much," he says, "but it's all I could find. I think the main problem is finding her skin. Unless it is in her possession, she can't return to her seal form. It must have been stolen from her when she was captured, or she wouldn't be so weak. A Selkie with her skin is as strong as a Lupine."

Diana straightens, always pleased with Lupines being used as the strength standard.

"I think I might be able to find out where the skins are kept," Rafe volunteers. "I know of some Gardnerians who frequent the Selkie taverns—"

"Selkie taverns?" I have a feeling I really don't want to know what this is.

"It's possibly where they keep them," Rafe explains, looking around uncertainly. "I'm not sure how blunt I can be here. It's not our custom, and I know it's not the custom of the Elves to speak about certain things in the presence of women."

"This is foolishness," Diana scoffs.

Wynter pulls her wings more tightly around herself. "There is nothing you could say that would be worse than what I have felt from her mind. It is…unspeakable."

"You're an Empath?" Yvan says to Wynter. He's looking at her strangely.

Wynter nods at him.

"Tell us what you know of the Selkie," Rafe encourages Wynter.

Wynter closes her eyes and leans to one side like a small tree bent by a raging storm, her face tense with pain. "She was brought to one of those taverns, along with others of her kind. All of them…undressed. Shown to men." Her brow knits even tighter. "The face of the groundskeeper looms heavy in her mind. She was claimed by this man. Money given for her. He took her for his own and…abused her. Many times." She tilts her head. "And there is another face. The face of another Selkie, this one younger, perhaps—captured at the same time. She feels crippling fear for this Selkie. Her thoughts are consumed by these images. It is hard to make out any more. She does not have a language that I understand."

Everyone is quiet for a moment.

"So we need to find her skin," Jarod observes, his expression grave. "Perhaps the groundskeeper has hidden it somewhere."

"Or destroyed it," Andras remarks.

"No," Yvan puts in. "It must exist."

"How can you be sure?" I ask him.

He turns his green eyes on me. "If it had been destroyed, she would be a soulless shell, with no emotion. Like the living dead."

A chill runs down my spine, and we all exchange dark looks, realizing the stakes are much higher than we thought for Marina, the newly named Selkie.

"Well, it's settled, then," Rafe says, his tone light, but his eyes hard as stone. "We'll just have to find it."

CHAPTER THIRTEEN

Camouflage

Over the next week Marina the Selkie slowly begins to shed her fear when she's around Diana, Wynter, Aislinn and me. And new friendships have been formed—Rafe, Cael, Rhys and Andras have fallen into an easy camaraderie and are now hunting together. There's even been tentative conversation between Yvan and my brothers when they're discreetly in their lodging.

Yvan stealthily speaks to me now, asking about the Selkie if we have a brief moment in the kitchen alone, quietly helping me with kitchen tasks when it will go unnoticed. I nearly fall over the first time he gives me a warm half smile, my heartbeat turning erratic.

But we have to be careful. Careful not to show that we're rapidly becoming friends.

I've decided to put my Gardnerian silks back on, wanting to blend in with my people and remain above suspicion—Marina's life might depend on it.

Marina watches me, her ocean eyes steady as I pull one of my fine Gardnerian-black, silken tunics over my head for the first time in a long time, my jaw clenched with resolve as I tug at the fabric and mentally beat back a swelling nausea. The shock of seeing myself in the washroom mirror sets me reeling even further.

A true Gardnerian—right down to the silver Erthia orb around my neck.

The very image of Her.

I glance over toward Marina, and the Selkie's trusting gaze sends shame coursing through me. Tears stinging at my eyes, I turn away from her and struggle to tie up the tunic's laced back, my fingers fumbling.

I hate Vogel, I want to tell her in a way she'll understand. *I'm nothing like my cursed people, even though I look like this. I don't want to look like this.*

The Selkie's fingers come over mine, gently taking the laces from my hands and deftly tying them tight as tears spill over and streak down my cheeks.

When I emerge from the washroom, Ariel catches sight of me and flinches back as if struck, then gives me a scathing look of pure hate.

"I have to fit in," I try to explain to Ariel, my palms out in surrender. "I have to dress like them. You know I'm not like most Gardnerians. But we're hiding a Selkie," I gesture toward Marina. "It's important that I fit in. You must see that."

A wave of guilt washes over me as Ariel ignores my words and scuttles clear across her bed, huddling against the wall and glowering at me. Her dark look is only mildly assuaged by Wynter taking a seat beside her, murmuring soothing words as Ariel buries her head against Wynter's chest, the Elfin Icaral's dark wings coming protectively around them both.

Wynter's eyes rest on Marina for a moment, the Selkie taking a seat on the floor by the fire, next to Diana. Wynter turns to me, takes in my garb, then nods once, her silver eyes full of steeled understanding.

Diana casually throws her arm around our Selkie and looks

me over, a shrewd gleam lighting her gaze. She raises her amber eyes and gives me a wide, sly smile of approval, baring her teeth.

I take a good deal of comfort from this—I can count on my Lupine friend to fully understand strategy in a fight.

I pick up my new white armband and turn to Diana. "Would you help me put this on?"

Her dark, knowing smile doesn't flinch. Diana gets up and strides toward me. She takes the Vogel band and cinches it securely around my arm.

Priest Simitri smiles broadly when I come into his History class early, pale rays of wintry light spearing through the windows. He takes in my conservative attire, complete with a white Vogel ribbon pinned around my arm.

"Ah, Mage Gardner," he observes with obvious relief. He's been dismayed for weeks by my dark brown, barely acceptable woolen garb, his vocal support for Vogel mirrored by his own ribbon. "You stand now in courage," he tells me. "Even though you have been forced to labor with Kelts and Urisk, and to live with Icaral demons, you have the courage to stand apart. To let your dress proudly declare both your faith *and* your support of our beloved Priest Vogel. I applaud you."

It's not courage, I think darkly, my stomach now a constant knot. *It's camouflage.*

"The armband, too?" Yvan snipes at me as he loads wood into the stove next to me that evening.

I'm deeply stung by his harsh tone. "Don't you think it's smart?" I snipe back.

He stares at the flames, his jaw flexing with tension. "It's smart." His green eyes flash at me before he throws the iron door shut and stalks away.

Anger burns at my insides.

I'm not these clothes, I want to yell after him, aware of the newly

stoked hatred bearing down on me from all the kitchen workers, Iris's brazen look of hostility the most open manifestation.
I can feel her look clear across the room.

I'm not this white armband, or these black silks, or this face, I continue to rail at Yvan wordlessly as he exits out the back and
shuts the door with a sharp slam I feel straight down my spine.

I'm not Her, I continue to rage toward him, an angry flush
burning at my cheeks. *You know I'm not.*

I'll never be Her.

CHAPTER FOURTEEN

Tightening Noose

It's late the next evening when I'm intercepted by a messenger from Lukas's division, the Twelfth Division River Oak pinned to his tunic.

Apothecary lab has just ended, and Tierney is by my side, a white band now pinned around her arm, as well. "Self-preservation," she told me when I first took in her white band with no small measure of surprise.

It seems I'm not the only one resorting to camouflage.

The uniformed messenger hands me a long package. "Mage Gardner," he says with a deferential bob of his head, his breath puffing out from the cold.

There's a note card affixed to it, my name on the small envelope in neat script, written with an artistic hand.

Lukas's hand.

A pang of regret rises. After what happened to Ariel, I've put Lukas firmly out of my mind, pointedly not responding to his sporadic gifts and notes. I was so mad at him for so many weeks, but guilt has gradually worn that down. I'm just as much to blame for what happened as he is.

I weigh this new gift in my hands, the box not as heavy as I would have thought it would be, given its size. The young soldier gives me another quick bow and sets off.

I sit down on a nearby stone bench. Tierney takes a seat beside me, smatterings of scholars passing by talking quietly, the chill wind picking up in fits and starts.

I hand Tierney the note card and tug at the stiff brown paper, ripping it open, pulling out the black leather case underneath.

A violin case.

Heart thudding, I open the case and gasp when I see what's inside, nestled in deep green velvet.

A Maelorian violin. Like the one Aunt Vyvian was given temporary use of the night of her dance.

Only this one is brand-new, the Alfsigr spruce varnished to a deep crimson, the edges gilded, the strings gleaming gold in the lamplight. A violin so expensive it could pay for my University tithe about ten times over.

With shaking hands, I take the note card from Tierney and open it.

Elloren,

If you wanted a portrait of me, all you had to do was ask.

Lukas

An incredulous laugh bursts from me, and a warm spark of affection for Lukas Grey is quickly followed by some remorse. I've been wrapped up in thoughts of Keltic Yvan while Lukas has been pursuing me from afar, and now this. Chastened, I hold the note out for Tierney to read.

Tierney's mouth lifts into a crooked smile, her eyes dancing with dark delight.

"It feels bizarre, but I kind of like him at this moment," she says, her smile growing wider.

I reverently close the violin case, heart fluttering at the sheer giddy excitement of holding such an instrument in my hands. *At owning* such an instrument.

I become suddenly conflicted—I don't deserve such attention from a man I don't plan on fasting to. I resolve to return the violin to Lukas the next time I see him, and to send a note of thanks in the meantime. Lukas deserves at least that.

Feeling eyes on me, I look up.

Gesine Bane and her friends are all staring at me and the violin in my lap, a nasty gleam in their eyes.

My elation instantly turns hard and sour, fear spiking on its heels.

Once Fallon Bane gets wind of this, I realize, *it will be open season on me.*

"She can speak, I'm sure of it," Diana observes to me that night as I send up a stream of music in the washroom, my fingers sore and unaccustomed to playing for so long. I don't care. It feels so good to have this violin in my hands.

And what a violin.

It renders my out-of-practice efforts into something heartbreakingly lovely.

Marina's in the bath, curled up naked under the cooling water, her sorrowful gaze rippling up at us. I finish my song and lower my violin as Diana cocks her head in thought. "She can speak, but she just can't speak in any form we can understand."

Marina opens her mouth and forces multiple tones through her mouth and gills, the sound transformed by the water, her multiple tones coalescing into a deep, resonating hum that sounds like an eerily mournful song.

Like she's grieving.

Our Selkie is a puzzle that can't be solved. Sometimes her animal-like movements and barking multitones are those of a wild thing, but her eyes are inquisitive and intelligent, and I know that Diana's right.

She's more than just an animal. More than a seal.

Jarod and Diana have not been able to find Marina's skin, and she can't go back home without it—her strength is sapped to the point where she often seems ill. I've written to Gareth, asking for information about the Selkie trade and where their skins are kept, but I know his response will be slow in coming. He's been gone for weeks with the other Maritime apprentices, all of them out to sea until First Month, when winter digs its claws in and all the ocean passes will start to ice over.

Every night an exhausted Marina methodically runs her fingers through our hair, pulling out the tangles more effectively than any brush as she softly mutters in her multitoned language. It seems to soothe her, and it soothes all of us in turn.

All of us but Ariel.

Ariel despises the attention Wynter pays to the Selkie and flaps her wings agitatedly at Marina and mutters obscenities. Fortunately, Ariel's attention is mostly consumed by an injured raven that now abides with us, along with the two chickens. The owl is long since healed and freed. The raven perches on the bed next to Ariel, the two of them spooky in their blackness and unspoken understanding, the bird's leg carefully splinted and bandaged.

And so my days wear on.

Sporadic notices flap in the bracingly cold wind. They're affixed to University streetlamp posts and outside building entrances, alerting passersby of the Selkie's theft and a monetary reward for any information as to her whereabouts.

At first sighting, the notices send a sharp spasm of fear through me. But as time passes, and they're battered down and lost to the relentless wind, my fears are dulled to a blunt point.

Once, thinking I'm alone in an alley, I tear down one of the last notices still remaining and stuff it in my cloak pocket. I look up to see Ni Vin, the young, scarred Vu Trin. She's standing across the street and staring at me, a curved sword at her side. She gives a subtle nod of approval to me as my heart skitters against my chest.

Then she turns and strides away.

"There's mention of it here," Tierney tells me, her finger coming down on the paper set before her. The two of us pore over the *Council Motions & Rulings* every week's end, late at night, feeding our ongoing sleep deprivation.

She's right. A small mention of an "escaped" Selkie and the posting of a reward, as well as a renewed motion—put forward jointly by Mage Vyvian Damon and Marcus Vogel, and struck down by a slim margin—to have every Selkie in the Western Realm shot on sight.

I rub at my aching temples. "My aunt's not going to win any awards for compassion, I can tell you that."

"You know what this means, don't you?" Tierney whispers darkly.

I nod gravely. If Vogel wins in the spring, it's not just Marina who will be in trouble—all the Selkies will need to escape back to the sea or risk being put to death.

We read on, finding there's been a failed motion brought forward by Marcus Vogel to execute anyone who defaces the Gardnerian flag. Another failed motion brought forward by Vogel to execute anyone who maligns *The Book of the Ancients* in any way. A motion brought forward by Vogel and five other Council Mages to declare war on the Lupines unless they cede a large portion of their land holdings to Gardneria. Another motion to execute all male Icarals held in the Valgard Sanitorium. A motion to execute anyone aiding Snake Elves in their escape east.

And a doggedly renewed motion, put forward for the sixth

time by Vogel, to expand iron-testing for Guild admittance and randomly at border crossings to "root out the Fae menace."

"He may not win," I remind Tierney, who's gone pale.

"Have you seen how many people are wearing white bands?" Tierney counters, her voice shaky.

"Still," I insist, clinging to hope, "the referendum's not until spring. And a lot can happen in so many months. He may not win."

"Perhaps you're right," she relents, slumping down into a crooked ball, looking small and scared and worn. "I hope you're right, Elloren Gardner."

The news comes at the end of apothecary lab.

I glance up as Gesine rushes in. Professor Lorel inclines her head as her Lead Apprentice breathlessly whispers to her and gestures excitedly.

I set down my pestle and study them with curious trepidation.

"Scholars," Mage Lorel announces, her voice uncharacteristically shaken. She appears to be suppressing some deep emotion. "Our beloved High Mage, Aldus Worthin, has joined with the Ancient One."

A shocked murmuring goes up.

"We have a new High Mage. By referendum this morning, the Council has chosen Priest Marcus Vogel." Her face lights up with a beatific smile.

Dread rips through me with devastating force, and I grip at the edge of my desk to steady myself as the other white arm-banded scholars gasp, then break out into expressions of happy triumph. Some laugh and hug each other, some chat excitedly, some cry tears of joy.

Marcus Vogel.

His sly face flashes into my mind. The remembrance of the feel of his hand on mine. His serpentine stare. The lifeless tree and the black void.

Ancient One, no. This can't be.

Tierney whips her head to look at me—stark terror in her eyes.

"Tierney..." I can only manage a choked whisper and reach out to grasp her arm.

"Please, scholars," Mage Lorel implores as she gestures for quiet. Her face is streaked with tears. A reverent silence descends. "A moment of prayer for our late High Mage."

Everyone lowers their heads and brings their fists to their hearts. Tierney's frozen, her face gone ashen.

The scholars around us bring fists to foreheads, then back over their hearts as their prayer goes up in unison.

Oh, Most Holy Ancient One, purify our minds, purify our hearts, purify Erthia. Protect us from the stain of the Evil Ones.

The prayer ends, and a cacophony of joyous celebration breaks out.

Tierney stumbles to her feet, almost knocking her stool over, and rushes out the back door, her distraught departure barely causing a ripple in the thick jubilation on the air.

I catch up with Tierney in the washroom. She's bent over one of the porcelain washbasins, violently retching into it. I wet a cloth and go to her, placing my hand on her heaving, crooked back, my stomach painfully clenched.

Tierney remains frozen in place as she grips at the basin, ignoring the strands of her hair that swim in it and my offer of the cloth.

"He'll close the border," she says, her voice low and coarse. "He'll make fasting mandatory."

"I know," I say, feeling light-headed.

"We'll have a year at most to find a partner. And if we don't, they'll assign us one."

"I know."

"And before he fasts us," she cuts in, still staring into the basin, "he'll test our racial purity." She turns to me, a wild desperation in her eyes. "He's going to test us with iron."

"Tierney," I say with hard defiance. *Enough dancing around the truth.* "I want to help you. You're full-blooded Fae, aren't you?"

She continues to stare at me. When she finally speaks, her voice is a strangled scrape. "I can't. I can't speak of it."

"Not even now?" I whisper urgently. "When your worst fears have been realized? Let me help you!"

"You can't help me!" Distraught, she wrenches her bent frame away from my hand and makes for the door.

"Tierney, wait!" I call out to her, but she ignores my plea and flees the room.

I follow her out, but it's clear she doesn't want me to—she weaves quickly through the crowded hall, and I soon lose sight of her amidst the happy Gardnerians with white-banded arms.

I make my way toward my Chemistrie class, eager to find Aislinn.

I don't have to search long. Aislinn is leaning against a wall, her eyes searching, her face stricken. As soon as she spots me, she rushes toward me down the Chemistrie lab hallway, jostling around celebratory groupings of Gardnerian scholars and subdued, strained-looking Kelts and Elfhollen. A small cluster of Alfsigr Elves stand apart, surveying it all with their usual cool, aloof indifference, which, at the moment, I find infuriating.

"They're drawing up their numbers," Aislinn forces out as she reaches me, her hand clutching my arm. "The Gardnerian Guard. Along the border of Keltania and the Lupine wilds. Vogel sent out the orders this morning. Randall's been put on draft notice. All the military apprentices have. Vogel's demanded that the Kelts and Lupines cede most of their land to us. The Keltanian Assembly just sent their Head Magistrate to Valgard to try and avert all-out war."

My mind's a spinning tumult. "But...the Lupines... Vogel can threaten them all he wants. They're immune to our magic."

"They'll send dragons, Elloren," Aislinn says, a thread of panic running through her tone. "We have over a thousand of them. If the Lupines and the Kelts don't cede, the Guard will attack them with dragons."

Every class I have today is transformed by Vogel's sudden rise. I can't escape it. Professor Volya can barely get the Gardnerians to settle down enough so she can lecture. Priest Simitri abandons lecture altogether and orders in food and punch.

There's a deliriously festive mood in Metallurgie, and a young Elf standing at Professor Hawkyyn's desk, riffling through his notes—as if getting ready to lecture. He's a white-haired, white-skinned Alfsigr Elfkin, and I glance around, confused, looking for Professor Hawkkyn.

Knots of excited Gardnerians talk animatedly, white bands marking all of their left arms.

The white bands are sprouting like malevolent weeds, along with the Gardnerian flags. Even Curran Dell has taken to wearing one, which I note with deep regret.

"Where's Professor Hawkkyn?" I ask Curran, who's talking animatedly with another military apprentice. Curran smiles at me in greeting and opens his mouth to respond, but he's quickly cut off.

"Hopefully the Snake Elf is back belowground," Fallon's voice sounds out from across the room. "Which is where the beast belongs."

Everyone grows quiet and watches as she crosses the room, her eyes tight on me. "He's probably run off," Fallon amends with a wild smile. "He knows what's coming." She thrusts her bottom lip out at me in cloying mock sympathy. "Awww. Are you *sad*, Elloren Gardner? Looking to fast to the Snake Elf?"

Shocked laughter sounds out and echoes behind me. I set my teeth on edge, Curran's apologetic look doing nothing to dampen my fierce response.

Anger whips up inside me so strong, I clench my fists and glare at Fallon with pure, undisguised venom.

Fallon's eyes widen with delight. She turns her whole self toward me, one hand coming slowly to her hip, her grin broadening as she revels in both my rage and the whole world working in her favor. She stares me down with mounting glee, and I fear I will abandon all caution, break down and strike her cruel, self-satisfied face.

Is it worth it, Elloren? I warn myself. *Getting kicked out of University for striking another Mage? Who will promptly cut you down with her Black Witch magic?*

Instead, I turn on my heels and leave the room, Fallon's cruel laughter sounding out behind me.

When I enter the kitchens, Fernyllia's face is haggard with dark worry, and she gives a start at the sight of me.

Olilly is crying, her heaving back to me. Yvan, Bleddyn, Fernyllia and Iris are grouped around her, consoling her in low tones.

They look like they've all sustained a powerful blow.

Head down, I cross the room and set right to work peeling potatoes, stiff and self-conscious, sharply aware of their eyes on me as the room quiets.

I know how I appear to them in my black silks and white armband, the threat of me heightened. My very presence has always been a symbol of Gardnerian might. But now, dressed like this, I'm an extension of Vogel—the monster about to come after them all.

I look up and feel the full, ice-water shock of their hate.

Yvan takes in the brutal glares they're all leveling in my direction, then turns to me, stricken, his expression pained but open. Wide-open.

And suddenly I'm wide-open to him as well, letting him see all of it—my fear and mounting desperation. My terrible isolation; my appearance reflecting nothing of my true heart.

We hold each other's gaze for a long moment as the room around us fades. The kitchen workers, the iciness of their stares, the crackling fires of the ovens, all of it dissolves like fog. There's only him.

Only us.

Olilly whimpers, distracting us both, rupturing our safe, protected bubble, the world rushing back in.

Iris is still glaring at me, her eyes flitting suspiciously to Yvan, then me and back to Yvan again as he pulls his eyes away from me and resumes comforting Olilly, his hand on the young woman's shaking arm.

Iris whispers something in Yvan's ear and gestures sharply in my direction. Yvan fleetingly meets my eyes, his face tensed with conflict.

Fernyllia speaks softly to Olilly in encouraging tones, and Yvan joins in.

"They won't send you back," I hear him say, his low voice resonating deep in me. "We'll help you get out. Your sister, too."

And then they all leave together, Iris being the last to exit. She shoots me a jarring look of hate, then steps out of the kitchen and pulls the back door shut with a slam.

My hands hurt when I finally leave my kitchen shift, my fingers sore from peeling so many potatoes, my chest a tight ball of despair. The sun has set, and night is firmly settled in the sky. The world is starless and dark as I move away from the lantern light by the kitchen's back entrance.

I take a deep, steadying breath, the cold air bracing. I'm halfway across the small field at the kitchen's back end, edged by a small stand of forest, the shadows tonight an inky, bottomless black, my steps dragging.

"Stay away from our men."

I halt, heart speeding, and look toward the shadows, my eyes searching for the source of the vicious words.

I can just make Iris out in the dark, cloudy night. She's leaning back against a tree trunk, arms confrontationally crossed, tall Bleddyn next to her, looking incensed.

My eyes dart toward a thinly populated path not far from here. Gauging whether or not Iris and Bleddyn can get away with attacking me again.

Iris stalks toward me, and I take a step back.

"I see the way you look at him," she grinds out, getting up near my face.

A hot flush prickles all over my cheeks, my neck. "I don't know what you're talking about..."

"You Roaches want to own everything," Bleddyn sneers, her voice deep and throaty, her eyes narrowed to furious slits.

"He's mine," Iris insists, the anger cracking open to reveal a pained vulnerability, her lips trembling. She gathers herself, her mouth tightening into an angry line, the hatred in her glare flaring. "Go back to Lukas Grey." She looks me over with disgust. "Where you *belong*. Stay away from Yvan."

Every muscle in my body tenses, and my hands clench into fists as I let my fear fall away and glower at her openly.

Bleddyn spits out a laugh. "He doesn't want her," she sneers, looking me over with contempt. "How could he? With her pretending to be a Kelt one day and a Roach the next?" She blows a disdainful breath. "She doesn't even know what skin she's in."

Iris looks to Bleddyn, vulnerable again, but infuriatingly heartened by her friend's cruel words. Iris shoots me one last look of pure hostility, then walks off with Bleddyn, the Urisk girl hissing out, *"Roach bitch!"* as she passes.

★ ★ ★

Rafe and Trystan are in the hallway waiting for me when I return to the North Tower. They're lit by lamplight, framed in black by the window behind them.

I swallow and fight back a swelling nausea as I take in their somber expressions, livid thoughts about Iris and Bleddyn whisked clear away.

Without comment, Rafe holds out a stiff, folded parchment, defiance in his eyes.

I unfold it, the sense of dread hardening in my gut.

Ancient One, no. It's a notice of impending draft.

"It's so quick," I say, staring at the notice with disbelief. "Vogel only took power this morning."

"It's like he was ready for this," Rafe says, his voice hard with suspicion.

"What?" I question, rattled. "You think Vogel knew this was coming? That our High Mage would die?"

Rafe's dark stare doesn't waver. "It makes you wonder. It's so well *planned*."

I remember Vogel's terrible presence, the black void, the dead tree. I stare back at Rafe, alarm rising.

Trystan is uncharacteristically on edge, his eyes haunted. Looking aimlessly around the cold hallway, he takes a seat on the stone bench, his head dropping into his hands, his fingers clenching his hair.

"It's a notice of *impending* draft," I say, trying to reassure them both, trying to reassure myself. "The draft might not happen for a while."

"This summer," Trystan says, not lifting his head, his tone devoid of hope. "He'll call us in this summer. There's a weapons shipment that's to go out just before that."

My heart is hammering against my chest. I look up to Rafe. "Where would they send you?" I breathe.

Rafe spits out a bitter laugh, like the question is horribly ironic. "To the military base in Rothir." His jaded grin falls away. "To wage war on the Lupines."

I feel a sickening drop of my gut. "What will you do?" I ask.

Rafe bares his teeth. "I'll use it for target practice." He flicks the edge of the notice. "Right through the Mage Council Seal." Defiant humor hardening to anger, Rafe looks toward the windows searchingly, then toward the door to my lodging. "Where's Diana?" His voice is uncharacteristically brusque.

I gesture loosely toward the northern wilderness. "Somewhere in the wilds."

His mouth set in a tight line, Rafe takes back the notice from me and hoists his bag.

"You'll never find her—"

"I know where she goes," he spits out, making for the door.

"What are you going to do?" I call after him, worried.

"Join the Lupines," he growls before leaving, shutting the door behind him with a hard thud.

I stare after him. Force myself to take a steadying breath. Attempt to beat back the thin line of panic as Rafe's heavy boot heels clomp down the stairs, the tower door slamming shut. Silence descends.

"They won't take him in," Trystan says with calm, terrible assurance.

Trystan's voice is muted, his head still in his hands, fingers clutching at his hair in tight fists.

"He's the grandson of the Black Witch," Trystan continues, tone deadened. "They will *never* take him in."

Thoughts spinning, with nothing solid to latch on to, I take a seat next to Trystan and put my hand on his shoulder to steady the both of us. His breath catches then stops for a moment. His slender body shudders, his hands coming down to tightly cover his eyes as he starts to cry. My heart catches in my throat—the silent way Trystan sobs is always more devastating to me than if he keened and wailed.

I put my arm around him and he falls against me, bending in, eyes pressed against my shoulder as I hug him and pull him in tight.

"I don't want to be part of this anymore." His voice is constricted almost to a whisper. "They've got me filling metal discs with fire power. Anyone who steps on them will be blown to pieces. I'm filling arrows with fire. And ice. For *what*? To kill *who*? I don't want to be a party to what's coming." He pauses, growing still. "And it's only a matter of time before they find out what I am."

Panic rears its head. "They don't have to find out."

He shakes his head side to side, hard against my shoulder. "Of course they'll find out. When I don't wandfast—"

"You'll have to wandfast." I firmly cut him off, brooking no argument.

Trystan goes very still. He's quiet for a moment, breathing against my shoulder. He raises his red-rimmed eyes to me. "How?"

The question hangs in the air like a tunnel with no escape. "You just will! You'll hide it. You'll hide what you are."

His calm deepens. He looks at me with unflappable incredulity. "Could you fast to a woman?"

"What?" I spit out, thrown. "Of course not!" A stinging flush rises on my cheeks along with a sudden wave of understanding. My mind casts about, desperately searching for a way out for him, but there's no clear way to escape this.

After wandfasting comes the sealing ceremony. And consummation is expected the very night of the sealing, the fastlines flowing down the couple's wrist as proof of consummation. The whole point of our joinings is to create more pure-blooded Mages.

It's impossible for Trystan to even attempt to pull off a charade of normalcy.

We're both quiet for a long moment.

"I could go to Noi lands," he finally says. "They accept…my kind there." His mouth twists in a cynical half smile. "But I'm the grandson of the Black Witch. Who will ever accept me?"

Incensed on my brother's behalf, I stamp down my panic, mutiny rising. "I don't know, Trystan. You might be wrong."

He looks to me with surprise.

"The grandson of the greatest enemy they ever had," I darkly muse. "A Level Five Mage. Trained in Gardnerian weapons magic. And disastrously at odds with Gardnerian culture." I shoot him a defiant smile. "Maybe taking you into the Vu Trin Guard would seem like perfect revenge against the Gardnerians."

Trystan's eyes widen. He blinks at me. "You've changed."

I give a deep sigh. "Yes. I have."

He breathes out a short laugh, affection lighting his eyes. "I'm glad of it." He wipes his tears away and straightens, shooting me a small smile. "You know there's very little chance any of this will turn out well."

I spit out a sound of derision. "Well, who needs good odds? Where would the fun be in that?"

Trystan coughs out another laugh, then takes a deep breath, eyeing me soberly.

"Go," I tell him, motioning toward the door. "Get some sleep. Down the road, when you're a rich and successful Vu Trin soldier, you can come back for Uncle Edwin and me and fly us back to Noi lands on the back of one of their dragons."

"And we'll all live happily-ever-after?" Trystan questions, a wry gleam back in his eyes.

"Yes," I staunchly assure him. "That's *exactly* what we'll do."

Trystan takes his leave, shooting me an appreciative glance before he goes, and my false bravado leaves with him. The North Tower hall is quiet, the walls solid, but the entire world has gone unstable beneath my feet.

The thought of losing both my brothers has my heart breaking to pieces in my chest.

★ ★ ★

When I finally open the door to my room, everything is wrong.

There's no fire in the hearth, and a bone-chilling cold has started to seep into the stone walls. And the atmosphere feels oppressive—laced with a heavy dread.

Ariel lies passed out on her bed, her chickens running about aimlessly, the raven staunchly at her side. A bowl of her nilantyr berries is tipped over beside her, her lips stained black. Marina the Selkie is curled up on my bed next to Aislinn, wide-eyed and afraid. Aislinn's face is pale and drawn as if she's withstood a disorienting blow.

"I didn't know you were here," I tell Aislinn, rattled by her expression. "What's wrong?"

"The Verpacian Council passed a resolution today in solidarity with Marcus Vogel," Aislinn says, her voice haggard.

My chest tightens. I glance around for Wynter and find her almost blending in with the shadows. She's crumpled up against the windowsill, black wings tight around herself, her expression despondent.

"What happened?" I ask, the dread growing.

Wynter's eyes flick to her desk, and I catch sight of the official-looking parchment.

"It was posted on the door," Wynter says despairingly. "The new Verpacian Council...they've...made some changes."

I swallow nervously, needles of fear pricking along the back of my neck. I go to Wynter's desk and take the parchment in hand.

It's an official notice from the Verpacian Council. All Icarals are required to return to their countries of origin after completion of this year's University studies. Verpacian work papers and Guild admittance will no longer be permitted for Icarals.

"How did they get two-thirds of the Verpacian Council to vote for this?" I ask Aislinn, swiping the parchment through the air. "The Gardnerians only hold a slim majority."

"The Gardnerians have been emboldened by Vogel's election, and the rest of the Council are scared. They want to placate the Gardnerians," she replies.

Wynter begins to cry.

Ariel will have to return to Gardneria. Where she will be imprisoned in the Valgard Sanitorium. And Wynter will be sent back to Alfsigr lands, where her people are debating whether or not to execute her kind.

My sickening dread begins a rapid slide into rage. I curse and hurl my bag at the wall. Marina cries out at the sound, and I immediately feel guilty for it. I slump down onto the bed, bring my hands to my face and force myself to breathe.

Over a thousand dragons.

When I look up again, a line of six mournful Watchers flashes into view. They sit on the long rafter above Wynter, wings tight around themselves, heads hung low.

They fade away as Wynter's sob deepens into a low, keening wail.

I huddle close to Aislinn in the North Tower's hallway as she takes her leave.

Her face is stark in the flickering lantern light, almost gaunt. A freezing rain has moved in, and it pelts the window beside us, a chilling draft seeping through.

Aislinn stops and turns to me. "Maybe Yvan Guriel needs to save his dragon after all," she ventures tentatively.

I eye her speculatively—it's such a brazen statement coming from my quiet friend. I cock my head in thought as her meaning dawns.

"Escape," I voice, a picture of flight forming in my mind.

Aislinn nods, her brow knit tight. "The Icarals...they'll have to get out, Elloren. And...maybe Marina, too. At some point. And the Lupines..." She breaks off, pained, and looks away.

Jarod.

There could come a time when the Gardnerians force the Lupines off their land, and that time could be soon.

Aislinn meets my eyes once more. "They're sealing off the borders. But...dragons can fly."

"Yes, they can, can't they?" I agree with a sly smile. "Straight over borders." I consider this possibility. "The dragon's in a cage," I warn her. "Made of Elfin steel."

She takes a steadying breath. "Don't you have Sage Gaffney's wand?"

I spit out a dismissive sound. "I do. And Trystan's powerful. But magic that can break Elfin steel—if those spells exist, he doesn't have access to them."

"What if I knew where we could find them?"

I stare at her. "How could you possibly?"

"There's a spellbook called the Black Grimoire," she says. "Only the Mage Council and military have access to it. It contains highly protected spells. Military spells. My father has a copy of it in his office, and he's away meeting with the Northern Lupines. He won't be back for at least another month."

I stare at her, disbelieving. "Aislinn, one does not simply *borrow* a military grimoire."

Aislinn slumps down, timid, her expression roiling with conflict, but then her jaw stiffens with resolve and she meets my eyes. "Well, I'm going to borrow it. And I'll have it back to him before he even notices it's gone."

I'm stunned by her boldness.

And proud. So incredibly proud.

"Well," I tell her, a smile spreading across my face. "I suppose it's time to speak to Yvan Guriel about freeing his dragon."

CHAPTER FIFTEEN

Military Dragon

The next evening, the atmosphere in the kitchens is as dark and oppressive as the day before, everyone's faces drawn and rattled. "I need to speak with you," I tell Yvan as he comes in from the cold and stoops to load wood into my stove, the heat blasting out like a hot wave.

He looks around warily, the evening shift thinly populated, Iris and Bleddyn blessedly elsewhere. "Now?" Yvan asks as he shoves a log into the stove, the lean muscles of his arms tensing as he does so.

"Soon."

He pushes the iron stove's door shut. "Meet me outside after you're done with whatever you're working on."

I finish prepping an apple pie, then find Yvan near the livestock pens, a lamp in hand.

He silently leads me around the pens and past the kitchen gardens. Then up a long, sloping field toward a ramshackle structure set just inside the wilds.

The abandoned barn is huge, enveloped in the evening's

lengthening shadows. The door creaks as he opens it for me, and I step inside.

The barn's ceiling is impossibly high with crisscrossing rafters. Bats flit back and forth, the lamplight illuminating them as they cast frenetic shadows on the walls.

"Is this your secret hideout?" I ask teasingly, glancing around as Yvan sets his lamp down on a dusty barrel.

Yvan nods, watching me as he leans back against a thick support beam.

I muster a small smile and he lifts his lips slightly in response, but the intensity of his gaze doesn't waver.

The shadows play across his face, highlighting his stark, angular appearance. A tremor runs through me, heightening my awareness that I'm alone with him in a very secluded place.

Ignoring the breathless pull I feel toward him, I look at him levelly. "I want to help you free your dragon," I say, steel in my voice. "There may come a time when flight is needed."

Yvan's eyes fly open with surprise, but he quickly gathers himself. "Elloren, my dragon can't be freed."

"Maybe not by you alone, but we have a large group…"

He coughs out a dismissive laugh. "Of inexperienced, naive youths."

"Of people with a large variety of gifts and skills."

"There's a big difference between stealing a Selkie from the University groundskeeper and freeing a Gardnerian military dragon."

Frustration flares in me. "What's the harm in letting everyone…have a look at the situation?"

"Besides getting arrested and shot? None that I can think of, really."

I press on, undaunted. "If that dragon can be saved…the Icarals might be able to go east. And others, too."

He stands there for a moment, looking stunned by my words. "I don't understand you," he says, his expression going harsh.

"Why are you even thinking about this? You're a Gardnerian. And not just any Gardnerian...you're Carnissa Gardner's *granddaughter.* Your grandmother..." He pauses, as if angry and struggling to find the right words all at the same time. "She was...a *monster.*"

My back goes up at the word. How was my grandmother different from any other successful military leader of any race? "She was wrong about many things," I counter, "but she was also a great Mage..."

"Who killed thousands and thousands of people." His angular jaw tightens, his green eyes boring into me.

"Your people were just as monstrous to the Gardnerians when they were in power," I challenge.

He glares at me as if struggling with strong emotion. "Your *grandmother,*" he grinds out, an unexpected fury breaking out around the edges of his words, "was responsible for the death of my *father!*"

Oh, Ancient One. I'm stunned into silence. But only for a moment. Pain seeps through me and quickly morphs into outrage.

"Your people," I counter, my voice breaking, "killed *both* of my parents!"

We're silent for a long moment, the constant, raw ache we both carry around suddenly unguarded and fully exposed.

"I know my grandmother did a lot of terrible things," I finally say with no small amount of effort. "Since coming here, I've learned that my people do a lot of really terrible things. But don't you think it's possible for someone to be different from everything you've heard about their kind? Even if they look... like I do?"

Yvan takes a deep breath, his eyes intent on my face. "Yes," he says, "I think it's possible."

I let out a long sigh and slump down on a hay bale, defeated. "I'm trying, Yvan," I tell him hoarsely. "I really am. I want to do the right thing."

"I believe you," he says, and there's kindness in his tone.

We're quiet for a few minutes, just staring at each other.

"I'm sorry you lost your parents," he finally tells me, his voice low.

Tears sting at my eyes, and I struggle to hold them back. "And I'm sorry about your father." The words are stilted as I try to bring my emotions under control. "What happened to him?" I ask.

Yvan's angular face tenses. "He was killed on the Eastern Front, a few days before Verpacia was liberated from the Gardnerians." He takes a deep breath, eyes narrowed, as if sizing me up to decide if he can fully trust me. "My father...he was a prominent figure in the Resistance. My mother didn't want anyone to know I was his son. So she moved me to a remote area and schooled me at home."

"You must look a great deal like your father."

Yvan smiles at this, as if I've inadvertently said something extremely ironic. "The resemblance is striking, yes."

"Our lives," I muse, "they've been similar..."

Yvan makes a contemptuous sound of disagreement. "There is *nothing* similar about our lives."

"No, there is," I counter, a bit put out by being so summarily dismissed. "When I was about five years old, my uncle moved us out of Valgard and to Halfix. It borders the northern wilds, in the middle of nowhere. I was schooled at home, just like you. I realize now he was trying to protect me from the attention looking *exactly* like my grandmother would bring. Just like your mother, he wanted me to be safe."

Yvan considers this, and I can tell he sees that I have a point.

"So," I say, after a few minutes of awkward silence, "you're becoming a physician."

"Yes." He nods. "Like my father. And you? You're becoming an apothecary?"

"Yes, like my mother," I reply. "I've always been interested in growing herbs, making medicines. But I never dreamed I'd be attending University. I always wanted to. Before I was sent here, I thought I'd be a violin maker, like my uncle..."

The words catch in my throat, and I can't help it. At the thought of Uncle Edwin, I start to tear up. "He's...he's very sick." I look down at my feet, struggling with my emotions.

"So...you know how to make violins?" Yvan's voice is low and kind.

I nod.

"From...wood?"

This strikes me as funny, and I smile, wipe my tears and look up at him. "With the right tools, yes."

He thinks about this for a moment. "That's...impressive."

"I suppose it is," I agree, feeling unsettled by the compliment.

"But the Guilds..."

I shrug. "Won't let women learn the trade. I know. My uncle taught me in secret."

He stands there for a moment, a surprised look on his face. "Have you played violin for a long time?"

"Yes," I reply. "Since I was a small child. And...and you? Do you play any instruments? Anything?"

"No," he says, shaking his head, looking as if he's distracted by his own thoughts. "I heard a Fae violinist once, though. I was very young. I can still remember it. It was...beautiful."

The look of longing in his emerald eyes as he says the last few words catches me off guard, and I find myself flushing and needing to look away.

As I glance around the barn floor, I become aware of papers scattered about. I pick one up. It's a page from *The Book of the Ancients*. Puzzled, I get up and pick up a few more of the papers. More pages from *The Book*.

"That's odd," I say as I continue to pick up pages, a stack growing in my hands. "Someone ripped up a copy of our holy book." When my eyes meet his again, I'm surprised by the look he's giving me. He's grown as still as stone, his expression gone cold…and defiant. "Did you do this?" I ask, very slowly.

He doesn't move, but his unwavering look of defiance is answer enough.

"Oh, take care, Yvan," I breathe. "This is a major crime in Gardneria." I hold up the stack of papers in my hands and gesture toward him with it. "Vogel wants to execute people for defacing *The Book*. Were you aware of that?"

"I suppose it's a good thing we're not in Gardneria," he replies, his green eyes hard.

"You're treading on very dangerous ground."

"Oh, really?" he shoots back. "And where would the safe ground be, Elloren? Because I'd really love to find it. Maybe if I looked *exactly* like Carnissa Gardner, it would be easier to find."

"That's hardly fair."

"What about any of this is fair?"

"I'm sorry. You're absolutely right," I say acidly. "My life has been so easy lately. I'm so happy that my looks offer me complete protection from all difficulties."

He looks momentarily surprised, then ill at ease as his brow knits tight. "We should be getting back," he says. "The other kitchen laborers will notice that we're both gone, and it will seem…odd."

"Why on Erthia would the two of *us* going off together seem odd?" I ask sarcastically.

Yvan smiles slightly at this, but his eyes remain serious and sad.

I reach up and touch his arm. "I want to help you rescue your dragon. What they're doing to her is *wrong*." My face tenses with frustration. "There's so much we can't change. But maybe…this is one thing we can do. And…" I think of the danger Tierney and the Icarals are in. And Trystan. And Yvan. My resolve hardens. "Dragonflight is a pretty good means of escape."

Yvan takes a deep breath and looks down at my hand. His arm

is sinewy…and so warm. It feels good to touch him. Too good. The air shifts between us, to something kindled and sparking. Flustered, I let my hand fall away.

"All right, Elloren Gardner," Yvan relents, his eyes steady on mine. "Let's see exactly how much trouble we can all get ourselves into."

"You want to break into a Gardnerian military base and steal a dragon?"

I'm facing Rafe, sitting on the chair by his book-strewn desk. Trystan, Rafe and Yvan are all poised on the edge of their beds, facing me in turn.

Rafe is grinning widely. Trystan wears his usual guarded, unreadable expression, and Yvan looks like he's recovering from finding himself firmly in cahoots with a bunch of Gardnerians from a family such as ours.

"You're serious?" Rafe prompts.

"Yes."

Rafe shakes his head from side to side as he tries, unsuccessfully, to keep from laughing. "Well, I tell you, Ren," he says, "things are a hell of a lot more interesting with you here at University."

"We always thought you were quiet and reserved," Trystan observes, and I can see a small glimmer of amusement in his eyes, as well.

"And now you want to steal dragons and rescue Selkies," Rafe continues.

"I don't think our grandmother would be proud," Trystan tells Rafe.

"No, I think Trystan's right," Rafe agrees, giving me a look of mock disapproval. "You are being a *very bad Gardnerian.*"

I glance over at Yvan, whose eyebrows are raised in surprise as he follows their unexpected banter.

As always, I feel a little off-kilter being in a room that Yvan lives in, too. It's intimate and strange. I can't keep myself from noting things about him whenever I'm here. The titles of his books, what type of clothing he has slung over his chair or on his bed. It seems to me, from the way he averts his eyes when we meet each other's gazes, that he feels the vague inappropriateness of it, too.

"Ren," Rafe says, his grin fading and his tone cautionary. "You do realize that, with the Selkie, if you're caught, you'll be fined for theft. If you steal a dragon from a military base, you'll be branded part of the Resistance, brought up in front of a military tribunal and most likely shot. By multiple arrows. If you're lucky, that is."

"I don't think the dragon can be freed," Yvan interjects. "I think they'll kill her long before anyone can figure out how to get her out of her cage...if that's even possible. Damion Bane's magicked the lock."

"What's the cage made out of?" Trystan inquires, suddenly intrigued. I can see that familiar light go on in his eyes. Trystan loves a mental puzzle.

"Elfin steel," Yvan replies. "It's so strong it can withstand dragon fire."

"Ah. I'm familiar with it," Trystan says. "It's what the Elves make their arrow tips out of. It can only be manipulated before it sets. Once it sets and cools, it can never be worked with again."

"Can you get your hands on some of it?" Rafe asks Trystan, a mischievous look in his eyes.

Trystan shrugs. "Some arrow tips, sure." Trystan narrows his eyes at Rafe. "You want to experiment with it, don't you?"

"Maybe there's a spell that can break it."

"Don't you need a military-grade wand for that?" Trystan points out. "Wands that powerful are expensive, and I'm assuming that Yvan here, being a Kelt, probably doesn't have one."

"Well, you're a military apprentice," Rafe points out to Trystan.

Trystan shakes his head. "They don't let us hold on to the wands. They keep them locked up in the armory. And we certainly don't have the money to buy one—"

"I have a wand," I blurt out.

Everyone stops talking and turns to stare at me.

"Are you stealing wands now, too?" Rafe asks, clearly ready to believe me capable of anything at this point.

"The morning we left Halfix, Sage gave me a wand. I think she stole it from Tobias, and... I didn't want her to get into any more trouble than she already was in, so I sewed it into the lining of my travel case. I took it out when I arrived, and it's been hidden in my pillow ever since."

"You've a wand in your pillow?" Trystan says, incredulous.

I eye him sheepishly. "Yes. I do."

"Why was this girl in trouble?" Yvan asks, and I feel my face beginning to flush as I struggle to put together the answer to his question.

"She...she fell in love with a Kelt." I look away from him and catch Rafe's eye as I do so. He's studying me closely, one eyebrow cocked. "She'd been wandfasted to the son of a member of the Mage Council," I continue, my eyes finding their way back to Yvan's riveting green ones. "She ran away with the Kelt. She had a child with him. An Icaral."

Yvan's eyebrows fly up. "This Icaral," he says, leaning forward, staring at me intently. "It's the one the Gardnerians are searching for?"

"You've heard of him?" I say, surprised.

"I heard that the Gardnerians are aware of a male Icaral hidden somewhere, and that many believe that this Icaral is the one of Prophecy."

"The Icarals that tried to kill me in Valgard thought that I was the next Black Witch," I say. "And that I was sent to kill Sage's baby."

"But it turns out Ren here can't even do a simple candle-lighting spell," Trystan tells Yvan. "So, as much as she loves to stalk babies so she can mercilessly slaughter them, she'll have to pass on this one."

"He already knows how pathetic I am," I tell Trystan, a little defensively.

"I don't think you're pathetic at all," Yvan says, his voice low and even.

I blink, momentarily disoriented by his defense of me.

Out of the corner of my eye, I catch Trystan and Rafe exchanging a quick, wondering glance. It makes me feel uncomfortably self-conscious, and I quickly look away from Yvan.

"Trystan," Rafe says congenially, thankfully changing the subject, "you get hold of some of those arrow tips, and Elloren, you can fetch that wand of yours."

Trystan shakes his head. "Even if Ren's wand is powerful, it might take high-level spells to break Elfin steel. Spells I don't have access to."

"Aislinn can get those," I confess.

They all gape at me, wide-eyed.

I turn sheepish and slump down under the combined weight of their stares. "Maybe, I mean. She's going to borrow a military grimoire from her father."

Rafe barks out a laugh. "Well, that's settled, then. We have a wand, we're soon to have a military grimoire—" he motions to Trystan "—and we've got our Level Five Mage here. Might as well see if we can tackle this cage."

"Does this mean you and Trystan will help us rescue the dragon?" I ask, astonished.

Rafe grins at me widely. "Certainly looks that way, doesn't it?"

CHAPTER SIXTEEN

Elfin Steel

"I don't even know where to begin," Trystan comments as he stands making neat slicing motions in the air with the white wand. The Elfin steel arrow tip is propped up on a tree stump a few feet away. "I've been learning spells to magic Gardnerian weapons, and that's about it."

We're in a secluded clearing in the wilds, about a half hour's walk from the University. We've all found it quite easily, starting at the edge of the field by the horse stables and walking straight toward a towering, vertical shard of salt-white Spine stone.

The morning sunlight cuts through the trees around us, our breath fogging the cool air. I look around warily, feeling as if the trees are pulling away, whispering about me on the wind. I take a seat on a moss-covered rock and pull my cloak tight to fight off the stiff chill. Yvan is leaning against a tree, facing me, his expression wary and watchful, his eyes always coming back to me.

He seems immune to the cold. I never see him wearing a cloak, but he's always so warm—heat practically radiating off his body the few times I've been close to him, brushed his fingers, placed my hand on his arm...

Yvan's eyes meet mine, and heat flares between us. I flush and glance away.

Rafe is flipping through the same type of grimoire that was handed to me for my wandtesting, the volume chock-full of basic spells. Diana sits on a long log next to him, her arms crossed, a determined expression on her face. Jarod quietly watches Trystan play with the wand.

Andras sits, sharpening his rather scary, rune-marked silver labrys—the usual weapon of choice for the Amaz. It's a huge weapon, able to deflect magic as well as split skulls, with the two axes attached to its long handle. Andras rubs a sharpening stone over the cutting edge of one side, a thin, rhythmic *screech* sounding from his steady, circular motion.

Yvan steps forward from the tree, his hands on his hips. "Why do you want to help me free this dragon?" He glances around at everyone. "I'm not even sure it can be done. And even if it can—"

"This is a dangerous idea," Andras puts in flatly, setting the sharpening stone aside. "I do not know if I can be part of such a thing." He gestures with his broad chin toward the arrow-head. "But I will help you try to break this steel. There will come a time when dragonflight east could help many." He sets his dark eyes on Yvan. "And my people despise the caging of wild things." He's silent for a moment. "I have always wanted to see an unbroken dragon. I have heard they are magnificent."

"They are," Yvan confirms with an edge of emotion in his voice.

"I will take a look at your dragon, Kelt," Andras tells Yvan. "And then I will decide if I will help the beast."

Yvan gives Andras a somber nod, then looks to Diana.

"Jarod and I also despise the caging of wild animals," Diana states vehemently, her arms crossed tight. "All Lupines do." She nods in my direction. "And Elloren Gardner asked for our help. So we will help you free your dragon, Yvan Guriel."

"And you, Rafe?" Yvan asks. "Why would you go against your own people?"

Rafe bares his teeth in a wide smile. "Oh, I don't know, Yvan. Because Marcus Vogel's a jackass, and the Gardnerians are really beginning to piss me off. What about you, Trystan?"

Trystan is only half paying attention to all of us as he focuses intently on the wand and slices it through the air in small swirls. "They're a bit self-righteous, yes," he comments absently.

"I wouldn't mind seeing them with one less military dragon," Rafe goes on.

"You never know when a military dragon might come in handy," Trystan agrees.

Rafe laughs. "That's quite true."

"I'll start with the weakest fire spell I know and work my way up," Trystan announces as he points the wand out in front of him, his other hand curled over his head gracefully.

"What? The candle-lighting one?" Rafe wonders.

"That would be the one," Trystan replies.

"*Illiumin...*" Trystan recites the words of the spell by rote. He flicks the wand in the direction of the steel.

A sharp, orange flash flies from the tip of the white wand and knocks Trystan backward with its force. I flinch sharply back, almost falling off the rock as the flash collides with the Elfin arrow tip and turns the entire log it rests on into a ball of churning flames.

Rafe's eyes have flown open wide. "That was the *candle-lighting spell*?"

Trystan nods, his mouth agape.

"Hell of a wand you got there, Ren," Rafe says.

I stare at the flames, stunned. A fantastical idea flashes into my mind—wouldn't it be incredible if Sage's wand actually was the true White Wand of legend? The thought is so outrageously impossible, it almost makes me smile.

It may not be the White Wand, I relent, but I'm glad it's a better than average wand.

"Did it do anything to the arrow tip?" I get up, walk over to the flames and peer in.

"You can't melt it," Yvan says patiently, not moving from where he stands. "If dragon fire can't melt it, your brother certainly can't."

Sure enough, the arrow tip is unharmed and unmarked.

"Perhaps we can break it," Andras suggests, getting up and grabbing his labrys. He takes the tip, places it on another stump, raises his weapon high above his head and brings it down onto the arrow with a deafening clang that leaves my ears ringing.

Again, the arrow tip remains unbroken and unblemished, albeit slightly recessed into the wood. Andras's labrys, on the other hand, has a large crack in one of the ax heads.

"Amazing," Andras says as he examines the labrys. He glances over at the arrow tip with no small amount of awe. "I do not think this Elfin Steel can be broken."

"We shall see," says Diana, irritated. She walks over to the arrowhead and glares at it as if it's purposely defying her. She focuses in, puts one foot in front of the other and goes into a slight crouch, then in a fast, graceful arc, she swings her hand over her head and down onto the arrowhead.

The stump splits into multiple pieces with an earsplitting crack.

But, again, the arrowhead lies whole and untouched on top of the mess of kindling.

"Ow," Diana says as she rubs the side of her hand and fixes the arrowhead with a look of extreme annoyance.

Jarod's eyes go wide. "I've never heard my sister say *ow* before."

"Have I ever told you that you have an extremely scary girl-friend?" Trystan asks Rafe.

"Multiple times." Rafe grins. He walks over to Diana and she holds up the side of her hand accusatorily. He takes her hand and kisses down its side.

"I really would try and avoid pissing her off," Trystan suggests.

"I'll keep that in mind," Rafe says, smiling at a very perturbed Diana as he pulls her into a warm hug.

Trystan pulls out the University's grimoire, and for the next hour or so, he goes through almost every spell in the book. He tries every type of heating spell, division spell, lighting spell, transformation spell and hurling spell he can find on the arrowhead, every incantation intensified by the wand. By the end of the hour, we're still left with an untouched arrowhead, sitting at the bottom of a large, scorched and partially flaming crater.

"You sure picked a challenge here, Yvan," Rafe remarks as we stare down at the arrowhead.

Jarod lifts his head and sniffs the air, surprise crossing his features. "Aislinn's coming."

I look around searchingly. Aislinn is back early from her trip to Valgard, the festivities surrounding Marcus Vogel's elevation to High Mage the perfect excuse for a visit to her family—and her father's Mage Council office. I've told her about this meeting, what we're trying to do and how to find us, just in case she was back in time.

I hear her light footsteps on the leaves, the rustle of her skirts, before she tentatively emerges from the trees. Stress is taking its toll on Aislinn, her face strained.

Jarod looks as if it's taking all the strength he possesses not to go to her, sweep her up in his arms and run off with her.

"I have something for all of you," she says. She pulls the sack off her shoulder, fishes inside it and draws forth a black leatherbound volume.

My breath catches in my throat, my hand coming up to cover my astonished mouth. "Holy First Children...you actually got it."

Aislinn glances at me soberly, then hands the book to Trystan, who eyes it with astonishment.

"Sweet Ancient One," he breathes as he takes it. "You did it."

"What is it?" Andras asks.

Trystan turns to Andras. "It's a Black Grimoire. Only members of the Mage Council and high-ranking military officers are allowed access to this. These are highly protected spells. Not just Gardnerian spells, either. Fae spells, too."

Trystan flips through the book with care as he speaks. "During the Realm War, the Gardnerians got hold of Fae Grimoires. There are some spells that the Gardnerians can use with wand magic, like the spells that break down a Fae glamour. Those spells are in here." Trystan holds up the book to Aislinn. "How did you get this?"

"My father," Aislinn says softly. "He keeps a copy hidden away in his Council office. So I…borrowed it. He doesn't know."

Rafe spits out an incredulous laugh. "I'd imagine not."

"This is dangerous," Trystan says to her. "Really dangerous."

"I know," she replies, the words tentative, but there's cold defiance in her eyes. "I'll slip it back after you copy the spells." She looks around at all of us. "There's something you should know. I overheard some of the Council members talking about a weapon the Gardnerians have now, something they're planning to use on the Lupines. It…it upset me. I got scared for… the Lupines." She steals a quick, troubled glance at Jarod.

Diana makes a contemptuous sound. "They've been threatening us for *years*. Always trying something new. Nothing ever comes of it."

"No," Aislinn cuts in sharply. "Something's different this time. Especially with Vogel in power. They seem sure of it. Smug, almost. They want to kill all of the Lupines. They want your land. And they want to send a message."

"Their magic doesn't work on us," Diana reminds Aislinn, a

tad condescendingly. "And we'll tear your dragons limb from limb."

Aislinn looks back at her gravely. "All the same." She gestures toward the grimoire. "Perhaps this can help with more than just freeing the dragon."

Everyone is silent for a long moment. We're officially playing with our lives now, stealing a Mage Council Grimoire and plotting to free a Gardnerian military dragon. And an unbroken military dragon, at that.

"I should go," Aislinn says, frowning. "I don't want to chance anyone seeing me with all of you. If anyone notices the grimoire is missing... I don't want anyone to think I may have passed it to any of you."

"What you did was very brave," Rafe tells her.

She nods at him and turns to leave.

"Aislinn, wait." Jarod steps toward her.

She holds up a hand to stop him, her face pained. "No, Jarod. Please... I have to go."

"We need to talk," Jarod insists, anguish breaking through.

Aislinn's hands grasp at her skirts as she shakes her head from side to side and begins to cry.

Jarod goes to her and takes her in his arms, pulling her close, kissing her head. She clings to him and weeps into his broad chest.

Diana stares at the two of them in shock, apparently having completely missed what's going on in her brother's life. Jarod whispers something to Aislinn, and she nods.

"I need to talk to Aislinn privately," Jarod says, noting his sister's hurt look. "I'll speak with you later, Diana."

His words don't seem to register with Diana as she stares after her twin brother, almost as if she doesn't know him anymore.

Jarod leads Aislinn away, the two of them quickly swallowed up by the woods.

"Diana," Rafe says gently.

Diana whirls around to face my brother. "Did you know?"

"I figured it out. It's been pretty obvious."

"Why didn't you tell me?"

"Well, for starters, it's really none of my business," Rafe says as he wraps his arms around her. "And besides, you're the one with all the superior senses, not me."

"I think her attention has been focused elsewhere," Trystan observes wryly.

Diana still looks a bit hurt, but Rafe's embrace seems to mollify her, and she leans into him as if absorbing some of his equanimity.

"The girl, Aislinn," Andras inquires, turning to me, his voice deep and resonant. "Her father...he is on the Mage Council?"

"Yes," I reply.

"It will end badly," Andras predicts, shaking his head. "You cannot break the bonds of your culture. It's like that arrowhead."

I glance down at the Elfin metal that still lies whole and untouched on the scorched ground.

When I look back up, Yvan's fiery eyes lock onto mine, alight with a defiance that kindles my own.

That night, I dream.

I'm in Yvan's barn, bathed in the faint light of a lantern's glow. Instead of just a few pages from *The Book* scattered thinly about, thousands of them carpet the barn's floor.

A figure emerges from the shadows. Yvan. His outline shimmers, fluid and indistinct, then rapidly coalesces into a solid presence.

He strides toward me, green eyes blazing. The pages swirl around his feet, the thin paper light as feathers. Without hesitation, Yvan pulls me toward himself and joins his lips to mine in fierce urgency.

I gasp, stunned by the intensity of his unexpected kiss. I feel the warmth coming off his skin through the rough wool of his shirt as I melt into his hunger, the feel and taste of him molten. Like honey warmed to scorched liquid, shuddering through me.

I slide my hand up the taut muscles of his neck, through his hair. Feel his hot breath on me as he kisses my neck, my face, my hair, my lips, as if starved for me.

"I love you, Elloren," he says, his voice ragged.

The warmth blooming inside me swells and fills my heart with a happiness so raw, it hurts. It feels so right to be with him. Like coming home after a long, impossible journey.

"Yvan," I breathe against the sharp line of his jaw. "I love you, too."

Out of nowhere, a fierce wind whips up.

The pages of *The Book* swirl and lift, then cyclone around us, taking on a fierce life of their own. I cry out as the pages push between us and force us apart, their sharp edges scraping mercilessly at my skin.

And then I can't see him. I can only see a wall of white as thousands of pages roar around me, the sound deafening.

"Yvan!" I scream.

But it's no use. He can't hear me over the roar of *The Book*.

CHAPTER SEVENTEEN

Naga

"So, Kelt," Ariel asks Yvan as we trudge through the woods en route to Yvan's dragon, "is there any chance that your dragon will eat the Black Witch here?"

I see the corner of Yvan's lip twitch up, but he keeps his eyes on the path ahead. "I suppose it's possible," he replies.

"Or perhaps it will envelop her in a ball of flames," Ariel muses gleefully.

I scowl at her as I trip clumsily over a tangle of roots. She knows full well how much I hate it when she calls me "Black Witch." But I'm worn down from arguing with her. It's impossible to reason with Ariel, and telling her I hate something just prompts her to do it more.

My brothers, the Lupines, Andras and Wynter silently accompany us. Unlike me, none of them trips over anything. They are all so annoyingly stealthy.

"Ariel likes to bait me," I complain darkly to Yvan, whose lip curls up a fraction more.

Diana was the one to convince Ariel and Wynter to accompany us, since they can talk to dragons with their minds. Aislinn has volunteered to watch over Marina.

Although Ariel views Diana as something of a barbarian, never quite trusting the Lupine not to snack on her feathered friends, there's something direct about Diana's manner that is often able to pierce the fog of rancid darkness Ariel seems perpetually enveloped in and tormented by. So, in the end, Ariel's curiosity won out, and she agreed to come, her decision bolstered by the fact that Wynter is joining us, as well.

"I'll be able to speak with the dragon," Ariel gloats at me, "and I'll be able to direct her as to which of your limbs she should tear off first. But you won't know what I'm telling her. It will have to be a surprise."

"Well, then, why don't you just practice your silent communication skills starting now?" I wearily reply.

Ariel smiles wickedly and flashes her long, stained teeth at me. "Perhaps I'd feel friendlier toward the Black Witch," she says to Yvan slyly, "if she hadn't kept me up all night."

A sickening panic shoots through me and halts my steps. Ariel slows then stops, as well, the rest of our party following suit as they regard the two of us with wary curiosity.

"Ariel, please," I plead as I become uncomfortably flushed.

"She talks in her sleep," Ariel explains to Yvan, her smile widening. "It was especially annoying last night."

I feel exposed and raw, ready to burst into tears at any moment.

"Ariel." Diana takes a menacing step toward her. *"Enough."*

"We should be on our way," Rafe breaks in. "There's only so much daylight left."

I nod at him stiffly, feeling bolted to the ground.

Ariel glances around slowly, taking her time, savoring my misery. "Don't worry, Black Witch," she finally says. "I won't tell Yvan what kind of dreams you have about him."

Yvan's eyebrows fly up, and he glances at me in surprise before looking uncomfortably away. Diana emits a low growl, her lip curling up.

Ariel hisses at Diana in turn and crouches into a defensive posture until Diana relents and lets Rafe lead her away, almost everyone following.

Wynter pauses, her expression of sympathy the only thing able to get me moving again.

I follow them in a daze of shame and fight back the urge to burst into tears.

So Yvan knows I've dreamed of him. So what? People can't control their dreams.

My painful humiliation dissolves when we reach Yvan's dragon.

The dragon lies on her side, eyes closed, in a large pool of blood, her spectacular onyx hide covered, just *covered*, with gashes and lash marks. One of her wings and a hind leg are bent at odd, unnatural angles.

My hand flies reflexively over my mouth, my breath cinching tight, overcome by such sadistic cruelty.

"Oh, no," Yvan gasps as he lurches toward the cage, dropping to his knees before it and grasping at the bars. Looking stricken, Wynter goes to Yvan, her wings wrapped tight around her small frame.

"Whoever did this needs to die," Diana snarls, low and menacing, her eyes lit up with wild fury. Fury that's reflected in both Jarod's and Andras's expressions.

Ariel is frozen, a look of shock on her pallid face. Unexpectedly, she bursts forth with a jolt of violent outrage and hurls herself at the cage, her eyes wild. "Get her *out!*" Ariel cries. "Get her out of that *cage!*" She crumples to the ground, her face ravaged, her fists clutching at the steel bars.

Trystan moves forward to speak to Ariel, cool and collected, as he holds up the white wand. "That's what we're going to try and do," he tells her gently. "But we won't be able to do it if you alert every soldier within ten leagues of our presence."

Ariel clings to the cage, her breathing ragged, her look of rage lessening to one of pure devastation.

Yvan's arm is stretched through the bars, his hand on the dragon's bloodied back. "She's still alive," he says, his voice uncharacteristically shaken.

The dragon opens her green eye halfway and looks right at Yvan, an ocean of misery in her gaze.

Tears sting at my eyes.

Andras goes over to where Yvan kneels and surveys the scene. "Her wing is broken," he observes with barely concealed outrage. "So is her leg, and she's lost a great deal of blood. Perhaps the Empath can tell us if there is any hope." He glances pointedly at Wynter, who takes a deep breath before kneeling down and reaching toward the cage.

The dragon's gaze shifts to Wynter as she places her pale hand on the dragon's gleaming, scaled hide and closes her eyes tightly, her expression pained. "She wants me to know her name is Naga. And that she wants to move, but she can't. She is in too much pain." Wynter's voice is a choked whisper, her thin mouth trembling. "Her thoughts are full of despair. All she ever wanted…" Wynter momentarily breaks off, tears trickling down her cheeks. "All she ever wanted was to fly free. To feel the wind on her wings. But…there's no fighting them. An image fills her mind. Yvan. Her good friend. Her only friend. She wants him and his people to flee before these Gardnerian monsters find them. Yvan thinks he can save her, but he can't. Even though he is a…" Wynter gasps, her eyes flying open with shocked realization, her head swiveling around to face Yvan.

Yvan blanches, and he stands up and backs away from Wynter. "Wynter, *please*."

"Yvan," she breathes as she shakes her head in disbelief. "It can't be. How can it be so?"

"I beg of you," he pleads.

Wynter bows her head as if attempting to collect herself.

She closes her eyes tightly for a moment, then opens them and regards Yvan calmly. "Give me your hand," she directs as she holds out one of her own, the other on the dragon.

"Wynter, I..."

"You *do not* need to fear this with me," she says firmly, her hand still outstretched.

Yvan looks positively stricken. But then he surrenders and gives his hand to her. Wynter closes her eyes as she reads both Yvan's thoughts and those of the dragon, her brow periodically tensing, her head nodding as if engaged in some private, hidden conversation. Finally, she opens her eyes, Yvan's hand still in hers. "Empaths are the keepers of secrets," she tells him.

I glance around in confusion. Jarod's and Diana's expressions are stern and unreadable, and Andras's fist is tight on his ax handle. Trystan and Ariel are looking at Yvan with wary concern.

"I don't mean to interrupt you," Rafe tells Wynter, stepping forward, "but if there's something we need to know about Yvan, I think you should tell us. If there's some danger..."

"He is no danger to any of us," Wynter states with calm certainty. "He can be trusted completely."

Rafe looks hard at her and at Yvan, eyes narrowed, before relenting. "All right," he says to Wynter, "what can you tell us about the odds of getting Naga out alive?"

Wynter concentrates once more on the dragon.

"Naga," Yvan asks the dragon, anguish breaking through, "who did this to you?"

The dragon's gaze tightens with pain. "A soldier," Wynter translates for the dragon. "Their Dragon Master." She winces sharply. "Mage Damion Bane."

"Ancient One," I fume, disgusted. "Of course it would be one of the Banes."

"We're going to get you out of here," Yvan tells the dragon, his lip curling with white-hot resolve. "We'll find a way."

"There is no way," Wynter translates. "He's going to come back. He's going to torture me until I break...or die."

"We'll stop him," Rafe says.

"Then they will send another," Wynter continues. "There is no stopping them."

"No," Trystan remarks as he runs his hands up and down the bars, studying them. "We're going to find a way to break this cage and get you out."

"Then you must find it soon, Gardnerian," Wynter translates, the dragon's eyes full of dark urgency. "*Very* soon."

We don't see much of Trystan over the next few days. He's careful to keep to his regular schedule, as we all are, all of us overstretched with exhausting work assignments and exam time looming. Even so, Trystan takes the time to disappear into the woods every evening to practice spells on the arrowhead with the white wand.

Ariel takes to pacing the room, her raven keeping a close eye on her from its perch on her bed. She's angry, morose and more on edge than usual. We all are. The Selkie seems to sense this. Like the raven, she watches us closely with worried eyes, curling up with Diana at night, her greatest comfort.

And Yvan seems troubled and distant, his private focus as intense on me as ever, but fully at odds with how he's holding himself back from me. He stays by the Keltic and Urisk kitchen workers, careful to pick tasks that don't send him into close proximity with me. And he avoids the small opportunities for conversation that he was starting to take advantage of, even though I can sense our intensifying pull toward each other from clear across the room.

It's upsetting and confusing, but I try to stuff the hurt down and focus on studying and remaining above suspicion.

I fall to brooding over what will happen if Marina is found, over whether or not Yvan's dragon can possibly survive and what it is that Wynter now knows about Yvan. There are so many strange things about him, like his speed and strength in dealing with Damion when rescuing the Urisk girl. How he seems to be able to communicate with the dragon just by staring at her. How he appears to sense my thoughts. The unnatural heat of his skin.

What secret is he hiding?

CHAPTER
EIGHTEEN

Yvan

"Are you still mean?"

The small child's voice coming from high above startles me. I strain in the darkness to make her out among the thick branches of the pine tree that stands outside the kitchen. I haven't seen hide nor hair of the little Urisk girl, Fern, in a long time. I'm surprised she's still here.

"Where are you?" I call up, keeping my voice as low as possible, remembering that she's illegally here, smuggled off the Fae Islands by her grandmother.

"But are you still mean?"

I think back, with no small amount of shame, to that day when Lukas came into the kitchen with me and threatened everyone so coolly, reducing little Fern to terrified tears.

"Iris and Bleddyn say you're still mean," she muses, her voice tiny, "but Yvan says you're not. Not anymore."

"Did he really?" A warm, pleasant flush prickles through me.

"Grandma says she doesn't know. And I don't know, either."

I consider this. "I *was* mean, but I didn't want to be. And I'm sorry. I'm not mean anymore. At least I hope I'm not."

"Oh, okay."

Everything is quiet for a moment.

"Fern?"

"Hmm?"

"Why are you up in a tree? It's not safe to be so high."

"I'm playing Black Witch."

My eyes widen with surprise. "Black Witch?"

"All the kids used to play it on the Islands. When the overseers weren't looking. Someone gets to be the Black Witch, and everyone else has to hide."

"What happens if she catches you?" I ask.

"She kills you, of course."

I freeze in place. "That...sounds like a scary game," I say, shame seeping through me.

This is my grandmother's legacy? A child's game where she's the evil monster out to kill them?

"You're pretty," the little voice says.

"Thank you," I reply, and I can hear her giggling through the leaves.

"Yvan thinks you're pretty, too."

"He does?" My cheeks grow warm with surprised delight.

"I told him you look like a princess, and he thought so, too."

"Oh," I say, charmed and lit up by this.

"He's my friend," she prattles on. "He plays with me sometimes."

"Does he, now?"

I try to picture it. Serious, intense Yvan playing with a child. But then I remember that time I saw him with little Fern when she spilled the bubbles all over his shirt. I remember the smile on his face. How patient he was.

"He makes me toys, too."

"Really?"

"Yup. He made me a bubble wand and a duck puzzle out of wood."

"That's nice."

"He's nice."

When it happens, it's so fast I don't have time to react. There's a loud crack, a high-pitched shriek and a sickening *thump*.

And then the screaming begins.

I drop my book bag and leap toward her small form, crumpled on the ground in front of me. She's fallen from the top of the tree, all the way down to land on the sharp end of a hoe that lies at the base of the tree. It's so dark, I can't make out much, but I *can* see that her right leg is very broken and that blood gushes from the wound.

"Oh, Ancient One," I breathe, my heart racing as Fern writhes and screams at the top of her lungs. Panicked, I look wildly around for help and see Yvan running toward us from the livestock barns.

"She fell. From the top of the tree. She fell on the hoe. She's bleeding. Her leg's broken." My words come out in a tangled rush as he kneels down and takes quick stock of the situation. His head darts around. Fern isn't supposed to be here. If anyone finds her here...

"Keep her quiet!" he orders.

"How?"

"Just *do it*!"

I sit down behind Fern, grab her head and cover her mouth firmly, her screams quickly and effectively muffled, and start to feel immediately sick to my stomach at having to do this. Her little body bucks and tenses against me as her hands claw at my arms and at the air. I try harder to restrain her. Yvan pulls up her pant leg and I can make out a shard of bone sticking clear out of her leg.

"Elloren," Yvan orders me sharply. "Hold her steady."

I keep one hand wrapped around Fern's head and covering her mouth, and grasp her arms with the other. Yvan takes her leg in his hands and feels around with dexterous fingers. Then, out of the blue, he jerks her leg back into position. Fern convulses and she moans with terror and pain.

"What are you doing?" I cry, wildly confused.

Now he's grabbing the newly straightened leg with both hands, completely covering the wound. He closes his eyes, as if in meditation, and holds the leg steady.

"Yvan!" I cry. "Why are you doing this? We need a real physician! Right now!"

But Fern's screaming begins to lessen, and her muscles go slack, her arms falling limply to her sides. She whimpers softly, and then even that begins to subside. Yvan stays where he is, eyes closed as if he's concentrating all his energy on her leg.

Fern is quietly trembling now, and I see the familiar figure of her grandmother hurrying over to us.

Fernyllia drops the scrap buckets in her arms when she catches sight of her granddaughter lying on the ground.

Yvan opens his eyes and looks over at me. "Release her, El-loren," he says.

Wildly unsure, I take my hands off the child and sit back, Fern's head limp in my lap.

Fern sniffles, her body still trembling, but she doesn't seem to be in pain anymore.

Yvan takes his hands slowly off her leg. The blood on his hands, on Fern's leg and her clothing looks like splashes of ink in the darkness. Incredibly, Fern pulls her leg in and holds out her hands to her grandmother. I sit back and stare at her, unable to believe my eyes.

How can it be? The bone—it was sticking clear through her leg!

Yvan steps back as Fernyllia takes Fern into her arms and hugs her tightly.

"My precious girl," Fernyllia says as she kisses her granddaughter's head. "What happened?"

"I fell out of the tree," Fern sobs, "and Yvan fixed my leg. But it *hurt*."

"It was just a scrape," Yvan tells Fernyllia.

What?

Did we just witness the same scene? I saw the odd angle of her leg, the bone sticking through it. And her blood is everywhere. Proof that I'm not mistaken.

Yvan takes in my wildly incredulous stare and looks back at me, his face harsh, as if willing me to remain silent. I glance pointedly at his hands, at the bloodstains all over his lap. I know that there are healers who can fix such extreme breaks over a span of a few months, but I've never heard of anything like this.

"Thank you, Yvan," Fernyllia says with deep gratitude. She turns to me. "And thank you, Mage Gardner."

"Elloren helped me," Fern tells her grandmother, her head flat against her chest, clearly exhausted by her ordeal.

Fernyllia kisses the top of the child's head before looking at me meaningfully. "Perhaps Elloren and Yvan would like some tea and apple pie," she says in that singsong voice people use with children, and her use of my first name stuns me. Fernyllia gently bops her granddaughter's nose with her fingertip. "And I'll make some hot maple cream for you, little one. Would that make you feel better?"

Fern's head bobs up and down weakly. Fernyllia stands up, her granddaughter cradled in her stout arms.

"Go ahead," Yvan says kindly. "We'll be right in."

A quizzical look flashes over Fernyllia's features before she nods and leaves us.

"How did you do that?" I demand in a low, urgent whisper as soon as Fernyllia is out of earshot. "That's healing magic. And Kelts don't have magic."

He won't meet my gaze. "I don't know what you mean, Elloren. Her leg was dislocated. I simply popped it back into position."

"That leg was *broken*. In *half*. I saw the *bone*, Yvan. With my own two eyes. And you're covered in blood. That was no scrape!"

His eyes meet mine, the angry intensity back in full force.

"And the dragon. You can talk to her, can't you?" I press on. "Just like Wynter and Ariel can. With your mind. How can you do that, Yvan? And when you went after Damion to help Olilly…you were so fast…you were like a blur. I thought I was imagining things, but I can't be imagining *all* of this. What are you hiding from us?"

"Nothing," he says, evading my eyes, his jaw tensing. "You *are* imagining things." He visibly struggles with his thoughts for a moment before setting his eyes back on me, his gaze now searing. He leans in, his tone sharp. "You need to stop."

I am undeterred. "I won't stop," I insist, leaning in, as well. "I won't stop until you tell me what's going on." My brow tenses, concern for him breaking through. "Tell me, Yvan. You can trust me."

There's a flash of tortured conflict in his eyes, and his lips part as if he's about to level with me. There's a chasm of sadness there, and my heart wrenches as I sense it.

But then his mouth clamps shut and the conflicted look is gone, only a hard anger remaining.

"I need to go," he tells me icily. "I have work to do."

"Yvan," I plead. "Wait…"

But I can only watch him, deeply discouraged, as he turns and stalks away from me into the night.

Wildly unsettled, I go to the kitchen, where I find Fern sitting next to her grandmother and sipping at a mug of maple cream.

Fernyllia has just finished cleaning up the child's wound, the leg straight and strong and marked only with a small, red bruise.

Fernyllia looks up as I enter. "Where's young Yvan?" she asks.

I take a deep breath. "He had to go. He…has a lot of studying to catch up on."

"Such a hard worker, that one." She clucks and shakes her head as she places her warm shawl cozily around little Fern's shoulders. The child sets down her mug and reaches for her grandmother, Fernyllia chuckling. "Up with you," she prods the child, who briefly rises so her grandmother can sit and then pull the child into her broad lap.

Settling in, Fern reaches for the maple cream and sips at it, her eyes shyly meeting mine.

"I misjudged you, Elloren Gardner," Fernyllia says quietly as she strokes her granddaughter's hair.

"I initially misjudged you, as well," I admit.

Fernyllia's eyes flick to the white band that encircles my arm. "You don't really stand with Vogel, do you, love?"

I shoot her a level stare and shake my head.

She gives me a shrewd look of appraisal, her mouth tilting up into a grin. "I thought not." Satisfied, she goes back to rocking and murmuring to the child.

I watch as Fern grows increasingly sleepy, until, at last, Fernyllia gently takes the mug of warm cream out of her granddaughter's hands and lets the child fall asleep on her lap.

"I'm sorry," I murmur. "I'm sorry I was so ignorant...and wrong, when I first came here."

Fernyllia looks at me appraisingly and then glances down at the child. "Apology accepted," she replies with a smile. "Have some tea, Elloren Gardner." She motions toward the teapot and mugs before her, minty steam wafting from the pot's spout.

I pour myself some tea and drink it with Fernyllia as she rocks her granddaughter gently back and forth, the scene full of comfort.

I'm stung by Yvan's anger and refusal to be honest with me, but as I watch the child sleeping and grip at my mug, the steaming heat seeps into my hands and some of my tension dissipates.

Fernyllia starts to sing a soft lullaby in Uriskal, the staccato language surprisingly lulling when lifted in song.

I slump back, sip at my tea and bask in this new, heartening friendship.

As I doggedly try to puzzle out Yvan Guriel's secret.

CHAPTER NINETEEN

Fae

"He must be Fae," Aislinn says as she flips through a leather-bound text with silver-rimmed pages.

The two of us are sitting on the floor of her room, her two Elfin lodging mates absent. We're squandering precious study time, poring over every book on Faekin that we can get our hands on.

"It must be strange," I observe, looking around her room, "living with two Elves."

Her face darkens. "I suspect I won't be for too much longer. Now that the Verpacian Council is being run by Gardnerians."

The University Council has always required the integration of lodging rooms, Gardnerians and Elves generally placed together since our countries are allied, our ways similarly reserved. But it's only a matter of time until this widely disliked policy is dismantled by the Verpacian Council, with its new Gardnerian majority.

A fire roars in the fireplace beside us, a variety of books strewn about. I glance over at Aislinn's bed, which is sequestered in a corner. Her things are finely made—her bed's deep green sheets are made of expensive, Alfsigr Ellusian cotton, and her books are crisp and new. Her clothes, while simple, are nonetheless crafted from silk and fine linen, and her comb and brush set is silver.

But these things pale in comparison to the ethereal living space of the Alfsigr maidens who reside with her. Canopied beds graced with ivory silken sheets have spiraling posts wound tight with living vines, their black-green leaves interspersed with delicate white flowers that give off a subtle scent as clean as a spring shower. Intricate tapestries done up in white, silver and black knot-work designs set off a complementary rug with a similar, darker design. A long bookshelf holds bowls of translu-cent crystals and black texts titled with embossed Elfin script. At the foot of one bed stands a lovely harp in the rich hues of the Tortoiseshell Mahogany tree, its strings glimmering gold.

"There are legends of Fae healers who can do miraculous things," Aislinn tells me, pulling my attention from the Elves' waterfall fountain. It's set near an arching window and sur-rounded by a variety of flowering plants in ivory pots with black knotwork designs. Its gentle rush is pleasing to the ear and sends a soothing moisture into the air.

I direct my gaze back to my own text, pausing to run my finger along a fanciful illustration of a Sylphan Air Fae. She's garbed in flowing, gray garments, riding on a cloud.

I trace along the Sylph's ear. "Yvan doesn't have pointed ears," I note.

"Could be a glamour," Aislinn postulates.

I point to a passage in my text. "Which, according to this, would narrow our choices down to Sylphan Air, Lasair Fire and Asrai Water Fae. It says here that they're the only Fae who can glamour." I pick up my mug of hot tea and sip at it, the weighty ceramic mug warming my hands. "Iron doesn't bother him. He touches it all the time in the kitchen."

"Maybe he's a half-breed," Aislinn replies absently, as she

runs her finger down the index of another text and begins to flip through it. "He might still feel an aversion to it, though."

I try to remember a time when Yvan seemed the least put off by the iron cookware or stoves, but I can't remember ever seeing him distressed by the contact. And, unlike Tierney, he always goes ungloved.

"There are so many types of Fae," Aislinn muses as she reads. "Hundreds. And all of them so different."

Fantastical images from the books' illustrations hang bright in my mind. The Laminak Fae, with their crystalline underground castles. The goat-herding Hollen Fae, their cities carved into mountaintops. Sylphan Fae, who could render themselves transparent.

"Look at these," I marvel, pointing out an illustration. "They have butterfly wings!"

"Hmm," Aislinn says with a nod. "Moss Fae. I've heard tales of them. They're trouper Fae. Put on plays for the monarchy."

I skim over descriptions of the Skogsra Fae, who dwell deep in the forest with the owls, and the stern Ymir Fae of the Northern Mountains, their sharp-spired dwellings formed completely from ice.

"Have you ever heard of the Vila Fae?" Aislinn asks.

"Are they elemental?"

She smiles and shakes her head. "No. Candela. Color Fae. Vila had an affinity for violet. They could transform themselves into the shade. The Sidhe used them as spies. That's why purple still isn't permitted in the Mage Council Hall."

"It's amazing they were ever a cohesive group," I muse as I flip through my text. "They're all so...different."

"Mostly cohesive anyway," Aislinn comments as she picks at another book. "Except for the Solitary Fae."

"Solitary?"

"Fae that existed independent of Sidhe Court politics. Renegades. Nomads. Like the Dryads. The Lasair Fire Fae." Aislinn's finger pauses. "Oh, here's something. The Lasair Fire Fae had powerful healing magic..." Aislinn's finger moves again as she skims down the section. "Powerful fire magic, gifted healers, fiercely independent, nomadic." She shoots me a significant look before continuing. "*Bright-green eyes*...extremely danger-ous..." Aislinn's mouth quirks into a small smile, her eyes lifting to mine again. "Physically very attractive. I know he's a Kelt, but...he is a bit attractive, don't you think?"

I shrug cagily. "A bit," I allow, not wanting to spark Aislinn's suspicion about my senseless crush on Yvan Guriel. "We should put that one on the list," I prod, attempting to sound nonchalant as I grip my mug and Aislinn scratches it down.

Fire Fae. Could Yvan be part Lasair?

"He's so strong and fast," I muse, remembering. "Always going off in the woods. I think I told you—for a time I won-dered if he was secretly Lupine."

I regret saying this as soon as the word leaves my lips. At the mention of Lupines, Aislinn's face becomes instantly strained.

"How are things between you and Jarod?" I venture.

She doesn't answer for a moment, just sits staring at the book. "I'm speaking to him, if that's what you mean," she says, her tone evasive. "Please, let's not discuss it any further. I've made my decision. I can't abandon my sisters and my mother. So there's no sense talking about it."

Troubled, I take in her wan appearance. Aislinn's been in-creasingly away, visiting with her family, gone now most weeks' ends. Partially to keep up appearances, in case anyone notices the grimoire is missing, and partially to avoid her feelings for Jarod.

"Aislinn," I tell her, "your happiness matters, too. Not just theirs."

Her expression becomes pained. "And how could I ever be happy, knowing I abandoned my family?"

"But you wouldn't be abandoning them."

She shakes her head, her eyes tight with anguish, and I know I can't sway her right now.

I let out a long sigh. "I miss having you around more. You're one of the few people I can really be honest with."

Aislinn knits her brow at this. "I know. I feel the same way. But at least you have Diana…"

I feel a pang of resentful bitterness pass through me at the mention of Diana's name, remembering something that happened between us a few days ago.

I was in the North Tower's washroom, naked after a long bath, faced with the scratched mirror before me.

Gardnerians do not, as a rule, keep mirrors in washrooms. It's considered unseemly and wrong to view oneself naked. But as I caught a glimpse of my reflection that night, I was struck by the beauty of my long, pale, glimmering form. Pretending, on a whim, to be Diana, wondering what it would be like to be as comfortable in my own skin as she is in hers, I stretched my arms high up over my head shamelessly, just as Diana always seems to be doing, mimicking her unself-conscious ways.

Just as I was doing this, Diana barged into the small room. Mortified, my hands immediately flew down to cover myself as I reflexively hunched over. I felt a sharp spike of shame, even though Diana, herself, was naked. I glared at her, absolutely hating her inability to knock.

Diana paused, taking stock of the situation. "Ah, good," she said approvingly. "You are admiring yourself, as you should. Youth and beauty are a gift from Maiya. We should revel in it."

"Get out!" I cried, wanting to literally throw her out of the room. "You need to knock! I've told you this a million times! It's like you're deaf!"

"I most certainly am not deaf," she huffed. "My hearing is *vastly* superior—"

"Get out!"

"But—"

"I said, *get out!*"

Diana made a great show of looking disgruntled and offended before padding out of the room in a snit. A few minutes later after my murderous feelings toward the Lupine princess had begun to abate, I heard a very perfunctory knock on the door.

"What?" I snapped. Did she ever give up? *Ever?*

"May I please come in and speak with you?" she announced with stiff formality.

"No!" I cried, still fuming as I pulled on a camisole and pantalettes.

After a few seconds there was another knock. "What about now?" she asked, sounding genuinely confused.

I let out a deep sigh. As easy as it is to get mad at Diana, it's just as hard to stay mad at her. "Come in," I relented.

Diana padded back in and took a seat on the edge of the washtub, eyeing me like I was slightly deranged.

I frowned at her and went about combing out my hair with a vengeance. "What do you want?"

"I need to talk to you about something," she said reluctantly.

That was something new. Diana was never reluctant. I paused and turned to face her.

"I wrote to my parents," she began. "I asked them about bringing you home with me."

Something warm and comforting dropped out of my center. The pain of anticipated rejection that replaced it was surprisingly sharp.

No. They said no. Of course they had. Diana was a fool to have thought it would be any different. A naive fool. *She thinks she's so all-knowing; that her people are so perfect. Turns out the noble Lupines are just like everyone else. Full of prejudice.*

"My father," she began tentatively, "suggested that they meet you first."

In other words, no.

I turned my back to her and kept combing at my hair, even more roughly this time, pulling hard at the tangles, glad that it hurt. It distracted me. Kept me from crying. It's better to be angry than pathetic.

"It's okay," I told her stiffly, swallowing down the pain of rejection. "I've been thinking on it, and I really don't think I want to visit your people anyway. My people are just too different from yours. I don't think I'd be comfortable."

"Elloren…" she tried, her tone kind. On some level, I knew that she was really trying, that she was on my side, but the part of me that wanted to hate her at that moment out of sheer hurt was stronger.

"Please get out, Diana," I said harshly. "I'd like to finish up with some privacy. I really don't want you here." I took some small, fleeting satisfaction in the look of hurt that crossed over her face before she left.

So much for sisters, I thought as she quietly closed the door. I pulled harder at my wet hair, tears stinging at my eyes. *So much for finding friends and family among her people. So much for not losing my brother, but gaining a sister. I'm not gaining anything.*

It's just as I thought.

"It's not possible to be close friends with Diana," I tell Aislinn stiffly. "She's just so…different. She'll never understand what it's like for us."

Aislinn is studying me closely, as if she can read the conflict behind my words. I look away and try to swallow back a hurt that still feels jagged and raw.

I close my eyes and reach up to rub my temples, a dull throb beginning to send an ache through them. After a long moment I open my eyes and survey all the books scattered about.

"What happened to the Fae?" I ask Aislinn. "Toward the end of the Realm War."

"They were brought to the Pyrran Isles," Aislinn says, cocking her head in question.

"And after that?" I press. "What then?"

Aislinn shrugs, her expression growing dark with unease. "They were resettled. Somewhere in the far north..." Her voice trails off. "What? You think something else happened to them?"

I can make out the paper-thin *click* of an Elfin pendulum clock and the small trickle of the waterfall as silence descends between us.

"I don't know," I reply. "I've looked all over the archives. I can't find out anything about it. There's nothing. And no Fae anywhere."

"Strange."

"Here's the thing." I lean in toward her. "I don't think they were just kicked out of the Realm. I think they might have been killed. And if they were, well, that means that anyone who's Fae or has Fae blood...their lives could be in danger." I swallow, attempting to beat back the creeping dread.

"There's more and more talk about rooting out mixed-breeds," Aislinn says ominously.

"And if Yvan's mostly Fae..." The clock ticks out a few more beats. "Then there's no more time to waste."

CHAPTER TWENTY

Asrai Fae

Tierney is waiting for me when I return to the North Tower. She's sitting on the stone bench in the upstairs hallway, stockstill, lit by a single wall lantern.

I come to a stop before her. "Tierney..."

"I was three years old when they came for me," she says, her thin voice low and hard. Her eyes are firmly tethered to the floor. "My parents, they were part of a small group of Fae. One of the last, hidden holdouts. It was over. The Gardnerians were closing in. There was no way out.

"My Gardnerian parents were close friends with my Fae parents. My father now, and my father then...they were both glassblowers, and they admired each other's artistry. Before the end came, my Fae parents...they brought me to them. Me and my baby brother.

"Before they left, they held me down. My Fae parents, and some other Asrai. I was frightened, and I fought against them, but they were too strong. I felt a terrible twisting of my back, a pinching of my face, burning all over my scalp. I was terrified... I didn't realize they were giving up their glamours for me and my brother. Making me into a Gardnerian. Ugly enough to keep me safe from fasting. Safe from the Fae Hunt.

"I remember screaming for my mother. And I remember her sobbing and trying to comfort me, then breaking down. My mother screaming for me as my father dragged her away, her nails like claws on my arm."

Tierney pauses, still as a winter lake, her gaze locked on to the empty space before her.

"My Gardnerian family—we were planning on getting out of the Western Realm before the spring referendum, in case Vogel won," she continues in a low, flat tone. "But now...we should leave right away, but we're not ready to take our whole family across a dangerous desert." She's quiet for a moment. "My Fae parents...my Fae family. They were never seen or heard from again." Tierney looks up at me, fear stark in her eyes. "The Mage Council voted today to make fasting mandatory for all Gardnerians eighteen and up. We have six months to comply."

My stomach clenches. All of us—fasted by the spring. By choice, or by force.

"Vogel's going to round us all up for fasting," she continues, "and he won't just be testing racial purity of the couple being fasted. He's mandated the iron-testing of the fasting couple's families at the ceremony." Tierney's mouth turns down in a trembling grimace. "My brother and I are Asrai Fae, Elloren. Full-blooded Water Fae. They won't just arrest my brother and me. They'll arrest my Gardnerian parents and brother for sheltering us. My *whole family*."

She breaks into tears, dropping her face into her hands as she sobs. I go to her and sit down beside her, pulling her thin, crooked frame into my arms.

"We'll find help." I console her as she cries, my resolve hardening. "We'll find a way to get your family out."

And if no one will help us, I silently vow, *we'll fly you all out on a dragon, straight over the desert to Noi lands.*

But I need more information, I realize. If we're going to help Tierney and her family, we need to know what the Gardnerians are likely to do to the Fae. Where they'll take them. And where the Fae disappeared to after the Realm War.

And I know exactly who to go to.

"What happened to the Fae?"

Professor Kristian pushes up his glasses and sets his pen down on his desk.

"I've been through all the archives," I stubbornly tell him. *And I need to know what happened so I can save my friend.*

His expression turns jaded, and he spits out a grim laugh. "You won't find anything about that in the archives."

"I'm not *in* the archives," I shoot back, shutting his door. "I'm here."

He eyes the white band around my arm, then shoots me a hard look.

"Really?" I say, responding to his unspoken question. "Do you honestly think I support Vogel?"

Professor Kristian rubs his fingers along the side of his mouth as he sizes me up thoughtfully. He gets up, walks to the edge of one bookcase, pulls out a pile of texts and reaches behind them, sliding out a thick volume set into the case with its spine against the wall. He moves back to his desk and hands me the book.

I look at the stained, scuffed leather cover, the title scraped clear off the front and spine. My brow raised in confusion, I glance at Professor Kristian as he gestures with his chin for me to continue.

I open the book and read the title page.

Accounts from the Pyrran Isles
By Cellian Rossier

"At the end of the Realm Wars," Professor Kristian says, his voice low, "the Gardnerians came in and purged the archives of certain texts they deemed 'Resistance Propaganda.' And the Gardnerian historian who wrote them…" Professor Kristian pauses until I look back at him. His eyes are heavy with warning. "He was sent back to the Pyrran Isles. Just like the Fae."

I read in the hallway of the North Tower, by the light of a dim, flickering lamp, hunched against the wall with Marina curled up beside me.

It's past midnight and the full weight of the night presses down on me, but I beat back against the fatigue and focus on the pages in front of me.

Toward the end of the Realm War, Cellian Rossier, an outspoken critic of the Mage Council, was arrested and sent to the Pyrran Isles. While a prisoner there, he took down secret, detailed accounts of what he witnessed, eventually escaping and smuggling his writings out with him.

They shackled the incoming Fae in Asteroth copper, the metal strong enough to sap them of their strength and power. Then they herded them into huge, stone island fortresses and locked them inside.

And then they rained iron shavings down upon their heads.

There was a toddler. A little girl no more than three years old. With jewel-toned butterfly wings that the child frantically beat as she aimlessly ran in circles and screamed for her mother. The Gardnerian soldiers laughed as they kicked at her, then, growing irritated at the noise, grabbed the child up by her wings, swung her around and slammed her headfirst into a stone wall.

The nightmarish accounts go on and on, and eventually I have to set the book down, unable to read anymore, my gut close to heaving with a nauseating mix of disgust and despair.

Devastated, I drop my head and sob into my palm, the force of the cruelty at play slamming into me like a riptide.

Marina's slender hand comes up to pat my head with a kind, gliding touch. She murmurs softly in her rough, flutelike tones, trying her best to comfort me as I slouch down against her and cry.

I agonize over Tierney's and Marina's plight the next evening as I tend to several pots at once on the kitchen stove, stirring each one in turn, vaguely aware of the workers going about their tasks around me.

My despair rapidly hardens to outrage.

We'll get Tierney out, I defiantly vow. *I don't know how, but we will. And we'll find Marina's skin and bring her home. Surely Gareth will be able to help us.*

I stir harder at the thick stew.

And we'll make sure the Gardnerians have one less military dragon.

Yvan enters the room and kneels down to load more wood into a nearby stove, careful not to acknowledge me in public. *Too careful*, I dejectedly note. I watch him out of the corner of my eye to see if the iron bothers him. He makes extremely quick work of opening the stove, not letting his hands linger on the iron handle any longer than they have to, but he doesn't seem hurt or repulsed by it at all.

My concentration on Yvan's movements evaporates when my brother Trystan unexpectedly walks in. Trystan is wearing his heavy winter cloak, his bag slung over his shoulder. Worried by the arrival of an unknown Gardnerian, the Urisk and Kelt workers quickly give us a wide berth and find tasks to do in the corners of the kitchen farthest from us, or even outside. Iris and Bleddyn shoot each other looks of alarm.

"I have a present for Yvan," Trystan announces in a delighted whisper. Trystan is smiling. Not a barely detectable smile of irony, but an actual wide, triumphant grin. I don't think I've ever seen him smile so widely in his entire life. Trystan looks pointedly at Yvan then discreetly at the back door.

I quietly follow Trystan out, Yvan exiting soon after.

Yvan joins us under the lantern that hangs by the kitchen's back door, the three of us huddled together in the cold, our breath fogging the air.

Trystan extends his hand and opens it, like a flower greeting the sun.

In his palm is the Elfin steel arrowhead. In pieces. Lots of them.

I gasp.

"But how?" Yvan breathes, like he's viewing a miraculous mirage. "I thought you couldn't break it..."

"Oh, you can break it," Trystan says, slyly, "if you freeze it first."

Understanding lights Yvan's expression. So incredibly simple. So obvious.

Trystan's eyes take on a dark, mischievous glint. "I don't know about you two," he whispers, still grinning, "but I'm in the mood for breaking cages."

CHAPTER
TWENTY-ONE

Ice

After my shift ends, I rush back to the North Tower, a spring in my step that even my heavy book bag can't weigh down. I'm elated by Trystan's discovery, only half aware of my surroundings. Thoughts of dragon rescue whir excitedly in my mind.

Saved. Everyone who'll need to get out as good as saved. Wynter. Ariel. Tierney. Yvan. We'll rescue Yvan's dragon, and no one will have to be afraid anymore.

It's dark and winter-quiet on the broad field leading up to the tower, and a sickle moon hangs overhead.

The wind picks up and whistles through the nearby forest. The eerie sound highlights a deeper silence, the surrounding wilds a tangle of bare branches.

Watching me.

I slow, then stop, suddenly rooted to my place on this broad expanse of sloping field. The walk from the University city to the North Tower is long and solitary, far away from everything. The wind shudders through the trees.

I swear I can feel eyes on me.

The hairs on the back of my neck go up, and I glance uneasily around.

The North Tower is still a distance away, a dim light shining from its upstairs window. The lower half of the tower has an odd glint, as if it's glazed with a thin layer of spun sugar.

Ice.

Alarmed, I stop and turn clear around, the lights of the University city mere pinpricks in the distance. From here, the mammoth stone buildings are as small as a child's toys. My heart picks up speed.

Movement by a solitary tree catches my eye, halfway between me and the wilds. I squint and make out the dark silhouette of a woman.

She steps toward me, moonlight flooding over her. Panicked recognition sweeps over me.

Fallon Bane.

Ancient One, no. No, please no. Not here. She can't be here.

I'm frantically aware of the North Tower at my back as danger floods my mind.

Marina. Marina. Marina.

My heart thuds high in my chest as Fallon approaches. My palms go moist as the wind whistles around us both and digs its icy claws into me.

Where's her guard? She never goes anywhere without her guard.

I nervously peer into the distance and can just make the four men out, waiting at the base of the field, quietly watching us.

I can barely think around the blood thudding in my temples.

She's come for revenge, I sickeningly realize. *Revenge for Lukas gifting me with the violin.*

Desperate, I go on the offensive, wanting to drive Fallon and her guards clear back from this field, away from the tower.

"What are you doing here?" I demand as I drop my book bag to the ground and stomp toward her on shaky legs. I shoot her a mocking scowl as I come to a stop just before her. "Did someone leave your cage open?"

Fallon coughs out an incredulous laugh and smiles broadly.

"Oh, I'm not the one who needs a cage," she purrs. She flicks the tip of her wand idly toward the North Tower. "I think the Icarals are the ones who need a cage, don't you?" She tilts her head and cocks her brow expectantly at me. Then she inhales sharply, as if surprised. "Oh, wait. I *forgot*." Her cloying sarcasm quickly morphs to venom. "They're your *friends*, aren't they?"

Marina. Marina. Marina.

An image of Marina screaming as Fallon and her guard drag her away flashes through my mind. Wynter, Ariel and I dragged away, too, and jailed for thievery.

And Diana—what if Diana's there? She'll kill both Fallon and her guard before she'll let them take any of us.

I take a threatening step toward Fallon and jab my finger at the ice-coated base of the North Tower. "What have you *done* to my lodging?"

"Just playing," she says, thrusting her lower lip out in mock apology. Eyes on me, she raises her wand, murmurs a spell and sends a thin stream of ice coursing through the air. It lands at the North Tower's base in a glimmering rope.

"Stop it," I demand, outraged. I lunge forward and push her wand arm roughly away. The rope of ice lassoes outward and falls to the field in a crystalline shatter.

Fallon is quick as a snake. Her hand comes around my arm, hard as a vise, her wand at my throat. I gasp and shrink back from the madness in her eyes.

"Or you'll do what, exactly, *Mage* Elloren Gardner?" She gives me a hard shove, sending me falling backward to the icy ground. Then she steps back, circles her wand toward my chest and hisses out a spell through gritted teeth.

Ice shoots from her wand and collides with the invisible shield just above my clothing, my tunic rubbed with Professor Hawk-kyn's metal powder.

Metal to block ice.

Fallon's eyes fly open then narrow tightly with understanding.

Her eyes dart toward the North Tower, then back to me with a knowing gleam. "Is the beast up there, too?"

"What beast?" I ask casually, my heart thumping. *Marina Marina Marina Marina Marina.*

Fallon's mouth twists into a lascivious grin. "You know *exactly* who I mean. The Snake Elf." Her eyes widen. "You've got him up there, don't you? Along with all the other creatures you're collecting."

My mind reels with confusion.

Of course, I realize. *The metal shield. She actually thinks I could be hiding Professor Hawkkyn.*

I spit out a stupefied laugh and glare at her, my anger spiking. "No, no Elves. Just my Icaral roommates." I flash a hard, taunting grin. "And my new violin."

I regret the words as soon as they leave my lips.

Ice blasts from her wand, and I cry out as my boots freeze to the ground, the cold searing my toes.

"Forgot to shield your boots, did you?" she crows, her eyes bright with hate. She circles around me, a hard gleam in her eyes as I frantically try to tug my boots free. "I've been keeping an eye on you, Elloren Gardner," she says with a sneer, as I manage to crack one boot off the icy ground. "Icarals. Lupines. The big Amaz. Elves. Maybe even a Snake Elf who's slipped by my watch." Her eyes flick toward the tower like a cat who's caught her mouse. "All coming and going. At odd hours, too." She stops, shakes her head and *tsk-tsks* at me. "*Why*, I wonder. And then I think..." She glances up at the tower thoughtfully. "What could you possibly have up there that's *so* interesting?" She smiles wide with manic glee. "Let's find out!"

She makes for the North Tower, and I cry out, desperately trying to grab her.

Just as my fingers grasp the silk of her tunic, her uniform bursts into illumination. Strange runes glow a fierce white all over her tunic and cloak, sending their light out onto the field like small searchlights.

Confusion barrels through me. *Where did those come from?*

Fallon looks down at the clothing, then to me with rising horror.

One of her guards yells out an oath, and each man sets off at a fast clip up the field. A silver streak whistles through the air to my right and slams straight into Fallon.

It's a huge knife, now impaling the side of her chest.

The moment slows and stretches out as Fallon's head jerks up and she sucks in a loud, whistling gasp of air. She falls backward to the ground with a sickening thud.

I take it all in, my eyes and mouth opening wide in stunned disbelief.

Terror, like a hot iron, sears into my chest, and the nightmare snaps back to vivid life with bracing speed.

Fallon grasps at her chest, her breath labored and wheezing. She lifts her wand, grits her teeth and sends up a bright, crystalline dome of ice over us, thin lines of blue light coursing over the translucent shield like small, crackling lightning, the air chilling to frigid. I'm awed by her skill as well as her fierce tenacity, even when seriously wounded.

I flinch back as another knife collides against the shield in a shower of ice crystals, its terrifying point piercing the ice.

Two men burst from the wilds. They're large men, all in shadows, black-garbed with dark fabric wrapped around their heads and faces. They raise curved swords marked with glowing gold runes as they run toward us. Two large shapes explode from the woods on either side of them and take flight with compact wings that send air currents down with powerful, rhythmic whooshes.

Dragons!

But like no dragons I've ever seen before—they're the size of large dogs, boxy and muscular, one black, one red.

The runic light from Fallon's clothing reflects off the collective riot of weapons, teeth, claws and wild eyes all hurtling straight for us.

A black terror swamps over me, and I frantically pull at the laces of my frozen boot with shaking hands.

Everything descends into chaos.

Fallon's guards frantically yell to each other as streaks of their wand fire spear through the air with staccato bursts of golden light. Fallon hurls out javelins of ice toward the assassins and the dragons, the spears scything straight through her ice shield as if it were mere air.

Breathless, I cower near the ground.

Fallon's guard runs toward the men and the dragons, wands raised as they continue to throw lines of fire out that are easily deflected by the assassins' curved swords. The black dragon swoops down and collides with one of our soldiers. I gasp in horror as the beast latches onto his throat and the soldier sends up a gurgling scream. Another soldier thrusts his sword into the beast's neck, the creature sending up a jagged shriek before slumping to the ground.

The red dragon crashes into our shield with an earsplitting shatter, the dome cracking apart. Ice rains down on us in a shower of frigid, clinking shards as the beast thumps down beside us, red-scaled belly up, eyes rolled back.

I pull hard at my foot, dizzy with fear. My boot lace is hopelessly knotted, the boot solidly frozen to the ground. The dragon's warmth courses over me in a wave and melts the ice near my toes, but it's not enough to free me.

Clutching her chest and propped up on her side, Fallon breathlessly grinds out a spell and points her wand at the dragon with a shaking hand, just as the creature begins to snarl and right itself. A line of ice knifes out from the tip of Fallon's wand and into the dragon.

The dragon freezes then wobbles, Fallon's spear of ice stabbed right between its eyes. The beast falls to the ground with a dull *thump.*

It's impossible not to be wildly impressed—she just killed a dragon with a huge knife sticking out of her side.

I duck as a glowing red orb whirs by overhead, along with stray wand fire, the orb exploding behind me into a circle of red flame that briefly turns everything in the world crimson.

Fallon lets out a harsh growl as she throws out a series of ice spears that collide with the assassins in a harmless spray of snow.

"They're shielded," she says more to herself than to me, her eyes latched on to the assassins as her guard relentlessly attacks them now with swords. One assassin fights with two guards at once.

Fallon cries out and rolls onto her back as she sends forth a ceiling of ice over the fighting men. She flicks her wand repeatedly, and ice spears rain down from the ice ceiling and impale the assassins' skulls.

The assassins slump to the ground.

The runes on her clothing still glowing a bright white, Fallon sets her fierce eyes on me, then promptly passes out.

It's at that moment when my boot finally cracks free of the ice, my ankle twisted and throbbing.

Wincing from the pain, I crawl on my knees toward Fallon. The hilt of the knife juts out mercilessly from her side.

I have no great love for Fallon Bane, but I certainly never wished for her to be this grievously harmed.

Lurching toward her, I grab hold of her arm with a shaking hand. "Fallon, can you hear me?"

Sweet Ancient One, she can't be dead.

"Get back," one of her guards orders harshly.

I get up on unsteady legs and stumble backward as he drops to his knees in front of Fallon, soon joined by the other two surviving members of her guard.

I stagger to the ground and reach down to absently massage my pulsing ankle, stunned and shaken.

More soldiers are running up the field, shouting. They're mostly Gardnerian, but some are clad in the light gray of the Verpacian Guard, one of them Elfhollen. Three Vu Trin, including Kam Vin and Ni Vin, bring up the rear. Ni Vin's eyes meet mine, her black scarf wrapped tight around the burned half of her head, sword drawn.

I turn and look over my shoulder.

There are dead men and dragons strewn across the field. I turn back toward where Fallon lies, incredibly still. A numbed horror washes over me.

Everyone's talking at once. Men yell out orders as a large contingent of Gardnerian soldiers arrives on horseback. They're accompanied by a Gardnerian physician and his apprentice, the physician yelling out for supplies.

All the noise is a disconnected mayhem in the face of my overwhelmed shock.

"Give me room!" the physician orders as he rushes to Fallon and drops to his knees.

She's momentarily blocked from my sight, healers and soldiers surrounding her, one soldier holding a torch, the outer ring of soldiers facing out, their weapons drawn, faces severe.

A young soldier comes down on one knee beside me. "Mage Gardner, are you all right?"

I flinch back from him, shaking with terror, his words barely able to pierce the storm of my emotions.

Someone wraps a blanket around my shoulders.

When the crowd around Fallon disperses, the physician is holding the large knife. Fallon's tunic is off, her chest covered with tight bandages, her rune-marked uniform and cloak in a tight, glowing ball that's quickly handed off and taken away.

She's not dead.

Her eyes are half lidded, but open and staring right at me with a hatred so intense, it jars me to the core.

"The North Tower," she rasps out. Her eyes loll backward, and she falls unconscious.

Breathless and heart thudding, I watch as two of Fallon's guards lift her stretcher and carry her away. A small army of Gardnerian soldiers draws protectively in around her, cutting her off from view.

"Who are they?" I ask a surviving member of Fallon's guard, motioning toward the dead assassins.

The young man's brow knits tight. We both take in the sight of the assassins as their bodies are thrown over the back of a horse. The men's dead eyes are rimmed with kohl. Intricate runes mark their faces, and their lips are painted black.

Chilled to the bone, I hug the blanket tight around myself.

"They're Ishkart mercenaries," the guard tells me with grim certainty. "Assassins from the Eastern Realm." He flicks his finger toward the dead dragons that are being loaded by more soldiers onto a cart. "And their pit dragons." He looks to the icy North Tower then back to me. "You should return to your lodging, Mage Gardner."

"But...what if there are more of them?" I worry, looking sidelong toward the dark wilds, the trees like hulking presences.

"They're not after you," he says. He nods in the direction they took Fallon in. "They're only after her. Our next Black Witch."

"Her clothes," I say, the glowing symbols bright in my mind. "What were those strange symbols?"

"They rune-marked her clothing with search runes," he tells me. "Tracked her here." He gestures toward the tower with his chin. "Unless you have another Black Witch up in that tower, no one will be bothering you there, Mage Gardner."

A soldier near the North Tower's door aims his wand and

sends out a line of fire around the door's frame, melting Fallon's ice. He wrenches it open and slips inside.

My stomach gives a hard lurch. Soldiers dot the entire field, quickly dispersing as they widen their search into the surrounding wilds. Panicked, I look up and catch a fleeting glimpse of an Icaral's silhouette in the upstairs window.

I get up and rush, stumbling, to the tower, just as the soldier reemerges. He stands aside, his face impassive, as I stride past him, taking the spiraling stairs two at a time, not caring about the flash of pain every stomp of my left foot brings.

Panting hard, I find Wynter waiting for me on the other side of the hallway, the door to our room open beside her.

Marina. Marina. Marina.

I run to the door and my feet skid to a halt just outside it.

Ariel peers back at me from where she lies on her bed, something rustling under the blankets at her feet.

The rustling thing shrugs the blankets off her head, and Marina peeks out at me with her ocean eyes.

"Ariel hid her?" I rasp out to Wynter, amazed and stunned, doubling over to catch my breath.

Wynter gives me a small nod.

"But..." I say, high-pitched with confusion, "Ariel hates her."

"She does," Wynter affirms with another nod then gestures outdoors, toward the soldiers. Her pale face darkens. "But she hates them more."

I look back to Ariel, and she glares at me with a hatred as hot as Fallon's.

"They came for Fallon Bane," I tell Wynter, my throat dry and tight. I'm overwhelmingly grateful that my grandmother's power has completely passed me by. "Ishkart assassins. They're trying to kill the next Black Witch."

"But they failed," Wynter says, more a grave statement than a question.

I let out a long breath and nod. I'm tense and still lit up with alarm, my ankle throbbing painfully.

"Why was Fallon Bane here?" Wynter's eyes are full of solemn concern, her voice a constricted whisper. "Does she know of our Selkie?"

I shake my head. "No. But she knows something isn't right." I tense my brow at Wynter. "We've got to free that dragon. No more waiting. We're going to need a way to fly a Selkie and more than a few Fae out of here. Before Fallon is healed."

The next day rumors abound that Fallon was brought back to Gardneria under heavy guard, some say to a military base surrounded by dragons.

Vogel uses the incident as an excuse to lock down the borders. Urisk seamstresses are interrogated, and all those who might have worked on Fallon's rune-marked uniform are shipped off to the Pyrran Isles. Random iron tests begin at all the border crossings.

The need for escape is getting more dire by the minute.

Breaking Cages

The Lupines, my brothers, Cael, Rhys, Wynter, Andras, Tierney, Yvan and I all peer through the dense brush and down onto the expansive military base that lies before us.

The Gardnerian Fourth Division base is like a small city unto itself—multiple Spine-stone buildings carved into cliff faces, a sea of waxed-canvas tents and dragon cages interspersed throughout. On the western end of the base stands a series of wooden barracks, only one lit from within by lantern glow, its chimney spitting smoke into the chilly air. Soldiers appear small as ants from our high vantage point.

I sense movement to my left and turn to see Jarod, then Diana, crouched low and rushing over to us.

"It's just as we thought," Jarod tells us. "They're operating with a skeleton crew."

"Everyone's gone to Valgard for Marcus Vogel's appointment of the new base commander," Rafe says with a smile.

"Who's the new commander?" I ask.

Rafe turns to me, his smile widening. "Mage Damion Bane."

I spit out a laugh. "We're going to get him in a whole lot of trouble, aren't we?" I crow.

Rafe nods. "Hopefully so much that Vogel will rescind Damion's power over the dragons and *feed* him to them instead."

I briefly meet Yvan's green eyes, and we share a brief glimmer of satisfaction.

Rhys turns to Rafe. "It appears they haven't bothered to post sentries." The young Elf points a slender finger toward the rows of dragon cages that border the entire base, edging the wilds. The cages appear isolated and unguarded, no movement around them. No torchlight.

Cael glances at Rhys, the older Elf's face taut, fully understanding the risk we're all taking, but desperate to have options for his sister to escape into the Eastern Realm. He moves protectively closer to Wynter.

"Damion Bane's not the only upper-level soldier in Valgard right now," Jarod goes on. "Vogel's reorganizing the whole Guard—there's a number of promotions being announced. All of Damion's lieutenants are in Valgard with him."

"Very good," Andras affirms with a nod, his fist tight around his labrys.

"It gets better," Jarod puts in, the late-afternoon light casting him in a bluish glow. "The soldiers who stayed behind? They're all fresh out of apprenticeships."

"Ah, wonderful," Rafe says with a smile. "Green as spring foliage. And while the cat's away..."

"Are the mice playing?" Trystan inquires wryly.

"With a large volume of illegal Keltic spirits," Jarod responds with a sly smile.

"And more than a few Urisk tavern girls," Diana spits out.

"Typical," Tierney snipes.

"Oh, this is almost too easy," Trystan gloats with a small smirk, the white wand hanging from the belt beneath his cloak.

We're quickly sobered when we find Naga in even worse condition than before.

She lies unconscious, both legs and both wings broken now, one ear cut clear off, her cage's floor smeared with fresh and dried blood, her forked tongue hanging limply out of her mouth. Shocked, Yvan kneels down by Wynter and puts his hand next to hers on the dragon's neck.

Tierney gapes at the dragon, her thin hand coming up to cover her mouth, eyes wide with shock.

She's with us now, Tierney, and eager to help create any chink in the Gardnerians' military might that she can—and to help us secure dragonflight escape for the Icarals and the Fae.

Our band of rebels is growing. All of us are here, save Aislinn, who's once again caring for Marina.

And Ariel.

After our last visit to the base, Diana and Jarod scouted out a hidden, expansive cave deep in the forest. Ariel is there, preparing the medicines and splints we'll need to heal our dragon.

"She's alive," Yvan breathes out.

"Gods...who did this?" Tierney murmurs.

"Dragon Master Damion Bane," Trystan succinctly tells Tierney as he pulls out the white wand and focuses it on a few different spots on the cage, his expression gone steely. "And I think it's high time we put an end to it."

Andras readies his ax.

We all step back as Trystan murmurs the freezing spell.

A thin burst of blue light surges from the wand's tip and collides with the bars of the cage, spiraling around them and turning the Elfin steel white-blue, a thick layer of icy frost growing beneath the spell's light. Trystan keeps at it for several minutes before murmuring the spell again, the light doubling in intensity.

As the spell fades, Trystan steps back and glances at the wand in frustration. "It's not working. They need to get so cold they turn white. The bars—they might be too thick."

"Try again," I prod. "You strengthened the spell the second time. Maybe you just need to work up to it."

Trystan takes a deep breath, nods then repositions himself and speaks the words of the spell once more. Again, the frost grows, and the steel glows blue. Every muscle in Trystan's body goes tense as he pushes at the spell. His body begins to tremble, and the wand starts to buck in his hand.

I reach out to steady him.

As soon as my hand makes contact with Trystan's back, a buzzing heat courses through me. Trystan's spell explodes in strength. The small spiral of blue bursts into a giant ellipse of sapphire light encircling the cage. And then the entire steel framework turns translucent as glass.

I recoil sharply as there's another burst of light, a deafening crack and the ellipse of light surges backward. I'm hit by a painful wave of frigid air that almost knocks me off my feet.

I pull my frozen eyelashes apart just in time to see the bars of the cage go white as snow then crumble to pieces, the shards of frozen metal smashing against each other, the sound like a million chandelier crystals falling on stone.

Before we have a chance to speak, the crashing sound echoes out from the forest over and over, near and far.

"What was that?" Tierney asks in a small, worried voice.

"It sounded like cages shattering," Trystan guardedly replies. "But...it couldn't be..."

"How many dragons are on this base?" Cael inquires, dead-serious urgency in his eyes.

Trystan swallows hard before answering. "A hundred and twenty-three."

Rafe turns to Cael. "Any thoughts on what they might do?"

"They're trained to kill intruders," Cael answers grimly. "And to go to their Dragon Master."

Yvan rushes at the tallest tree in the vicinity, a great, towering pine. He scrambles up it with breathtaking speed, deft as a river monkey. I blink up at his form as he hangs one-armed from the treetop, not quite believing my eyes. I rack my brain and try to remember what type of Fae can climb like that.

Something snarls in the distance. One man shouts then more. A series of vicious growls rise that set the hairs on the back of my neck on edge. And then a base alarm sounds—a high-pitched, spiraling whistle as dragons begin to shriek.

"They're everywhere," Yvan calls down. "They're *all loose...*"

Yvan leaps from the top of the tree and lands in front of me with a heavy *thwump*. He's crouched low, a look of fierce resolve burning in his emerald eyes.

I've no time to marvel over his effortless leap from such a great height. He grabs my arm and practically throws me out of the clearing into the shelter of the trees.

I scrape my arm, and a branch slashes at my face as I hit the ground.

Three dragons shoot into view, soaring over, just above the treetops, beating foul wind down onto us with powerful wings, their undersides covered in hard, ebony scales. One of them lets out a rasping shriek. I become acutely aware of the softness of my skin—how easily it would yield to teeth and claws.

Easy prey.

Cael and Rhys have taken to the trees, arrows nocked in ivory bows as Tierney shrinks down by a large oak. The base below us has become a cacophony of shrieking and growling. Men shouting. Women screaming. Horses panicking.

"*Wyn'terlyn,*" Cael calls out to his sister in Elvish, his eyes seared on to her. He points to Naga and barks out an order in their tongue. Wynter quickly slides under Naga's broken wing, disappearing from sight.

"I can hear dragons," Diana says, cocking her head. "A number of them. Coming this way."

"How many?" Andras asks, his jaw going rigid as he brandishes his ax and flexes muscular arms.

Diana levels her eyes at him. "Too many to count."

Rafe readies his bow as Diana and Jarod crouch low. Yvan's hand finds my arm, every part of me on high alert, heart racing. I remember the broken dragons' horrible teeth, their soulless eyes...

"Stand ready!" Diana commands as she morphs her hands into clawed weapons, one arm arced above her head, a low growl emanating from her throat.

A dragon bursts into our clearing, wings beating. I gasp and reflexively shrink back behind Yvan as arrows shoot down and bounce off the beast's neck. The creature immediately zeroes in on Diana, tilts its horrible head and hisses, showing off murderous, spiked teeth.

Diana darts forward and smacks the side of the dragon's head. Her blow sends the creature slamming to the ground with a loud shriek. In a blur of speed, Diana is astride the dragon, its neck in her hands as she jerks it around with a cracking twist. The creature slumps limp and lifeless into the dirt, black foam bubbling up from its mouth.

Jarod's and Diana's heads jerk upward. Two more dragons fly into the patch of sky above. They crash down, bending back trees with beating wings, branches cracking off and raining down into the clearing.

Yvan falls on me and pushes me flat onto the ground. Huge tree parts rain down on us. Arrows whistle by from multiple directions, one piercing the bark of the tree behind me with a dull *thwunk*.

"Stay down!" Yvan cries as he pushes himself off me and into a crouch.

A flash of steel glints amidst the thrashing confusion of dragon limbs as Andras curses and swings his labrys. There's a metallic thud, a terrible, ground-shaking roar, the *whoosh* of more arrows, Diana's low growl as she kills another dragon. Complete chaos ensues as the dragons fall, writhing on the ground, a new one bursting forth from the trees, its face twisted in ravenous fury.

Trystan raises his wand at the beast as it stalks toward him. Fire bursts forth from the wand's tip in a powerful surge. The wave of fire engulfs the dragon and flames toward Yvan and me. A great burst of water drenches us both from the side, dousing the fire and chilling me to the bone. I sit up and rub at my eyes as I choke on rancid smoke.

I look over to see Tierney putting out Andras's flaming cloak hem with another burst of water from her palms as Andras pulls his labrys from the dragon's neck.

"What are you *doing*?" Diana yells at Trystan. "Stop setting people on fire!"

"Sorry!" Trystan calls to Andras, his voice rattled.

"Fire won't hurt them!" Yvan cries out to Trystan as he rakes his hair in frustration. "They're *dragons*!"

Without warning, another dragon crashes down from the sky to land in front of Yvan and me.

I scuttle backward into the woods as Yvan leaps at the creature.

Dizzy with panic, I hear a soft rustling to my left. I turn to see, amidst the dense brush, the head of a dragon. It's motionless, with opaque eyes that watch me coldly. I stare at it, transfixed and realize I'm about to die.

The attack comes from behind as yet another dragon slams me into the ground. Claws scrape at my back with a red-hot slash, then there's an unbearable pressure as a heavy foot comes down on my back, pinning me in place, the beast snarling behind me. I scream at the top of my lungs as the other dragon's terrifying face slides into view, inches from my head.

And then Yvan is there, grappling with the dragon before me, his hands tight around the creature's horns. Baring his teeth, he jerks the beast's head back, blackened blood spurting out from the creature's mouth.

The pressure on my back abruptly releases as the dragon behind me roars and lunges for Yvan. I spring free, scramble to my feet and break into a panicked run.

I race through the woods, my breath coming in deep gasps, not daring to look back at the snuffling creature that's now crashing through the woods behind me.

I burst into another clearing and leap over the remains of a cage. A powerful blow to my side sends me flying toward a tree. My head collides with it, a shower of stars bursting to life behind my lids. A terrible, ripping pain on the side of my thigh reduces me to a wild state as I claw at the ground. I scream at the top of my lungs, the sound disembodied, taking on a life of its own.

Through my screams, I hear Yvan snarl out something in a strange language, the words quickly morphing into a bizarre hiss. Trapped in a blaze of pain, I roll over to see Yvan rip the dragon's head clear off its body.

I stop screaming as the searing pain grows numb and the world begins to spin slightly off its axis. "Yvan..." I croak, as he runs to me and views my leg with horror, the green of his eyes having taken on a bright, otherworldly glow.

He drops down and grabs at my shredded skirt hem and rips off a long shred of fabric. His form blurs in and out of my vision, and I'm vaguely aware of him wrapping the long shred around my thigh and cinching it tight.

Trystan bursts into view. *"Oh, Ancient One. No!"* He runs to me, his eyes flying to Yvan in desperation. "What can I do?"

"We've got to get her out of here," Yvan says. "There's not much time. She's losing too much blood..."

And then there's an unbearable heat around my shredded thigh. The pain halves, and my leg feels knit tight again, but the world is a blur, and I'm ebbing.

"How did you..." Trystan's voice breaks off in shocked awe.

"Does it matter?" There's a fierce challenge in Yvan's tone.

"No," Trystan demurs, his voice calm and sure. "No, it doesn't."

Yvan's arms come around me, lifting me as the world spins and goes in and out of view.

I'm vaguely aware of the voices of the others, sounding like they're momentarily underwater as we move through the forest. The world briefly comes back into focus as we slow to a stop.

"They're...leaving," Cael marvels. I weakly glance over toward where the Elf is pointing. My head lolls strangely, like it's partially disconnected from my body, my arms limply wrapped around Yvan's neck. We're high up, afforded a panoramic view of the military base. Naga is unconscious and being carried by Diana and Jarod, one wingtip scraping along the ground.

What looks like over a hundred dragons are rising and flying off into the west, as frantic soldiers try in vain to subdue them with hooks and spells.

"Where do you think they're going?" Andras asks.

"They seem to be headed in the direction of Valgard," Trystan says, incredulous.

"They have a mental connection to Damion Bane," Yvan says. I can feel the subtle vibration of his deep voice along his warm chest. "So they probably are headed for Valgard."

Complete chaos has broken out in the military base, soldiers yelling out to each other, shooting arrows and blue streams of wand light at the dragons, the majority of the beasts now a swiftly moving black cloud barreling toward Valgard.

One of the dragons, a straggler farthest from the others, rounds back, lets out a horrific roar and begins to fly straight toward us. I should be terrified, but I'm dizzy and so weak. It seems like a surreal dream as the realization hits me.

Before, when I touched Trystan—the latent power in my blood seemed to amplify his magic.

"Trystan," I rasp as I set a weak hand on my brother's back. "The cratering spell. Blow a hole through it..."

Trystan grinds out the words to the spell as the dragon swoops in. I gasp as heat shudders through me, through my hand and into Trystan's shoulder. A beam of white light bursts out of the white wand and spears toward the dragon, colliding with the creature's chest, piercing the dragon clear through. An explosion of limbs, flesh and blood streaks through the sky as the white beam barrels onward and crashes into the vertical cliff face of the mountain before us.

An explosion of rock and dust follows, the sound deafening, the ground shaking beneath us. Multiple avalanches rumble to life and rain down huge stones onto the military base, the largest of the structures quickly reduced to smoky rubble.

"Is that..." Jarod says, his voice dazed.

"Damion Bane's new military headquarters, yes," Trystan finishes for him.

Everyone flinches as another avalanche of stone breaks free from the mountain and takes out the last of the stone buildings. The soldiers below, small as ants, have grown silent as they stand near their small, isolated barracks and stare, along with us, at the destroyed base. One soldier yells out and points in our direction.

"They're regrouping," Cael says grimly as gruff voices begin to bellow out orders. "And they'll come after us."

"Let's go," Yvan prods, his arms tight around me. "I need to tend to her leg. *Soon.*"

"They'll send trackers out after us," Rafe says, his voice ragged. My brother is pale, his face streaked with blood.

Tierney raises her hands in the air, closes her eyes and begins to hum, low and clear. Gray clouds pull in from every direction, like dogs heeding a master's call, growing and mushrooming above, their movement dizzying and strange, like time speeding up. Thick, fat flakes begin to rain down on us, first scattered, and then thick as an upended sack of flour.

"There," Tierney says, barely visible through the frigid white. "That should hide our tracks nicely."

Aftermath

I'm drifting in and out of consciousness, half-aware of Yvan's arms around me, my head lolling over his shoulder, the terrible pain in my leg muted into a throbbing ache that grows and then recedes, over and over, like the rhythmic sweep of the ocean's tide. I can taste blood in my mouth, smell it on Yvan's taut neck.

And then I'm dipped down, and the air around me grows damp, the voices more distinct as I'm laid out on a cold, stone-hard floor. Everyone is fuzzy, some of them grouped around me. The dragon being carried in by Diana and Jarod briefly comes into focus, her scales scraping against the stone floor of the cave as she's lowered down, her hide giving off a dusty, wood-smoke smell. The warmth from her body rushes toward me, loosening my muscles. The pain spikes. I cry out as flashing spots of light block out my vision.

Yvan's voice. Yelling out orders as I writhe in pain. My clothes being pushed up and over. Hands tight on my leg. Other hands around my arms. Grasping me firmly as I struggle against them.

"Ren." Trystan's voice, coming from right behind me. I moan again. "You've got to try and stay still, Ren."

I scream out like a wild animal as the pain of a thousand

knives stabs at my leg. I buck against the hands grasped tight around my thigh, the pain seeming to go on forever and ever.

Finally, the pain begins to fade and the room comes into focus, like I'm surfacing from deep water, gasping and choking.

Yvan is staring at me, his face full of an intense relief, his arms still tight around my leg, the pain now tamped down to a small ache. My head throbbing, the room begins to spin, my vision blurring. I slump back against Trystan.

"You fixed my leg," I weakly marvel.

Yvan smiles, a desperate relief evident in his eyes. He moves up to sit beside me as Trystan places something soft under my head. I sink back into it.

"You've lost a lot of blood," Yvan says gently. He takes hold of my tunic at the waist and rips open the side seams with one quick jerk.

Even in my haze, this strikes me as odd. "What are you doing?"

He pauses. "Do you trust me?" His eyes are steady on mine.

I nod, my head feeling weightless as if it could just float right into the sky.

Yvan slides his hands through the ripped seam and finds his way with deft fingers. He slides one hand behind my back and the other to the center of my chest.

I draw in a small, languid breath. "You're so warm…"

"Shhh," he says, his deep voice soothing. "Close your eyes."

I obey as his hand moves up my breastbone with slow, deliberate care. Warmth radiates out from his fingers and flows through me, coursing from his hands into my entire body. The light-headedness fades as the warmth grows, my breath strengthening in my lungs, the long, stinging slashes on my back muting to tingling ribbons.

I open my eyes and meet his gaze, my vision clear again, the pain gone. He's so close to me, his ministrations like a lover's caress.

Perhaps sensing the shift, Yvan's touch becomes tentative and featherlight. He slides his hands away and pulls back. As I blink up at him, Yvan's serious expression wavers and becomes momentarily boyish and unsure. He glances at my leg then quickly away.

I sit up, surprised that the room isn't spinning. My skirts are pushed up to the top of my thigh, only a faint, pink scar where the gaping wound was. I stare at my leg, amazed, the blood on the cave floor and Yvan's hands and forearms proof that I've not dreamed this.

Yvan goes next to Rhys, who's slumped against a wall. His tunic is being cut off with a small knife by Cael. Rhys's upper torso is crisscrossed with bloody gashes, one ivory sleeve soaked with blood, the arm beneath hanging at an odd angle.

Ariel is bent over the unconscious dragon, lining up her torn wing. Wynter's hands rest gently on the beast's side. Naga's chest rises and falls in weak breaths, smoke periodically sputtering out of her nostrils and spiraling white toward the cave's ceiling. Andras kneels down beside the dragon and begins to straighten out her bent leg.

Ariel leaps up and grabs roughly at his shoulder. "Get away from her!" she snarls at him. "She's not a *horse*! You have to line up the greater tarsal bone with the lesser tarsal bone or it will fuse *all wrong*!"

Andras pulls his hands away from Naga's leg and lifts them, palms up, in surrender as Ariel glares at him murderously.

Wynter gently places her hand on Ariel's arm. After a moment Ariel's manic look recedes. She sits back down, focusing in on Naga's wing, and sets back to work with nimble fingers, cursing to herself as she works.

"Where's Diana? And Jarod?" I ask, my eyes darting around the cave and quickly lighting on the Lupine twins' clothing, piled up against one wall.

"They're out in wolf form," Trystan assures me. "Standing guard."

Alive. All of us, miraculously still alive.

Rafe is slumped down near Rhys, holding on to his own arm, a strained expression on his pale face as if he's gritting his teeth.

I pull down my skirts and cautiously rise with Trystan's support, holding tight on to his arm as I wiggle the toes of my left leg, scared to put weight on it. Screwing up my courage, I bear down on the leg, amazed to find it flush with more energy and strength than the other.

"Rafe," I call out. "Are you okay?"

Rafe smiles, his head slumped to one side. "Oh, I've been better." He looks to my healed leg with obvious relief, then glances over at Yvan who's laying his fingers over Rhys's gashes one by one. "But I suspect Yvan here could reattach our heads if he had to, so I'm feeling hopeful."

Yvan's eyes flash at Rafe.

We all know you're Fire Fae, I want to tell Yvan. *Stop the charade.*

"Can you heal Naga?" I ask Yvan bluntly.

Yvan hesitates, his jaw tensing as he holds on to Rhys's wounded arm. "No," he finally says, guarded. "Not when she's in this form. And she isn't able to shift to human form."

Rafe's eyes widen, along with my own. "She's a shifter?" Rafe asks with surprise.

Yvan gives a tight shake of his head. "The Gardnerians use geomancy to bind their ability to shift."

I stare at him, amazed. "Are you saying that all of our military dragons...are wyvern-shifters?"

Yvan meets my stare head-on. "They were."

I try to wrap my mind around this—there's a human form bound somewhere inside Naga, unable to get out.

Tierney leans against the cave wall, stoic and unhurt. She's looking at Yvan, her jaw set forward, her gaze full of concern and solidarity.

Two Fae. The both of them. Water and Fire.

Cael stands and begins to grab up his weapons and secure them one by one.

An Elfin bow and arrows. Knives.

In case they come for us.

The terrible reality of our situation seeps in. "We've destroyed a Gardnerian military base," I state flatly, not quite believing the words.

Everyone turns to look at me, the gravity of what we've done, and the extreme danger we've placed ourselves in, stark in everyone's eyes.

Tierney is the first to speak, her voice soft, her eyes gone hard. "Good."

"We cannot all stay together here," Cael puts in, his gaze narrowed at us all. "Ariel Haven can care for the dragon. As soon as Yvan is done, the rest of us need to separate. And quickly."

I rush back toward the North Tower, the sack over my shoulder containing the white wand.

Emerging from the wilds, I step onto the large, sloping field that lies before the tower, the irregular, frozen ground rough against my boot heels. I pause, overcome by the immensity of the black dome of sky reeling overhead. It's ribboned with silvery clouds, sharp as talons.

Something moves in the sky to the northeast. *Flapping.*

Legs buckling, I'm seized by a sudden, crippling terror.

Dragon. Another dragon.

I stumble back into the shadowy woods. Shuddering with fear, I frantically search the northeastern sky.

A cloud. One of the ribbony clouds. The dragon shape has dispersed and split into three separate slashes against the black dome of the sky.

I brace myself against a large stone, struggling to breathe as it all washes over me—the dragon attack, the beast's terrible claws, the wild pain, the mountain falling apart.

We'll be caught. They'll find us and arrest us all. And then...

"Elloren."

I flinch at the sound of Yvan's voice and the feel of his hand on my shoulder.

He's so warm. I can feel the heat straight through the layers of my cloak, my tunic and my camisole. His warmth steadies me.

It's a cloud. Nothing but a cloud. I force down my panicked breathing.

"Are you all right?" he asks, the angular lines of his face thrown into sharp relief by the moonlight.

"The cloud," I force out, peering into the night sky. "It moved." I swallow, fighting back the memories. "I...I thought it was a dragon."

Yvan nods and looks up at the sky, his expression darkening. He lets his hand fall from my arm, leaving a void for the cold to rush back in. He looks tired. And worn.

"What are you doing here?" I ask, the wind stinging at my face. "We're supposed to separate."

"I wanted to thank you," he says.

I shake my head tightly in protest. "You don't need to thank me."

"No, I *do*."

"For what?" I ask, incredulous. "For almost getting us all *killed*?"

Yvan shakes his head in surprise and disbelief. "Naga's *alive* because of you. I needed help. I couldn't do it alone. Before you came here...before I met you..." He seems to be having trouble finding the right words. "Naga...she was..."

"Your friend. I know." I finish for him softly, feeling suddenly defeated, and as tired as he looks. I fix my eyes on his. "I know you can talk to her, Yvan."

He grows quiet, his expression turning carefully neutral.

I study him in the moonlight, the vivid hue of his eyes muted to silvery gray. I remember how his eyes glowed a fearsome green. His inhuman strength. His strange language. His terrible hiss.

"What *are* you, Yvan?"

The line of his jaw hardens.

Perhaps it's the exhaustion, or the lingering fear that makes his stubborn silence feel so piercingly unkind.

"I don't understand," I press. "After everything that's happened...why can't you tell me what you really are?"

His face tenses with frustration, but he doesn't say anything, and I'm inexplicably hurt by his silence. Tears sting at my eyes.

"But the dragon knows what you are," I force out. "And so does Wynter, doesn't she?"

"Elloren..."

I bite my lip, horrified that I'm so close to bursting into tears. I struggle, to no avail, and pathetically start to cry right there in front of him.

He just stands there, staring at me with those intense eyes of his, and I'm suddenly terribly aware of how my skin must shimmer in the darkness—highlighting how irreconcilably different we are.

A cloud shifts, and the panic rears its head again. I struggle to fight it back, trembling. "I could have died..."

"You didn't."

"But I *could* have. We *all* could have."

Again, he retreats into silence.

"They might catch us," I insist, my voice growing shrill. He doesn't respond, and his continued silence sends a flare of hysteria through me. "They might find us...and arrest us...and *kill* us..."

His face grows hard, his eyes flinty. When he speaks, his tone is as hard as his eyes. "Yes, Elloren. They *might*."

I'm oddly steadied by his terribly blunt reply. He's faced this fear and moved past it. It's possible to move past it.

And then his hand is on my arm again, his gaze searing, but his touch gentle and warm.

"Go on," I relent as I wipe roughly at my tears with the back of my hand. I gesture toward the twinkling lights of the University city with my chin. "Go get some sleep. You look exhausted. Your dragon will be fine. Ariel may be a bit... unstable...but she knows what she's doing when it comes to caring for any winged animal."

He nods tightly, his face incredibly tense as if he's desperate to say something, but just can't. Unexpectedly, he steps toward me, eyes burning. "Elloren," he breathes as he brings his hand up to cup the side of my face, his long fingers sliding back through my hair.

I gasp. His hand is so hot on the cold skin of my cheek, his fingers threading back through my hair. His touch...it feels so good.

He leans in, his face close to mine as if he's about to kiss me, and for a moment it seems like everything is about to right itself.

I tilt my head up, my heartbeat erratic, suddenly wanting nothing more than to feel his lips on mine.

He steps back sharply and pulls his hand away from my face as if he's been burned.

I'm so shocked, I don't know what to do.

He looks furious with himself.

"Good night, Elloren," he finally says, his voice strained.

And then he turns and strides quickly away, leaving me to the ice-cold night, too hurt and dazed to react. I watch his darkened form recede, then disappear, swallowed up by the University.

CHAPTER TWENTY-FOUR

Revolutionary

The wanted postings appear the next morning.

They're affixed to the message boards of every tavern, lodging house and hall.

I skid to a halt at my first sighting of the crisp sheets of parchment. A newly vicious cold has swept in with the morning wind, and it burns at my exposed skin and chills my lungs. It sets me shivering and hugging my winter cloak tight with woolen-gloved hands as I peer at the notice before me.

It's nailed to a board outside the apothecary lab. Across the street, three Elfhollen scholars slow then stop in front of another posting tacked onto a lamppost. Their circle tightens as they murmur gravely to each other, their faces growing troubled as they read.

By joint order of the Verpacian and Gardnerian military forces, a search for those connected with the destruction of the Gardnerian's Fourth Division military base is being aggressively conducted and a reward has been posted.

Rebels… Revolutionaries… Resistance. As I skim the posting, these words stand out in sharp relief. Each of them sends a fresh stab of fear through me. I'm seized by a sudden, startling under-standing that my brothers and I, our strange circle of friends...

My stomach gives a hard lurch.

We've become all of these things.

I read on, light-headed, struggling to see the letters through a fog of disorientation.

Information regarding those connected with the destruction of the Gardnerian Fourth Division base is to be immediately brought to the attention of the base's newly appointed military leader: Commander Lukas Grey.

Just above the poster hangs a fresh advertisement for the up-coming Gardnerian Yule dance. Next week's end.

He'll be back, I realize, heart thudding. To bring me to the dance, and to find those responsible for the mayhem.

My knot of fear pulls tighter.

How on Erthia will we possibly evade Lukas Grey?

We're avoiding each other, all of us. The stakes raised im-possibly high.

"Bring Tierney to Professor Kristian," Yvan tells me in pass-ing, late that night in the kitchens, his voice terse, his eyes averted, as if the very sight of me burns his eyes. He stalks off toward the other Kelts, and my heart aches.

The way he's avoiding me—it goes beyond what we all have to do for self-preservation. No, this is more than that. Some-thing between Yvan and me has fractured, and I don't know how to fix what we've broken.

I drag myself back to the North Tower that night, a dulled fear humming inside me. There's a package for me there, Wyn-ter handing it to me with no small amount of alarm.

"There was a soldier here," she tells me in a small voice. "He almost saw her." Her silver eyes dart toward Marina, who's watching us intently, fear etched on her face.

I take the package into my hands and turn it over, concern spiking.

Another gift from Lukas. But small this time. I open the card first.

Elloren,

It seems our finest have misplaced a dragon. I'll look for you when I arrive.

Lukas

I open the small package as Wynter watches with wary curiosity.

It's a necklace, and I pull up the silver chain, letting the pendant dance in the air between us, glinting in the soft lantern light of the upstairs hallway.

A tree. Intricately carved in white wood.

I grasp the pendant in my hand and breathe in a deep, startled breath as a huge, branching Snow Oak bursts into view, caressing my mind, sending out branches through my limbs, clear down to my hands and feet.

It roots me right to the floor, this wood, steadying me, a pulsating echo of pleasure coursing through me.

I release the wood, breathing hard.

"Careful, Elloren Gardner," Wynter cautions, eyeing the pendant in the same way I've seen her look at Ariel's nilantyr.

"I know what I'm doing," I tell her uneasily.

It's the right thing to do, I reason with myself. *To stay on Lukas's good side and pretend that everything is fine and normal. I'll wear it every day so that he finds it on me when he arrives.*

I can picture him now, spotting the chain, sliding his pianist fingers along my neck to guide the necklace into the open, closing his palm around the tree pendant as he smiles at me.

A prickling flush heats my cheeks at the thought of him, and I'm instantly ashamed of my imaginings.

I slip the pendant's chain around my head, drop the tree inside my tunic and attempt to push thoughts of Lukas out of my mind.

But I can feel the wood of the small tree pulsating against my skin, like a warm, unsettling heart.

CHAPTER TWENTY-FIVE

Two Hundred and Fifty-Six

An icy wind rattles the diamond-paned windows as I sit with Tierney in Professor Kristian's cluttered office.

It's late evening, and a throbbing ache pulls at my temple like taut fishing line, the scar along my thigh tingling.

All day I've held my breath, waiting for an arrest that never came as my friends and I stolidly went about our usual lectures, work and tasks, all of us trying to blend in unobtrusively— nothing but harmless, hardworking scholars, the lot of us.

But I saw the Verpacian and Gardnerian soldiers questioning scholars and professors, the military presence growing through-out the day. It sent a cut-glass fear straight through me.

This is bigger than just us now. And we need help.

Tierney and her family need to get out of here.

Professor Kristian sits behind his desk, eyeing Tierney and me with somber concern. Tierney looks like a rabbit tensed for flight, her knuckles white as she sits forward, gripping at her chair, frozen in place.

"What's the matter, Elloren?" Professor Kristian asks me, his eyes flitting to Tierney and back to me again.

Heart racing, nerves primed, I jump off the cliff. "Yvan Guriel. He told us...that you might be able to help someone who might be—" I take a deep breath "—glamoured Fae."

Professor Kristian's brow rises, and he's silent for a long moment, frozen in place like Tierney.

"You know Yvan Guriel?" he finally asks.

I blink at him, surprised by the question.

A bit, I think, with wry hurt. *He almost kissed me.* I nod cagily.

Professor Kristian spits out a sound of amazement and narrows his eyes. "Surprising. Yvan hates Gardnerians. Quite a lot."

It stings bitterly to hear it. I push the hurt aside.

"We have a common goal," I tell him, straightening.

"Transporting glamoured Fae east, I would imagine," he says matter-of-factly. "Is that what you're getting at?"

Tierney and I glance at each other, and the jumped-up fear in her eyes jolts me into remembering what the stakes are for her and for her family.

"Yes," I tell him definitively. "That's exactly what I'm getting at."

He takes a deep breath, nodding, lets it out and clasps his hands together, his forefingers steepled in thought. His lip lifts with amusement as he sets his eyes on me. "Flirting with the Resistance, are we?"

I let out a deep breath. "I'm afraid I've jumped clear into bed with them."

A bark of surprised laughter bursts from his lips, and I can't help but cough out a small laugh, as well. I massage my aching head and look back up at him, resigned to the wild path I've veered onto.

Laughter still swimming in his eyes, Professor Krisitan sits back in his chair and stares at me with amused incredulity. "That's...not a very Gardnerian thing to say," he says, still chuckling.

I let out a resigned sigh. "I'm feeling less and less Gardnerian every day."

He nods with understanding, and then his expression goes odd, like he sees something in my face, something he finds troubling. He swallows audibly and then...his eyes sheen over with tears.

"What's the matter?" I ask him, immediately concerned.

"Nothing," he says with a shake of his head, his voice breaking. He clears his throat and leans forward to set out tea mugs for both Tierney and me from the chipped tea set ever-present on his desk. His eyes flick toward me, and there's a raw pain there. "You...you reminded me of someone, just then," he says, his tone still ragged. "Someone I used to know."

"Who?" I ask, confused. "My grandmother?"

"No, someone else," he says cryptically, now closed off. "It's nothing."

He shakes his head again and pours tea for us, the steam rising in the air.

It's comforting, the familiar burble of the tea as it's poured, the scent of minty steam on the cool air, a chill seeping in from a strong draft around the windows.

Professor Kristian eyes Tierney as he pushes a cup toward her. "You would be the glamoured Fae, I presume?"

Frightened, Tierney looks sharply toward me, eyes wide, and I nod encouragingly to her.

"I can help you," he tells her, his voice low and kind. "You've come to the right place. You have *nothing* to fear."

Tierney stares at him blankly for a long moment and then bursts into tears, her thin shoulders heaving, her body bunching up into a protective ball.

"Oh, my dear. It's all right." Professor Kristian gets up and comes around to lean against the front of his desk. He hands his handkerchief out to Tierney and places his hand gently on her arm.

Tierney takes the handkerchief with a shaking hand.

"What are you, dear?" he asks her. "What type of Fae?"

"Asrai," she chokes out.

"That's a lovely thing to be," he says reassuringly. "Maybe not here, but it will be when you and your family get to Noi lands, hmm?"

Tierney chances a look up at him and starts crying harder, nodding her head in pained assent. She looks small and scared and so young.

"Have some tea," he tells her with a pat to her arm.

"Thank you," she manages. She roughly wipes at her eyes, gets hold of her staggered breathing and takes the mug he's patiently holding out to her, sipping at it as Professor Kristian sits back against the desk.

His expression turns oddly amused as he turns his attention to me. "Well, you have been busy, haven't you?"

"I don't like to be idle," I reply tartly.

"Hmm," he says, eyeing me with friendly suspicion. "You wouldn't happen to know anything about a missing dragon, would you, Elloren?"

My breath catches tight in my throat.

Professor Kristian looks to Tierney. "Or a freak snowstorm that fell *only* on the Gardnerian Fourth Division military base?"

Tierney's eyes fly open wide, and she almost chokes on her tea.

Professor Kristian nonchalantly removes his glasses, fishes another handkerchief out of his pocket and begins to clean them. "You've both probably heard by now that over a hundred military dragons flew straight into Valgard yesterday evening and headed straight for their Dragon Master—Mage Damion Bane."

I swallow hard. "Yes. I heard...something about that. It's... surprising."

"Is it?" he asks, his brow cocked. He goes back to cleaning his glasses. "Surprised Mage Bane as well, apparently. It took him and seven additional Level Five Mages to kill most of the dragons and subdue the others. Mage Bane is likely to be under a physician's care for a few months to come. He sustained a nasty claw slash down the side of his face and neck, I've heard."

I struggle to keep my face impassive.

"The Gardnerians rarely talk about...embarrassments such as these." He chuckles as he slides his spectacles back on. "But more than a hundred dragons—that's not so easy to sweep under the carpet now, is it? And it happened just in time for the glorious celebration of Damion Bane's rise to Commander of the Fourth Division base." Turning slightly, he points his thumb toward the window. "Coincidentally, that's not too far from here."

He knows. He knows. My heartbeat picks up speed. *And if Professor Kristian knows, who else might?*

There's a perfunctory knock at the door.

"Come in," Professor Kristian says nonchalantly.

Vice Chancellor Quillen sweeps into the room.

A new surge of fear shoots through me, and I shrink back against my chair.

Ignoring Tierney and me, Vice Chancellor Quillen removes her winter wrappings, hangs them on the worn, wooden stand already crowded with our cloaks, then takes a seat near Professor Kristian. She smooths out the black silk of her skirts, a silver Erthia orb bright around her neck.

"Horrid weather, Jules," she comments, sliding off fine calf-skin gloves.

"Yes, quite," he absently responds, the two of them disconcertingly oblivious to our presence as they take a moment to complain about the frigid cold that's moved in.

Finally, there's a break in the conversation, and a long silence as the Vice Chancellor settles in and levels her eyes at us.

I struggle to hold her penetrating, green-eyed glare.

As if suddenly remembering we're there, Professor Kristian

looks at me and gestures toward the Vice Chancellor. "I believe you've met Vice Chancellor Quillen."

Panicked, I glance over at Tierney. Her eyes are riveted on the very Gardnerian Vice Chancellor, her fear dangerously apparent.

"Relax, Mage Calix," Vice Chancellor Quillen says dismissively. "You're among friends." She turns to Professor Kristian. "How many Fae children did we hide during the war, Jules?"

"Two hundred and fifty-six," he responds without a pause. "Not including Zephyr."

My head is spinning. "Who's Zephyr?" I ask.

"My adopted daughter, Mage Gardner," the Vice Chancellor replies succinctly. "She's Sylphan Fae. And far away from here. In Noi lands, with my brother, Fain."

"How is Fain?" Professor Kristian puts in congenially.

"Enjoying the East," she replies just as cordial. "He's keeping pit dragons now."

"For sport?" He seems surprised.

She smiles mischievously. "No. You know Fain. They're his companions."

Professor Kristian coughs out a laugh.

"Anyway," Vice Chancellor Quillen continues, turning to me. "Zephyr is quite safe there. For the moment." Her expression turns reflective as she looks at Tierney and shakes her head from side to side. "But so many more in hiding. And now—" she lets out a deep sigh "—it seems we've got to get you all out." She shakes her head again and purses her lips at Tierney. "Don't fret, Mage Calix. We've some unexpected friends, it turns out." She looks to Professor Kristian. "It seems that someone dissolved the Elfin steel dragon cages. Did you hear about that?"

The side of Professor Kristian's lip twitches into a smile. "Clearly the work of a Level Five Mage, Lucretia."

The Vice Chancellor pins her eyes tight on me. "Isn't your brother a Level Five, Mage Gardner?" I open my mouth, desperate to find a convincing lie, but she doesn't wait for my response. "Tricky spell, too."

"A protected military spell, I believe," Professor Kristian idly comments, glancing over at her.

"I am so glad you brought that up, Jules," the Vice Chancellor says, her gaze uncomfortably tight on me. "Because it turns out there's a military grimoire missing. They just can't seem to find it." Her eyes sharpen. "Might you know anything about *any* of this, Mage Gardner?"

I can barely breathe. All our secrets, secrets no more.

Except for the white wand, I note with some relief.

Professor Kristian laughs lightly. "Come now, Lucretia. You know these girls are ignorant of all these matters."

"Oh, that's right," she agrees. "How silly of me. They were with me last night, Jules. Mage Gardner and both of her brothers."

"And why's that, Lucretia?" Professor Kristian asks, blithely playing along.

"Well, there's the matter of Mage Gardner being behind on her University tithe. And her younger brother's acceptance into the Gardnerian Weapons Guild." She shakes her head wearily. "We were in my office. All evening."

"Putting in late hours again, Lucretia?"

The Vice Chancellor rolls her eyes and clicks her tongue. "Oh, it's never ending."

"Well, that is a relief," Professor Kristian comments. "Especially since the Gardnerians are investigating every Level Five Mage's whereabouts last night. It's good to know Mage Gardner and her brothers are well accounted for."

I sit there, speechless, blinking at them.

A smile lifts the corners of Vice Chancellor Quillen's mouth as she eyes me with open approval. "Welcome to the Resistance, Mage Gardner."

★ ★ ★ ★ ★

ACKNOWLEDGMENTS

It takes a village to bring a novel into fruition, and my village of readers/editors/authors is a talented one.

First of all, a huge thank-you to my husband, Walter, for all his years of support, child/teen care, reading, editing and all-around book-widowerhood—and all that tree information!

Thank you to my daughter Willoughby (for her spot-on, unflinchingly honest feedback); daughter Schuyler (for her great editing and ideas); and daughters Alexandre and Taylor for putting up with my writing habit and helping to "hold down the fort."

Thank you to my parents, Mary and Noah Sexton, for their enthusiasm, ideas and encouragement.

Thank you to the Burlington Writers' Group—Cam M. Sato, Kimberly Ann Hunt and Denise Holmes (three of my favorite writers and talented editors); the amazing Diane Dexter (editor, reader and good friend); the incredible Eva Gumprecht (esteemed writer and editor); everyone at Harlequin TEEN who worked on this project; Liz Zundel (reader, editor and font of intrepid moral support); Leslie Ward (for her feedback and encouragement when this project was in its infancy); my mother-in-law, Gail Kamaras; my sister-in-law, Jessica Bowers (without whom none of this would have happened); my brother Jim and M.J. Bray, two of my earliest readers; Bronwyn Fryer (genius friend) for teaching a novice how to format my editing; Anne Loecher; Tanusri Prasanna; the fabulous authors/editors Dian Parker and Kane Gilmour; The Burlington Writers' Workshop; Lorraine Bencivengo Ziff (for amazing editing and encouragement); Susan Shreve; Crystal Zevon; Geof Hewitt and everyone else who read and gave feedback on parts or all of my various novels/novellas. Thank you, Beanbag, for loaning me your mad writing skills and genius wit!

A big thank-you to Mike Marcotte, computer whiz extraordinaire, for tech support and my fabulous author website, www.laurieannforest.com. And thank you to everyone else who helped with tech support.

Thank you to Natashya Wilson, Executive Editor at Harlequin TEEN, for taking a chance on this series—I'm thrilled to be working with everyone at Harlequin TEEN (the most fabulous and fun imprint EVER). Lauren Smulski, you are the best (and wittiest) editor I could have imagined for this project—you've brought this book to a whole new level. Thank you for your endless patience and incredible editing/ideas.

Above all, I want to thank my tenacious agent Carrie Hannigan (Hannigan, Salky, Getzler Agency) for believing in The Black Witch Chronicles for so many years (and through so many edits). I couldn't ask for a more encouraging or talented agent/reader/editor.